UNCAGED LOVE

RAFE & HARPER

KALYN COOPER

Uncaged Love

KaLyn Cooper

Cover Artist: Drue Hoffman

Editors: Devin Govaere, Marci Boudreaux Clark, Trenda London, Rebecca Hodgkins

Published 2016, 2020

ISBN: 978-1-970145-04-5

This is a work of fiction. The characters, incidents and dialogues in this book are of the author's imagination and are not to be construed as real. Any resemblance to actual events or persons, living or dead, is completely coincidental.

Dear Reader,

Uncaged Love is a deeply edited version of *Explosive Combination*, which is no longer available. If you read my debut book, please be aware changes have been made to bring it back into the **Black Swan series**. The basis of this story remains the same, but several changes have been made. One small part of the ending has changed to coordinate better with *Rescuing Melina*, the **Guardian Elite** crossover with **Susan Stoker's Special Forces: Operation Alpha World**.

For those of you who have read *Unrelenting Love*, you'll remember the Ladies of Black Swan attempted to call Harper Tambini, their friend working for the ATF as an explosives expert. *Uncaged Love* explains why she was unavailable.

There are many books in the **Black Swan** series with

more coming soon. Be sure to check out the **Guardian Elite series,** a spinoff from the **Black Swan series**. All books are listed on www.KaLynCooper.com with links to all formats.

Thank you for reading my books! Reviews are always appreciated.

Always,
KaLyn Cooper

DEDICATION

To the women in our military who have taken on a man's world and, through intelligence and determination, succeed every day.

ACKNOWLEDGMENTS

I'd like to thank my editor, Marci Clark, for all the wonderful things she does for me. Many thanks to Drue Hoffman for this stunning cover and the many things she does for my career. And to all those other incredible romance writers who encouraged me, advised me, and hugged me when I needed it. Thank you, ATF Special Agent Rick McMahan for his inspiration. Last, a special thanks to Cindy Marini for helping me discover Harper Tambini.

Rara avis in terris is Latin for "a rare bird in the lands."

In the ancient world, it was believed that the landing of a single black swan created a change that would affect the entire world. In today's world, that change can be seen almost instantly…9/11 is the best xample.

Fact: Scientists at the University of Michigan discovered that co-crystallization of two common explosives creates the most lethal, non-nuclear bomb on the planet, casually called Chaz.

Fact: In September 2012 Popular Mechanics magazine published the formula to make Chaz, which is similar to a process used in pharmaceuticals.

Fact: In 2003 the ATF was moved to the Department of Justice and became the Bureau of Alcohol, Tobacco, Firearms and Explosives.

CHAPTER 1

HARPER TAMBINI IGNORED THE TINGLING THAT NIPPED AND niggled at the back of her neck. She blamed the cool breeze sweeping down from the snow-topped Andes Mountains and automatically looked that direction even though she couldn't see them in the dark of night.

"Who'd believe spring this close to the equator would be so chilly?" She rubbed her bare arms and considered digging a windbreaker out of the bag slung over her shoulder.

"We'll be on the jet soon enough," her teammate, Marcus Hernandez, reassured her. "The cold wind sure cuts right through."

"What do you expect?" Robert Sanchez flipped up the collar on his nylon jacket and hunkered into what little warmth the lightweight material offered. "We're at almost nine-thousand feet."

"Yeah, I know." She scoffed at herself. Tambini, you're getting soft. After some of the most rigorous training in the world, including a month in Alaska for cold-weather drills, this night breeze shouldn't bother her as much as it did. For a fleeting second, she considered the chill might not be the external temperature, but her internal sixth sense. She brushed the possibility aside, but glanced around the poorly-lit parking lot as they made their way to the hangar on the private aircraft side of Bogota's international airport.

She didn't see anything unexpected for two o'clock in the morning. Besides, she could handle whatever came up. Like an overprotective big sister, she scanned the five men she'd lived and traveled with for the past three weeks. They were all capable agents for the United States Bureau of Alcohol, Tobacco, Firearms, and Explosives, but none had intensive special operative training like hers.

Three years ago, Harper had been selected for a top-secret program to prove women could be as effective as men in the clandestine world of SpecOps. Out of one hundred candidates, less than half had successfully completed the same testing of mind, body, and soul the military puts Army Special Forces, Navy SEALs, Air Force PJs, and the Marine Corps' Raiders through. She'd been designated as an elite special operator for the United States government before additional training with the CIA. Even her boss on this task force had no idea of her extensive skills.

"I can't wait to get home and hug my wife and kids," Senior Special Agent Mike Estes told his team. "I feel like I've been gone for months rather than a few weeks."

Harper moved the long strap on her duffel bag to her other shoulder. "I'm just glad we didn't find anyone who could make Chaz." While working on her master's degree, she'd been instrumental in the development of the most lethal, nonnuclear explosive on the planet. The unique process was supposed to be classified, as was her involvement in the DOD research. "I'm still pissed that scientific magazine published an article, including major portions of the formula, then referenced our research in the damned footnotes."

What scared her more than anything else, was her name was included as a member of the development team. For her protection, when she entered the special operative training program, her identity had been scrubbed from social media and flagged with any reference to her military service. No one had thought to redact her name from a research project she'd worked on during college, even though technically she was still on active duty.

Robert Finch chuckled as he walked beside her. "Like the bad guys don't read English or smart people magazines."

"Y'all can just thank the Freedom of Information Act for our vacation in Colombia," her mission boss said from her other side, his Tennessee accent creeping in as it often did when he was tired. "I'll be happy when we touch down on U.S. soil once again. This has been one hell of a trip. I despise Third World hotel rooms."

Harper glanced over her shoulder to watch their local CIA contact pull his beat up brown van through a gate in the chain-link fence and disappear into the obscurity of the country's largest city. Keeping up with the conversation, she noted, "I can't wait to sleep in my own bed. I swear the hotels put rocks in the mattresses."

It had been a brutal mission. For three intense weeks, from one end of Colombia to the other, Harper had constantly been on edge. More than once, she'd felt as though someone was watching her, which was to be expected. At five-feet ten inches, she was tall by American standards. She was gigantic compared to most South Americans. Then, there was the fact she traveled with five men. Her unease went far beyond the furtive glances she received almost everywhere. The whole trip, she'd felt as though she were in the crosshairs of an expert sniper. The hyperawareness had emotionally drained her. She was more than ready to go home.

"At least you get to go home to a nice place," Marcus said. "I'm still bunking in with Robert in the bachelor pad that always seems to look like Thursday morning after a hump day party."

Robert laughed. "Hump day is right. You're still just jealous both those twins ended up in my bed, and you slept alone."

"TMI, gentlemen." Harper dramatically stuck her index fingers into her ears. With a grin of satisfaction she gazed at her complaining teammate. "I can't believe I was able to find such an awesome apartment."

"Do you think your friend, Katlin, can find one for me?" Marcus flashed her a lady-killer smile. "How about I move in with you? Didn't you say your place has two bedrooms?"

"Not only no, but hell no." Harper threw him a look that she hoped he interpreted correctly. There was no fucking way she was going to allow him to even visit her new place. She was well aware of his hound dog reputation. A thought crossed her mind, and she didn't bother to hold back the evil grin. Her girlfriends would eat him up and spit him out. She might invite him to one of their clubbing nights just to watch that happen.

Harper was excited about her new beautiful apartment in Washington, D.C. Finding such an awesome place down the hall from the women she had covertly trained with for over a year, was a godsend. Sweat and blood created an unbreakable bond only those who had endured the journey together could understand. She couldn't wait to get back home and tell her friends about this latest mission. Because they all held one of the highest security clearances in the United States, they never worried about comparing adventures.

She couldn't wait to see the faces of Katlin, Grace, Nita, Tori, and Lei Lu when she told them about going undercover in a Cartagena bar on a Caribbean beach to seduce a drug lord wannabe. As their CIA training had predicted, within a few hours, and a few chemically laced cocktails, Harper had been able to get the man alone by making him believe he was God's gift to American women. The corners of her mouth turned up as she remembered him, naked, tied spread eagle to the four-poster bed.

By the time she was finished with her interrogation, she was sure he'd legally purchased the CL-20, a key ingredient in Chaz. Fortunately, the inebriated idiot didn't have the HMX which was needed to complete the formula. He also didn't seem interested in purchasing the popular explosive. His plan was to sell the CL-20 in its solid state to the Revolutionary Armed Forces of Colombia, better known as FARC. Her team had quietly speculated the purchase was one of the CIA's means of supporting the subversive guerrillas when after they reported their findings, they had been ordered to follow up several leads on HMX smuggling.

For nearly two weeks, the six members of the International Explosives Task Force chased a gunrunner who'd smuggled the HMX explosives into the country and was holed up in the far western regions. There was no way to ferret him out. It didn't matter since no connection could be found between him and the hopeful drug lord. Harper had personally confirmed neither had the technology—or brains —to complete the complicated process.

Mission accomplished, they were headed home, and none too soon in her opinion. She was tired of beige hotel rooms that wouldn't get a one-star rating in the United States and restaurant food that was either tasteless or so spicy her mouth burned for hours. Harper longed to slide between the soft yellow sheets of her own bed in her new condo. She'd fall asleep, the monuments around the National Mall in D.C. as her personal nightlights, and refuse to wake up for a week.

"Someone get the hangar doors," Estes called to the team.

Jarred from thoughts of home, Harper yelled back, "I've got it." She trotted to the exterior control panel and reached for the button to power open the gigantic hangar doors facing the tarmac.

Huge rough fingers gripped her wrist and squeezed. For a nanosecond, she stared in confusion at the sun-browned hand and an arm covered in night camouflage utilities as the man tried to pry her hand away from the red button. His acrid body odor nearly turned her stomach before training took over.

She whirled and brought the heel of her free hand to the tip of the man's nose and jammed it upward with complete focus on her immediate duty to silently take out her aggressor so she could then stealthily assist other team members. The crunch of cartilage and the hiss of his breath through clenched teeth gave her temporary satisfaction.

She continued her spin to bring her knee up. He must've anticipated the move because she contacted his thigh instead of his groin.

He still had her wrist and pulled it behind her back, drawing her closer to his body to reduce the impact of any more of her moves. He caught her arm just before her arrowed knuckles connected to the windpipe-crushing spot above his prominent Adam's apple. He stepped between her legs and pinned her against the cool metal sheeting of the hangar. His huge hand covered her mouth and pinched her nose.

She couldn't breathe. Her rapid heartbeat was using up what little oxygen was left in her lungs.

Harper glared into the shadowed eyes of her enormous attacker as she twisted, seeking any advantage.

She instantly stilled when the cold steel barrel of a gun was pressed into her temple.

"Move and you're dead, perra." The gunman growled with a thick Spanish accent.

He was right to call her a bitch. She was one, especially when her life was threatened. But she wouldn't acknowledge his intended insult with as much as a twitch of a muscle.

"I take my hand away. Scream if you want." The glint in her attacker's eyes said he'd like to hear her beg. "Do you no good. Your team is—"

"Shut up, fool," the gunman snapped in Spanish and sneered.

As if in a dance move, she was yanked from the building and spun around so her back was to him. She sucked in a much-needed breath, replenishing her dazed brain. He had her wrists secured with flex-cuffs within a second. Before she could fight free, another set of large male hands had grabbed her at the hips and bound her kicking legs with strong arms and they'd placed plastic restraints on her ankles.

Once she was secured, the gun returned to her head. She furtively scanned the area. She hadn't heard gunshots, but that didn't mean her team was still alive.

The minimal light from the crescent moon revealed only shades of black, but Harper observed movement everywhere around her. Well-camouflaged men rushed about like ants before a rain, purposeful and under time constraints. Sicarios, if she had to guess. These were a drug cartel's armed men who carried out assassinations, theft, extortion, and kidnappings.

Had they been targeted simply because they were

Americans? Or had her ATF team angered a capo to the point he wanted retribution before they left the country?

Harper ignored her attackers as they patted her down, choosing to scan the area for her team. The sicarios brutalized her breasts and buttocks, then roughly rubbed between her bound legs. They wanted to humiliate her, but she'd been trained by the best in the world. Their hands on her body meant nothing, and neither did their crude suggestions and taunts. They removed all her communication devices and weapons—even the knife hidden in her ankle boot.

She found the rest of her team.

Relief washed over her. They were alive. Distinguished by their casual American traveling clothes of jeans and polo shirts, they stood bound, side by side, guns to their heads. In the diminished light, she still caught the glances they shot her way. Damn. She hated when they checked on her because she was female.

This was her fault. She'd let her guard down, eager to get home. They had been minutes away from boarding their jet that would whisk them away to freedom.

She twisted and turned the plastic ties on her wrists, but they only cut deeper into her tender flesh. She was flexible enough to slip her tied hands to the front, but the pistol at her temple kept her from trying more.

What do they possibly want with us? Good luck if it's money they're after. They obviously don't understand government jobs don't pay very well. As team leader, Mike Estes carried cash in both U.S. and Colombian currencies, but they'd gone through a lot of money between living expenses and bribes. Harper vaguely wondered how much he still had left.

CHAPTER 2

ONCE AGAIN HARPER SURVEYED THEIR CAPTORS. THESE MEN were unusually tall, not the run-of-the-mill gun toters. The average Colombian man was only five-feet seven inches. Obviously, they'd been imported mercenaries or selected for the intimidation value of their height.

But she'd put a serious hurt on one. She loved it when men underestimated her.

Drops of blood glinted in the moonlight before they were absorbed into the dark shirt of the man who'd attacked her. A few feet away, another sicario was on his knees, cupping his groin, and a third rolled on his back, holding his knee. They all swore profusely in guttural Spanish. She smiled inside, but kept her expression blank. She was proud her team had fought back.

Off to the side, the tallest man stood with a distinct military bearing. He barked orders in Spanish as he constantly scanned the area for trouble. Harper held his gaze when their eyes met. She refused to show weakness.

The tall man's body language caught and held her attention. The precise carriage, the way he placed his feet exactly shoulder-width apart, knees slightly bent, and back straight, indicated an authoritative stance she recognized but couldn't place. Ironically, it reassured her somewhere deep within.

Bright headlights from an approaching vehicle caught the hard angles of his face, and his light blue gaze seemed to bore through her, all the way to her soul. Holy shit. He wasn't Colombian. But he was absolutely in charge.

Had they been trapped by an American ex-patriot? What the hell was happening?

A black Hummer limousine stopped ten feet from her team, coating the scene with a bright white glow. The interior light came on when the back door opened. Nothing covert about this entrance.

A man exited the vehicle with more grace than she'd expect for someone of his girth. Black curls fell over his collar, framing a stern brown face.

Oh fuck. She recognized him. Every ATF and DEA agent knew of Carlos Narváez. He had been on their top ten most wanted list for years. Although he'd packed on more than a few pounds, that cocky grin was unmistakable.

With the confidence of a well-protected king, he strode to the man in charge of the ambush. In the wee hours of morning, in his tailored gray suit, Narváez looked as though he were prepared for a skyscraper corner office rather than a clandestine meeting at a closed airport in South America.

In a calm, sophisticated voice, he asked the man in charge, "Segundo, were my guests hurt?"

"No, but the tall bitch broke José's fuckin' nose, and that one"—Narváez's second pointed at Marcus Hernandez—"got Valez in the balls. Garcia had his knee taken out by that one." The pointed finger designated Mike. At the mention of their names, the hurt sicarios tried to appear unharmed and unaffected by the pain

"It's probably the first time a woman surprised José and fought back," Narváez said with an exaggerated shrug. Then he lifted a hand and gestured toward himself. Her teammates were manhandled and placed in front of one of the most feared drug lords in all of Colombia, a true capo. He had money and power and, it seemed, an army of giants.

Her gaze drifted from the affluent bastard to the man on his right, Segundo. Damned if he wasn't staring at her again. His silver-blue glare scanned the length of her body with obvious male appreciation before returning to her face. She felt stripped naked, but a small part of her relished his approval. Men were so easy. Maybe she could use his attraction to her advantage.

Defiantly, she lifted her chin a fraction and glowered back.

"Carlos Narváez," Mike Estes said in conversational Spanish, "did you come to wish us good-bye?" He then switched to English. "But, excuse me, you speak perfect American English. You were educated in the States. Graduated from the Citadel, wasn't it?"

A slow smile wiped away the harshness of Narváez's frown and replaced it with a startling flash of perfect white teeth, which had to be caps. He looked almost angelic, but like an Old Testament angel—handsome, yet a fierce warrior who could strike with wrath.

Narváez's smile didn't reach his eyes. "Virginia Military Institute."

Harper let out a deep breath. Estes—Testes as they called him behind his back because the man had big brass ones—seemed to be taking some control.

"Well, I knew it was one of those Southern military-type

schools."

Harper mentally rolled her eyes as her boss pushed the notorious cartel leader.

Not a good idea. Find common ground. Negotiate, damn it.

Estes was evidently pissed they'd been ambushed and had decided to take some of his aggression out on Narváez. This might not end well.

Narváez stepped closer to their team leader. "And you, ATF Senior Special Agent Mike Estes, where did you get your education?"

How the hell did Narváez know Mike's name?

Estes hid his surprise, but Harper recognized his shock in the slight shift of his posture. "United States Naval Academy then five years in the Marine Corps. My master's is from Georgetown. I believe your MBA is from Darden at UVA, correct?"

More on edge than before, Harper shifted within her constrained stance and considered a duck-and-shoulder-shove move followed by a head butt. She needed an offense in case Estes called for it.

"Very good, Agent Estes, you've done your homework." Narváez tilted his head.

In full Testes mode, he said impatiently, "Okay, Narváez, you have our attention, and you obviously have us. What do you want? If you wanted us dead, you would have killed us by now."

Mike was right, but Narváez could still kill them. Easily.

Every member of their team had muscled thugs holding pistols at their heads. There was also a perimeter of armed guards facing outward. Even more men were in the hangar with their plane. The odds were all on Narváez's side. But where there was life, there was hope.

"Yes, you are correct." Narváez paced carefully down the line of his captives, inspecting each from head to toe. He stopped in front of her and stared at her face.

She would show no fear. She tilted her chin up slightly and glared back at him.

"What do you want?" Estes enunciated each word, calling from the far end of the line.

"Miss Tambini." Harper wasn't sure if Narváez meant to address her or to answer Mike's question. Her confusion must've shown on her face because the drug lord went on to say, "Harper will be joining me for a while."

The bottom of her stomach dropped, flipping and twisting like an Olympian diver. *Me? Oh, hell no.* Her ATF pre-mission preparation had included a complete study of torture techniques preferred by Colombian cartels, and there was no way in hell she'd let this monster touch her.

"No, take me," Marcus yelled, his eyes open wide with fear for her.

"I came to make Miss Tambini an offer she can't refuse." The left side of Narváez's mouth turned upward in a smirk as though he'd made a joke. He sniffed and rubbed his nose.

Damn it, he's using his own products. He could be unpredictable, possibly paranoid. He hadn't shown any of those characteristics, yet. Perhaps he was still in the grandiose stage; that might account for the ballsy move to ambush their team.

"Narváez, take me," Mike offered in a controlled voice. "Let my team go. Now. Safely."

Narváez cocked his head and seemed to consider this for a minute. "I doubt you have what I need." He looked toward his Segundo, who still stared at Harper.

"Segundo, I can tell you like her. She's tall, a good match for a man your size. You can't keep your eyes off her. I can see why. She's beautiful." Narváez leaned in closer and carefully examined her face. "Maybe I'll give her to you… when I'm done with her."

"Don't touch me, you bastard," Harper snarled and twisted her face away.

He caught her chin between his thumb and forefinger and held her still, forcefully but not painfully. She stared into eyes so dark brown they were nearly black.

"You know who she looks like?" Narváez was so close she smelled the coffee on his breath and the tang of cocaine-laced sweat. He withdrew a stark white handkerchief from his pocket and wiped away the small beads of moisture on his brow. He was jonesing. He continued, "The actress, the one who was Miss America but lost the title because she'd posed nude for Penthouse." His smile broadened, and she knew he was picturing her naked.

Harper shuddered but controlled it quickly.

"She starred with Arnold in that movie, you know the one." Narváez released her chin and, thankfully, leaned back.

"Yes, Eraser. She does look a little like Vanessa Williams, especially in the shadows." The Segundo had spoken in perfect American English, and, if she wasn't mistaken, a hint of a Southern accent flavored his vowels.

Harper thought she saw a flicker of embarrassment in his light blue eyes.

Why would this thug be uncomfortable?

Narváez ran a long finger down Harper's cheek. "On second thought, I'll give her to you now, Segundo. She seems spirited, yes? You'll enjoy her. Besides, I have my new wife to keep me entertained."

Her skin crawled with revulsion. The click of her teeth mashing together was so loud everyone close had to have heard. She would be no man's property. Human trafficking was very profitable and prevalent in South America, but as an ATF agent, she'd never been involved in that area of smuggling. No way in hell did she want to experience it from the inside.

"I'll die before I become your whore," Harper told the men who looked at her like a commodity. She was beyond fear now and well on her way to fury. If anyone touched her, she vowed to kill him. He wouldn't be the first man whose life she'd ended.

"You'll do exactly what we ask of you." Narváez ran his thumb over her dry lips. It took all her self-control not to bite it. "But you have no need to fear, Miss Harper Tambini, it's not your body we need."

Narváez's eyes never left hers as he ran a finger down her throat toward her breasts. Unblinking, she held his gaze until he stepped back. He sniffed and scowled as he rubbed his nose. She wondered how often he used.

"No, Narváez! Take me," Estes demanded again. "I'm the one you want."

Narváez ignored her team leader. "Bring her."

The gun at her head was gone. Her captor slung her over his shoulder as though she weighed nothing. No one would ever consider her small or petite at nearly five feet ten inches of honed muscle, but the man carried her with ease. Her shoulders ached in the uncomfortable position. Like an inchworm, she writhed and wiggled in an attempt to make him drop her.

"Carlos," Segundo called out to his boss's back, "what about the others?"

"Kill them. They're of no use to me," Narváez said without hesitation or pausing his stride.

"You don't want to start an international incident where four…tourists, who are very important to the United States government, suddenly disappear or, worse yet, turn up as dead bodies. Every U.S. alphabet agency and some foreign ones would be crawling all over Colombia within twenty-four hours. That would be bad for business." Seconds later, Segundo added, "Besides, you have what you need."

Not for the first time, Harper wondered why they needed her. She was sure she'd find out all too soon. All she had to do was withstand their torture and stall for time. The U.S. government would send a SpecOps team for her as soon as they could. Hopefully it would be her friends, and new neighbors, the Ladies of Black Swan. They would gladly allow her to kill Narváez. She wondered if she could get a message to Katlin, Grace, Nita, Tori, and Lei Lu.

"Do with them as you think best." Narváez strode to the back door of the limousine.

Harper had been gently placed on her feet next to the rear door with the gun back at her temple.

Segundo gave a hand signal, and the men holding her teammates stirred. Horror ripped through Harper as one-by-one the men were choked out and sagged to the tarmac.

She turned to protest, but the prick of a needle stole her voice before she could utter a word. The warm drug, pushed by adrenaline, raced through her body and numbed her senses immediately. The world blurred as her teammates were dragged into the hangar.

Her knees buckled.

Before she hit the unforgiving concrete, strong arms scooped up her limp body and gently placed her in the limousine. With heavy eyelids, she looked into sea-blue eyes livid with anger. Her senses fogged by the drug, she thought she heard someone whisper in her ear, in southern-accented English, "I've got you. I'll take care of you."

Her eyes drooped closed and the world faded to black.

CHAPTER 3

FUCK. FUCK. FUCK! WHAT THE HELL WAS CARLOS THINKING? Rafe Silva gently placed the long-legged woman onto the rear seat of the limousine then crawled in next to her, much to the dismay of his soldiers. His men would cop a feel if given half a chance, and he didn't want anyone to touch her. Hell, if he wasn't back there, they'd probably gang bang her unconscious body.

Men in this country had very little respect for females. They looked at beautiful women as toys to do with as they wished, and Harper Tambini was gorgeous. That didn't make her a whore, but Rafe doubted she was an angel either.

In Colombia, there were basically two kinds of women; those available to any man and then there were good girls. The latter grew up in the same neighborhoods as his men, attended Catholic school, and went to church with their parents. They married good boys who worked in the fields next to their fathers and grandfathers. But Rafe's men hadn't seen a good girl since they left home as teenagers to work in the trade. In Colombia, outside the cities, men either worked the land sunrise to dusk, or they carried a gun for the operation. The women worked in poorly lit processing rooms or in the kitchens preparing food for the hundreds who kept the cocaine trade moving.

To his men, Harper was the worst kind of woman: powerful, both physically and emotionally. She'd fought rather than given up and had seriously hurt José. She was also a professional and, as an ATF agent, not only better trained than they were in their militant field but better educated as well. Agents had college educations, and most of his men could barely read and add. She threatened everything they'd been raised to believe about male and female roles.

Rafe's gaze ran the length of her fit body that limply leaned against him. Her shoulder-length brown hair waved as it fell across high cheekbones. Glints of gold and deep reds were highlighted when several of the men lit hand-rolled cigarettes. The scooped neck on her T-shirt revealed only the top of rounded breasts begging for a man's kiss.

"Can I have the woman when you're done with her, Segundo?" Ruis asked.

"What are you talking about?" Valez unabashedly readjusted his obviously sore balls. "You might as well go ahead and take her now because Saint Segundo will never touch her. He's too good for any woman Uncle Carlos offers him. He only fucks high-class bitches he finds in the city."

One of these days Valez was going to push him too far. Rafe didn't care that the insubordinate upstart was the heir apparent to one of the largest cartels in Colombia. It might've been tonight, but Rafe was too concerned about Harper's safety.

The malicious young man leaned forward. "Give her to me now. Maybe releasing into her will help relieve the pain in my balls." He had the audacity to wiggle his fingers when he held out his hands.

"Sit. Down." The glare Rafe gave the man a decade younger than him should have cowered Valez back into the leather seats. "And you'd better shut the fuck up before I remove those precious balls of yours with a spoon and feed them to Ruis."

At the mention of his name, Ruis threw his hands up in the air. "Oh, no. I have no part in this." His gaze darted back and forth between Rafe and Valez, unsure of which master to follow.

It was times like this that made Rafe wonder why he remained in this godforsaken country. Harper moaned as she shifted in the seat beside him then snuggled into his shoulder.

What the fuck was Carlos thinking? Kidnapping a federal agent had to be the most idiotic thing his friend had ever done. And a female to boot. She was a rare and valuable commodity to the U.S. government. He knew for a fact they'd come for her and kill them all for taking her. He'd led many such missions as a Navy SEAL.

And where the hell had Carlos found out about the ATF agents? Rafe thought he knew everything and everyone his boss did, but evidently not. Carlos actually knew the woman by name. Damn.

He was sure the kidnapping was Carlos's idea, but based on information he'd received from whom? They'd been separated for only a few hours while Rafe had taken care of cartel business, and he'd left Carlos chasing his newest wife into the bedroom.

As he inhaled, Rafe caught the faint scent of feminine shampoo. This entire cluster fuck had to be reported immediately to his superiors. He'd call Langley at first chance.

The need to protect this woman had been triggered from the moment he'd watched her break José's nose. Damn, she was good. She'd taken his man by surprise and would've kicked the shit out of him had Juan not been there with a gun to her head.

Had Beth fought as hard when she'd been kidnapped? No. He couldn't let himself think about his former fiancée. He couldn't go there.

Harper's head lolled against Rafe's shoulder as the drugs pulled her deeper into sleep. Good. They still had hours of traveling.

Harper thought she heard men speaking but the need for sleep tugged insistently. She was so tired. It had been a long operation, but was finally over. Her undercover work and expertise in explosives had proven the cartels didn't know what they had. Yes, the drug runners understood both explosives, HMX and CL-20 individually, but they didn't know they could be combined into the world's most lethal non-nuclear weapon. Thank God.

American lives had been saved once again.

The stench of homemade cigarettes and sour male odor was overwhelming. The men on her team needed a shower. Maybe she did, too. She should wake up, take a long hot shower and wash her hair. But she was so tired.

She nuzzled into a hard shoulder that smelled shower clean with the distinct scents of spicy male deodorant and expensive aftershave.

Hmmm. Nice. Maybe she'd just go back to sleep. When her bottom left the seat, her consciousness jolted awake. She was being jostled around too much, but she needed to sleep. The plane must have hit a patch of turbulence. Damn, it was hot in there. Somebody needed to turn the cabin temperature down. Sleep wrapped around her like a man's arms as she let out a long slow breath and fell into the depths of sleep once again.

Deep chuckling, and overwhelming heat, brought Harper awake.

In Spanish, she heard a man say, "Segundo, the woman, she's all wet. She sweats. I think she's sick."

At the word sick, Harper came fully awake with a horrible feeling if she didn't move this second she was going to throw up where she lay. Bile bubbled up her throat.

She started to take a deep breath, but acrid body odor assaulted her nostrils and turned her stomach. She tried to move her hands to cover her nose, but her arms wouldn't work. She fought to wake up, hoping to make sense of her situation. She was supposed to be on the ATF jet headed home but something told her that's not where she was.

The plastic restraints binding her wrists cut deep into her flesh as she sat up as best she could with her hands tied behind her. The pain cut through her mental haze.

Cracking her eyes open as she had been taught in survival school, Harper determined she was in a bouncing vehicle filled with large men in black camo carrying automatic weapons. It was the Hummer limousine that had pulled onto the tarmac in Bogotá.

Now she remembered everything. The ambush. The prick of a needle.

Harper's stomach rolled and tried to climb up her throat. In desperation to keep her supper where it belonged, she attempted to gather saliva but her mouth was so dry she could only swallow a drop.

"Segundo. We need to stop." The sicario next to her started to move to another seat.

"She's white like a ghost," another man shouted.

She was going to be sick all over this car in just a minute.

There was little in this world Harper hated more than throwing up. She'd rather take another bullet than lose her lunch. She never understood how bulimic women emptied their stomach then went back to whatever they were doing.

All these thoughts of throwing up weren't helping. She was going to be sick. Now.

"Move," she screamed. "Let me out!"

Strong hands grabbed her as she pulled herself to a sitting position. She started wiggling toward the limousine door.

"Let go of me." She fought to be free of several pairs of male hands, less concerned with what they were grabbing than her upset stomach. "I'm going to be sick. Let me out. Now!"

Segundo yelled orders into the front seat for the driver to pull over.

She looked at the men in the large limo and realized she had spoken in English. They probably only knew Spanish. Changing languages, she screamed at them in Spanish to fucking let her out because she was about to puke all over them. Served them right if she did.

The men's eyes grew huge. Several scooted away from the door while the long vehicle skidded to a stop. She fell atop two of the men, and they pushed her back upright. Segundo lifted her out and carried her to the side of the Colombian excuse for a road.

Instantly her belly flipped, and she could no longer hold its contents. She bent over and emptied her stomach. Sweat dripped off her face, and her nose ran as her body rebelled.

"What…what did he inject into me?" she rasped out.

"Just a little something we make." He sounded proud. Fucker.

"Is it—" she gasped in warm air hoping to get her

stomach under control. "Is it cocaine-based?" She turned her head to look up the men next to her.

He narrowed his striking blue eyes to slits but said nothing as another bout of nausea overtook her. Sweat poured out of her as she shivered, freezing in the oppressive heat of the Colombian night. They had obviously left the mountains.

"You fucking son of a bitch. I'm allergic to cocaine. It's killing me," she said as she shook uncontrollably. She bent over, dry heaving because her body had already purged everything from the bottom of her digestive system.

Segundo shouted, "Carlos, we have a problem."

Harper watched Narváez stick his head out the window then scrunched his nose. Good. She hoped the smell offended him. Although she could barely see him in the reflected headlights, she forced herself to watch. As the two men kept up a conversation in rapid Spanish, too fast for her to catch anything but the highlights, she knew the instant Narváez understood she might die. A flash of panic crossed his arrogant face. He wanted her for something and needed to keep her alive until he got it.

Segundo returned to her side and held a handkerchief down toward her face without looking at her. He explained, in Spanish, Narváez's personal physician would meet them at the compound and treat her, but she needed to get back in the car now.

After several minutes of forced deep breaths, she straightened but remained slightly bent so as not to stretch her still-fragile stomach. She'd regained control of her body, but the ordeal had sapped so much energy from her.

Harper looked at the small white cloth in Segundo's hand and yearned for a clean, cool washcloth but managed to ask, "Are you going to cut these cuffs so I can use that to wipe my face, or are you going to do it for me?"

He contemptuously looked at the handkerchief then at her cuffs. With unexpected care, he gently wiped her brow, cheeks, and finally her mouth. With each stroke, another slice of her strength dissolved, leaving exhaustion in its place.

He held a bottle of water to her lips. "Sip and rinse. Don't drink." His words were in English kind and caring, a contrast to the hard planes of his face.

She could see the sympathy in his oddly tender blue eyes. She did as he ordered. Part of her wanted to spit in his face, but something about him stopped her. Besides, she didn't have much fortitude left. She filled her mouth with a cool wet liquid, swished in every crevice to remove the acidic taste, then turned her head and spat.

Louder, in a cold hard tone, he asked in Spanish, "Can you travel now?"

She nodded, too weak to speak. The determination to bolt from the car, combined with the exertion to empty her stomach, had used all her physical reserves. She felt warmth envelop her as the drug took over again.

Harper collapsed.

She would later vaguely remember the sturdy arms which had come around her so gently before she hit the ground. She thought someone whispered in her ear, in English again, he was getting her help. That was ridiculous. She must be hallucinating. It was the drugs. It had to be.

Then there was nothing but darkness.

CHAPTER 4

HARPER ROUSED TO INSTANT ALERT AS SHE FELT HER BODY being lifted. Someone had picked her up under her knees, his other arm around her back.

"Sick!" She'd tried to scream the word, but it came out as a whisper. Obviously, though, she'd spoken loud enough for the man to realize the meaning of her word. He gently set her unbound feet on the ground and let her bend over.

Mostly dry heaves again. She hadn't counted the number of times this had happened, but Harper was aware this wasn't the first.

The whomp whomp whomp of slowing rotors caught her attention. Head down, she glanced to the side. A flat-green Huey helicopter, gunned out for war, wound down atop a round landing pad. She filed that information into her foggy mind. She couldn't fly, but maybe she could seduce the pilot into helping her escape…once she felt better. Damn it, she couldn't see who'd flown the bird.

Sweat dripped off her face as Harper wobbled and tried to stand straight. She took deep breaths and turned into the breeze to cool her sick-dampened skin. The blue of an ocean filled her view, but maybe it was just the color of Segundo's eyes, as he once again picked her up and carried her into a palace. She thought it was a palace. It was a pretty beige color with high walls and turrets on the corners. Every little girl's fantasy.

She was going under again. She had to fight it.

"Sleep now, baby." She was sure this time. She'd heard him speak in English, just a whisper directly into her ear. She felt like a child in his arms. She wanted to curl into this man and let him protect her. "The doctor will take care of you."

His words were the last thing she heard as blackness won over her willpower.

As though from the other end of a long tunnel, Harper heard, "Undress her, please." It was the now familiar voice that commanded everyone.

Through her fog-clouded brain, she heard him order in Spanish, "Doctor, why don't you wait outside until she's in the nightgown? Show my woman some respect."

My woman? Did he think he owned her? She was no man's property.

"Certainly, Segundo." There was a hint of fear in the man's answer.

"Yes, sir," repeated several men, their voices fading as they stomped away in rapid retreat.

Harper still felt ill and didn't want to move for fear of disturbing her fragile stomach. She hated to be sick but truly despised the feeling of helplessness. She'd promised herself as a teenager she'd never be at the mercy of another person again.

Yet, there she was. Captured. She hoped her teammates were safe and had made it home. She was sure someone would come for her. Maybe a SEAL team or a Marine Corps Special Operations team. Most of the Army's Special Forces were busy in the Middle East, but she'd certainly like to see some of the men she'd trained with and worked alongside in the desert. Hope soothed the fear that grew in the pit of her now-empty stomach.

In English, just above a whisper, Segundo spoke so close to her ear she could feel the moist heat of his breath. "I know you're awake, querida. You'll be all right now. The doctor is just outside, and he'll give you something for your stomach. Don't fight the injection, or I'll get the guards to hold you down." He brushed a wet curl from her clammy forehead and traced her jaw line with a gentle finger. His touch was comforting, not creepy as Narváez's had been.

Surprisingly, she wasn't worried he'd hurt her. His touch was so compassionate, almost sensual. He'd even called her darling. Normally she hated such terms of endearment, but she liked the way he'd said it.

What the hell? Sicker than she'd ever been, throwing up every few minutes, and now she was thinking about the way the man touched her.

What was wrong with her?

He'd kidnapped her.

Drugged her.

He was one of the bad guys…wasn't he?

He'd spoken English to her. Hadn't he? Her brain was so confused. She'd grown up speaking both Spanish and English, so her brain automatically translated. Did the drugs have her that muddled?

"I won't let them hurt you. We didn't know you were allergic." He moved away quickly as the light patter of feet became louder.

Someone with small hands gently spread cream over her face and neck. Harper cracked her eyes open and saw a teenage girl's face with pretty brown eyes almost too large for her delicate features. She used a warm washcloth to remove what little makeup remained and the dried sweat. It felt as if pounds had been lifted from Harper's face.

Harper could have kissed her, but then she would've been forced to open her eyes. Not happening.

"Segundo, she's very tall. Will you help me with these clothes?" the small pensive voice asked.

"Of course, le chiquita." Segundo had called the young woman little one. Was she his daughter? Was he old enough to have a daughter that age?

Limp, in the drugged stupor, Harper was unable to offer any resistance to the large hands that brought her to a sitting position as small ones efficiently stripped away her clothes. Long, rough fingers massaged her shoulders, sore from being pinned back for too many hours while her arms had been cuffed behind her back. She ran her cheek over the back of his hand and blamed her action on the drugs they'd used.

"Quickly finish getting her dressed and cleaned," he demanded.

"Yes, Segundo," a young, frightened voice answered.

Cool soft material seemed to float over her body. Small hands unhooked her bra and unwove it through the gown. The girl unsnapped Harper's jeans but struggled to pull them down.

"Here." Segundo picked Harper up under her arms and stood her on shaky legs.

Her bare feet absorbed the coolness of the tile, and Harper sighed.

"Are you going to get sick again?" He scooped her up, and his long stride had her in a bathroom within a second. He placed her on her feet in front of the commode.

"No, I'm not sick," Harper croaked out. She looked at the American-style toilet and suddenly had to go. "But I could...

um…use some privacy." She looked at him now, focusing on what had mostly been blurred facial features as the planes of his face became clear. His confused expression was suddenly replaced by understanding.

"Yeah. If you don't mind." She glanced around and found the door, her gaze remaining on it.

He nodded once and started to leave but stopped mid-stride. He stared at her for the longest minute, studying her face. "You can't escape, so don't even try." Scowling at the young girl, he ordered, "Finish getting her cleaned up, quickly. If she tries anything, scream." Looking back at Harper, the man warned, "I'm right on the other side of this open door. Make it fast."

The second Harper's jeans and panties hit the floor, the teen was there to collect them, eyes pleading for compliance. Her large brown eyes darted to the doorway before she pointed to the sink where a plastic-wrapped toothbrush sat next to a new tube of toothpaste. A recognizable bottle of blue mouthwash stood beside it.

"For you," was all she said.

Thank God. Harper's mouth felt sticky, yet dry, at the same time. She made use of everything provided as fast as she could, including the floral-scented soap and washcloth. But she obviously wasn't fast enough.

She sensed him before she saw Segundo standing behind her, watching her in the mirror as she rinsed and spit into the sink.

"Bed. Now." The determined look on his face bore no questioning or resistance.

Although she felt somewhat better, she'd expended what little energy remained. Her legs were weak and unsteady. She'd taken two tentative steps before she was whisked up and carried back to the bed. Such impatience. She could've made it on her own. Probably.

Instead, she floated in the air as if she were a young child, safe in loving arms.

Harper forced her eyes to remain open and looked into his aqua blue depths again. His nearly black hair fell across his forehead. She wanted to push it back, as he had done for her. When she attempted to lift her hand, it felt too heavy, detached as though she'd fallen asleep on it.

He whispered in her ear again, "You'll be all right, Harper." He gently placed her back on the bed. The soft mattress and cool sheets lulled her. She wanted to sleep but felt the need to remain awake.

She'd been unconscious for much of the trip, so she wasn't sure how long she'd traveled over bumpy roads. She didn't remember getting into the chopper. It was daylight now, and from the position of the sun, she guessed midday. The humidity there would be oppressive if not for the warm ocean breeze that cooled her skin.

The door creaked when Segundo opened it to allow in an older, heavy-set man with a worn backpack. "Watch your hands. She's mine." He then took a Sentinel stand in front of the door with arms crossed over his powerful chest, feet shoulder width apart and a scowl on his face.

The man Harper hoped was a real doctor, took her vitals. Though heavily accented, he asked her in English, "Are you allergic to cocaine as they have told me?"

Her throat was raw but she managed to answer, "Yes."

The man pulled up her eyelids and closely examined her eyes with a penlight. "The worst is over. What you need now is sleep and fluids to flush the remaining drugs from your system."

He glared at Segundo. "You're very lucky the cocaine was only a small portion of what you gave her."

After digging in his bag for a moment, he pulled out a syringe and small vial of liquid. "I'm going to give you something to relax your stomach and to help you sleep. Water and crackers, only, for the rest of the day, and by tomorrow you should feel much better."

She didn't fight when he gave her a shot, not because beautiful Blue Eyes had threatened her, but because she simply didn't have the strength. The doctor packed up his bag and left immediately.

Harper watched through slitted eyes—she couldn't open them any farther without wasting a great deal of effort—as the girl brought an ice bucket filled with bottled water then placed it on a nightstand. She gathered Harper's clothing and worn boots.

Segundo told her, "You may go. I'll call you when she awakens."

As soon as the girl had left the room and the door clicked closed, Segundo helped Harper sit up and held her with his arm around her shoulders. He ran an ice cube over her dry, cracked lips. Her tongue instantly sought the melting liquid and darted out to capture every drop.

He drew in a ragged breath.

Her gaze flew to his, now the color of the deep ocean. His hand stilled, and she licked the ice cube, eager to replace the lost fluids.

Segundo blinked then glanced toward the door. When his eyes returned to hers, they were the blue found only in deep mountain snow and just as cold. He pressed the ice cube between her lips. "Let it melt in your mouth. We'll see if that stays down before we try any water. Lie down now. The shot will help you sleep."

He laid her back to the mound of pillows and pulled the sweet-smelling sheets up to her chin. With a deep breath, Harper relaxed for the first time in hours, maybe days. Somehow she knew he'd protect her while she slept.

Segundo stretched out on top of the covers next to Harper. She curled into him as if they'd been lovers for years. They fit, which amazed her. She'd always felt big and awkward, but next to him—he had to be six feet four—she felt just right.

Must be the drugs, she considered again, or the smell of a man after a long mission.

~

Rafe tucked Harper into his side, an arm around her shoulders.

Thank God, she's going to be all right.

From the moment he'd learned she was allergic to cocaine-based drugs and might die, he'd become increasingly pissed at Carlos. What the hell was the man thinking? This woman, who nestled into him so perfectly, needed to stay alive, and he'd do everything in his power to make sure she did.

The heat of every breath she exhaled covered him in a soothing balm. She'd fallen asleep, this time restful.

Why did Carlos need her so much he was willing to risk everything to kidnap her? A woman on an international ATF team was unusual, and thus more valuable to the U.S. government. Did Carlos intend to hold her for ransom? And why was she there to begin with? Colombia was not known for its tobacco or alcohol production, and guns most often came into the country rather than being exported out.

As he gazed at her soft face, perfectly arched eyebrows

and long lashes that created gentle curves under her eyes, he wondered what a woman like her was doing in a violent country like this.

Rafe replayed the hangar scene and paid attention to every word. Carlos had called her Miss Harper Tambini. Miss. Rafe didn't know why her unmarried status pleased him. He hoped Carlos was right. She didn't wear any rings, but he'd look more carefully for an indentation on her left hand. He didn't want to lift the covers and disturb her beauty sleep—not that she wasn't beautiful enough—because she was exhausted.

How did Carlos know her name? Who had he been talking with lately? And why hadn't he shared this information with me?

Damn it. Rafe was the second in charge of the entire operation, including thousands of acres of farming, cocaine production, and transportation, as well as the private army that protected everything Carlos held important.

Harper rolled and placed her left hand on his chest as she tucked herself closer to him. No ring had circled her finger long enough to leave permanent depressions.

He smiled.

The awareness of her he'd tried to ignore since they grabbed her in Bogotá nudged something deep inside him. No woman had affected him this way in years. He could spend hours dining and dancing with the most beautiful women in Colombia, but he'd never felt as strong an interest for any of them as he did for this stranger.

Beth had stirred him this way the first time she'd walked past him, totally concentrating on her next high board dive. Swim team bathing suits hid nothing, and hers had clung to every curve of her luscious body like a second skin. She hadn't even noticed him. But he'd sure as hell noticed her.

Goddamn, how he missed her.

Rafe stretched cramped muscles in his arm then cupped the back of his head. Maybe he was attracted to Harper because they were lying in bed and it had been far too long since he'd had a woman. Yes, lack of sex had to be why.

His gaze traveled from her dark hair to her high forehead. Someone had once told him that was a sign of intelligence. She had to be smart to become a U.S. federal agent. A bachelor's degree was the minimum requirement.

He mentally traced each gently arched eyebrow. Even with her eyes closed, he felt the power of them. Large, oval-shaped Bambi eyes and the longest black eyelashes he'd ever seen. Their shadows hadn't darkened the hollow place above her high cheekbones, lack of sleep and dehydration was the cause. He had to be sure she drank the next time she awoke, but not so much it would upset her stomach again.

She had a small nose that turned up ever so slightly at the end. Her lips pouted in sleep. They were pale right now, but he could imagine them reddened and even fuller from his kisses. He could also imagine them doing hundreds of things to his body. His erection pulsed.

Her hair fell over surprisingly muscled shoulders, and he suspected she could do as many pull-ups as most of his sicarios. Although her arms were tucked in close to her body once again, he could see her rounded breasts and almost picture them tipped with dark brown nipples. Damn how he wanted to taste them, take them into his mouth and savor them, make her demand more and give her everything she wanted.

But would she want anything from him? Would she accept his touch?

Stop that. She was sick, and he was there to protect her.

Rafe brushed away an errant strand from her darkly

tanned face, and she sighed as his fingers found their way slowly down her jaw to a slightly pointed chin. Her cheeks were tinged pink from the receding fever. She was gorgeous even when she was sick. The image of this attractive woman, content in his arms, seared into his brain.

He wished he knew more about her.

Fucking Carlos. What's his plan? Did he intend to kill her after he'd used her? And exactly what skills had he referred to? And why hadn't Rafe been brought in on this plan?

Since they'd been roommates at VMI, they'd discussed everything, like the brothers neither of them had. They'd talk for hours about their shared dreams of improving Colombia's economy and helping the people with legitimate agriculture while not letting it become a Communist country like most of South America. Those pipe dreams had all disappeared in the last few years, along with his respect for Carlos which decreased with every white line his old friend sniffed.

Rafe closed his eyes in disgust and matched the breathing of the mysterious woman who lay pushed against him. He fell asleep with her warm breath on his neck and her hand resting gently over his heart.

CHAPTER 5

HARPER ROUSED FROM THE DEPTHS OF SLEEP, GENTLY THIS time. Her nausea had receded in the previous hours. With only glimpses of her surroundings as she'd been helped into a bathroom, she wasn't sure where she was, but she knew she wasn't alone.

She snaked her hand cautiously over the bedspread. The man was gone. Maybe he'd never been there. Maybe he hadn't been real. Drugs could make the mind believe weird things. Hell, in the depths of Colombia, she'd thought she heard him speak Southern-accented English.

There had been a limousine, she was pretty sure.

A helicopter? She wasn't confident about that memory. It might have been from the mission. She was sure her team had flown through mountains in a chopper.

Someone had carried her, at least once. No, at least twice. A castle. She shuddered as she remembered large hands holding her body while small ones stripped off her clothes.

Someone had forced her to sip water beside the road. Blue Eyes was to thank for the small kindness.

In the bathroom, it had been a small gray mouse of a girl.

In the bed, oh God, he'd been in bed with her. Had he…
No. She was sure he hadn't raped her.

With an audible sigh, she rolled onto her side. Sleep. She needed more sleep.

There had been so much sweat pouring out of her body she'd used the sheet to wipe her face, and then someone with a cool, wet cloth had delicately washed her face. Small hands, like a child's.

And Blue Eyes, again, concerned and gentle in his touch. With the memory came a sense of security.

That's just fucking weird. Had to be a hallucination.

She took a deep breath. This time she felt better. She hoped her body had purged the majority of the poison. A warm breeze bathed her face and brought with it moisture and the unique smell of salted air. The ocean, she concluded. As she forced air to the bottom of her lungs, she rolled to her other side. No nausea, finally.

At some point they'd untied her. When, Harper had no idea.

It would be best if they thought she was still asleep, so she barely cracked her eyelids and discovered the sun reflected on an ocean. The dark yellow circle had slipped a fraction beneath the blue water horizon. Okay, she faced west, and the sun was setting on the Pacific Ocean. She marveled for a moment about how Colombia was one of the few countries in the world with two ocean coasts only a hundred miles apart. She estimated they had traveled over two hundred miles from Bogotá. At least it was warm there.

Army torture training had taught her the best way to force any toxic from her system was through a strenuous workout, but first she needed water then food. She couldn't remember when she'd eaten last. Her muscles would start to cramp if she didn't get some electrolytes soon.

Driving oxygen progressively deeper into her lungs, Harper began to systematically stretch her muscles. The unique scent of roses drifted over her with a cooling ocean breeze. Raising her eyelids a fraction of an inch more, she discovered fresh flowers in a cut crystal vase filled with a rainbow of roses and fragrant greens on her bedside table.

Really? Somebody put flowers in my room?

Well, she had been sick. The gesture struck her as oddly civil.

She heard a quiet, twittering voice call to her in rapid Spanish. "Miss. Miss. You are waking up now? Are you sick again?"

"No," Harper croaked. "Hungry." She hoped she'd replied in a Spanish dialect the young woman understood. The Puerto Rican Spanish she'd learned as a child was a little different from the Colombian dialect, but over the past few weeks, she'd assimilated the verbiage and colloquialisms.

Wooden chair legs scraped against tile before the scurrying sound of soft shoes faded. From what seemed so very far away, she heard a bird-high voice calling for Segundo. Maybe he could her find some food and something cold to drink.

Harper sat up in bed and swung her legs over the side. So far, so good. She gave her stomach a moment to be sure it was settled. As she shifted her feet closer to the floor, very soft lace brushed against her bare breasts like a lover's caress. She looked down at the satin negligee in deep gold. She wondered who'd put this on her, although as sick as she'd been, she didn't really care. If it had been Segundo, she hoped he'd enjoyed the thrill of her naked body because he'd never get the chance to see it again. She'd break his neck before she'd let him touch her.

She stood, walked carefully on unsteady legs to the misty

sheer curtains hanging from ceiling rods at the edge of the open-air bedroom. A live postcard spread out below.

A golden sun washed the world in peach tones, warming the white stucco walls of her room. Ocean waves crashed on jagged rock spires before they frothed onto a small sandy curve of beach. Down the steep mountain, workers in woven straw hats continued to pick in green sentinel rows. At the far reaches of her view, evenly spaced banana trees blocked her gaze, but deep green mountains loomed above the tall fronds. High stucco walls surrounded the large house and also encompassed several one-story buildings with many doors giving it the appearance of a worn 1950s beach motel. The compound had been built in terraces, like so many in mountainous areas of the world. Harper's room was several levels up, so she had a bird's eye view of what looked to her like a huge agricultural operation.

Breathing deeply, she was overpowered by the scent of flowers again. She stepped through the gauzy curtains that kept most of the bugs out and onto the balcony overlooking beautifully tended gardens. Roses, iris, bird of paradise, hibiscus, and many plants she couldn't identify were artfully arranged to capture each color and saturate the senses. The sweet smell lofted to her was almost too much for her tender stomach.

"Planning to jump, Harper?" Segundo's deep voice was close.

She held in the jolt and refused to turn and look at him. She hadn't heard him enter the room or approach. He was so close to her back his breath wisped over her nearly bare shoulder. Realizing she was scantily clothed, she crossed her arms over her breasts to conceal her hardened nipples. She was more off her game than she'd imagined.

Not planning to jump, but she had been scoping out the

place to find an escape route. She was weak and had to get her strength back before she could try, so she would play along, for now.

"No, I was absorbing the view. It's picturesque," Harper managed in a deep, sleep-heavy voice. "Although I'm not sure where here is."

She sensed his eyes surveying every inch of her body as he stepped beside her. The sunset had turned pastel pinks and purples. She hoped it gave her sun-browned skin a healthier glow than it deserved.

The ocean breeze brought his spicy male scent, replacing the floral mix that had lured her out of her room. She'd call it fresh, earthy, like the fields outside the walls. Not sweet like the garden below.

"You are in the Narváez Western Compound, surrounded by fruits, vegetables, flowers, and loyal sicarios who will capture you, or kill you, if you try to leave. But you are Carlos's guest. We've removed the restraints and expect you to join us for supper in thirty minutes."

Unconsciously, Harper rubbed her wrists, raw from fighting the plastic cuffs. Someone had put a salve on them, taking away the pain.

From the corner of her eye, she got a good look at Segundo in the setting sun. He was a magnificent specimen of a man, well over six feet with wavy dark hair falling beyond the collar of his button-down dress shirt. He had the kind of soft curls that begged for a woman's fingers to rake through them. His light blue eyes with an even lighter outer circle currently seemed too serious. It had obviously been a long time since they had reflected his laughter, but the few lines fanning from their corners indicated he'd been happier in his past.

He was very handsome by anyone's definition. Delicious,

she decided. The edges of her lips curled up slightly at the thought of tasting his sun-kissed skin.

What the hell are you thinking?

This man had kidnapped her, almost killed her with his despicable drugs, and now held her captive so she could… what? Why had they taken her? Narváez had said they didn't want her for her body. Thank God.

When the man turned his broad shoulders and stepped closer, heat surged through her entire body. It was like an uncontrollable chemical reaction she had to him. She wanted to step back, but held her place. Invasion of personal space was a common interrogation technique, one of many she'd been trained to resist. She would show no fear, although she wasn't afraid of this man. No, she had a totally different reaction to him. And wasn't that just the damnedest thing?

Segundo's gaze never left her face. "You're looking much better. I thought for a short while we might lose you. We had no idea you were allergic to the drug we used to knock you out. Shall I send the doctor in again?"

"Again?"

"Yes, he's been here several times. He tended to you as soon as we landed and has checked on you regularly."

Landed. So there had been a helicopter or a plane. Good. At least part of her memory was real.

"No, I'm better. I probably still have traces in my body. What I need is to go for a run or a hard workout to force the rest from my system. I don't imagine you're going to allow me to do either." She stepped away from him. He was too close. Unless it was a required part of an operation, she kept her distance from all men, especially the strong, virile, and commanding kind.

"We have a gym, and you may use it at your leisure." He

said as though she should already know. "As I said, you are a guest. But your presence is required at supper."

"If I'm a guest, then I'd like to leave immediately." Could this all have been a nightmare? A misunderstanding?

He smiled down at her. "Certainly not. Carlos will explain everything." His eyes looked more hopeful than confident.

He gestured for her to move back into the bedroom, where the slight teen with the tweeting voice carried a shimmering golden evening gown that sparkled under the recessed lighting in the room. She cautiously laid it on the bed before she disappeared through a doorway.

"I believe this should fit quite well. Carlos picked it out for you himself." When the young woman reappeared, she carried a sheer lace halter bra and matching thong in one hand and gold spike heels in the other.

Segundo plucked the thong from the girl's hand. He ran a large thumb over the small V of satin and lace. His darkened eyes ran the length of her entire body and back up before he took in her face. "I'll be back for you in twenty-five minutes. Be dressed." He dropped the thong on the bed and strode out of the room.

A metallic snick confirmed Harper's fear. The door only locked from the outside. She was a prisoner, no matter Segundo's lies.

CHAPTER 6

HARPER NEEDED A SHOWER AND HAD TO WASH HER SMELLY hair. She would be alone in the shower and able to think. As she turned, the small woman handed her a bamboo tray with a glass and an unopened sweating bottle of ice-cold water next to a perfectly ripened banana. Harper cracked open the water and thanked the girl then took the tray with her into the bathroom.

Earlier, when she'd been allowed to use the facilities and brush her teeth, she hadn't cared what the bathroom looked like. Now, feeling better by the minute, she saw a large jetted tub sunk into the floor, surrounded by colorful tropical plants. There were many shades of green with bright red flowers, some with leaves as large as a bath towel, while others were delicate ferns. A three-foot-tall bird of paradise reached out from the corner as though in greeting. A honeymoon suite in a tropical paradise came to mind. Except it was part of Harper's jail.

The glass-fronted shower boasted two showerheads on opposing walls. Diamond-shaped tiles of white marble streaked with green were accented by its reverse; green marble with rivers of white covered every wall. Two opaque white vessel sinks sat atop sculpted green marble counters with bronzed waterfall faucets. A sculpted green vase overflowed with fresh-cut flowers filled a corner of the counter. Shocked by its classic beauty, Harper stood admiringly in the center of the large room. Okay, not a stark prison cell…a velvet cage. Nonetheless, she was still a captive bird.

The corners of Harper's mouth kicked up. Not so long ago, her handle had been Lady Osprey during several missions in the Middle East. She wondered if USSOCOM would send her friends after her. Technically, she still worked for the United States Special Operations Command. They had temporarily assigned her to the ATF because of her work on developing Chaz.

Harper's thoughts were interrupted by a knock on the door just before it cracked opened six inches.

"Miss, may I draw you a bath?"

"What's your name?" Harper asked instead of answering the question. She motioned the small girl into the room.

"My name?" The girl looks scared to death.

"Yes." It was a simple question, and she'd asked in Spanish.

"Here, they call me Carlotta."

Harper knew what it was like to be called something other than your given name. After her mother was murdered, she'd been forced to live with an aunt she'd never met, who insisted upon calling her Annie, a version of her real first name. Although Annabelle Harper Tambini was on her birth certificate, her mother, and everyone who knew her, had called her Harper. No shortened nickname and never her first name.

"No, I want your given name. The one your parents and

the church gave you." Harper picked up the banana and peeled it halfway.

"Oh, I am Cesara Magdalena Rosado." She straightened and squared her shoulders as though very proud of her name.

"What do you like people to call you?"

"Maggie," she said with a huge smile. "It's American, right?"

Harper had to snicker. "Yes, Maggie, it's American." She now looked at the waif and asked just before she took a bite of the fruit, "Who dressed me in this sleeping gown?"

With lowered eyes, Maggie admitted, "I did, miss. Your clothes…they smelled very bad. You were sick, you see. Segundo, he helped me, but he turned his head. He's nice like that. He stayed with you for a long time. They ordered me to take care of you. I did my best, miss, but I'm not a nurse."

Harper finished the banana and laid the peel on the tray. "You obviously did just fine. I'm alive and feeling better. Thank you, Maggie. Now talk to me as I shower. You've apparently seen me naked so don't be embarrassed."

Harper had never been concerned about being naked around women. She'd played several sports during high school and college and showered with more women than she could count. The Army was the same way.

She nudged the thin straps off her shoulders and allowed the satin and lace gown to fall to the polished tile floor. She stepped free of the pooled fabric and strode naked to the multi-head shower then adjusted the hot water.

"Maggie, do you know why I'm here?" Harper stepped under liquid heaven. She let the warm water drench her from head to toe as it washed away the feelings of helplessness with the smell of sickness.

"No, miss. Banita, she's the head housekeeper, she said that you are a guest. A very guest especial."

"Do you get many guests here?" Harper surveyed the bottles lined on the shelf. She flipped open one of the body washes and sniffed. Fruity. Not her personal style so she replaced it and moved on to the second. The familiar designer logo held promise. She breathed in one of her favorite perfumes and proceeded to use the liquid soap.

"No, miss. Not very often. You're the first woman guest, I think." Maggie paused for a long minute before she admitted, "I was a little afraid when Banita asked me to be your...helper."

"Why?" Harper asked as she shoved her head under the warm spray.

"Because I didn't know what you'd need me to do. What they'd expect." She spoke quickly then, adding. "Momma went straight to Segundo as soon as you landed, and he explained everything. And Momma saw how sick you were. She told Banita it was all right for me to take care of you, but no men. Never I am allowed to take care of the men." Maggie's little voice was adamant, no doubt an echo of her mother's words and sentiment.

"So Narváez has men guests? And they get personal helpers, too?" Harper wondered just how personal the helpers were as she soaped away the stench of the day and the previous night.

"Yes, but the house whores take care of them most of the time, and housekeeping just cleans the rooms."

"The what? Did you actually call them house whores?" A chill ran from Harper's wet hair to the soles of her feet that had nothing to do with the water temperature.

"Yes, miss. That's what Momma calls them. They are here to entertain the sicarios and some of the other men who live here, whenever they want a woman."

"Well, hell," Harper muttered and wondered if Narváez

was in the sex trade, too. Was she to become his perverted toy? No. She remembered him saying he didn't want her for her body. What then? She needed to get everything she could out of this girl.

"Maggie, who lives here? I'd like to know who to expect at dinner." Her request sounded reasonable as she tested the young woman's knowledge and willingness to share. Harper placed a dollop of the matching shampoo in her palm and lathered her hair.

"Carlos Narváez and his new wife, Bunny," Maggie said. "His last two wives are still here in the compound, but not in the big house anymore. The one before them now lives in Cartagena, according to most of the household staff."

"Four wives? What's up with that?"

Maggie snickered. "Not him." She giggled this time. "He's out shooting at nothing."

Those words didn't make sense. Harper had translated wrong. Out shooting. Oh, he's shooting blanks. Harper laughed out loud, at herself and at Narváez. Maggie got to giggling harder.

Finally under control, Maggie added, "He wants a son to carry his name, someone to take over the business someday."

Understandable. Most men wanted an heir, and in this part of the world, that meant a son.

"I wish he'd have a son soon. I do not like his nephew, Velez." At the hate in her voice, Harper looked at Maggie who visibly shook. "He is not a good man."

Harper made a mental note to find and keep an eye on Velez. "Has he hurt you?"

"No, he knows if he does Segundo will hurt him." She crossed her arms over her small developing breasts and rubbed her biceps. "I don't like the way he looks at me."

Changing the subject, Harper asked, "Who else will be at dinner?"

Maggie continued. "Segundo, of course, and probably a few of the house whores."

Guess Harper would get a first-hand look at these women. If she had the opportunity, she'd try to talk to them about their situation. She had no idea what she could do to help, but if they were being held against their will she'd do whatever she could. Hell, she wasn't sure what she could do to help her own predicament.

Harper shook her head slowly as she repeated washing her hair. The heat and mist permeated the glass shower with the spicy scent she liked to wear out on dates. She took deep breaths of the moist, warm air as though cleaning out her lungs as well. "Is se…is that their only purpose here? Do they cook or clean or work?"

"Oh, no, miss. We staff cook all the food and clean all the rooms. The men are not allowed to touch the staff. Segundo makes sure."

"Good for him." Harper liked Blue Eyes for his protectiveness. She rinsed the expensive shampoo from her thick hair before working the coordinating conditioner into her scalp and hair. Someone here had good taste. She couldn't afford this lifestyle, but she could enjoy the amenities as Carlos's guest-slash-prisoner. Drugs and guns—and maybe human trafficking—made for high living.

"So, who else is in this house, Maggie?" Might as well ask the real questions. Harper had always been amazed at what people would reveal, especially staff. More than once she'd disguised herself as a maid or cook just to hear the household gossip to get to know a situation better. She liked gathering human intelligence and was good at it.

"Always guards."

Figures. "Do they carry guns?"

"Yes, big rifles and pistols. Most have several guns all the time."

"Great," Harper mumbled as she took the hand-held showerhead and rinsed her hair. "How many people are in the whole compound?"

"Maybe forty." The little girl was a wealth of knowledge, and so willing to share.

"Do they all sleep here in this house?"

"No, the men have a barracks, but some have rooms here in the big house…Valez." Maggie practically spat out the man's name. She continued, "The staff, we have our own place. Some have apartments because they are married. I still live with my parents above the garage. Since Father drives the limousines and takes care of all the cars and trucks, we have a big place—four rooms. My sister and I have our own bedroom. Mother is the second floor maid here in the big house. She has an important job." Pride emanated through Maggie's voice.

"I'm sure it is, and you're very proud of her, I can tell." Through the glassed enclosure, Harper saw red tinge Maggie's cheeks. "So how many people sleep in the big house?" Harper asked as she stepped out of the shower. Maggie handed her a warmed towel for her hair and a bath blanket that she stood on tiptoe to wrap around Harper. How nice it was to have a personal attendant.

"There are ten bedrooms in the big house, but how many sleep here depends on how lonely the men are at night, and if Mr. Narváez takes one of the house whores or stays with his wife."

"What about Segundo? Does he have a wife, or does he bed the whores most nights?" For some odd reason, Harper wasn't sure she wanted to know the answer.

"No, Segundo has no wife, and he doesn't like the house whores. He says they are for the men. I think he goes into town and finds a woman. Maybe he has a special one at the East House. I've never been there," Maggie offered as she plugged in a hair dryer and handed Harper a new brush.

Maggie bent and retrieved a white tray filled with new, boutique brand makeup. Harper tested a few foundations on her hand before she found one that matched her facial tones. A light blush and waterproof black mascara gave her face color once again.

Inching closer, Maggie watched her every movement as if she'd never seen anyone apply makeup before. Her skin was so young and smooth, she didn't need a drop of color enhancement.

Noticing the girl's interest, Harper asked, "Do you want to use this?" She pointed to the tray. "There are some colors here that would go well with your pretty brown tones."

"Oh, no, miss. Mother says makeup is for whores." Her innocent eyes told the rest of the story. "But you don't look like a whore when you put it on. You are like a magazine lady."

"Thank you. Where I come from, women use makeup to enhance their looks. Sometimes less is more. It's a lesson every American girl learns soon after she starts wearing makeup." Changing the subject, she asked, "So is this a farm? What is raised here?"

"Yes, miss."

"Call me Harper, please."

"Yes, Miss Harper, it's a big farm, the biggest in this area. We raise flowers and vegetables and coca plants. Farmers from all around bring their crops here." Maggie pointed toward the tall, slim windows which allowed the ocean breeze to wisp away the steam. "Over there are the processing rooms. They just built a new one last week. I heard some of the women talking about how tiny it is and wondering how they are supposed to work in such a small space. One of the men who helped build it said it kind of looked like a big kitchen, so maybe they're moving the cooks out of the big house. They're not happy about the idea."

Maggie looked at her watch then said, "You should hurry. Segundo does not like to be kept waiting. You have five minutes before he opens the door for you. Please hurry. You can't be late."

Harper didn't miss the urgency in her voice. As she quickly applied the final strokes of mascara, she asked, "Would Segundo hurt you if I was late?"

"No, Miss Harper, not Segundo."

Seeing the fear in the young woman's eyes, she pushed. "Then who?"

"The boss man, Mr. Narváez. He can be mean. Momma says he's sampling the crops, and that's a bad thing."

Harper bent over and hugged the girl then dashed from the bathroom. As she slid on the thong, the image of Segundo fingering the lace popped into her mind. Part of her wanted to be grossed out, but another part of her wondered what it would feel like as he stroked his fingers over the lace with it on her body. Slipping into the halter bra, she had to readjust her breasts to fit comfortably in the barely-there cups. The meager cloth didn't cover much more than her nipples and offer basic support.

She slid the dress easily over her head and adjusted her breasts again so the low V in the front revealed just a shadow of cleavage. She knew how to use her body to distract a man from her questioning, but she didn't want them to get the idea she was sexually easy.

She liked the way the soft satin of the dress clung to the

curve of her small waist and slightly rounded hips before draping to the floor. Slits up the sides, nearly to her hips, allowed glimpses of her shapely legs. She was proud of her body. Not bad for a twenty-eight-year-old. Her body was just another trick in her arsenal she'd use to escape.

She smoothed the luscious fabric over her hips and reached for the zipper at the small of her back. It moved a few inches and caught.

"Damn it." Harper tried to move it downward and restart, but it wouldn't budge.

Maggie emerged from the bathroom, damp towels in hand, and scooted to Harper's back. "Let me," she said and tapped on Harper's hands.

There was a knock seconds before the door opened. Segundo stood framed in the doorway, broad shoulders nearly touching each side, his posture straight, his mere presence a command. When he stepped in, Harper took in his perfectly tailored navy blue suit with red striped tie expertly knotted at his thick neck.

Power. The word shot through Harper's mind as her blood heated in reaction to his proximity.

CHAPTER 7

Standing in the open doorway of the guest room, Rafe let out a deep breath.

Harper was ready.

Backlit by the remaining traces of the setting sun, she looked like a goddess. The rays caught the slight golden highlights in her almost black hair. The long strands fell in soft waves over her shoulders and framed her heart-shaped face.

The maid's dark brown hands dealt with the low zipper on the almost backless dress.

Rafe took in Harper's fully curved lines and gym-toned muscles. He didn't care for the skinny, model-thin look. He preferred women with a little meat on their bones. In truth, an athletic build did it for him every time. Beth's body flashed through his mind but was quickly replaced by the woman in front of him. A body like hers was perfect in his opinion.

"I'll do that." Rafe knew his tone was harsh as he strode toward Harper. He softened his voice and looked at the maid whose hands shook. "I guarantee I've dealt with more zippers on formal dresses than you."

Maggie bowed her head and stepped away.

Harper had recovered considerably, but Rafe didn't trust her. As an agent, she was trained in hand-to-hand combat, perhaps she could even kill with her bare hands. He was sure he could counter anything she threw at him, but fighting with her was not what he wanted.

She carefully watched his every move as he approached.

He stopped, just out of arm's reach. "May I?"

Harper gave him a short nod. "Thank you."

He could tell she shoved down the urge to flinch when he touched the base of her spine. The open zipper revealed the tiny strings to the thong he touched less than half an hour ago. The idea of that tiny piece of cloth covering the most private part of her body stirred him like no woman had in years.

She stood, vigilant and still, as he examined the zipper. But he was too distracted by her bare skin, so smooth, laying open to his touch. Rafe wanted to run his hand up her back. He fought the urge to turn her around and take her face in his hands then gently kiss the thin line of her lips until they parted for him, letting him into the heat of her mouth. He'd then peel the dress off and caress every inch of her exquisite body. Carlos had given her to him after all.

He was not that kind of man nor would he ever be.

He forced himself to look at the dress and found the problem. Although he had large fingers, he gently released the cloth before succeeding with the zipper.

He shouldn't touch her. He was Segundo, and she was Carlos'…guest. More accurately, his prisoner. Rafe had vowed to protect her, but who was going to protect her from him?

His position in her life at the moment didn't stop him from desiring her, though. Rafe trailed his fingers up her backbone before fine light pink lines on Harper's left shoulder caught his eye. He traced them with the tip of his finger. Nearly a dozen radiated from a single source about the size of a quarter. Exit wounds were nasty, shredding the surrounding skin like a fist bursting through paper, especially when compared to the pencil-sized entry point. He had an urge to kiss every inch of stitched skin, then to follow the raised lines with his tongue.

Rafe leaned in and spoke in his native English so the maid wouldn't understand. "You were shot."

He could tell his slow Southern drawl had its intended effect. When she turned and looked into his eyes, he watched them slightly soften.

"Yes, twice," Harper told him quietly in English.

Facing him now, he could see where the bullet had entered her body. "This one was a through and through. Tore your soft skin somethin' fierce, darlin', but it looks like you had a talented plastic surgeon." He touched the straight pink scar, not quite an inch long, just under her collarbone, and felt a jolt pass through him. Her slight twitch and small gasp confirmed she felt it, too. That had never happened before, even with Beth.

"Yes, I did. Would you like her name? She has a prolific practice in West Palm Beach, Florida. Usually she's tucking up aging movie stars, but you might need a little work around your eyes. They look so sad." Harper touched the outer edge of his eye and ran a finger to his cheekbone.

He sucked in a breath. They were so close now. He considered kissing her, just a light brush of his lips on hers.

As he slowly slid his hand down her well-toned arm, he read the intelligence in her chocolate brown eyes. Her makeup was so slight, just a little to cover and warm her illness-paled skin, the total opposite of the house whores he was forced to dine with every night. It was such a pleasure to see a beautiful woman from his homeland.

The women in the big house were all painted bimbos, ready to do whatever he asked of them. All it took was a glance their way and they'd be in his lap, pawing at him, nothing seductive at all. He was Segundo, a very powerful man within this household, within the Narváez business, and even within the cartel. Women considered it a privilege if he so much as touched one of them casually.

He hated what they'd been subjected to, whores paid to keep the men on the plantation entertained and happy and, most importantly, to keep them there and working hard, miles from the nearest city. Some had arrived at the compound gates willingly, selling their bodies as a way to feed their families. Others had been sold by parents with too many hungry mouths at home. Narváez kept the prettiest ones for himself and to work in the main house. A few others worked the barracks, but all too many were sold to a human trafficker. Rafe did what he could for the women, but, as his old friend often reminded him, he was Segundo, second in command and he did what he was told to do.

Rafe was pretty sick of taking orders, too.

He'd never sought the attention or quick relief from any of the women who passed through the organization. That's not how he'd been raised. In Charleston, South Carolina, a man got to know the woman, enjoyed her company, and dated before he touched her body and shared his with her.

He missed intelligent conversation with a woman. He and Beth would verbally spar at every meal. The topic didn't matter; each would argue an opposite side. Or they'd share information on the same subject. She had been so smart and had the ability to see things from many angles yet never lose sight of the goal. It seemed only natural she went into Naval

Intelligence after graduation and commissioning. At heart, she wanted to save the world from itself. Instead, it had killed her.

Rafe slowly ran his hand up Harper's arm and over her bare shoulder to the curve of her neck. Her pulse raced against his fingers when he ran his thumb over her jaw line. Her glossed lips begged for his when her little pink tongue darted out to moisten them. His eyes met hers, not quite asking permission, more in warning he'd take what he wanted.

A flicker of calculation crossed her eyes, and he knew he was being played. Like a slap in the face, he remembered she was a U.S. agent and had been trained in the world of shadows and lies, same as Beth.

On his fiancée's brutalized, dead body, he'd sworn to never love again. He couldn't get involved with a woman who worked in the shades of darkness that was his world.

Rafe took Harper's hand and jerked her toward the door. "Let's go." His voice was gruff, but he didn't care.

Almost as tall as he was in her high heels, Harper strode easily beside Segundo, hand-in-hand. His fingers were intertwined with hers, likely to keep a good hold should she decide to bolt, not for the intimate palm-to-palm contact. There had been a moment in the bedroom when she'd seen desire in his eyes.

She could use sex against him. It was one of many tricks the CIA had taught her as part of her special operations training.

When he'd touched her scar, gently traced its pencil-thin lines, and his breath brushed on her neck…her body had betrayed her. She'd wanted to turn and kiss him. Somehow he'd known the pain of her wound had hurt more than just her body.

There was no way he could have known the two bullets before that one had murdered her mother and how the stream of "uncles" her aunt paraded through what was to be a safe home over the next six years had stained her view of men forever. Harper shoved the memories of her teenage years back into the recesses of her mind, where they belonged.

Focusing on escape, Harper mentally mapped the house as they walked down the hallway from her bedroom to a larger corridor and turned left. Thankfully, Segundo slowed as they descended a grand marble staircase to the main floor where an Italianate fountain sprayed water through its top and carved cherubs peed into the lower pool.

"At least someone here has a sense of humor," Harper mused. Her only answer was a slight upward twitch at the corner of his mouth. She'd like to see him smile.

"We're late," he announced as he tugged her into an ornate room just off the foyer.

From Harper's point of view, it looked as though someone had bought an entire French hotel lobby, and when it got there, they'd dumped it in with the Ikea furniture from a well-used college apartment. Dust clung to the magnificent eight-tiered crystal chandelier hanging in the middle of the room over a cheap pool table that had seen better days a decade ago. French provincial chairs with delicate tapestry seats sat next to a black block cigarette-scarred coffee table, one essential to every man's first apartment. At the far end, at least forty feet away, furniture had been carelessly moved aside, and a mounted basketball hoop reigned over the wooden polished floor. This was Boys Gone Wild.

Segundo dragged her to the bar at the opposite end of

the large room from the basketball court where Narváez stood chatting with the man Harper thought she recognized from the kidnapping. "My apologies, Carlos," Segundo began.

Unsure why, Harper interrupted, "It was all my fault," she explained in a slow, sultry voice in English-accented beginner Spanish. She turned to show off her naked back and toned buttocks. "My silly zipper got stuck." She placed a possessive hand on Segundo's chest. "He has very good hands and"—she paused dramatically—"took care of the problem. I'm sorry it took longer than we expected. He was very… thorough." She batted her long black lashes at Narváez as she forced a slow, sexy smile to cross her face.

Seduction was actually a class she'd taken at CIA Headquarters in Langley, Virginia. Those lessons had come in handy during this Colombian mission. Harper was always amazed what men would tell a woman in order to impress her. She wondered what she'd learn from Carlos Narváez tonight.

Segundo grabbed her wrist and removed her hand from his chest with a glare. Was he upset at her insinuation they were intimate before coming down? Had it infuriated him? True, he'd been a gentleman, but she wasn't about to apologize. There had been that little heat wave she'd felt when he touched her, and she was positive he'd felt it, too.

Narváez handed her a glass of wine. Harper wasn't sure her stomach would tolerate alcohol yet—plus she needed to keep a clear head. She gingerly touched her abdomen and begged in her novice Spanish, "May I please have bottled water? Let's be sure I keep that down first. I'm not sure my tummy is ready for alcohol just yet."

"I'll bet," the younger man said. "You were really puking your guts out last night."

Narváez grimaced then handed her a bottle of unopened water he retrieved from the small refrigerator under the bar.

"Looking good now, though." Dark eyes, identical to Narváez's, ran the length of her body but stopped on its way back up, focused entirely on her breasts. "Since Segundo doesn't seem to want her, Uncle Carlos, I'll be more than happy to see to her needs."

Segundo snaked an arm around Harper's waist and pulled her to him. "I will see to anything she needs."

Narváez glanced between the two men and laughed. "Pablo, my sister has taught you well, and I'm sure you learned a few things in that private high school in California, but you have a long way to go before you play in the same league as Segundo." He then smiled at Harper. "Please forgive my rude nephew, but let me introduce him. Pablo Valez is my older sister's oldest son. After getting kicked out of three colleges, she sent him to me hoping I could straighten the boy out. I'm not sure I'm doing a good job."

Quick as a whip, Narváez whacked the young man on the back of the head. "Mind your manners. Miss Tambini is a guest, and you will treat her with the utmost respect."

Clack. Flap. Clack. Slap. Clack, resounded in the high-ceilinged room. Female giggling followed. Three women emerged from the other side of a gaudy modernistic statue. A figure in jiggling electric lime green stood out among the rest. Harper had difficulty focusing. The woman wobbled across the marble floor on six-inch stilettos, shaking fringe that covered every inch of the cropped halter top and low riding mini skirt. Longer fringe barely covered her dark midriff and thighs. The blurring movement of the material made Harper's stomach roll with what felt like sea sickness this time, not cocaine poisoning.

A nearly naked woman with bleached white hair piled on

her head strutted with an exaggerated rolling gait beside the first. Her bright blue bathing suit bra had a puff of short blue feathers matching the bikini panties decorated with varying lengths of longer ones designed to create a skirt. Thigh-high sky-blue boots stretched up her legs so tight they appeared painted on. She stopped to pull them up, and her abundant breasts almost fell out of her bra.

Harper's mouth fell open slightly, and then she saw the third woman. The yellow sports bra covered some of her buxom bosom. The belt to the matching yellow leather chaps held in her belly, but a scrap of her red lace panties peeked through. Red cowboy boots completed the outfit.

Harper clamped her lips closed to suppress the laughter threatening to bubble up her throat.

Segundo must have seen her attempts to withhold her humor and laid a restrictive hand on her back. He bent down, his lips almost touching her ear. When he spoke, she felt the heat of his English words. "The blonde in feathers is Bunny, Carlos's wife. Think twice before laughing and insulting her. Everyone in this room has a gun except you."

Harper plastered on an overzealous smile and whispered, "Where does the one in the green dress keep her gun? That outfit is so tight I can see her naval. She's got an outie."

"You are so bad." His suppressed laughter came through in his voice.

Loudly, Harper answered in mutilated Spanish, "No, Segundo, I'm very good."

Narváez proudly brought the colorfully feathered woman to her. "Harper, please let me introduce the love of my life, Bunny."

Both women held out a hand, but Harper gave a good squeeze before releasing the silly-dressed woman's knuckles.

"Nice to meet you," Harper said, although the sentiment was far from true.

Harper assessed the woman to see if she might use her to gain her freedom. She saw a loyalty to Narváez that matched Segundo's, but hers was laced with fear. As the man's fourth wife, she had reason for concern.

Carlos wrapped a possessive arm around his wife and signaled for the other women to approach. As he introduced them, they snuggled into his large body, his eyes tracing each with apparent lust.

Harper dutifully nodded at each when introduced.

Narváez pulled all three women into him and spoke to them in low tones.

"Are they guests? Friends of Bunny's?" Harper asked Segundo.

"No, and yes." He pulled her a few steps away from the now giggling women. "The women are…um…they work in the house."

She just stared at him. She had a pretty good idea what they actually did in return for their keep but waited to hear how he'd explain it.

"They're here to keep the men content," he finally managed.

"But they're Bunny's friends? She must be really hard up for female companions."

His eyes changed to a cold blue. "Bunny used to be one of them, before she became Carlos's favorite."

They both glanced at the tight group and watched Carlos stroke the cowgirl's nearly bare ass.

"I hope she's not the jealous wife type," Harper couldn't resist saying.

Segundo chuckled. "No, she knows she has to share. As his wife, though, she gets status and credit cards."

Male rumbling came from the far end of the bar where Valez and two bodyguards snorted lines of cocaine, leaving several other sicarios to watch over the festivities. From her peripheral vision, she caught the way Valez watched her, not as a potential threat, but as a potential treat. He grinned at her and blatantly adjusted his erection. His initial male appreciation was morphing into animalistic hunger, no doubt enhanced by the cocaine.

The Narváez lovefest huddle now broken, the woman in the slime-green outfit jiggled with anticipation as she and the cowgirl kept eyeing the nearby men, but they remained at Bunny's side. They obviously knew their place. When Bunny nodded, the two women trotted to the bar and plucked small straws suggestively from the guards' fingers before they bent to inhale the white powder.

Velez never took his gaze off Harper, ignoring the other two women.

Bunny dragged her husband to join them. Each took a new straw from a cup before they too inhaled a white line.

Harper cringed and glanced at Segundo. Would he join them? A flash of disgust glinted in his blue eyes, and he looked away.

Carlos moved behind the bar and made drinks for the women while they cackled incessantly about each other's choice of clothing for tonight's special supper.

Before the drinks were finished, all three women glared daggers at Harper from over-painted eyes. She ignored them and discussed world politics, in English, with Carlos and Segundo. Both were amazingly well-informed.

Harper tracked the conversations of Bunny and the women as they debated fashion and celebrities. Harper was surprised at how much attention the women paid to U.S. movie stars and their apparel. She'd never cared what stars wore to social events and awards, but it was a serious topic with these women.

Whenever Bunny tried to draw Carlos into their conversation, he waved her off without so much as a glance in her direction and continued to focus on Harper. She could see jealousy building in the new wife as well as a slight flicker of fear.

Did the inane peacock really think she was looking at her replacement? No way in hell. The idea was so repugnant Harper shuddered.

A bell rang somewhere in the mansion.

CHAPTER 8

"I'T'S TIME FOR SUPPER," CARLOS ANNOUNCED AS HE HELD out his hand to Harper. She laid her fingers on his upward palm, and like a princess, she glided into the huge formal dining room. Bunny scurried to Carlos, who simply looked at Segundo and tilted his head toward his wife.

When Segundo held out his hand in an after-you gesture, Bunny grabbed it, held it up as she mimicked Harper's action, and tottered into the next room.

Carlos guided Harper to the head of the formal table, which was set for royalty. Only half of the twenty-four seats were elegantly prepared for the meal.

"We seldom get guests here, and I do so enjoy a grand dinner party." Carlos seemed intent on impressing her. "Does this meet your approval?"

It was truly extraordinary. The crystal water goblets were already filled, and a waiter was pouring a light-colored white wine for the first course into one of the five glasses on the upper right. She counted five forks to the left of the fine bone china plate, three knives, and three spoons to the right. A small bread plate held a butter spreader and another spoon lay horizontal at the top of the plate.

Harper knew very little about stately dinners. She'd been raised by a single mother who'd sold real estate, and fancy eating out usually meant sitting down at a chain restaurant rather than their usual fast food grab and go. Only once, while she was in the Army, had she attended a meal like this: a Battalion Dining In. This table was laid out as similarly.

"It's beautiful," she admitted. "I feel honored you'd go to all this trouble for me."

Segundo parked Bunny in the chair to Carlos's left, then rounded the table behind them.

"It's my pleasure. You are an important guest." Narváez seemed to gleam.

Yeah, right. Important enough to kidnap.

Carlos practically shoved Harper into the chair to his right. Segundo took the next one, sandwiching her between the two men.

The colorful women argued for a moment about who was to sit beside Bunny then sat quickly when Carlos cleared his throat. The bodyguards lumbered in with Velez who plopped down next to Segundo.

Harper played the charming guest throughout the first two courses, eating little. She cut the toast point laden with caviar into small pieces and sampled one, quickly deciding she was not a fan of fish eggs. The cold soup was more to her liking, and she'd eaten half of it before she set the rounded spoon aside. When the poached salmon with mousseline sauce and cucumbers was served, she again tasted a bite and lied as she voiced her approval to Carlos. Covering her dislike of seafood, she started into a long, amusing story about literally running into Peyton Manning in an airport so she wouldn't be expected to eat more.

Before everyone had finished that course, two guards dressed in rumpled uniforms entered the dining room, all but zipping up their pants. They were followed by two women, barely covered by robes, with tousled hair and reddened, swollen lips. Everyone at the table stopped eating and stared.

After a terse look from Carlos, the men turned tail and slid away. The women weren't as observant, but when Bunny shook her head almost violently, they got the message and left.

Harper tilted her head toward Segundo and declared in English, "Obviously they didn't get the memo."

Carlos burst out laughing, and everyone else at the table followed his lead, although Harper was pretty sure only Segundo and Carlos understood what she'd said.

Throughout the meal, Segundo and Harper bantered subject after subject. From impressionistic paintings to Middle Eastern politics, baseball to soccer, they spoke in Spanish and sometimes slipped into English when the arguments became heated. Carlos often interjected an opinion and was occasionally caught on one side or the other.

Segundo's grimace at the beginning of the meal had evolved into a grin and finally a genuine smile. It changed his whole face. He looked younger, less burdened. The bright white flash of straight teeth and teasing blue eyes dashed Harper's defenses. For a few minutes, she enjoyed his personality, forgetting this man had kidnapped and imprisoned her.

"Segundo," Bunny called across the wide table, "you are smiling. I've not seen you like this before."

"Forgive me, Bunny, but it has been many years since I have enjoyed such a sharp mind."

Harper winced at the verbal slam to Bunny.

Obviously realizing his faux pas, Segundo added, "Our

business keeps me so serious and focused, I rarely take time to enjoy the company of a woman."

"The House Honeys have noticed," Bunny reprimanded.

Harper choked on her lamb until Segundo patted her on the back. His touch on her bare skin instantly made her stop coughing. His open palm sent tingles through her entire body. When he casually rubbed his hand up and down her spine, she tried to hold back her shiver, but couldn't.

"Are you cold?" Segundo asked with what sounded like real concern.

"No," was all she could manage to say. She was hot. This time drugs weren't to blame…it was the man.

When the dessert dishes were cleared from the table and strong Colombian coffee had been poured, she'd had enough. Harper was exhausted from playing the good guest, drained from her illness, and irritated the man beside her could stir her simply by his nearness. He'd help kidnap her, and that pissed her off. She was ready to move on.

Harper looked at Carlos. "My compliments to your chef. I haven't eaten this well in months." It was the truth. ATF agents ate like cops, fast food eaten fast. Her cooking was so far from the gourmet supper they'd just finished, it was laughable.

"I'll be sure to pass along your compliments." Narváez tried to grin, but the lax muscles in his face didn't work. He was too drunk and high to remember his wife's name. After getting it wrong the third time, he reverted to calling her querida. With multiple Spanish meanings, Harper decided lover was most appropriate.

"If you'll excuse me, I'm very tired." Harper started to stand. At a look from Carlos, Segundo placed a firm hand on her shoulder.

"Harper," Carlos started then paused, acting as if he'd just thought this, "would you like to see the gardens? Perhaps Segundo would show them to you."

Suppressing her impatience, she pasted on a smile though she gritted her teeth. "No, thank you. As I said, I'm tired." She was tired of playing games and irritated with the whole situation.

Carlos sipped the liquid sludge they called coffee from a cup that looked as though it belonged in a child's tea set when compared to Narváez's huge hands. The heavy-set man drunkenly smiled at her. "Have some more coffee, my dear." He reached for the silver pot in front of him.

"I don't want any more damn coffee." Harper'd had enough. What she wanted was answers. "What do you want from me, Narváez? Why did you kidnap me, knock me out—almost killing me—and forcibly bring me here?" Fury and impatience pulsed in every muscle in her body.

The eyes of the women across the table went wide and starkly white with a woman-to-woman warning.

In the way of South American men, Carlos gave an exaggerated shrug and poured more coffee into his fine china cup. He sat back and sipped, saying nothing.

"I've had enough of this." Harper rose from the table and threw her napkin next to her untouched cup.

Faster than she thought possible, Narváez shot out of his seat and grabbed her arm. She looked down at his bulky hand on her bicep and ordered, "Get your hand off me."

She never saw it coming.

Narváez slapped her across the face.

Her head was knocked to the side where she saw the flare of anger in Segundo's eyes.

Harper spun on Narváez. She swept out a leg, taking his large body to the polished Italian tile floor in one swift move. She pinned his arms above his head and pressed a gold stiletto heel to the carotid artery pulsing wildly at his throat.

"Don't you ever touch me again! I've killed men for less than what you just did," Harper said, growling the warning. Her face stung. Anger roiled within her, but she held it in check. Emotions only got in the way.

She heard several safeties click during her takedown of their boss and knew there were at least three guns pointed at her, ready to protect him. Ready to shoot her.

With her eyes still riveted to Narváez's, she spoke softly, but in the silence of the large room, everyone heard, "Tell them to put the guns away, or I'll punch my heel through your soft neck and right into your carotid artery. You'll bleed out within minutes…and I'll ruin this beautiful golden dress. What's it going to be, Narváez?"

As Carlos thought about his situation, Harper increased the pressure on his throat. He finally choked out, "Put them away. I seem to have upset my guest."

Without letting him up, she said, "Good choice." She heard the click of guns placed on safe and the brush of metal on leather. "Now, are you ready to talk business?" She chanced a glance around the table and saw all guns had been holstered. Velez grinned back at her. The man gave her the creeps.

Narváez looked up at her. "Can we now sit and talk like the civilized people we are?"

She let him up but stepped far enough away from him so she was out of reach. Segundo picked up the chair that had tipped over when he'd stood up and drawn his gun. He offered a hand and a kind glance to Harper then seated her before taking his own beside her, once again.

The splash of neon women across the table huddled together, breathing loudly and squeaking like tortured mice.

Harper took one look at them and abruptly commanded, "Shut up!"

Gently, as though speaking to an injured small child, Narváez took Bunny's hand in his own and patted it. "Now, now, my dear. I'm sorry that frightened you. Run along, my darling. I'll be up soon." With no more encouragement needed, Bunny and her entourage scurried from the table.

Harper let her anger show as she purposefully said in English, "Well, now the children are off to bed, perhaps we adults can get down to business. What the fuck do you want from me?"

He ignored her as his gaze followed the retreating women. Only Bunny looked back. Narváez blew her a sappy kiss.

"I refuse to become one of your house whores. You wouldn't like it when I started killing your men." But several would die in her escape. And she would escape, after killing Narváez.

Carlos finally looked at her. He raised a hand and moved to touch the reddened fingerprints he'd left on her arm but stopped an inch from her bicep. Reconsidering, he quickly snatched his hand away and picked up his coffee cup.

"I want you to cocrystallize HMX and CL-20." He spoke off-hand, as if she should have known.

Harper felt every drop of blood drain from her face. Her stomach flipped once again. She swallowed hard against the rise of the meal she'd just finished.

"Don't be surprised. The cocrystalization process was initially invented to improve the effectiveness of drugs. I am in the pharmaceutical business." Narváez, the calculating cartel boss, was back. Almost no trace of the drunk, lust-struck man remained.

She opened her mouth to speak but nothing came out. She

closed it and tried to compile her thoughts. No, she couldn't give this drug lord the most dangerous non-nuclear explosive on the planet. Yes, she knew how to make it, and had made the compound before, but she wouldn't do it for him. No. Never.

"It was very clever how you got Diaz and Ortega to trust you so quickly." Narváez set his empty cup onto the saucer.

He knew the men she'd been sent to investigate. Her team had spent weeks and traveled all over Colombia and…oh God…She'd assured the U.S. government no one there could make the explosive. No one but her.

"You didn't think those idiots bought the explosives without my knowledge and my money, did you?" The look Narváez gave her said gotcha.

"I…I…" she stammered. Get it together Harper, she scolded herself. Lie. "I can't do it. I don't know how."

Narváez's jowls flapped as he shook his head. "Not true, Miss Tambini. You worked with Dr. Matzger on the process while getting your masters at the University of Michigan last year. You are the ATF's explosives expert, are you not?"

Damn, he knew a lot about her.

She didn't answer the question. "I won't do it."

"Yes, you will." Narváez snapped his fingers and one of the guards who had been silently standing next to the door handed him a tablet. After swiping the screen a few times, he smiled and handed her the device.

The picture of Hernandez as he stepped off their plane made her sigh in relief. Her team had made it home safely.

"This picture was taken at nine o'clock this morning as the rest of your team arrived in D.C. My U.S. contacts have orders to follow each member of your team, but if you refuse to do as I say, I'll change their orders. They'll start killing the men you work with…one by one." Narváez watched her face as he spoke, but all she could do was stare at the clear shot of Hernandez. The photographer could just as easily have taken a shot with gun.

Narváez smiled and grabbed the tablet from her shaking hand. "Should I start with Hernandez?" He swiped the screen and showed her the next picture. Estes walked from the new ATF Headquarters in D.C. "Or perhaps your team leader? He's been grilled all day by his superiors about the little… incident at the Bogotá airport."

Narváez turned the tablet and looked at the picture. "He doesn't look very happy. Maybe I should put him out of his misery."

"No." Harper's voice squeaked. Get a grip. Take a deep breath, she ordered herself. But all she could think about was Estes showing her the picture of his little baby boy being held by his three-year-old daughter. She forced another deep breath. "No, I can't let you do that."

"So you will cook for me." It was a definitive statement. A satisfied smile spread across his pudgy face and turned her stomach. Harper closed her eyes and wondered how she'd get out of this predicament. Maybe she could escape before she was forced to create the bomb.

Escape, hell, the USSOCOM was already figuring out how to extricate her. "You know plans are already in place for U.S. forces to come get me." True, standard operating procedures required initial attempts through the Department of State, but she also knew her boss. He'd send the troops in for a raid and rescue.

"They don't know where you are," he replied smugly.

She was sure they knew exactly where she was. During her first mission with the ATF, she'd lost her tracker, and its replacement. She'd schmoozed the guys in tech to let her try the newest device, which was no bigger than a flash drive. To be sure she didn't lose the little critter, she'd sewn a small section of her front right pocket in every pair of pants she owned. It fit perfectly in the dip of her hip. When the sicarios searched her, their hands slid right over it. The techies assured her it was waterproof, so it currently resided wherever her clothes were, hopefully still in the big house.

Smiling, Harper said, "Narváez, are you willing to wager your life on that assumption?"

He considered this for a minute but in his drunken and drugged state must have decided she was bluffing.

"Of course. Besides, nobody is going to come for you. I have friends in Washington. So far, your State Department is doing little more than stomping their feet and demanding to talk to you. I'm a former ambassador's son, and my word goes a long way in those circles. Too bad you've been ill when the Embassy has called, but I assured them you were resting comfortably, as my guest." He emphasized the last three words, his toothy smile an unsaid gotcha.

Damn State Department was in negotiations to get a tourist back. Her team wouldn't wait for those goody-two-shoes, thank God. The military had invested far too much money in her training to leave it up to the bureaucrats. She just wasn't sure who they would send, or when, but they would come for her.

Narváez's eyes darkened as he threatened, "And if you don't do exactly as I say, I'll give you as a present to the Cali Cartel, and I assure you, they won't be so kind. Here you have a lovely room with a magnificent view of the Pacific Ocean overlooking my gardens. I allow you to move about as you please." He added with a shrug, "Within limits."

He refilled his coffee, his pudgy hand steady as he lifted his cup to his smug lips. He sipped the thick, black liquid. "I give you the freedom and comforts of my home, and you'll make me the most feared man in Colombia. If you refuse, I'll drug you again, and when you awaken, you'll be in the hands of my companions. They won't care about your skills, just that you are a woman. Your team will be hunted down one at a time and brutally murdered. Trust me, Harper, none will die painlessly."

No, not her team. She knew he could follow through on his threat. But not if he was dead.

He sipped. "But, as long as you do exactly as I say, they live." It was then she knew he had a hold on her until she could find a way to eliminate him and escape.

"Until I kill you, Narváez," she taunted.

He spit out coffee in his abrupt laughter.

"You? You can try. Many have. All have failed. You don't think I've been a target before today? Why do you think I have my own army?" He waved toward the men who'd drawn guns on her mere moments before. "I protect what is mine. If you do as I say, and be good to Segundo, I'll feed you and clothe you in the finest. Each time I use your services, you'll gain my trust, and I'll grant you more freedom."

She felt Segundo's arm come possessively around her shoulders. He gave her shoulder the slightest reassuring squeeze.

"I won't touch you. No one will." He smiled at his second in charge. "Except Segundo. You are his. But I assure you, if I order him to beat you for disobeying, he will. He's faithful to me and has been for years." He gave a nod to the man holding her.

She didn't dare look at Segundo, afraid of what she'd see in his eyes.

Narváez looked to where his wife had disappeared only

moments before and smiled rakishly. "We'll discuss this more tomorrow. Right now I have to see to my wife."

Harper knew all too well his adrenaline had skyrocketed during her attack and a testosterone spike would follow. The human survival reaction, based in everyone's cells, most often resulted in the need for procreation, or just sex in most.

As Narváez rose from the table, she also stood.

"You are responsible for her, Segundo." His glare should have been enough, but he added, "Don't disappoint me."

She saw a flare of anger in Segundo's blue eyes but doubted Narváez caught it.

"Harper, I will see you in the morning. Sleep in. You still look exhausted from your illness. I'll meet you for lunch at precisely eleven-thirty on the garden terrace." With a dismissive nod, he left the room with his two bodyguards trailing behind.

After Narváez's footsteps receded, Segundo faced her, raised his palm to her cheek, and then tenderly ran his thumb over the bruise she knew was reddening on her cheekbone. His touch was so careful.

He spoke in English, presumably because the walls had ears and staff gossiped. "I'm sorry for this. He was drunk. He's not usually violent toward his guests. I think you provoked him beyond his control. He's not used to anyone talking back to him or refusing him, least of all a woman. You did it in front of his wife and, more importantly, his men."

She didn't care whom she'd embarrassed Narváez in front of. He'd kidnapped her and now wanted her to create bombs for him. She wouldn't do it. He could use them against Americans, and as an Army officer, it was her job to protect American lives.

Segundo bent and lightly kissed her bruise. Her insides

quivered when his soft lips touched her cheek. He was so gentle, and it felt reassuring.

It was the adrenaline. Had to be.

Harper stepped back knowing Segundo, too, had experienced an adrenaline rush and was feeling its aftereffects.

"I won't work for him. But I promise you this, Segundo, I'll kill Narváez before I leave here. As his second, that will leave you in charge. Be ready for it," she warned the man who held a possessive hand on her bare back.

His warm eyes slipped to frosty blue once again. "I'll walk you back to your room." The heat in his voice from seconds ago had been replaced by ice.

Harper followed his gaze to her arm where red stripes could be seen against her darkly tanned skin. She needed a shower to wash off the feel of Narváez's ugly hands. Unfortunately, no amount of water and scented soap could clean her soul of her hatred for him.

She and Segundo said nothing as they walked past the fountain and up the marble stairs. Harper confirmed the map she was mentally building. She would escape. And she would kill Narváez.

At the door to her room, Segundo unlocked it and opened it wide for her to enter. Then he pulled the door closed and locked it from the outside, without a word.

CHAPTER 9

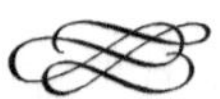

The encrypted message had said: Important call at 0245.

Segundo, known only by a handful of people in Colombia as Rafael "Rafe" Silva, slipped into the night dressed totally in black and climbed to the top of the first mountain ridge. A clear crescent moon cast a spear of white on the unusually calm Pacific Ocean.

The satellite phone in his pocket vibrated softly. He dug it out and answered. "School Boy here." He hated that code name, but it had been his since he'd been recruited into the CIA as a freshman in college—when he'd been Narváez's roommate. Since Rafe's parents had been Colombian refugees, and United States citizens by choice, and Carlos Narváez was the Colombian ambassador's son, the residency office at Virginia Military Institute thought it was a good idea to place the two young men together.

Rafe had always wondered if the CIA had instigated that decision. As he sat on the cool rock outcropping and breathed the earthy jungle scents, he felt as though they'd controlled him his whole life. He'd had enough. He'd thought many times about just packing his few things and leaving Colombia.

The information he'd passed along never seemed all that important, but tonight would be different. He'd known something big was up two days ago when Carlos had him pack the chopper with his best men and they'd lifted off for Bogotá. His friend had seemed almost giddy with excitement when he'd given Rafe orders to watch the hangar and capture the men who would come for the jet inside. There wasn't time, or privacy, to discuss it. Rafe hadn't known there'd be a woman with the team. Carlos had forgotten to mention her, too. It had been a bad idea from the start.

"Control here. Hold for incoming call." Before he could ask whom he'd be speaking with, he'd been placed on hold. He normally reported facts and findings to Operations Control and that was it, unless he was meeting with his handler.

"School Boy, this is Deputy Director Thomas Gillpatrick."

Oh fuck.

"Yes, sir." Rafe actually sat up straighter. This could be bad.

"I understand that Narváez has kidnapped an ATF agent. Can you confirm?"

That didn't take long. Interagency communication was usually nonexistent, and cooperation even more rare.

"Yes, sir, he has. She's here at his western compound."

"Do you have access to her?" She must be very important for someone so high in the agency to be concerned.

"Yes, sir."

"What is Harper's condition?" The familiarity, and real concern, of the DD with Narváez's captive couldn't be missed.

Rafe quickly explained her allergic reaction to the knockout drug and following illness for over twelve hours. Then he told the man who was second in charge of the CIA about the slap at supper and Harper's takedown of Narváez.

"That's our girl," Gillpatrick said with pride in his voice. "I want you to know just how important Harper Tambini is to our government. She has knowledge and skills that could change the balance of power in the world. Now, tell me exactly, how is she?"

Holy fuck. Could this get any worse? "She's weak but getting stronger."

"No torture, though, right?"

"No, sir, not for her. Narváez has threatened to kill her whole team if she doesn't cooperate with him."

The DD was quiet for several beats. "Where's he getting his information?"

"I have no idea, but he knew the names of everyone on her team and when and where to set the ambush. He's also having them followed stateside. He refuses to talk to me about his intel, but it's on the money."

"Damn." The DD drew out the word. "I'll take care of the U.S. tails."

"When is her extraction, sir?" Rafe hoped it'd be soon.

"We're working on it, but it's a unique situation." He heard the deep exhale on the other end. "To be honest, it's a clusterfuck. The ATF contacted me when your name popped on the Narváez file. State Department had to get their worthless nose in on it under the guise of Standard Operating Procedures. Harper doesn't work for us, although she's trained with us in specific areas. Don't be deceived. There's a lot more to her than meets the eye. Her Army training parallels yours as a SEAL. Speaking of SEALs, you'll get to say hello to an old friend when they arrive to retrieve her.

Matias Rivas asked to lead this mission when he heard you were involved."

Rafe hadn't thought about Mat in years. It would be great to see Preacher again, and Harper would be in good hands with his old running buddy. "That's wonderful, sir."

"What does Narváez have planned?"

"He wants her to make some kind of special bomb out of CL-20 and HMX."

"Fuck."

Rafe barely heard the whispered word but was sure that was what the DD had said. Rafe said nothing.

After a long pause, DD Gillpatrick announced, "That's what we were afraid of. Does he have the components?"

"Yes, sir." Rafe had wondered what his old friend was up to when he began to stockpile HMX, an explosive that had been around since World War II and Rafe had used often as a SEAL. When containers of CL20 arrived last week, curiosity had been replaced by worry. What kind of war was Narváez starting and with whom?

"What's Narváez's mental condition?"

"He's been sampling his own merchandise with increasing frequency. He's getting paranoid." It was a sad fact for Rafe. Carlos was no longer the man he'd roomed with in college.

"I expect you to keep her safe, School Boy."

Great. It seemed everyone wanted the same thing, especially him.

"Yes, sir," was his only response.

"Very well…hold." Rafe heard faint voices in the background. "Extraction is set for tomorrow night. SEALs are in motion."

This was his chance. He had to take it. Rafe knew, deep down inside, that he might not get another opportunity in a long time, and Narváez would be a target for elimination after his kidnapping stunt.

"Sir, I want to leave with her. I'm ready to come home, and this is an excellent opportunity to exit. Is Narváez sanctioned now?"

"Of course, from the moment he ambushed the ATF team."

Rafe didn't miss the fact that his request wasn't answered. "Thank you, sir. I plan to execute him myself."

"You may have to fight Harper for that privilege. Keep her safe. Make sure she's fit and ready to go. You're a long way from nowhere, and extraction won't be easy. I'll notify the SEAL team that there's two to extract."

"Thank you, sir." Yes, thank you. He was headed home. Spending time with Harper Tambini on the way there was just another benefit.

"Gillpatrick out." The line went dead.

An hour later, Rafe stood on Harper's balcony and watched her sleep. He'd slipped undetected over the railing from his rooms next door. Christ, the Deputy Director of the CIA was involved. Rafe was responsible for Harper's safety, and he vowed he'd die before he'd allow anything or anyone to hurt her.

He glanced at the mechanism in his hand. To most, it looked like any hunter's GPS. He pointed it slowly around the room to detect audio or visual equipment. Good. None. Carlos had become so paranoid in the past few weeks that Rafe wouldn't put it past him to bug Harper's room without telling him, even though he was in charge of security. Satisfied, he slid the device into a side pocket in his black cargo pants.

For nearly two years, Rafe had run the entire operation. From growing the flowers, fruits, and vegetables—and yes, the coca plants—to the picking, processing, packing, and shipping to the United States.

Harper stirred. He crept to the bed and bent to shake her shoulder to awaken her.

She grabbed his arm and flipped him onto the bed face down, arms locked behind his back. She held a knife to his throat. His legs splayed, and her knee nudged his crotch.

"Harper," he choked out in English, "I'm CIA. I'm one of the good guys. Let me up."

She held her position. "You're very high ranking in this organization to be CIA. How long have you been under cover?" She kept her face close to his and spoke in undertones.

She was good. He'd never expected that move. "I started at the top. Narváez and I were college roommates. Now can you get off me?"

His heart beat rapidly for what seemed to take forever. The cold steel at his throat didn't quiver. He heard her sigh and the pressure of her knee at his crotch ease. She finally removed the knife and slid off his back.

"I'd hoped someone was inside, but I didn't think it was you." She moved quickly away from him and braced herself on her knees, the knife still held in fighting position.

Rafe rolled onto his back and sat up. He rubbed where the blade had pressed, thankful not to feel any blood on his neck. "You're better than I thought you'd be. I never saw you steal this from the supper table." He glanced at the satisfied look on her face.

"Yes, I am good. The hardest part was to find some place under that dress that it wouldn't imprint. The last thing I wanted was Narváez to strip-search me at the supper table." She shuddered.

He fluffed a pillow and leaned against the headboard as

he stretched out his legs that had gotten a nice little workout in the past two hours. The climb up the mountain wasn't strenuous, but a gain of a thousand feet over two miles wasn't a stroll on the beach. It was his crotch, not his burning thighs, that he wanted to rub. He was too much a Southern gentleman to make such a crude move.

Harper's tan, rounded breasts swayed under her lace nightgown as she crawled into the bed beside him and pulled the sheet over her naked legs. Damn, she had great legs. All the right curves, and well developed, too. He wanted her to wrap those legs around his waist as he drove into her. She made him instantly hard. He hoped the night and his baggy utility pants would keep his condition hidden.

Remembering how close she'd come to hurting him just a few seconds ago, he forced himself to study the room.

"Did they recruit you in college?" Harper settled next to him, a polite distance away.

"Yes. I had a five-year commitment to the Navy after graduating from VMI. Carlos went on to grad school. He came home to Colombia while I finished out my Navy tour. They approached me again and asked if I'd come here. Nothing was holding me in the States, so here I am."

All his plans to get married to Beth after they'd completed their tours had been buried with her in a closed casket. The Taliban had abused her body beyond recognition. The forensic team at Dover had used DNA to identify her remains.

No, nothing had been left to hold him in the U.S.A. back then. But now, five years later, he was ready to return home.

"How about you?"

"I was Army ROTC at the University of Michigan. I also had a physics scholarship and was able to finish my master's before I went into the Army. I've always liked working with demolitions, bombs, munitions, but as a female, those military occupational specialties were banned. Fortunately, I was able to get assigned to the ATF as an explosives specialist, but I still work for the Army."

Huh, Army. He'd never seen any soldiers as beautiful as Harper, but there were many good-looking women who wore uniforms. There had been a growing number of women in all the military services in the past ten years. Beth had worn Navy uniforms, except when she went under cover.

"They let you finish your master's?" Rafe asked. "They had us shipping out within days of graduation."

"Yeah. ROTC took a lot of my free time, so I worked in the lab year round to make up for it so I could keep my scholarship. Within four years, I had both a bachelor's and a master's degree."

"Year-round school, huh? Didn't you ever go home?" He treasured his time away from school and with his family. He'd needed the breaks.

"I didn't have a home." Her statement was spattered with pain. "Well, I guess my dorm room was my home back then." She exhaled a long breath. Changing the subject, she asked, "So what's the plan? When's extraction?"

CHAPTER 10

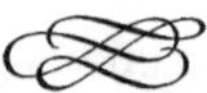

So much for small talk. Harper got down to business, and Rafe liked that for some odd reason. There was something special about her. She definitely had physical strength, but it was more an internal power that shone through and undeniably drew him to her.

"Tomorrow night. SEALs are on their way. I'm supposed to be sure you're fit and ready to roll, so we'll get in a run and maybe some gym time later this morning." He looked forward to seeing her in workout gear and sweaty. Still, he'd rather have her sweaty in this bed. "By the way, I'm leavin' with you."

"Who is there to take over the business then? Not that I really care, but I am going to kill Narváez, you know."

Truthfully, Rafe didn't care what happened to this place, or any other property that he'd been forced to manage over the past several years. The other members of the cartel could fight over it. He'd feel bad for the workers, though. Some of the capos beat the workers, tortured them if production was down. They had no idea how to lead people.

He and Carlos had a strong workforce and treated them

right. At least they had until the past few months. Four months ago, he'd watched Carlos put on a show for a visiting capo by grabbing an old man off the processing line and beating him because he didn't work fast enough. Rafe could have killed Carlos right then.

"He's been sanctioned, by the way."

"I'm sure. Probably from the minute he took me."

"You may have to fight me for the privilege of killing him." He hated what his friend had become. This paranoid, trigger-tempered sadist wasn't the save-my-country economist he'd known in college.

"We'll see." Harper smoothed non-existent wrinkles in the duvet and crossed her ankles under the sheet. "So, you're to protect me until the rescue. Do you plan to stay by my side until the SEALs arrive?" Her gaze met his. "I don't trust your guards, and I'm still too weak to fight them off if it came to that."

"I know. I saw the way they looked at you last night." Rafe recalled the hungry glances that started during the ambush. He was also sure some had copped a feel while in the limo. He wanted to kill any man who dared put a hand on her. Unfortunately, it was impossible for him to keep her within arm's reach all the time.

"We know they're coming within twenty-four hours," Harper said, "but no one else does, so whatever we decide, it needs to appear long-term. We should also consider a contingency plan, in case they can't get to us. How do you want to play this?"

Harper was right. His SEAL team had been delayed, turned around mid-mission, and even had ops called off before their gear was packed, usually due to politics. The DD had insinuated those games were in play, so they'd better plan longer term.

Rafe had ideas. All involved him and Harper naked in this bed. He shifted his hips to accommodate his throbbing erection. "I think we should be lovers." Rafe rolled over and cupped her face. He bent in to kiss her.

"Pretend to be lovers." Harper quickly pushed him away. "We're professionals here."

"Fine. We'll pretend to be lovers." He propped his chin on his hand. "Narváez already thinks we're headed that direction, thanks to your little performance at supper tonight. It's a good cover for us to be alone a lot. Also, if you're mine, no one will dare touch you. They know I'm your protector, but that wouldn't mean much to some men. As my lover, the other men will keep their distance and show you respect."

"Will Narváez buy it?" Her tone was more businesslike than worried.

"How good an actress are you?" Rafe was only slightly worried. She'd proven Oscar worthy a few hours ago.

"Very good. We should start tonight. How did you get in here?" Harper was very take charge. Rafe wasn't sure how he felt about that but he was totally in favor of this plan.

"Balcony. My rooms are next door. It's more like an apartment than a bedroom."

"That's convenient." She rolled on her side to face him. "Go back to your room and come in through my door. We'll make appropriate noises. The whole house will be discussing our tryst at breakfast. Do you normally spend the night, or are you a bang-and-go guy?"

"I don't ever sleep with women in this house or any other Narváez property." He most often found satisfaction in Cali with Melina, or if they were in the Narváez East Compound, he'd go into Cartagena and spend quality time with Isabella or Valentina, but he wasn't going to tell Harper that. He got up from the bed and strode to the balcony.

"Oh, that's right," Harper teased, "the house honeys were so disappointed that I made you smile and they couldn't."

He cringed at the thought of those women and wondered how many were in Carlos's bed right then.

Rafe watched a sly smile spread across her gorgeous face as she suggested, "Take off your clothes before you come back in. You were supposed to be asleep, dreaming of me, so now you want me. Wear your boxers."

"I sleep naked." He smiled, a sexy grin that usually melted women. Her return smile was more a dare than shock at his words.

"I usually do, too, but I think I'll wear a nightgown while I'm here. This bedroom has too many people who just walk in. Maybe you should wear a robe. We're only pretending to be lovers. You leave here with a hard-on, and they'll know something isn't right."

"What makes you think you turn me on?" Although he was hard as a rock under his black cargo pants, he'd hoped she hadn't noticed in the dark.

"Reach down…and we're just talking." She looked right at his crotch then back up. She grinned. "Wait until we start making sounds like lovers."

He turned to leave.

"Hey, Segundo, if we're going to be lovers, I should know your name."

That stopped him. He turned to look at her.

"Rafe. Actually, it's Rafael Silva, but call me Rafe. I'll be back in a minute, through that door." He pointed to the hall door and disappeared over the side of the balcony.

~

Sixty seconds later Harper heard the click of her door unlocking. Knowing her role, she ran to the door. "Who's there?'

"It's me." Rafe strolled in as if he had the right to her room…and her.

In nothing but dark silk boxers riding low on narrow hips, Rafe was outlined in yellow by the dim hall lights. His broad shoulders filled the doorway. As he moved toward her, light caught raised pectoral muscles and flashed off well-defined six-pack abs. His swagger defined testosterone in motion. He was a specimen of pure male confidence and dominance.

He addressed the guards at the door. "Take a break. I'll let you know when you need to come back. I'm going to enjoy my woman for a while." He left the door open long enough for his guards to watch as he claimed Harper, yanking her into his arms and covering her mouth with his.

His kiss was heaven and sin wrapped in one hard body. And he was hard everywhere.

Rafe slipped his hands around her, and she felt their heat through the thin silk of the nightgown. Intensity built quickly within her, and she grabbed his head, shoving her fingers through his silky dark curls. He pulled her forcefully against his body, but she didn't resist. No man had ever made her feel this way so fast.

At the click of the door, Harper pushed Rafe away. She had to get away from him before she lost her senses.

"That should get them talking." Her voice was roughened, but she kept it low. "The whole compound will know you were in my room by breakfast." She walked over to the nightstand and pulled a bottle of chilled water from an ice bucket. She needed to cool down, from the inside out. After cracking the seal, she chugged down half of the cool liquid before setting it on the nightstand. "I'm going to bed." She glared at Rafe. "And to sleep."

"We need to make this convincing." He moved toward her. "Maybe we should—"

"Yes, we should make the appropriate noises," she whispered. Much louder, in a breathy voice, she said, "Oh, yes, kiss me there again."

From ten feet away, he looked at her as if she was insane. With a palms-up motion, she mouthed, "Come on." She slid onto the bed, fluffed a pillow, and sat with her back against the headboard, her bare legs stretched out on top of the duvet.

Harper hoped she looked nonchalant when she picked up a magazine from the floor and flipped a page. Rafe's kiss still had her belly quaking. "Oh, Rafe, please, please," she begged in a slow, sultry voice. She pointed to the empty space beside her on the bed.

He rounded the king-sized bed and started to crawl under the covers. She shook her head no, so he lay down beside her. She continued to flip through the magazine, trying to ignore the nearly naked man next to her.

When he said nothing for several long minutes, she leaned over and whispered, "Are you always silent during sex?" She could almost see the light turn on in his head.

In a louder than necessary voice, he said, "You are so beautiful." He leaned in to kiss her, but she moved away and gave him a warning glance.

"I'll bet you say that to all your women." And the thought of Rafe with other women irked her, but she chose to ignore the twinges of jealousy.

"Oh, querida, that feels so good."

From the other side of the bed, she cocked her head and just looked at him then whispered, "Really? Darling? Is that the best you can do?"

He shrugged.

"Oh, Segundo, there's so much of you to explore." She gasped then turned the page of the magazine. Something caught her eye, and she ignored Rafe as she read, or tried to read. She didn't dare look at him as he held up his side of the imaginary scene with low moans.

Harper felt a poke on her arm. She glared at Rafe with a what-the-fuck look then realized that she had been engrossed with his words while she stared too long at the same page. She mouthed, "Sorry" and claimed loudly, "Oh, Segundo, I want you. Now." She started bouncing up and down on the bed. He bounced, too.

"Oh, yes, yes, more." Her demands grew louder as they bounced in unison. "Yes," she all but screamed and flopped on the pillows with a sigh.

In a quiet voice, she teased, "Was it good for you?" When he smiled, her stomach fluttered. He had the best smile.

Rafe liked this playful side of Harper.

"Well, it certainly sounded good for you." He chuckled quietly.

"If I made love with all those noises, you'd know I was faking it."

Interesting. He thought back to the women he'd bedded over the years and tried to remember if any of them were loud.

"You're not a screamer?" He rolled up on his elbow to look at her and propped his chin on his hand.

"No. But we needed it for our performance." She continued to indifferently flip pages.

She was either good at this, or he was out of practice.

He'd never had to fake an intimate relationship before. As much as he wanted her, he wasn't sure how long he'd last before he had her for real.

"Ready for round two?" He was. Actually, he was ready for round one, but this time he would kiss every inch of her soft skin, open her wet folds and taste how much she wanted him before he slid into her and made her scream his name as she came around his cock.

"Well, Rafael Silva, I'm going to sleep." The finality in Harper's voice left no room for debate.

He moved close to her and tried to put his arm around her.

"Get over there." She pointed to the other side of the bed.

"Can't we at least cuddle?"

She'd tucked into him earlier in the day, in this very bed. But that was when she'd been sick. Her warm body had spooned perfectly into his.

"No, this is just pretend. If you can't keep these roles straight, then we're ending it, right now." Her words were firm, but the heat in her big brown eyes said she wanted him.

"I can do this," he said to reassure her as much as himself, and he slipped under the covers on the far side of the king bed. It just wouldn't be easy with her so close, and him with a raging erection.

He wondered why he was always drawn to strong women like her—those who led a dangerous life. Beth had gone into the Navy Expeditionary Intelligence Command, and after only two years, they'd let her do field work. It was part of the test to see if women could actually work in combat roles. She had gone under in Iraq with another agent as his wife and successfully integrated into the community. That assignment had only lasted a few weeks, more a test than a real mission.

NEIC then loaned her to a joint task force in Afghanistan for the same kind of duty. Some son of a bitch had blown their cover. The Taliban had her for two days before the Marine Raiders arrived only to discover it was a recovery rather than a rescue. They'd brought her maimed body out of the cave while he was in Alaska training with his SEAL team. Her parents were told she'd been in a vehicle when a roadside IED exploded on her side.

Unfortunately, Rafe knew the truth.

Damn, he missed Beth, even after all these years. She and Harper were a lot alike, playful in private and all business when needed. They were both proud of their work and very good at it.

Why the hell was he so attracted to women who worked in the shadows? After Beth's death, he'd decided he wanted a Southern belle for a wife. A woman more concerned about what to serve at a Junior League luncheon than sharpening her skills in hand-to-hand combat. He needed someone who didn't know, or care, about the dark world where he worked. Someone who only lived in the light. Someone who wouldn't die in the darkness.

Love, of course, wouldn't have anything to do with his marriage. He wanted a family, a wife to come home to, and kids. He liked children and the idea of having his own. Men had married for hundreds of years without love being involved. He'd do the same so he'd never have to suffer the pain of losing the love of his life.

Just before daybreak, Rafe gave up on the idea of sleep. He'd tossed and turned for hours. It wasn't possible for him, knowing he could reach out and find a beautiful woman he wanted under the same soft sheets, but he couldn't touch her.

He'd promised the deputy director she'd be healthy enough to leave. Maybe he should wake her up and make her sweat beside him in the gym since she wouldn't let him show her how much fun sweating in bed could be.

In the gray light of early morning, Harper looked so tired, her eyes shadowed from lack of deep sleep. She'd been sick most of the previous day. He'd let her sleep so her body could recover.

Rafe rolled off the bed and quietly slipped out the door in search of the guards.

CHAPTER 11

AT NINE-THIRTY, HARPER STILL WASN'T UP WHEN RAFE entered the big house and asked the staff for her location. He'd already checked the day's production schedule, examined the crops, got the workers started, and been ribbed by a dozen men about the American woman. Their ploy had worked.

"You wore her out last night. I heard her scream for you." The older guard on duty outside Harper's room slapped Rafe on the shoulder with a proud smile.

Rafe remembered Harper's explanation of screams during sex and wondered if the guard's women had faked it also. He examined the lined face, prematurely aged by drugs. Probably.

"You come back for more? Morning sex is good for a man," the guard said with a chuckle.

Rafe stopped short on his way through the door. With an effort, he controlled his contempt. He was playing a role, and he had to make it look good. He dug deep to find a convincing tone.

"I've got this. Leave." Rafe closed the door behind him.

Harper stirred, but he could tell she was asleep, not pretending. The cocaine reaction had taken a lot out of her. Several empty water bottles sat on the nightstand. Good. She was smart to push fluids.

"Harper." He leaned over her. She needed to get up and moving. They'd go running later and maybe hit the gym. Sweating the remainder of the poisons out of her gorgeous body would be the best thing for her.

He reached down and shook her shoulder.

"Mmmm," she moaned. Great, now she moans for me. He leaned so his lips were an inch from her ear.

"Harper. You need to wake up now. It's late morning. Time you were out of bed."

She arched her back and exposed her neck to his lips as if to beg for a kiss.

Oh, how he wanted to press his lips into her neck and kiss his way down the rest of her body. But this was all pretend. She was deeply asleep, and he couldn't take advantage of her.

He smacked her butt and said, "Time to get up, darlin'."

She rolled away from him and pulled the covers up. Had he stayed in that bed, she'd be cuddled up against him right now. Damn. He could all but feel those soft curves gliding up against him. He was half-hard at the mental picture.

It had been a long time since he'd slept the whole night with a woman. Well, he'd awakened with Melina many times, and yes, they'd had sex. But it was usually after they'd worked a black op all night, stealing data from the Cali Cartel's computers or observing a high-level meeting or following someone to see the newest connection. So many bad things happened in the dark of night, it was no wonder they called it the shadow world.

There had been a time in his life when he loved waking up next to the woman he'd shared his body with for hours. He and Beth had lived together for nearly a year after he'd finished BUD/S and she'd completed indoctrination into NEIC. It had been the best year of his life. But it all ended right after his twenty-fifth birthday. Hell. It had been eight years. A lifetime ago.

Many other women had passed through his life since then. He'd mourned for over a year until his best friend, Mat Rivas a.k.a. Preacher, had taken him out on three days of binge drinking and fucking women after they'd wiped out the cell responsible for Beth's death. His last years as a SEAL were a repeated cycle of successful missions and celebrating their return alive.

He'd moved on from that life and into this one as watchdog over Carlos Narváez. Rafe had always planned on a career in the Navy until time came to re-up. Rafe remembered with clarity the clandestine meeting where the senior CIA agent had spouted continued duty to their country, the fact that only he could get close to Carlos and how all he'd have to do was report in.

Even Rafe had been surprised when Carlos had bought into his cover story. Disgruntled as a SEAL, constantly putting his life on the line for a thankless country that had allowed his fiancée to be captured and killed because the U.S.A. doesn't negotiate with terrorists. It was logical and, at times, seemed almost too real. Convincing his old friend he wanted to help make Colombia—the country of his parents' birth—a better place by instigating all those plans they'd created as idealistic college boys was easy.

Rafe had been welcomed with open arms. They'd soon fallen into the close camaraderie of their college years. At first, he'd hated deceiving Carlos, but then he saw the good things the two of them could do. They had torn out coca plants and replaced them with flowers and vegetables.

Together they introduced twenty-first century farming techniques, not just on Narváez land, but in the surrounding communities. Small farmers began growing more and making more money, improving their lifestyle. The legitimate side of Carlos's business boomed.

Like too many others, though, Carlos had let success go to his head. He started personally testing his cocaine products and the slide downward was swift. The last two years were a totally different story. Carlos had become as corrupt as the rest. He used the overpowering aroma of the flowers to mask the cocaine hidden underneath from U.S. Customs Inspectors. The good Narváez name of his father as former Ambassador was used too many times to cover the laundering of drug money. His focus had been diverted to criminal business endeavors…now even kidnapping.

All that would end soon. Within hours, that chapter would also close. Rafe couldn't wait.

It was time to fulfill his original dreams, to find a woman to sleep with all through the night. But it wouldn't be the woman curled on the bed in front of him. Harper's job was too dangerous; she could be taken from him too easily. No. He'd never again give his heart to a woman with such a perilous job. But he'd sure as hell share his body with her, over and over again.

Rafe slid onto the bed and curled up beside her. "Harper," he whispered into her ear as his fingertips moved a pesky strand of hair from her face. "You either get out of this bed, or I'm getting into it then into you."

Her eyes shot open, but she remained still for a few seconds before she rolled over. They were nose to nose.

"If you ever attempt to rape me, I'll cut off your dick and stuff it down your throat. Then I'll shove your balls up your ass with my fist. When you beg me with your eyes, I'll finally kill you. One shot. Right here." She touched the middle of his forehead.

"I like it when you talk dirty." He smiled, and she looked a little frustrated.

"Sharing my body is not part of my work. I don't have sex while on the job. This is all pretend. Keep that straight. Now, get the hell out of my bed. I'm getting up." She shoved his shoulder.

Damn. She had guts. And he liked that. It took a lot, but Rafe stood and stepped away. He knew she would carry through on her threat. She was more than capable. But he'd glimpsed, just for a second, that undeniable desire. He wanted to wrap himself in her heat and make them both explode.

"So you never have sex as part of the work." It was a statement not a question. "What about after the work is done? I'm sure Harper Tambini has sex."

"You'll never know," she quipped as she slid out of bed and headed for the bathroom.

Rafe stepped into her path. He slowly, gently, cupped her smooth face in his hands.

"I think if you got to know me, the real me, you'd see I'm a lovable guy." He wanted her, but he also wanted her to know the real Rafe, the man who'd served his country for the past five years and hated every minute of his life as Segundo.

Rafe watched her large fawn eyes soften briefly as she saw him for the man he was underneath the hard-ass exterior. Then they were hard as topaz again.

"Harper Tambini, the ATF agent, is here now." Slowly, a seductive smile crossed her goddess-like face. "When we're out of Colombia and safe, maybe you can meet Harper Tambini, the woman. She loves men. Often."

He thought he felt the brush of her lips as she turned her face into the palm of his hand before she stepped around him.

It was so light he couldn't be sure. When she shut the door to the bathroom behind her, he closed his fist as if to hold her touch.

Accepting that he couldn't join her in the shower, he headed for the kitchen to have the staff send up a light breakfast for her. Even though he and Harper had to meet Narváez in just under two hours for lunch on the terrace, she needed food, now.

Harper really liked the red sundress smattered with gardenias and wedged white sandals that showed off her darkly tanned skin. Like the other clothes in her room, these seemed to have magically appeared when she needed them. Although, it was creepy if Narváez had actually picked them out for her. They were so close to her personal taste and always the right size.

As she descended the stairs, exactly on time, she knew the men watched her every move. She could feel their hungry stares hidden behind dark Oakley sunglasses. The dress hugged her ribs and breasts, but the scooped neckline was lower than one she would usually prefer for a luncheon because it revealed several inches of cleavage.

Rafe sat in a sturdy wrought iron chair with green padded cushions and sipped what looked like thick lemonade from a tall cut-crystal glass. His seemingly endless legs were clad in khaki cargo pants and crossed casually at the ankles. A brilliantly white safari shirt fit loosely over well-developed muscles, and his dark brown hair curled just below the collar.

He was mouthwatering.

When he threw her a heated smile, her icy shield thawed at the same time she pulled her cloak of professionalism around her to stave off Carlos Narváez.

The two men chatted amiably about the crops as she drew near. Narváez filled the oversized chair across the round table from Rafe while Bunny flitted between the table and sideboard, ceaselessly fussing at the staff.

Narváez gestured to the seat next to him, but Harper wasn't going to give him the first point in this game. She chose the chair beside Rafe and pulled it even closer to him. When he draped his arm across the back and stroked her bare arm possessively, she didn't even try to withhold the shiver.

"So, the rumor is true, Segundo." One side of Narváez's mouth quirked up. "You have claimed Harper as yours."

"We're enjoying each other's company," Rafe replied.

It was true enough. She had enjoyed being with him, especially at supper last night. Their rapid changes of topics with shared and opposing points of view had been quite entertaining.

"Harper, did you sleep well?" The other man asked with a mocking smile.

"Of course." Harper casually laid a hand on Rafe's thigh. "I slept in late this morning. I'm afraid the drug reaction has kicked my ass."

"And what a pretty little ass it is," Narváez missed the envious green darts Bunny threw at him from the sideboard where she arranged fruit on a hand-painted plate.

Maggie appeared with a bottle of cold water and set it next to a chilled glass. Harper quietly thanked her and gave her a genuine smile which was quickly replaced by a contemptuous grimace as she watched Narváez's gaze follow the small girl who retreated to the kitchen. "Is your personal maid taking good care of you?"

"She's doing very well." Harper resented the way he'd looked at Maggie. She was a good kid. Harper would kill

Narváez before she'd allow him to touch the young girl and ruin her life.

"Excellent." He turned his head back toward Harper who chose that moment to admire the garden that surrounded them.

"Your gardener should be commended." She needed a benign topic before she lit into the cartel capo. "He put a lot of thought into the design. I like how he hid the walls of the compound with the vibrant red climbing roses then contrasted them with the bright yellow sunflowers. The ponds are a clever way to water the orchids. There must be a dozen different varieties. The colors are magnificent and show off so well against the green of the dieffenbachia."

"You seem to know your plants," Rafe noted. "Are you a student of horticulture?"

"No. My degrees were in chemistry and physics." She'd made her point, so she removed her hand from Rafe's thigh and sipped the orange colored juice. Surprisingly, it was delicious. She couldn't identify all the fruits, but it was close to a health club smoothie. She took a large drink before continuing, "I enjoy flowers as much as the next woman."

Bunny flounced over to the shaded glass table with a plate in each hand and presented them to the men, as though for their approval, before she set them in the middle. One contained an assortment of giant apple wedges arranged around a lump of white cheese that seemed hurriedly plopped off center. The colorful array of local fruit halves on the other plate had already fallen over each other during transport and now slithered around the plate quickly combining juices.

The men paid no attention as they carried on the conversation. "I am so glad you enjoy my flowers," Narváez said as he reached for piece of fruit. Bunny bounced beside him as though expecting a compliment or, at the very least, acknowledgement. She received neither and finally took her seat next to him.

Two maids in gray and white uniforms carried trays of food and gently placed plates on the table for the men and Harper. Bunny's food was all but dropped in front of her with a disgusted sneer.

Harper didn't bother to hide her smile as the kitchen staff scurried back to their domain.

"Tell me, Harper, how do you do it?" Narváez asked between bites of seasoned fish.

"I usually use my fork and carefully lift the flakes away from the skin and bone."

Narváez chuckled. "Seriously, how do you do it?"

"Like this." She demonstrated her forking technique in answer to his question.

His voice lost all mirth and became harder. "Tell me exactly how will you cocrystallize the explosive? I believe you call it Chaz."

Well, hell, maybe she could think up something, like a rare piece of equipment that would take him a few days to purchase.

"It's been a while. I'll need a computer to access the formula." Yes, and she'd use it to get a hold of USSOCOM. Even though Rafe had told her they would be extracted that night, she'd learned years ago to double check everything she was told.

"No need." Narváez smirked. "A complete copy of the original research you did at the University of Michigan is in the lab. Everything you should need is already there."

Damn him. The bastard was pushing her into a corner.

Then he announced, "The CL-20 and HMX is due to arrive in an hour. The wash chemicals are already present."

Harper's appetite vanished. How could she do this? But

how could she not? They would kill her team members if she didn't make the explosive.

"Today, you will make a small amount for me, and we'll test it tonight." Narváez sat back with a smug expression. "We've been invited to a birthday party in Cali. You will"—he paused and waved his hands as if trying to pick the right word from the hot morning air—"ah, yes…eliminate…Turi Solis."

What the fuck? He wants me to use a bomb to kill one man? No way. I won't do this.

She stared at him and didn't bother to disguise her hatred. Before she could verbalize her protest, he recapped, "Do I need to remind you we'll be in Cali? One phone call is all it would take." Narváez withdrew his phone from his pocket and played with it for a minute before he handed it to her. "I've taken out a little insurance." He chuckled. "Actually, he's quite large."

Marcus Hernandez. Harper shoved down the urge to call his name.

Live feed showed her bloodied friend tied to a chair, gagged. "Say hi to the pretty lady," a Spanish-accented voice demanded as the man pulled down her teammate's gag.

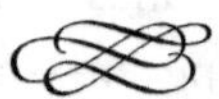

"Harper, don't do it. Whatever they want, don't do it. They're com—"

A fist met his jaw, and her teammate's head flew to one side.

Harper gasped.

"I warned you." The heavy Spanish accent seemed to intensify his words.

Hernandez's chin rested on his chest.

Harper exhaled raggedly as her heart broke for what they had obviously already put her friend through.

Narváez grabbed the phone from her and yelled at the picture. "Don't kill him yet, you fucking idiot. I need him."

He looked up at Harper. "Do as I wish, and he'll remain alive."

He touched the screen, and her friend was gone.

Harper's stomach flipped, and bile rose in her throat. Her unsteady hand grabbed the water glass. She carefully sipped. "What guarantee do I have that you'll keep your word?" She knew he'd lie to her to get his damned explosives. She sipped again and focused on her options. She had none. "After the demonstration tonight, I want proof of life before I'll make another drop."

"Certainly, me dulzura."

She wasn't his sweetness. At the moment, there wasn't a single sweet thing in her body. She would kill him before she left Colombia. The sooner, the better.

He had her and knew she'd protect her teammates.

Resigned, Harper focused on what she had to do. Turi Solis. She knew his name was on the sanctioned list. She'd studied all the capos before this mission. He'd gone to college in the U.S.A. under the name of Justin Soli and traveled back and forth as an international entrepreneur. Since he had close ties with some power brokers in D.C., they'd looked hard at him. It wasn't unreasonable that he'd have underlings purchase the HMX or CL-20 plus the connections to get all the technology to cocrystallize, but they'd found nothing to connect Solis/Soli to explosives. His dirty fingers were in lots of other illegal trade such as human trafficking; drugs, of course; and supplying guns to South American mercenaries— all allegedly and not provable in a courtroom.

The more Harper considered it, the loss of one more scumbag wouldn't bother her, but there would be innocents at the party.

"Why him?" she asked nonchalantly.

"Let's just say he's made some bad decisions lately."

A few months ago Solis had wrongly identified a tourist as a U.S. agent, had captured, and then tortured him. The bastard had sent body parts to the CIA for weeks before Solis realized he had the wrong man. She wondered if there was a government agent buried inside the Solis organization. Probably. It would make sense.

As she raked her memory for other details, she recalled Solis had flattened a rival's compound over a deal gone bad.

His competitor hadn't been at home at the time, but his wife and young children were all killed in the gas explosion. That's how it was reported by local authorities.

While Solis wasn't the head of the Cali Cartel, he was a powerful member. She shuddered at the thought of being turned over to that organization.

Harper decided she'd try to take out Turi Solis. Him and only him.

"We'll leave at four o'clock," Narváez announced as she mentally rejoined the table conversation. "Let's plan on staying overnight at La Comunidad."

Harper gave Rafe a questioning look. She'd never heard of that place.

Rafe mouthed, "Later."

That meant they'd be in Cali tonight…not at the Western Compound.

They wouldn't be rescued that night.

Her heart dropped, and the pain of lost hope followed it to the pit of her stomach.

As if Rafe knew what she was thinking, he patted her shoulder. His touch comforted her at the same time it sent threads of electricity through her body.

Narváez caressed Bunny's hand and suggested, "Let's get massages for two, side-by-side, at the spa. You've had such a stressful week, mi amor." His love, the over-bleached blonde, bubbled with excitement and babbled about the pleasure she'd show him in thanks.

Harper felt like gagging.

"The spa is wonderful, but so is the pool and Jacuzzi," Rafe agreed.

Harper turned her attention to Narváez, "Carlos."

He finally tore his gaze from his wife and looked at Harper.

"Shall we arrive in time for me to do a little shopping?" She wondered if he'd let Rafe take her to the open market where she would buy a disposable cell phone and call the operations center or, better yet, simply disappear.

"I've already chosen your dress for the party and matching handbag where you'll carry my present for Turi's birthday." His grin became hungry. "I also can't wait to see you in the bikini I've selected for you. We'll arrive early enough for a swim." He flashed an envious glance at Rafe.

"What if the explosion takes out others?" Harper had always worried about the collateral damage of explosives. It was the innocent lives that bothered her to the point of haunting her dreams.

He cocked his head and was probably calculating whom else he could kill with one blast. Or perhaps Narváez liked being up close and personal with the kill. Maybe she could kill them both with one kaboom.

His interest faded quickly. Narváez gave an exaggerated shrug. "So be it. I'm not concerned who else dies, only that you take out Solis."

"What if I make too much and don't need it all? Although it's an exacting science, this is still a new explosive. Testing will be involved."

"Do you think me a fool?" He smiled rakishly. "You might decide to use it on me."

Well, he was right there.

"Smart man. You already know I plan to kill you." She showed him two rows of perfectly straight white teeth that hid her worried soul. She had personal feelings about this assassination. She wanted to kill Narváez for kidnapping her. Hatred for the man grew with each hour she remained his captive.

"As I told you last night, Harper, many have tried, and

yet, here I sit in the open air of my terrace, eating without a care. Tonight, we'll walk among my friends and enemies, eating Turi Solis's food and acting properly social. I've been a target for years. I don't fear you. You won't kill me."

He looked at Segundo. "He won't let you."

She wondered for a split second if Rafe would try to stop her. He'd been Carlos's friend for more than a decade. Then, she recalled him saying that she might have to fight him for the right to kill Carlos. Rafe wouldn't stop her—she was sure of it.

"Besides, the more you get to know me, the more difficult it will be for you to try to kill me." He lifted his chin in defiance.

True. This was new for her. Every target before was simply that, a target. In the Army, her team was given orders, and they carried them out successfully. The small group of women she commanded as a Special Forces test team was so effective the military announced in 2013 that they would allow women into combat specialties previously closed to anyone with two X chromosomes.

But killing Carlos Narváez was different.

Yes, assassination had often been a part of her previous job, and she had done it very well. But she had no personal feelings toward those men. They were simply targets. Narváez would be a first for her. She knew him, and she hated him. There were emotions attached which only got in the way for an assassin. She'd overcome that to do her job.

"I have treated you well, yes?" Narváez brought her out of her thoughts. "You have not been tortured, as assuredly my fellow capos would have done. You have the freedom of my compound and your own personal protector. I dress you in designer clothing, and all I ask is that you make me a small bomb. Tonight, you'll kill Solis with it."

Yes. She would. How the fuck was she going to do that though? All her kills in the past were planned as a group with lots of intel and executed with precision with several backup plans. Tonight, it would be just her. And she'd be close, exponentially increasing her chances of getting caught. Damn Narváez.

Rafe nudged her to him and back into the conversation.

"Carlos, I think I'll take Harper for a run before we leave. We'll try to work some of the remaining poison out of her body."

She knew Rafe wanted to show her the compound and be sure no one overheard their escape discussions. She liked the idea that he was leaving Colombia with her.

"I have some plantation business to oversee first." Rafe rose. "I'll pick you up in two hours." He bent and brushed a kiss on her cheek. She was sure it was for show, but heat radiated down her throat and warmed her whole body.

She lowered her eyes, afraid he'd see the desire in them.

With minutes to spare, a navy blue designer sports bra with light blue piping and matching running shorts were delivered to her room. How the hell did Narváez do that? Harper ripped the outlandishly high price tags off and slipped into the perfectly fitting workout clothes. She readjusted the bra as she heard the lock click.

"Ready?" Rafe stepped in the doorway.

She took a step back. In worn navy running shorts and professional, nearly weightless shoes…and nothing else…the man was sex on two legs. Every inch of his powerful body moved as muscles stretched and bunched when he sauntered toward her.

"Harper?" he whispered.

He was so close she shivered. When he cupped her cheek, her breath caught. Her heart beat way too fast, as though she'd already been running.

"Babe, are you sick again?" He looked so apprehensive. But of course he wasn't worried about her. He couldn't be. He barely knew her. It wouldn't matter anyway. No one, except her team, was ever really concerned about her. Men least of all. They used her body and left.

"I'm fine." Her words were curt as she stepped away from him. Sitting on the bed, she laced the dark blue running shoes that had appeared with the jogging outfit. Looping the last lace, she stood and announced, "Let's go."

Minutes later, Harper sensed Rafe watching her as they stretched in the tiled courtyard using the steps to extend their hamstrings.

"Ready?" He asked, his eyes never meeting hers.

"Lead the way," she told him. They jogged through decorative iron gates onto a well-traveled dirt road.

As soon as they were far enough away for others to overhear, Harper said, "I want to see as much as possible. I need to be prepared for extraction, and I'd like some idea of where I'm headed."

Rafe kept his voice low and spoke only in English. "Damn Carlos. This fucking Cali trip put a hold on our escape."

"Would the SEALs try to get us out of Cali?" Harper doubted it, but while on a Special Forces team, she'd had to be prepared for in-theater changes.

"I'll send a message to ops letting them know the change in plan. They'll probably wait until we return here tomorrow and come then."

It was just one more day. Harper could hold out and do whatever she had to do to stay alive.

Rafe's words interrupted her dismal thoughts. "Don't look at them, but there are turrets on every corner of the compound. The guards have been given orders that you are not permitted beyond the three-meter walls without either Carlos or me at your side. Same goes for the guards throughout the plantation."

Harper noted guard towers every thousand feet, each with at least two machine-gun-toting soldiers.

Rafe continued, "Their orders are to shoot at your feet with a command to stop. If you disobey, they have permission to shoot you. Trust me, my soldiers are trained and loyal to Carlos. They are so good some of the other capos in the cartel borrow them for kidnapping, assassinations, and protection."

"The other drug lords use your hit men?" She was surprised that Narváez would lend them out.

"They are Carlos's men, not mine. And yes. This cartel is very loosely allied, and many of the men are not professionally trained. Since Carlos owns the land that grows the crops and the trucks to move the goods to market, and with his import connections in the U.S.A., he's a very powerful capo. Most cartels are limited to one geographic area, but Carlos owns several plantations scattered throughout Colombia. There's another even larger compound on the Caribbean Sea and some farms on the far side of the mountains."

"So, does that make you a lugarteniente?" Harper jogged easily beside Rafe.

"I'm more than a lieutenant, although I do closely oversee all the lugartenientes and sicarios. I rarely bother with halcones, the cartel's eyes and ears on the street. I don't have time to listen and sift through local gossip to see if someone is after Carlos's operation. I already know they are, and I have plans in place to deal with any attempt on his life. I've arranged the chain of command for Carlos closer to that of the military with Carlos a commanding officer. I guess that makes me the executive officer, the tip of the funnel for information going in and out."

"He trusts you." As if given an unseen signal, they both lengthened their stride and established their breathing.

"Yeah." Rafe then added, "Usually. But I didn't know anything about kidnapping you. If I'd had even an inkling about what Carlos had planned, I would've tried my damnedest to talk him out of it."

"That's good to know." Harper thought for a moment then asked, "Where does Pablo Velez fit into this organization?"

Rafe chuckled. "Everywhere and nowhere. He's Carlos's nephew and self-appointed heir apparent. He showed up here about six months ago, his mother screaming and yelling at Carlos to teach the boy some respect and convince him to get his ass back in college. I'm pretty sure the only thing the kid has learned is that Carlos is worth a fortune and how to enjoy all the free sex, drugs, and rock 'n roll that any kid his age could ever want." He shook his head. "He's also a conceited, mean little bastard."

"You don't like him," Harper noted.

"The little fucker thinks he knows everything, and he's dumb as a box of rocks." They turned and jogged down toward the Pacific Ocean, past fields of neatly pruned coffee trees clinging in rows to the steep slope. "He has no leadership skills whatsoever, yet thinks he should have my job. He doesn't understand that this is a very complicated international business. All he sees is what the money buys."

The closer they came to the shore, the more overwhelmed Harper became at the sweetness of the flowers. She was shocked to see acres of red roses on tall straight stems, carnations that waved gently in the constant ocean breeze, and dahlias the size of dessert plates in every color imaginable.

"Why flowers?" She'd seen them everywhere in the house, but this was more than the entire country could use.

Rafe said with a smile, "When we were in college, Carlos did a paper for his merchandising class that showed Colombia was perfect for flower production because of its constant year-round temperature. Bet you didn't know that Colombia is the second largest producer of cut flowers in the world."

"I had no idea." Puffs of dust rose around her ankles as her shoes slapped the steep dirt road.

"Carlos and I made great plans back in those days to transform Colombian agriculture into legitimate exports. Now he uses the flowers to overpower the U.S. Customs drug dogs and the flower and coffee industries to launder his money. He calls it being vertically integrated. He owns the land the flowers and cocaine are grown on, the transportation to market, and the legitimate U.S. bank accounts that process the sales."

"I guess he learned something from that MBA," Harper admitted.

"Too bad cocaine is killing all those intelligent brain cells," Rafe said with disgust.

"He's still your friend." Harper had noted the warmth and concern in Rafe's voice when he discussed Carlos. Their friendship went deep.

"No." Nodding toward the big house he said, "That man isn't my friend. He's becoming more paranoid every day, more violent. Just last week he nearly beat the hell out of a maid because he was high and slipped in his own bathroom on water Bunny had splashed out of the tub. I had the chopper take the poor woman to the hospital in Cali."

Chopper. That's right. Narváez had a helicopter. They could use it to escape, and since Rafe was going, too, maybe they could get past the guards. That made a potential Plan B.

They turned to jog on what there was of the beach—little more than a half mile of sand. Harper looked out at craggy spires of tortured rock that jutted from the tempestuous ocean. She sped up and cut in front of him to run in the waves.

"It's cold, you know," Rafe warned. "The strong Peruvian Current brings ice-cold water from Antarctica up the South American coast then makes a circle here on the West Coast of Colombia."

As far as Harper was concerned, that water never became warm enough for swimming, not even in California. Forget a possibility for escape via the ocean, especially without wet suits. On the other hand, SEALs were known for swimming. She hoped they didn't plan on that route, but she was scuba certified and could swim out if necessary.

They turned at a narrow rock path that led up the mountain toward the compound. It was more like climbing the steps of a skyscraper than a jog. Harper was thankful for the first time for all the hours she'd spent on a stair stepper. When the land finally leveled, she glanced back to see the ocean hundreds of feet below. It truly was a beautiful place, but she'd never be sorry to leave.

"Come on, this way," Rafe called as he made a right turn and they started down a relatively flat road toward the compound gate.

Sweat seeped from every pore as she trudged the final yards toward the house. The metallic stench of the medicine surrounded her when she slowed to a cooling walk. Rafe hadn't even broken a sweat. Damn him. The allergic reaction had damaged her body more than she'd imagined.

"Sorry. That's about all I can handle right now," she confessed as Rafe shook out his muscles.

"I understand. Let's hit the showers. You have a bomb to make." He held open the iron gate and gestured for her to enter.

CHAPTER 13

RAFE TWISTED THE KEY TO UNLOCK THE SMALL BLOCK building that stood a hundred yards away from any other. He pushed the door open for Harper and flipped on the lights.

Her mouth fell open.

"Narváez wasn't kidding when he said he'd replicated the lab at Michigan." It looked almost exactly the same. It even had the solid block of granite that levitated on forced air, required for the highly volatile CL-20. In one corner sat a red sphere that looked like a WWII oceanic mine with steel protrusions in every direction. She was glad to see he'd purchased the newest version detonation chamber since they'd blown up one during testing. The cocrystallized explosive was potent.

"So, tell me about this new bomb." Rafe's gaze swept the room. "We used HMX in the SEALs all the time. It was great, impervious to almost everything. You could beat it with a hammer, and it wouldn't explode. Not like CL-20. That shit is as jumpy as nitroglycerine. If you looked at it wrong, it would blow."

"You're absolutely right. Octogen"—Harper looked his way—"HMX or octo, as many call it, is a wonderful explosive. Its impact sensitivity is relatively low for a nitrosamine high explosive, unlike hexanitro—" She stopped herself in the beginning of the multi-syllable chemical name and smiled at him. "What you call CL-20. The researchers at China Lake made it as a rocket propellant. It actually produces twenty percent more energy than HMX, but its instability makes it a poor choice for military applications."

"No shit." Rafe stepped beside her and laid his flat palms on the long stainless steel table. "During EOD training, we had to use CL-20 just so we'd know what it looked like and its capabilities. I was happy to carry HMX, especially when in plastic form."

Rafe sounded interested. Good. Harper tried really hard not to get too technical with him, which was so easy as she stood in one of the most modern labs in the world, ready to mix a state-of-the-art explosive. She was one of five people who could do this. Although parts of the formula and an explanation of cocrystallization had actually been published in Popular Mechanics, there were procedures and chemicals that only the five knew. There was a damn good reason for that.

To keep things light, Harper asked, "Did you know that its code name in World War II was Aunt Jemima? The underground factions used to mix HMX with flour to smuggle it into occupied countries. If anyone got wise, they'd cook it into pancakes and eat it."

Rafe laughed. "There's an explosive farts joke in there somewhere, right?"

Harper laughed, too. "No joke. They really did."

She looked around the room. All the equipment she

needed was there. Plastic bottles were lined like soldiers on a tall shelving unit. More than enough to make what she needed for tonight's demonstration.

"So what's the big deal with this new explosive?" Rafe asked.

"Basically, cocrystallization takes the best of both chemicals and combines them. It has the velocity of CL-20 and the stability of HMX."

"Is it really that significant an increase?" His face was doubtful.

She nodded. "Yes. It's nearly two hundred fifty miles per hour faster."

"Holy shit." His response was a whisper.

Harper went on, "If shaped with polymers, like they do to create C-4, it can easily reach deep bunkers. We thought about selling it to oil companies to replace slow drilling apparatus, but our research was funded by the Department of Defense." She and the team she'd worked with had kicked around dozens of civilian applications, but they knew what it was designed for…the biggest bang for the least bucks.

"What do you call it?"

"Chaz, but don't ask me why." Harper snickered. "Scientists aren't known for their marketing creativity. We always called it by its chemical name, which wasn't even confirmed when I visited the lab last year."

"Okay then, Chaz. If it's even close to the HMX I've used, it's going to smack his ass all the way to hell and make a fucking mess of everything around what used to be Turi Solis."

Harper had to agree. "That's relatively accurate."

"So, what do we need to do to make Chaz go boom?" Rafe had a grin across his strikingly handsome face. The fluorescent lights washed out his tan, but his blue eyes glittered. Here he was, in a lab—where she was very comfortable—volunteering to help her, knowing full well that they might get blown up. At least he'd handled explosives before.

Rafe looked around the room then grabbed two chemical-resistant aprons off pegs on the wall next to the door and handed her one. She slipped it on and looked up at him.

Harper giggled like a little girl. The sight of six-feet plus, broad shoulders, and alpha attitude in an apron made her giggle faster.

"I've been in a lab before," Rafe reassured her. Harper tried to control her spasmodic outburst, but it took several tries before she got it under control.

With a deep breath, she asked him, "Will you please get the HMX from the safe over there?"

"Yes, ma'am." Rafe headed for the thick-walled box next to the explosives chamber.

Harper tied her hair in a bun at the back of her neck and began the process. "Have you ever been to a party at Solis's?"

"Unfortunately, yes. This will be the third year he's thrown himself a birthday party. The food is always great at these ordeals. Solis can be long-winded, though. Some men would be humble and just say thank you. Others use it as a political platform. Solis likes to tell the crowd—and there will be a crowd—just how great he is. And why use five words when twenty-five will do?" Rafe carried a small, but heavy, box to one of the stainless steel tables.

"So he speaks from a podium?" She could plant the bomb under the lectern and maybe she'd get only him. But if his guards checked it before he spoke, they'd find it and remove it.

"No, he likes to walk around as if he's talking to individuals. He's a real showoff. I mean showman." Rafe's dislike for the drug runner was obvious.

"Does he use a microphone?" That idea had possibilities.

"Yes."

"Excellent." Harper went to work with Rafe by her side. This felt right to her—too right, too comfortable.

Harper and Rafe leaned on the second-floor balcony railing of their two-bedroom suite at La Comunidad and examined the manicured grounds filled with blooming red and yellow hibiscus under straight towering palms. She wondered if she —no, it was now they—could escape from here and disappear into the large Colombian city.

"What is this place?" Harper wondered. "It's like a hotel, but not. Are these individually owned condos or like a timeshare resort? My room is beautiful. The Jacobean four-poster bed is divine."

She'd never stayed in such rich surroundings but was schooled to identify wealth when she saw it. The hand-woven Persian rug had no doubt been imported a hundred years ago via Spain and held up today due to proper care. The heavy Mediterranean style furniture had been crafted from Brazilian hardwoods more than two hundred years ago. For her personal tastes, the rusts and gold brocade were weighty but fit in with the ornately-curved wrought iron chandeliers and side tables.

"It's a safe haven for the members of the cartel Carlos belongs to," Rafe explained. "You saw the armed sicario at the gate. Most capos will stay here while they conduct business because the rooms are swept for listening devices at least twice a day and the surrounding walls won't allow directional microphones to be effective. The huge palm trees block snipers' lines of fire. The capos can relax and enjoy all the comforts of a first class resort and know what they say will never be repeated by the staff." Rafe smiled. "Several escape the daily grind here with their puta rather than their wives."

"Is that what they think I am, your whore?" Harper shot him a glance. Sex was never expected as part of the job, but the promise was often a means to get a man alone without bodyguards. Men were easy. Their guard dropped with their pants, and they never considered women a threat to their lives. Fools. Mere flirting was how she'd gotten the information she needed about the HMX and CL-20 purchases.

For some unknown reason, she didn't want anyone to think she was Rafe's whore. It bothered her more than it should.

"No." Rafe looked over his shoulder at her. "The story Carlos is feeding his friends is you're an American socialite and my lover. Can you deal with that?"

"Now that's a role I can play." The only part worrying her was she feared she might like it too much. This attraction she had for Rafe was palpable. As he stood next to her, she felt their connection on some basic level. She'd never had that with a man before.

She didn't have time to think about that now, not with what she had to do tonight. Would the miniscule amount of explosive she'd made and polymer-bonded that afternoon take out Turi Solis...and only him? Would they be able to covertly steal the microphone and replace it once she rigged it?

On the helicopter ride to Cali, she'd feigned a queasy

stomach so she could sit in the co-pilot seat next to Rafe. Thankfully, he was Narváez's pilot. Stealing the chopper was high on her list of escape routes, especially since the rescue was off for tonight. Rafe had managed to send a message to CIA Operations Control Center notifying them of Narváez's plans to travel to Cali.

Harper had memorized the terrain as they flew over the Cordillera Occidental range of the Andes Mountains and dropped into the wide Cauca River valley to the metropolis of Cali. Colombia had very few navigable roads; most transportation was by water or air. Of its nearly one thousand airports, only one hundred were paved, a necessity to land the small corporate-style jets like the one used by the ATF, but half of those weren't long enough. SEALs used lots of different kinds of helicopters and planes. Hopefully, she and Rafe would be rescued from the Narváez western compound tomorrow night.

The front seat of the helicopter had given Harper an aerial view of the snow-capped Cordillera Central range dotted with volcanoes and serrated peaks. She watched Nevado del Huila —the highest active volcano in Colombia—spew a thin stream of smoke and steam that lazed its way into the atmosphere.

To the Southwest, Puracé sat majestically, still crowned by winter's pure white snow. Only fifteen thousand feet tall, it was much shorter than many others, but was the most active volcano, threatening to blow nearly every ten years.

She'd occasionally seen the Cordillera Oriental range with its somewhat shorter mountains in the far distance. Harper was once again thankful their travels hadn't taken her into the vastly unexplored river basin that drained the melting snowcaps of the Andes into the Amazon River. At this point in her life, she'd experienced more than enough remote area survival and hoped the SEALs wouldn't consider it a viable option for escape. She couldn't wait to get home to her D.C. condo.

"Have you been to Cali before?" Rafe's voice brought her out of her longing for home. He sipped eighteen-year-old scotch from a short crystal glass delivered from the bar as he leaned his forearms on the railing.

"No. There was no intel that any of the cartels in this area had purchased either HMX or CL-20, so we didn't need to investigate here." She wasn't thrilled to be here now either. She was in the heart of the Cali Cartel, and before they'd lifted off, Narváez had reminded her how easy it would be to give her to them. She shuddered at the idea.

"If we were going to be here longer, I'd take you out to some of the salsa clubs." Rafe gave her a warm smile. "People come from all over the world to Cali just for the nightlife."

Harper had heard of the hedonistic lifestyle that made this city famous. Their team had visited a few clubs in other cities to gain HUMINT, human intelligence. It never ceased to amaze her the things drunk sicarios or halcones would tell a beautiful woman to impress her. The lugartenientes were the worst, or best, depending on your point of view. They bragged constantly about their kidnappings and killings with details only those present would know.

She changed the subject. "The weather here is so much hotter and muggier than at the Narváez compound. I miss the ocean breeze that's blocked by the mountains. I'm sure being in the middle of such a big city has a lot to do with it, too. Cali has become quite a metropolitan area."

"Yeah, it has." The disgust in his voice was unhidden.

"Last year Cali had nearly two thousand murders. That's a lot considering there are just over two million people who live here. Compare that to Miami, which is only slightly bigger and had less than eighty homicides."

That statistic astonished her. She'd known it was a violent city, drugs and politics mostly. Maybe they could focus blame on one of those when she added to that number tonight.

Harper didn't want to think about killing a man in a few hours. It would be her first solo assassination. She'd always had her team to help plan and carry it out, as backup and encouragement. They were always there in case it all went to shit, and she knew all too well that it could go very wrong, very fast. She needed to change the subject.

"Are you ready to go back home to your family?" She was fishing for information about Rafe. His assimilation back into American society could be difficult after being under cover for so long. Maybe she could help him, to show her thanks for his protection the past few days.

"No, I don't want to live in Charleston, South Carolina. It's too close to my family and all their drama. I need a bigger city. Don't get me wrong, I love my parents and sisters, but I prefer to visit rather than be drowned in their microscopic problems. Which high school friend is cheating on his wife or who overcharged my sister for her latest house renovation seems so petty compared to who is going to shoot at me next."

"Will you stay with the government? Move to D.C.?" The possibility of seeing him after this was over sparked somewhere deep inside Harper since she owned a two-bedroom condominium near DuPont Circle and worked in the nation's capital.

"No, I need to get away from the job completely. They'll want me to go back under somewhere else, I'm sure. I know this is going to sound weird to someone like you, but I'd like to find the right woman, settle down with a big dog, and go to work in the morning five days a week. I'd leave the work at the office when I come home at night. Someday have a few kids. I'd be their swim coach. Live a normal life."

"And forget about this other world we work in now?" Harper felt compelled to share. "Someday I might want that life. But, for now, I love the thrill of my job. I live for the adrenaline rush." She took in his weary eyes that had seen too much and wanted to kiss away the bad and replace it with good memories. Memories lasted, even though men didn't. "At least I get to go back to the United States and live my own life between missions, and each time we're sent out, it's different. You've been stuck with Narváez for years." It dawned on her he'd been as much a prisoner of Carlos Narváez as she—and perhaps even more so, given how long he'd been with the man.

They were quiet for a long time. She watched vibrant red and blue parrots call to each other and swoop between trees and plants. Harper finally broke the silence. "What was your degree in?"

"Criminal justice. Think I should become a cop?" he teased.

She laughed at that idea. "Certainly not."

For some unknown reason, Katlin Callahan popped into her mind. Briefly, Harper thought it would be absolutely awesome if her friends, the Ladies of Black Swan, were to be the ones to rescue her. But they had left on a mission to the Middle East the same day she'd been sent to Colombia. After training with those women for over a year, and now living next door to them, they remained close. Harper knew Katlin had some kind of connection to Guardian Security, the company that protected their condos.

"You do have a lot of management skills." She slid Rafe a glance. "There's a company you might want to consider when we get back. My friend knows the owners. Have you ever heard of Guardian Security?"

"I don't think I'd be happy as a rent-a-cop walking around some warehouse or construction site at night with one bullet and a Maglite."

"I'm not sure they offer that service." Harper had partied with her friends down the hall and met some of the men who worked for Guardian. Although from different branches of the service, all were former special operators who'd seen several tours in combat. Harper was sure they had seen plenty of the shadow world. More than once she had wondered if the company was really a black ops front.

From their brochure, she could tell Rafe in all honesty, "Guardian does high-tech surveillance, but they do have bodyguards. They offer home and business security systems and monitoring. You might be surprised to learn just how big they are. I want you to know that once we get back, I'll help you if I can." She hoped he realized she was sincere. He seemed consumed by what lay ahead tonight or their impending escape.

"Thanks. I'll think about it. Let's get dressed." Rafe finished the last drop of expensive whisky before he walked back into the suite. Harper stayed on the balcony for another minute and watched his tight ass swagger away. She was attracted to Rafe, but she'd never break the rule about sex during a mission. It could get her killed. After they were out of this country? Maybe. He'd be fun to play with for a while, but only a short time. She never kept a man around long enough to build a relationship, long enough to be hurt when he left.

She had a job to do tonight.

In the limousine on the way to the resort, Narváez had said nothing, but he'd shown her another live feed of Hernandez. Her teammate was unconscious, still tied to the chair, his face bloody and bruised.

With her last thought about the remainder of her team, she opened the sliding door to the suite.

CHAPTER 14

Rafe adjusted his black bow tie as he stepped into the shared living room at the same time Harper emerged from her bedroom.

He took one look at the beautiful woman in the dark green gown before him, and his fingers stopped. She'd curled her shoulder-length hair, or maybe it was the humidity. It didn't matter because dark curls framed her pretty face and made her look vulnerable when her eyes closed. He could tell she was gathering her emotions, but when her high cheekbones tinged pink, and she bit her bottom lip, he was sure she knew what he was thinking.

He wanted to run his hands over her bare shoulders and use his tongue to trace the edge of her halter gown where it barely covered her rounded breasts. Then he'd start with her instep and kiss his way up those long legs until he reached their apex and bury his face into her softness.

But no. They had a party to attend. And surrounded by a hundred people, she'd kill Turi Solis, a capo in the same cartel as Carlos. Damn Carlos for making him kidnap her. On the other hand, Rafe was also thankful to him for bringing Harper into his life.

She wasn't just his gorgeous date for a party. He was supposed to be her personal jailer. At the same time, he was her protector. Either role he was required to play, he would be at her side all night.

Harper was part of the dark world where he'd already lost too much. He'd never keep her in his life after this was over, but, damn, he wanted her in his bed tonight, all night.

He traced every curve of the emerald body-hugging dress with his gaze. "You are so beautiful." He walked to her. "Christ, you're stunning."

She didn't step back. That was a good sign.

He slowly lifted his hand to her face but stopped, not touching her. He hesitated, giving her time to retreat.

She didn't move.

Harper splayed her hands on his chest, and he feared she'd push him away. He held her tempting brown gaze and tried to read her thoughts. A flash of heat was his permission.

He lifted her chin with just two fingers until her lips met his. The pulse that tore through his entire body was new. It raced past his heart and kicked it hard, awakening feelings for the first time in too many years.

She slid her arms around his neck, and Rafe felt her surrender to the kiss.

This kiss wasn't for show; this was for him. He pulled her to him. She was almost as tall as him in her high-heeled sandals. Their bodies fit perfectly.

He deepened the kiss, teasing her lips to open for him. When she did, he dove in, exploring her mouth with his tongue. She gave as good as she got and probed his mouth demandingly. Rafe liked that she wasn't shy about what she wanted.

He ran his hands up her bare back and down the length of her well-toned arms. He broke from her mouth and kissed his way down her throat with light nips. Her rapid pulse told him she liked what he'd done.

Slipping his hand from her back and around the side, he slid his fingers under the halter top to her left breast. He'd wanted to touch her like this since he'd first seen her. He lightly drew his fingertips over her rounded breast before his thumb brushed her nipple. It instantly hardened for him. She shivered, and he took possession of her mouth again while gently kneading her breast.

"Hey, Segundo, we're going to be late," accompanied a pounding at the door.

Fuck.

Rafe ended the kiss and slowly removed his hand from her breast as he looked into her fiery eyes. He wanted her, and for more than an instant there, she'd wanted him. Right there. Right then.

"Segundo, she'd better damn well be ready. We've got to go." Narváez's cold voice brought them both back to the reality of the evening.

Harper stepped away from Rafe. She looked as shaken as he felt, but with a deep breath, she regained her composure. She checked her makeup in the mirror next to the door. He needed to be close to her again, so Rafe stepped beside her and needlessly straightened his tie. He used a perfectly white handkerchief to wipe her lipstick off his lips, but he couldn't erase the evidence of their passion. Before he reached for the door, he softly kissed her neck, just below her ear.

"To be continued," he whispered and took her hand.

~

As the limousine exited the iron gates of La Comunidad, Harper picked up the small beaded bag and checked its contents; lipstick that was really Chaz, dental floss that was actually fine det cord, and a tiny blasting cap appropriately hidden in the cap of her perfume. She was ready.

She folded her hands over the bag and stared at the fresh manicure, compliments of the resort spa. She didn't dare look at Rafe. She was afraid of what he'd see. She'd kissed the far-too-handsome man as a prelude to the role she needed to play. Then she'd lost her ever-loving mind. When his lips had touched hers, heat had drenched her body and mind-numbing need replaced common sense. If they hadn't been interrupted, she would—

No you wouldn't have, she reassured herself. Taking a deep breath and refocusing on the present, Harper looked up.

Valez was all but licking his lips as he stared at her. Hunger poured from him, but not for the pretty woman at his side who fawned over him.

Rafe must have read her mind when he whispered in her ear, "Provided by the resort. She's been vetted by the organization and knows if she talks, she's dead."

At her surprised look, he added, "Don't worry. She's very well-paid. And she'll keep Pablo happy, and occupied, all night."

He caught Valez's salacious grin at Harper and lit into him, "Boy, play with your pet." He threw his arm around Harper and tucked her in close before he kissed her temple. "This one is too far out of your class. You couldn't begin to handle one with brains like hers."

At the hiss of voices, Narváez ignored Bunny to watch the other two men in the car.

"You think you're so fucking smart," Pablo snarled.

"I am fucking smart," Rafe leaned forward, "and don't

you ever forget it. Even if you could make it through college, you'd never be as smart as me…or Carlos."

"Pablo, Segundo makes a good point," Narváez nodded toward Harper. "Miss Tambini is one of the most intelligent women you will ever meet. You cannot treat her like your whore. Did you not learn anything from supper last night?"

The young man made his second mistake. He chuckled. "Yeah, I learned a mere woman could knock you on your ass and threat—"

The man-child never saw the fist that crossed his jaw.

Narváez spoke to the young woman who held a limp Valez. "Take him back and tend to his headache. Tonight is too important for him to fuck up again." He turned his gaze to Rafe. "I don't think I could even beat any manners into the boy. He is simply too stupid. You are right."

As though nothing had happened, Narváez turned toward his new wife, gently caressed her cheek, and asked, "Now, sweetheart, what were you saying?"

Bunny babbled thanks for her new dress that barely covered her nipples, exposing bodacious amounts of breast. Harper hoped the woman didn't sneeze. Wardrobe malfunction wouldn't cover that incident. At least it would keep the focus on her rather than on Harper.

"You okay?" Rafe leaned in front of her, blocking her view of Valez and Narváez.

"I'm fine." She thought about it for a second then added, "I think the kid just got a valuable lesson. I hope he learned something from it."

One side of Rafe's lips quirked up. "I doubt it. He's really dumb. To be honest, I was afraid he'd do something tonight to give us away."

Rafe leaned in and briefly pressed his lips to hers.

"Everything will work out. I've got your six." He then moved back into his seat and took her hand in his.

Harper stared at their joined hands. She'd been nervous when she'd stepped out of her bedroom, not so much about tonight's activities, but about the man whose body heat radiated next to her. He'd looked devastatingly attractive when he strode into their shared living room, yet he had a little boy's frustrated frown on his usually hard-as-stone face. The way he'd twisted at his black bow tie made her grin.

Rafe's tailored dusky-gray tuxedo brought out the silver flecks in his light blue eyes. Not many men could pull off the double-breasted suit, but his tall, tapered lines and wide shoulders were perfect for the style. With his absolutely straight posture, he looked almost militaristic.

When he'd touched her so tenderly, she couldn't resist. His words made her feel cherished, something she'd never felt before. It made her want him. And, damn, she wanted this man. More now than ever.

His kiss had sent a jolt through her, of not just desire and need, but one so different from any she'd experienced with any other man. She wasn't sure what it was about Rafe Silva, but he was so unlike any man she'd ever been around.

She liked the way he kissed. Some men were all slobbery and choked her with their probing tongue. Rafe's kisses were gentle and warm, and he'd allowed her a taste of him as well. He'd given her a degree of control. She liked that most of all.

The limousine stopped, bringing Harper out of her thoughts. Rafe took her hand as she gathered the floor-length gown in the other, lifting it so she could step gracefully from the car.

Rafe kept a possessive hand at the small of her back. She knew his hand-tailored tuxedo hid a holstered .40 caliber pistol. They'd discussed the possibility of needing it. He promised to protect her, but if it all went to hell, she'd find a gun and protect herself.

When they entered the grand home, Harper saw hundreds of sophisticatedly dressed women and black-tie-clad men. Even so, she and Rafe made a distinctive pair. She was possibly the tallest woman in the room, and the three-inch heels pushed her towering over most of the men. Rafe's lanky six-feet-four gave him a few inches above the tallest bodyguard.

She caught glances from both men and women, but the magnificent beauty in the sparkling ruby dress with flowing black hair was the most noticeable of the group gathered. Her stare was piercing. There was hurt and envy in the nearly black eyes that met Harper's before the other woman looked away.

Rafe couldn't take his eyes off the woman in the red gown that embraced each curve of her Marilyn Monroe body. Harper felt like a flat-chested giraffe.

"Who is she?" Harper kept her voice quiet as they strolled through the crowd.

"My handler." His voice was rough. "I should've known she'd be here."

"How long have you been sleeping with her?"

He stopped in mid-stride and backed her into a private corner hidden by a white marble pillar and a fern taller than both of them. "I never said I did." His words were clipped, his manner defensive.

"You didn't have to." Harper fought down the green monster. "The look in her eyes when she saw the two of us together told me."

Rafe closed his eyes and swore.

"It's okay. I don't care." She placed a reassuring hand on his arm. "Yes, I know it's against the Company rules, but I'm not about to tattle. You're the one who needs to keep in mind our relationship is all for show. Introduce me. We should tell her our plan so she doesn't get hurt."

A flash of uncomfortable hesitation crossed his bright blue eyes before he nodded and led her into the crowd.

The striking woman with latte-colored skin, much darker than Harper's suntan, kept slyly glancing their way as she and Rafe approached.

In proper societal Spanish, Rafe said, "Melina Costaneda, I'd like you to meet Harper Tambini."

"It's a pleasure to meet you." Harper grabbed the woman's hand and shook it lightly. "I understand we have a lot in common. Rafe, I see that both of us ladies are in need of a drink. Would you mind?"

"The bar is in the garden," Melina offered in a smooth-as-satin voice.

"Why don't we all walk that direction?" Rafe suggested with a purposeful glance toward Narváez and Bunny, who were headed their way.

CHAPTER 15

THE GARDEN WAS LIKE A FESTIVAL OF LIGHTS. PALM TREES were wrapped in golden miniature bulbs, and spotlights drove beams into their giant green leaves sixty feet above. Candles floated on the turquoise bend of the pool, and green lights accented the edges of progressive ponds.

Stepping stone paths appeared gray from the downcast blue solar lights and wound through trees and tall bushes to the wings of the palatial home. Each curve, hidden from the last, revealed another private, picture-perfect setting.

The scent of blossoming roses overpowered the most heavily perfumed woman. Plate-sized dahlias splashed fire reds and sunrise yellows against the white-spattered green dieffenbachia and elephant ear leaves.

Admiring the garden, Harper walked Rafe and Melina to a deeply shadowed section. She checked the area around them to be sure no one was hiding, wishing she had the equipment to test for listening and video devices. She spoke in English when she was sure they couldn't be overheard.

"Melina, I know you're Rafe's handler." And his lover

went unsaid. "I work for the U.S. government, but Narváez kidnapped me two days ago."

Relief and recognition fell over the woman's classical Spanish features, her worry gone in an instant. She was all business now, no longer a jealous lover.

She revealed, "I received a call from the deputy director himself about you. You must be very important."

"I don't know about that," Harper admitted.

"She is," Rafe asserted.

"My orders are to help you any way I can. What do you need?"

Harper liked her direct approach. "Turi Solis is going to die tonight in an explosion. We could use your help to distract the bandleader while we steal the microphone and plant the bomb. Is there anyone else we should warn?"

"Yes, I have a man inside Solis's organization." She scanned the crowded room. "I'd warn him if I could, but he isn't here. He missed his last two contact checks. I'd hoped to find him. That's the real reason I came to this party." Melina shot a glance to Rafe in apology.

"I hope you find him. If he needs extraction, we're waiting for the final go," Harper offered.

Dark eyes glanced at the blue topaz of Rafe's with a hint of regret. "I know it was scheduled for tonight, but then you traveled here."

Harper closed her eyes, pissed at Narváez for spoiling their escape. She couldn't think about that now.

Melina continued, "I am to contact Mr. Gillpatrick directly if I see you. Any message for him?"

Rafe looked at each woman then said, "If it goes bad tonight, Harper and I will try to escape from here. Otherwise, we'll head back to the Narváez compound tomorrow morning."

Melina nodded as if another message had been sent and received. "I understand."

Harper smiled. "Let us know if you see your inside man. In the meantime, what do you know about Solis and tonight's party?"

Melina looked Harper up and down. "He likes beautiful women who call him by his American name, Justin."

Harper wasn't sure if she needed that information. She had no intention of meeting the man. "I'll keep that in mind. What else?"

"He'll switch to bourbon just before he gives his birthday speech, which should happen around midnight. Until then, he'll drink vodka and tonic, heavy on the tonic. He likes to keep his senses with this many people around."

"Thank you, Melina. You've been a great help." Harper looked to Rafe. "We need to find Narváez and tell him to slow down. We'll be partying all hours, and we can't afford for Carlos to even hint about our plans or, worse yet, brag. He needs to stay sober."

As the three emerged from the darkness of the gardens, they scanned the party for Solis, Narváez, and Melina's inside man. The first two were easy; they were talking ten feet from the bar.

Harper pasted on her best party smile as Rafe guided her through the crowd that had left the house to enjoy the warm evening air.

Narváez gestured to them when they were several feet away, and in a loud voice announced, "Turi, my old friend, I'd like you to meet Ms. Tambini." He gave Harper a smug smile. "She's staying with me for a while."

Mentally Harper rolled her eyes, but they remained fixed on Narváez, narrowing ever so slightly.

He noticed.

Turi Solis raked cold, dark eyes the length of her body with overt male appreciation. She couldn't help herself; she feared and hated this man instantly for his arrogance and the brutal heart she knew hid beneath his expensive tuxedo.

"Is she my birthday present? Or perhaps you might lend her to me for a few days, on a trial basis, before we negotiate a price." His eyes lingered on the cleavage exposed by the deep V of her emerald dress. He grabbed her chin and moved her face to examine each side.

Rafe stepped toward Solis and was immediately grabbed by two of Solis's bodyguards, who promptly restrained his hands behind his back.

"Your Segundo doesn't like me touching her." Even the man's voice was slimy.

Narváez laughed heartily, although a bit nervously. "You misunderstand. Miss Tambini is visiting me from the United States."

Solis's gaze held a lusty gleam as he met her eyes.

Harper grabbed his thumb and bent it back to nearly breaking. His smile strained visibly as she looked into his dead eyes. She spoke very quietly in English, "If you ever touch me again, I'll kill you."

Narváez nearly choked.

In English, Solis began, "Please, Miss Tambini, accept my sincere apology for assuming that you were…available. Many of the women here tonight are professional escorts and thus paid for their services. As a single man, I am open to paying for the right attributes."

She released his thumb, but not his eyes.

He continued, "Please, call me Justin, all my American friends do. Although I know American women have a sharp tongue they rarely withhold, a word of advice: it's not wise to threaten a man, especially me."

The corners of her mouth turned into a genuine smile. "Mister Solis," she emphasized his formal name, purposefully defying his request. "Underestimating a woman could be the death of you."

Narváez coughed repeatedly.

Solis winced as he rolled his thumb in a circle. "What brings you to Cali, Miss Tambini. I'm sorry, I didn't catch your first name."

"Mr. Narváez brought me here, and I prefer you call me Miss Tambini." It was true, Narváez was responsible for her being in this garden.

Solis was an idiot. She couldn't wait to see amber liquid in his glass.

She breathed a sigh when a portly man with a voluptuous bleach blonde on each arm approached their small group. He gave Narváez a wicked scowl before he flashed a used-car-salesman smile at Solis.

"My friend Turi, knowing your taste I have selected these two for you." The women left the man who was as tall as he was wide and went directly to Solis, distracting him with groping hands.

Harper took this as her cue to leave. "Mr. Solis, I'm sure we'll see you later this evening." She turned her back and headed to the bar.

Rafe shook off the hulking bodyguards. He signaled to Narváez with only a tilt of his head to join them.

They found a standing table and gathered around it, fresh drinks in hand.

At an unseen signal between the two men, Narváez suggested, "Bunny, my sweetheart, why don't you go freshen up."

Instantly, the woman dug out a mirror from her purse and began examining her face.

He took pity on her and added, "Give us a few minutes."

Grudgingly, she gazed across the table at Harper.

Rafe slid his arm around her and said, "We need to talk to Harper. It's business."

At that, she turned and started to march away, dejected until Carlos smacked her playfully on her abundant ass. She spun around and blew him a kiss, then added an extra swing to her step as she disappeared into the crowd.

"Harper, my apologies for Turi's misconception." Narváez said in an attempt to be a gentleman.

It didn't work. Turi Solis was a pig and no one could apologize for his actions.

Narváez tried to explain, "Colombia is a very different culture from the United States."

"I understand its differences, but that doesn't mean I approve of the sale of women for sex." She wished she could wash off the feeling of Solis's hands on her face.

Narváez glanced around and quietly asked, "So, now that you've seen the place, how will you do it?" He had a conspiratorial edge in his voice.

Harper wasn't sure she should trust him with the details, but needed them all to cover her.

"We need to wait until he switches his drink to bourbon," she explained and rolled the stem of her wine glass between her fingers. "I'll rig the microphone to explode when he turns it on. He'll be standing alone, and away from others at that point, so it will reduce collateral damage. I need all of you to be scattered around and mention that it must be a rival cartel."

Harper took a deep breath. "It'll be ugly. Gross. Just be

prepared to run out the door with the other guests." She slid the wine away, her stomach churning, again.

"Change to soda," Rafe suggested to Narváez. "We need to keep aware of Solis's men. We can't afford for anyone to suspect you."

As though Narváez suddenly realized this could lead back to him and the repercussions would be deadly, he turned serious. "We need to be out of here as quickly as possible."

"Agreed," Harper said.

Walking companionably in silence, Harper regained control of her emotions and focused on the mission. They had a lot of time to kill. What an appropriate phrase, she decided.

Time passed slowly, but the crowd never thinned as the hours drew on. In fact, Harper believed more people arrived the closer it got to midnight. She watched as Bunny became a needy drunk hanging all over Narváez, who grew increasingly irritable.

Harper kept a shrewd eye on Solis, waiting for the short bourbon glass to replace his tall ice-filled vodka and tonic. For a while, he'd disappeared with both blondes then reappeared alone nearly an hour later with damp hair and a crisp white shirt under his tailored tuxedo. He brought a glass of amber liquid with him.

"It's time." Harper and Rafe casually walked toward the band. On a small side table lay a black microphone atop a white cloth next to a black notebook with songs the band knew how to play.

Rafe opened the book in front of them both as Harper slipped the microphone into her purse.

"Darling, I'm going to visit the little ladies' room while you decide on a song," she called as she stepped away from Rafe.

He nodded then motioned the bandleader over to the edge

of the stage and began a lengthy discussion about songs they could play.

Inside the house, she saw the usual line to use the closest restroom so she turned down a hallway. She was immediately met by a lanky man in uniform carrying an automatic rifle.

"Where are you going?" he demanded in Spanish.

Thinking quickly, Harper answered in his language, "I really need to use the ladies room and there's such a long line to the one in the hall. Can you please show me to another?" She placed her hand on her stomach and faked gagging.

The man blanched and all but shoved her down the hall and into a bedroom. For effect, she slapped a hand over her mouth and made retching noises.

He pointed to the attached bathroom. "In there."

She chanced a glance back at the guard as she closed the bathroom door. He'd returned to his post in the hall.

After locking the door, she quickly disassembled the microphone and withdrew its contents. With shaking hands, she twisted the lipstick from the tube.

Get a grip, Harper. You can do this. Deep cleansing breath, exhale slowly and focus.

She followed her own advice. Instantly, she felt better. She could do this. She'd rigged hundreds of bombs, even with the sensitive CL-20. Chaz was much more stable, especially polymerized. She rolled it into a ball and hooked up the detonation cap. Ever so carefully, she put the microphone back together after making sure it was in the off position.

When Harper sighed in relief, her bladder screamed at her. Well, she was in the bathroom so she took advantage. While turning on the water to wash her hands—she had to scrub them well to be sure no traces of the Chaz remained—there was a knock at the door.

She jumped. Who the hell would that be?

"Harper, is everything all right?" Melina's voice sounded hurried.

"Yes. I'm fine." Harper cracked the door open and whispered, "It's finished. I'm just cleaning up."

Melina glanced at the microphone lying next to the sink then over her shoulder at the empty doorway. "I'm going to assist Rafe. Make it quick. Solis was working his way toward the band."

"Let me wipe the place down real fast." A few seconds later, Harper heard heels clicking in the hall then Melina telling the guard her friend was feeling better and would be out shortly.

Harper looked at herself in the mirror. *This is it. I'm really going to kill a man.*

She'd killed before, but that was with an M4 rifle and the bad guys were shooting at her and her team. Yes, Lei Lu had shot their boss seconds before and they were running like hell to reach the extraction point, but that was a different situation completely. She was part of a team who had her back.

This really wasn't that different. Her team was no longer all female. She had Rafe and Melina on her side. They'd have her back. She hoped. But Narváez had her ATF teammate.

Time to go do this. She just hoped it wasn't too late for Hernandez.

With only a nod for the guard, she quickly moved outside.

Near the end of the path, yet still hidden within the garden, Narváez shifted from one foot to the other. "What the fuck took you so long?"

Harper looked at him. In the dark shadows, his pupils were pinpoints. The bastard was high. She held up the microphone and covered the on switch with her thumb.

"Release Hernandez, now, or I'll show you the way to hell." Harper's voice came out stronger than she expected. Thank God. She could show no weakness to Narváez. He had to believe she'd do it.

He stared at her thumb. One breath, then two. His eyes finally met hers. Yes, she'd do it too. She'd sworn to kill him and was willing to become a suicide bomber if he refused.

Sweat beaded over his top lip, and droplets formed at his hairline. Narváez must have seen her conviction because he reached for his cell phone.

"Proof of life first," she demanded.

With swipes of his fat fingers, he managed to connect to the live feed. He spoke quietly into the phone then extended his arm so she could see her teammate.

"No, Harper. No." Hernandez's voice was raspy and slight, but she understood him.

She knew what she had to do. "Release him. Now." Harper held up the microphone so he could see. "As soon as he's released, this goes to Solis."

Narváez nodded and gave the order. She watched as Hernandez struggled to stand and staggered to the door.

With every ounce of determination she could muster, she glared at Narváez. "If they go after him, or any other members of my team, I'll hunt them down and kill them. I want you to video this tonight and send them a copy. Let them know I'll find them, and when they least expect it... kaboom." She dragged out the last word.

He quickly spoke her warning into the phone. There was a glint of disbelief in his eyes, but all it took was one look at her for confirmation.

"Give me your phone," Harper demanded. She dialed Estes's number. Before he could say anything more than hello, she blurted, "I'm alive. You'll find Hernandez at…" She held the phone toward Narváez, who gave him an address in Virginia. "We're in Cali, and I'm about to leave Turi Solis's party with a bang."

Quicker than Harper thought possible, Narváez grabbed the phone from her. "She's mine now and works for me. My lugartenientes are expecting your SEALs so don't bother sending them to my western compound, ever." Narváez disconnected the call. "I did as you asked. Now give me the microphone." His sneer probably worked on others, but she was running on full adrenaline, and it made her bold.

"No. Go get into place in the crowd. We need to blame a rival cartel. Hurry. I'll put this back."

After a long minute, he seemed to agree with those instructions and left.

She counted to ten then nonchalantly walked to the table where Rafe joined her with the book.

"Good job," Rafe said as he pointed to nothing in particular in the book.

Hiding her actions with what looked like a musical discussion, she replaced the microphone on the tabletop.

Harper glanced to where Melina had the bandleader deeply enthralled in a conversation, or, more aptly, he was enticed by her cleavage that was amply on display from his perch on the raised platform.

"Let's get the hell as far from here as we can," Rafe suggested and cocked his head toward Solis.

The man of the hour looked pleased as he headed toward the band, his steps filled with purpose.

"What took so long?" Rafe's tone was chastising as he placed his hand on the small of her back and guided her through the crowd. "I had to send Carlos up to the band to make a request."

"I was nervous and shaking," Harper admitted.

His eyes softened, and he put his arm around her. It felt so good there. He kissed her temple.

"It's ready to go, though, right?" He whispered in her ear then kissed the sensitive spot just below.

She nodded, but doubts filled her. What if she'd done something wrong? What if it didn't go off? What if it wasn't enough to blow Solis all the way to hell? They'd tested it in the blast chamber in the lab. The teaspoon-size of Chaz had impressed Rafe, and her calculations worked out every time she ran them.

This would work. It had to.

Solis approached the bandleader at the end of the song, who pointed toward the microphone.

He crossed and picked it up.

Harper held her breath.

She looked at the gathering crowd who had moved off the dance floor. A low murmur of groans filled the air. Guess they all knew what was next. Several hit the bar for fresh drinks.

Harper and Rafe moved farther back into the crowd toward the house and the exit.

The bandleader walked over to Solis and began talking. Shit, that wasn't supposed to happen.

Go away, she mentally yelled at the band member. Go far away.

Both men looked at the band, and then Solis smiled. He

spoke a few unheard words. The other man nodded, and Solis moved to the middle of the dance floor.

He began to speak into the mic. "Thank you for joining…" He looked down at the microphone in his hand, directly at the button. With an almost sheepish grin, Solis looked back at his audience.

He moved his thumb.

The noise was so much louder than Harper expected even though she'd covered her ears with her palms. Inside the explosives chamber, it had been significantly muffled.

The instant force pounded her and threw debris at lightning speed into the crowd. At the last nanosecond, she remembered to duck her head and close her eyes.

As Harper became aware of her surroundings, she saw more than heard people screaming.

Even though his lips were next to her ear, Rafe sounded distant. "Let's go." His arm still around her, he guided her through the house. On the way out the door, they met Melina. She put her arm around Harper like a good friend, and the three speed-walked to the limo.

"Are you all right?" Melina asked loudly enough for her to hear.

Cold as steel, Harper glanced at her. "I'm fine. He was a son of a bitch. How about you?"

At the door to the limousine, Harper hugged Melina briefly. "Thank you so much. You were a big help. I hope you find your inside man. You may want to search for him now during the confusion."

Harper turned to Rafe, who just stared at Melina. Emotions ran over his face too rapidly for her to read, but she caught regret.

"I'll be in the car. You might want to say your goodbyes quickly." She ducked into the back seat. From her window, she watched Rafe take Melina into his arms and kiss her gently, sweetly. When they parted, she saw tears streak down Melina's perfect face.

Harper thought about the way Rafe held the other woman and remembered their heated pre-party kiss in the suite. She felt a twinge of jealousy but knew Rafe was leaving Melina tonight and heading to the U.S.A. He was leaving her with tears in her eyes.

Harper knew what that felt like. For years, men had left her broken. But not anymore. She left them now before she had the opportunity to become attached. She knew that kind of pain. Compassion for Melina coated her jealousy.

Rafe folded his tall body into the limo and sat next to Harper. He looked away and remained silent for a moment, his hands clenched in his lap. In a roughened voice, he said, "Thanks, Harper. That was harder than I ever imagined."

"Do you love her?"

"Yes, but not in the husband-wife way. She's a good friend"—he glanced down at her—"with delightful benefits. I could never love a woman like her…forever. Her job is too dangerous. She likes living on the edge, and I'll be done with that life very soon."

"I completely understand." Harper admitted. She loved the rush of adrenalin, knowing she could live or die at any minute made her feel alive.

"Do you?" Rafe's gaze pinned her.

"Yes. I've had several friends with benefits. They're the best kind." Or so she'd discovered over the years. Being dumped soon after sex had been an on-going saga starting with Bobby Neels, who had humiliatingly broken up with her in the high school cafeteria the day after she'd succumbed to his pressure and given him her virginity. The few college boys she'd dated weren't any better. But in the Army, she'd learned that she could be friends with a man, sleep with him, and still be friends with him. She'd had a few go-to guys who had understood her sex-only mandate, and the sex had always been so much better with them. Now, she had to really enjoy the man's company before she'd allow him in her bed. Friends with benefits were the only men in her life now.

"Are they?" Rafe's question had too many depths to it for her to handle.

"Yes. Sex is always better with a friend and no strings attached."

"I like women who know what they want and are driven to get it." He looked at her now with a feral smile. "In bed as well as out."

She captured those deep blue eyes with hers. He wanted her, but only temporarily. She saw that now.

Before she could stop herself, she had to ask. "So, there's never been anyone you wanted to keep for the long term?"

Rafe looked away and out the window. She waited. When she didn't think he'd answer, he spoke but didn't turn toward her.

"I was engaged. Beth and I lived together for almost a year while we were in the Navy."

Harper heard the pain in his voice. "You don't have to tell me what happened."

He ignored her and continued. "She was part of a special project for the Navy Expeditionary Intelligence Command."

Oh shit. Harper instantly saw the parallel with her own military career. She wanted to tell him to shut up. She didn't want to hear any more, but he kept on talking.

The next word he said was, "Taliban."

She knew the exact situation. It had been a case study for every female agent training with the CIA. The class had dissected the whole op from original orders through autopsy.

She hoped Rafe didn't know the extent of abuse his Beth had endured, especially the gang rape and sodomy.

Tears spilled down her cheeks from eyes that had seen too much. Fear that a similar capture and abuse could happen to her was the reason she'd considered resigning her commission and joining the ATF full time when her contract was up. She'd thought she'd be safe in that organization… until Narváez kidnapped her. He could still give her to the Cali cartel who could do much worse to her than Rafe's fiancé experienced.

She finally managed to say, "I'm so sorry." She wrapped her arms around his waist, and repeated the words over and over again.

Eventually, Rafe turned, and they held each other. Nothing more than meeting the other's need for comfort.

"It was a long time ago." Rafe kissed her temple.

Before he could say more, Bunny and Carlos crawled into the limo and sat across from them.

Narváez overflowed with excitement. As the car left the Solis house, he jabbered. "The police are on their way. The chief, who was there as a guest, was grilling Turi's bodyguards, but the cartel rumor was rampant. That was a good lie." He looked so pleased with himself. Bunny leaned against him and started snoring.

"It worked." Narváez was ecstatic.

"Yes, it did." Harper stared out the window into the night, hoping to end this conversation. She was beyond exhausted, and her body demanded sleep. The adrenalin rush had lasted for hours and pushed all her physical resources to the limit. The culmination of events in the past twelve hours left her empty.

"Come here." Rafe pulled her to him, and she nestled her head onto his shoulder.

Safe. The word spread through her, smoothing the razor-sharp edges she'd been walking on for too long. Her SpecOps training flashed through her head. On your way down the adrenalin slide, pick an "s": sex, sleep, or sustain. Harper added 'safe' to that list. She closed her eyes and was asleep instantly.

When the car stopped, she awoke and walked hand in hand with Rafe to their suite. As soon as the door clicked shut, Rafe pulled her to him. "I believe this is where we left off before we were rudely interrupted and forced to go to that dreadful party."

CHAPTER 17

Harper guided Rafe's hands around her waist as she stepped into him. Revived from her twenty-minute combat nap in the limousine, she was ready to pick another "s" from the post-adrenaline choices.

When she moved her hands to his solid chest, his pectorals twitched at her touch and she knew he felt the charge that ran through her.

Every nerve ending rushed to alert, sensitized to his body. The small of her back tingled where his big hands caressed her bare skin. She shifted closer, slowly so she could enjoy the spread of their contact. Thigh to thigh. Hips to hips. Her nipples hardened when her breasts touched his chest. She raised her head. Rafe's eyes were half-closed, as if he enjoyed the heat they created just standing together.

When he lowered his lips to lightly touch hers, the explosion of sensation took her breath away. He was so tender, soft, and caring. She hadn't expected the gentler emotions. For her, it had always been nothing more than sex. Hot and fast. Hard and sweaty. When it was over, it was over. Either she left or the man did. Admittedly, there was often a second round and occasionally a third. Harper liked sex. But that's all it had been.

She wanted to stay in Rafe's arms forever. She could kiss him and be satisfied. Well, maybe not. She really liked sex.

He pressed into her and deepened the kiss. She opened for him, welcoming his tongue. She dug her nails through his dark, wavy hair and pulled him closer. She needed more.

Rafe swept his hands down her back and unzipped the designer gown. She unfastened the halter clip at the neck and the dress fell to her feet in a pool of dark green fabric.

"Oh, Christ, Harper. I've wanted to touch you like this since you stood in the Bogotá moonlight giving me attitude." He kissed his way to her ear then sucked on her lobe.

Her ears were extremely sensitive. She squeezed her thighs together and sucked in her breath. It was as if he were touching her, sucking her clit.

She moved to nip his throat and found where his heated blood rushed just under the skin. When she licked his pulse line, it raced faster.

He ducked to recapture her mouth. His large hands found her bare breasts.

He moved around her tongue and mouth in sync with encircling her breasts with a single finger. The motion was dizzying as he spiraled his way to her taut nipples.

He dropped his head and took a beaded point into his mouth. When he sucked gently, she clenched her fingers in his hair and pressed his head to her. She loved this and wanted more.

At the feel of teeth on her over-stimulated nipple, she whimpered on an exhaled breath. He moved to the other side.

She was already wet, but she loved what he was doing to her body right now.

They'd get to the rest.

She stroked his back, assuring him she liked it. When she ran her nails down his spine, he arched in pleasure and looked up at her with a sexy grin.

He kissed his way down her tight stomach and ran his tongue in a circle around her belly button before licking inside. Continuing the path downward, he trailed small kisses to the edge of the green lacy thong that barely covered her tight dark curls.

"Mmmm." Enjoyment resounded in his hum. Now on his knees, he ran his hands the length of her legs. They'd never felt erogenous until Rafe's hands skimmed her calves and thighs. On his next pass from hip to ankle, he took the thong with him then raised each sandaled foot, removing the scrap of cloth.

He cupped her bare bottom and nuzzled his face into her dark curls as he inhaled slowly.

"I've wanted to know what you taste like for days," he growled through gritted teeth.

"I'm not stopping you."

He'd immediately find out just how ready she was for him. How much she wanted him thrusting inside of her.

With his thumbs, he gently parted her. His tongue swept into her softness, claiming her. It felt cool on her most sensitive spot where every nerve congregated and begged for his caress. In seconds, his tongue brought her close to the edge. Her leg muscles tightened and shook in anticipation.

"Easy, baby. Let's move this to the bed." He picked her up as he stood. For the first time in her life, she felt small, almost delicate.

He set her on his bed then shucked off his tuxedo jacket and tossed it onto the padded chair. His shoulder harness, gun tucked securely in its holster, followed it.

When he started on his shirt, Harper jumped up to her knees. "No, I want to do that."

She was hungry to explore his magnificent body. Any man of hers had to be in as great of shape as she was. Rafe met every one of her requirements and exceeded them.

With experienced hands, she pushed the onyx studs from their slits in his silk shirt. She ran the tips of her nails over muscles that quivered then gently scraped them down his back.

He pressed into her touch, begging for more.

She did it again before she placed her spread hands on his chest and smoothed them over his wide shoulders, taking the shirt with them. She ignored the garment as it dropped to the floor. After running her nails through the sparse dark hair on his chest, she opened her hand so it tickled her palm.

"You like that. I can tell." Rafe clasped the back of her hand and brought her palm to his lips where he placed his soft lips in its center, then traced each line with the tip of his tongue.

Her thighs tightened once again.

When he released her hand, he started to unbuckle the designer belt, but Harper laid her hands over his.

"No, I wanted to undress you." She brushed her lips over his then looked down to unfasten the belt and top button on the slacks. Before unzipping, she ran her hand down the full, hard length of his erection.

Rafe hissed in a breath.

"Oh, I knew this would be good," she told him as he nipped at her neck.

Momentarily distracted, she stretched her neck, offering him more. He lightly used his teeth before she remembered what she'd been doing and unzipped his pants. Anxious, she reached inside and stroked him once again before following the waistband to the sides and shoving his pants, briefs and all, to the floor. He toed out of his shoes and made quick work of his socks.

Harper looked down and was impressed. She'd been with many men. They'd run the gamut; tall yet small, to short but well endowed. Rafe had it all, packaged in a killer body. One that would fit her so well.

"Like what you see?" Rafe's voice was deep and coarse.

She'd been staring. And smiling. She couldn't resist stroking him once more. The soft skin that covered the steel beneath fascinated her as she ran her hand up and down his shaft.

He drew in a ragged breath and fisted his hands at his sides.

"Definitely." She pulled him onto the bed and down on top of her.

"Now, where were we before you got sidetracked with my clothes?" Rafe rolled to the side and traced her body with his palms, gliding over her every curve, dragging fingertips in their trail. He kissed her slowly at first, but as soon as the heat hit her, she deepened it. She was ravenous.

They were both breathing hard when his deft fingers parted her wet lips and encircled her clit. Everywhere he touched her, caressed her, kissed her, sent sensations to that nub. As he pressed and massaged her, she shook in anticipation.

Rafe kissed his way down her body, never changing the pressure or speed of his touch, until his tongue finally replaced his fingers. She loved the feel of his warm breath on her inner thighs, but when he licked her sex, she raised her hips and moaned his name.

He slipped a finger inside her wet channel, and her internal muscles clenched around it. She felt his chuckle between her legs before he looked up and grinned. Her hands fisted the bed sheets as his tongue circled, teasing her. He slipped a second finger in, stretching her gradually. When he began to suck and rhythmically move his fingers in and out of her, she couldn't bear it any longer.

"Rafe, now! I want you inside me."

He didn't stop but increased the speed and intensity.

When she hit her peak, his mouth took hers. His tongue mimicked his fingers as he took her over the edge.

As she shuddered through post-orgasmic waves of pleasure, he continued to kiss her and hold her tenderly.

Before she regained her breath, he kissed a path from her jaw to her ear then lightly ran his tongue around each sensitive outer curve. Her legs tightened reflexively, and he resumed the circling motion of her drenched softness.

"Give me time to recover." Harper kissed him on his neck, the only part she could reach at the moment.

"No. Again. Now. You can do it." He pressed two fingers deeply into her, and her hips involuntarily pushed to meet him. There was a desperate urgency in his eyes.

Rafe looked toward the side tables but couldn't reach either of them with his free hand. "I don't ever want to stop touching you, but the condoms are in the top drawer."

"Top drawer," she repeated, breathless. She reached blindly and opened the drawer, grabbing a packet. "Convenient."

"This place gets used a lot for sex."

Had Rafe had sex with someone here before? Not a thought she wanted to pursue. He stroked her hard, and all thought was gone.

"Very considerate of them."

"You can thank the staff in the morning. But, right now, you're going to thank me."

Normally Harper didn't like domineering or demanding men, but she'd do anything for Rafe as long as he kept touching her, giving her more pleasure than she'd ever had.

She watched with hungry eyes as he ripped open the pack and tossed it aside. She reached for the condom and silently begged to do the honors.

"I'd let you, but I'm not sure I'd last through it. Just listening to you come, I almost lost control." His hands shook a little as he slid on the condom.

"Next time," she commanded.

He grinned. "Next time."

Harper was sure she'd met her match in bed.

His touch alone ignited her and brought her higher, faster. He nipped her over-sensitive nipples, and she thought she might come right then. She pulled his head up from its path to her other breast and gazed into his ocean blue eyes that sparkled with silver.

"Now." Between breaths she demanded, "I want you inside me now."

"Your wish is my command." Rafe moved up to kiss her and slid inside then stopped.

She knew there was more. And she wanted it all. She wrapped her legs around his waist and pulled him in. "Don't hold back."

"Don't let me hurt you." He watched her carefully as he pulled out then slowly slid into her, completely. She smiled up at him as he pulled out then thrust this time. She met him with raised hips. They soon found their rhythm.

He grit his teeth, fighting his release to prolong both their pleasure.

She was close. "Almost," she managed between gasps.

He reached between them and found her center. His first

nudge shoved her over the edge. With the next thrust, he arched his back and groaned, and she took him with her.

Rafe lay on top of her, biceps shaking as he held his large body off hers. He finally caught his breath and pushed over, pulling her on top of him. She started to move off him, but he held her in place.

"Where do you think you're going?" he asked between pants.

"I'm too big," she insisted. He wouldn't let her move.

"Honey, I'm five inches taller than you and have at least fifty more pounds of muscle. You're not too big. Fact is, I think you're just right for me, everywhere."

There was that damnable grin again. Harper might actually be blushing.

And it was a fact. Rafe was a big man...everywhere. She'd never had a man like him before. He cuddled her to him and caressed her back with soft strokes.

"Stay right there for a few minutes, and we'll try this again. I'm sorry I was a bit quick, but it's your fault. You've had me primed for hours...hell, days." He was teasing her. That was new to her, too, especially in bed.

"You don't mind the female superior position?" She rose up a little to watch his face. She could tell when men lied to her. They'd done it enough. She'd made it her business to be able to read people, and she was very good at it.

"I prefer it," he said.

No pupil dilation. No side glances. His eyes crinkled at the edges with a hint of devilish smile.

"You really do." She was shocked. Few men really liked giving up control.

He cupped her breasts as if they were a precious gift and ran his thumb over her nipples, which peaked immediately.

"This way my hands are free to play with you." He slid a hand down and rubbed his thumb over her clit.

She tightened her legs involuntarily as the muscles deep inside her grabbed onto his growing erection.

"We'll both enjoy it more this way."

For the next three hours, Harper's body oscillated between a mindless state of pleasure and very short recovery naps. She and Rafe couldn't seem to get enough of each other.

Then Rafe's cell phone rang.

CHAPTER 18

"Melina, are you all right?" Rafe asked, troubled after he'd checked the caller ID. At the mention of his handler's name, Harper stiffened against him. He soothed her with long strokes from the crown of her sweaty hair over one sturdy shoulder and then curving over her bare hip to cup her gorgeous tight butt.

Although he was concerned about the safety of the woman on the phone, he was more interested in the naked woman lying in bed with him. The past few hours had been beyond wonderful. She was so responsive to his touch, as if they'd been lovers for years. She drove him beyond the point of control, and still he wanted more from her. No other woman had made him desire her so much, or so often.

"Rafe. They're looking for Harper." The urgency in Melina's voice was unmistakable.

He sat up straight in the huge four-poster bed. "Who is?" he shot back then leaned toward Harper when she sat up alongside him. He tilted the phone so she could hear.

"Solis had her checked out after their encounter. His men

know she is an explosives expert and have decided it had to be her."

Rafe's heart sank all the way to his groin as his balls drew tight against his body.

Solis's men are coming for her, and I'm naked with my gun ten feet away.

"Fuck!" was all he said as he jumped out of bed and headed for his weapons and clothes. He covered the phone with his hand. "Get dressed."

Harper leaped from the bed and ran to her room.

"You need to leave, now," Melina urged. "They know you're Carlos's Segundo and they can get into La Comunidad. Hurry. Come to my place. I'll do what I can to get you out."

Rafe dressed as he listened to his handler. "We're on our way."

Buttoning his black camouflage shirt, he entered the living area of the suite. Harper sat on the couch in blue jogging clothes while she tied navy running shoes. Even though she had a dark tan, her long legs were exposed to her barely covered butt, and the tank top left much of her shoulders and all of her arms uncovered.

"Don't you have anything else to wear?" Rafe sat beside her and tied his boots. "Your skin will show up at night."

"No. Fuckin' Narváez gave me white capris pants, a yellow tank top, and brightly colored skirts and blouses. Thank God I slipped these into the suitcase he had packed for me." She'd given this a lot of thought and understood their need to run without him even telling her the details. They were already on the same page. Good.

Rafe went back to his room and grabbed a dark brown T-shirt and black sweatpants. He tossed them to her as he slipped into his shoulder rig and checked his gun. By the time he glanced back, she was dressed in his clothes. She'd tied the excess shirt with a knot at her trim waist and rolled the sweats to fit the curves he'd memorized in the past few hours. Damn, he wanted her again, and he started to grow hard as his gaze raked her body.

Her eyes zeroed in on his gun. "I'm not leaving here until Narváez is dead."

"Babe, we gotta get outta here, now." He heard the elongated vowels of his Southern upbringing and realized he'd spoken more English in the past two days than he had in years. That could be a good thing since he was headed home. Right now. Elation he hadn't dared think about bubbled up.

"Goddamn it, Rafe." Fury laced every word. "The bastard kidnapped me. He made me kill Solis for him, and we wouldn't be running if he hadn't. He's sanctioned. I have the opportunity to fulfill that order. Give me your gun."

She was now badass ATF Special Agent Tambini, no longer Harper, the warm, loving woman who had fucked him blind four times in the past few hours.

Fisting her hands on her small hips, she narrowed her eyes. "Rafe, if you don't give me your gun, I'll kill him with my bare hands."

Christ. He didn't want her to do that. She might get hurt in the process. But Narváez's had to die. Now.

Rafe took a deep breath and steeled his soul. "He's mine." Memories of the poor old man Carlos had nearly beaten to death in the processing plant popped to the forefront. The over-painted faces of the house whores he knew Carlos abused all times of the day and night floated past on a mental screen. Out of all the atrocities the man had committed, the kidnapping of Harper and the look of dread on her face when told she had to make Chaz held for several seconds.

He would kill Narváez for that alone. Rafe reached under

the bloused pant leg just above his right ankle and removed a small Glock 26.

"It's hot. Cover me," he said.

She ejected the magazine and checked that it was full as he dug out the extra clips. She took them and slid them into her cleavage, the only place to secure them given her loose pocketless clothing.

"Thank you." To his surprise, she leaned in and brushed a kiss on his lips. "I've got your back."

Rafe strode toward the door, but before he reached for the knob, he turned around and pulled her in for a quick, but deep, kiss. He needed the reassurance as she kissed him back with equal desire. He was doing this for her on so many levels.

Harper smiled at him with warmth and a hint of promise. In the next breath, Special Agent Tambini was back, fixated on the mission as she nodded toward the door.

He took her hand and strode boldly down the wide marble hallway, acutely aware of his surroundings and on the lookout for Solis's sicarios.

There were no hidden cameras here. No one would dare video the comings and goings at La Comunidad. If anyone saw them, they knew him as Narváez's Segundo, higher ranking than any lugartenientes in the cartel. At the corners, though, he stopped and peered around cautiously.

When they reached Narváez's door, Rafe turned the knob slowly and was surprised to find it opened. His friend had obviously been too drunk to remember to lock it, or he'd felt secure enough in the private suite to forego basic security measures.

Sparse forty-watt wall sconces barely lit the halls, so very little light followed them into the living area. It was larger than the one he and Harper shared. The LED nightlight in the kitchen at the far end cast the great room in a bluish-purple hue, which allowed them to see a fully set dining table, a living room with a fireplace, and the open door to the only bedroom.

Rafe gave them a full thirty seconds for their eyes to adjust after silently closing the outer door.

Light snoring accompanied thick grunts and snuffles, another side effect of snorting cocaine. Rafe grabbed a small, fringed pillow from the dark couch to muffle the shot. He assumed a shooter's stance, feet spread shoulder-length apart, knees bent, weight forward on the balls of his feet, ready to move in any direction as needed. He looked down the sights of his Kimber 1911 at Narváez. This part was muscle memory from years of training.

While in the SEALs he'd killed many men on three continents with bare hands, knives, bombs, rifles, and pistols. Sometimes it was fast. Other times he'd sat patiently behind a sniper rifle for hours. They were all merely targets assigned to him by someone higher up the chain of command. He had no connection with them other than through the kill.

His friend's familiar smell reached his nose and Rafe's stomach turned over. What the hell was he doing? A clear picture of their stark VMI dorm room flashed across his brain. Small single beds, covered in wool blankets tucked so tight a quarter would bounce, shoved against opposite gray block walls. Cadet uniforms hung neatly in golden oak built-in closets with cabinets above, and drawers underneath covered the entire wall on either side of the solid door. Matching desks sat against square pipe footboards that had seen better days three decades ago. There, face to face, at all times of day and night, the idealistic young men had planned to make Colombia a better place to live for all its people.

Hours of idealistic debates, years of working the land….and it had all come to this.

Rafe realigned the sights on Carlos's head fifteen feet away.

What had happened to that good man? Drugs had corrupted his ethics and his mind. He'd become a stranger.

Through blurred eyes, Rafe refocused over the barrel of the flat black gun and slowly pulled the trigger back.

Harper knew all too well what mental state one had to be in to shoot a person in cold blood. She'd wondered if Rafe could actually pull the trigger. There was a fine line between hate and love.

For her, it was black and white. Narváez was sanctioned for elimination, and he'd kidnapped her. Although her prison had been an elegant one with a small degree of freedom, he'd held her captive for his own purposes. He'd had his men beat the hell out of Hernandez and threatened the safety of her team. She had no doubt the next time he wanted her to cook Chaz, he'd find and torture someone else. That plainly pissed her off and was reason alone to take him out.

She heard Rafe's fast, uncontrolled breathing as she approached the open door to the bedroom. She dared a peek into the unlit room. Rafe stood, barely inside the bedroom, gun down at his right side, pillow clutched in his left hand.

Harper stepped into the room, close behind Rafe. She placed her hand on his back before she whispered into his ear, "It's all right. I'll take care of it. We need to go, now."

Narváez stirred, rolled to his back, then seemed to settle.

In the faint blue light, she saw tears glistening in Rafe's eyes. She understood his mixed emotions and, on tippy toes, gently kissed his cheek. "Cover me. We've got to get out of here." She grabbed the pillow from him as he turned and walked silently into the other room.

She raised her gun, pillow over the muzzle.

Narváez sat upright in the bed, the gun in his hand pointed at her. Harper didn't hesitate. Her two shots took less than a second. She double-tapped Narváez, putting one bullet in his head and one in the heart, but not before Narváez had gotten off a shot. It had gone wide, splintering the doorjamb.

Harper turned quickly to run and looked into the end of Rafe's barrel. She raised her eyes to his and knew he would pull the trigger without hesitation.

Bunny's shrill scream cut through the dark room.

"Put the gun down, Bunny. I don't want to shoot you." Rafe's voice was steady and clear.

Oh shit. Harper was in his line of fire with her back to the shooter.

"You killed him, you bitch." Bunny's voice was so high it hurt Harper's ears.

Harper watched Rafe's cold blue eyes for a clue.

"I'll kill that fucking bitch," Bunny screeched.

"Down, Harper." Rafe's voice was low and authoritative.

She dove to the floor.

Two fast shots echoed in the large bedroom.

Harper glided into a kneeling shooting position and brought her gun muzzle to face Bunny. She was dead.

"Move." Rafe grabbed her hand and pulled her to her feet. He practically dragged her to the suite's door.

He was all business now. There'd be time later for him to mourn the young man who had once been his brother at heart.

When Rafe cracked the hall door, she stooped and peered through. Two men with M4s at the ready stepped off the elevator.

Rafe shut it quickly, but quietly.

"Solis's sicarios. Jump over the balcony. Tell the gate guard they shot Carlos and Bunny. I'll meet you on the corner two blocks east, one block north." He grabbed her and smashed his mouth to hers. The kiss was brief, but sent an intense jolt through her body all the same.

"Hurry," Harper begged him.

She dashed to the other side of the room, whipped the heavy drapes back, and slid open the doors. She was over the balcony railing before she heard Rafe accusing Solis's men of murdering Narváez. Running as fast as she could, her long legs eating up the distance across the neatly mowed lawn, she reached the glass door of the guardhouse and stopped.

The guard didn't rise as she approached so she pounded on the locked door.

"Solis's sicarios just shot Carlos Narváez," she screamed at the man through bulletproof glass. He simply shrugged, comfortable in his office chair, sub-machine gun propped next to the door.

"What you want me to do about it, puta? Did they get blood on you?" Then he looked at her with earnest. She saw recognition flash in his dark eyes.

The guard rose like a crouched tiger after easy prey and was through the door just as she stepped back. He grabbed her left arm and held it in a vise-like grip.

"I don't give a shit about Narváez, but I have orders to detain you, American bitch. There's a bounty on your head."

She could see he was already spending the money in his miniscule brain.

They both heard the shots at the same time. When the guard looked toward the private resort, Harper took advantage of his momentary distraction, grabbed her gun from under her shirt, and shot him. In all the confusion, it'd just be one more gunshot. She removed his sidearm, which he hadn't bothered to un-holster.

"That she's-just-a-woman attitude can kill you," she murmured and shoved his pistol in her sweats next to hers, grip pointed for a left-hand draw. She pulled the T-shirt over both guns.

Harper hoped Rafe was all right. She stepped over the guard who'd fallen in the doorway and pressed the button to release the personnel gate lock. In less than ten seconds, she was on the other side, headed east on the empty street.

At the end of the block, she stepped into the darkness of a deeply recessed storefront, watched La Comunidad, and listened to the street sounds of Cali. No one would call the police. The cartels ran the city, and each owned a great number of policemen. This was cartel business, and no citizen or government employee would dare interfere. Harper was more worried about Solis's men calling for backup and if Rafe would escape before the cartel's reinforcements arrived.

She'd give him five minutes…then she'd go back for him. She never left a team member behind.

CHAPTER 19

THREE MINUTES AND THIRTY SECONDS LATER, A MALE FIGURE burst through the same small gate Harper had used and left open. Running full out, gun in hand, he looked back over his shoulder when the gate clinked shut automatically, locking their carnage inside.

It was Rafe. She knew that body, every masculine inch of it. He moved swiftly, silently, among the shadows.

She let him pass her and watched him duck into a narrow alley when a dark SUV whipped around a corner three blocks down then raced toward La Comunidad. Another vehicle followed mere yards behind. Both stopped at the closed vehicle gate. A uniformed man with a battered rifle in hand jumped out and ran to the ornate iron gate that was wide enough for two trucks to pass through.

She heard him announce that the guard was dead. He went to the personnel gate and unsuccessfully shot at the solid lock several times, the report echoing repeatedly off the three-story buildings. Someone from inside the vehicles hollered at him, and he returned to his seat. The first SUV rammed the decorative gate numerous times before its hinges broke. As both sped through the new opening, she watched taillights disappear.

Harper shook her head. Men. They all wanted a piece of the action so not one of them stayed behind to guard the gate.

My good luck they weren't trained in the U.S.A.

She bolted from her hiding place and ran toward the alley where she'd watched Rafe disappear. Slowing only a little, she slid into the darkness between the two stucco buildings and plastered her back against the rough wall. She looked down the alley. The small space seemed to intensify the aroma of the rotting garbage in the dumpsters over-filled by the apartments above and the street-level stores and restaurants. She slowly breathed through her mouth.

"Harper?"

Not sure she'd actually heard her name, she let her peripheral vision search the alley. Maybe it was the rustling of rats hunting tonight's supper.

"Harper." It was barely a whisper. Closer this time.

"Rafe?" she called back.

He stepped from behind a dumpster, kicked an insolent rat out of the way, and jogged to her. His embrace was fierce. So was the kiss.

In her ear, he whispered, "You're supposed to be three blocks away."

"I couldn't leave without knowing you were okay."

He kissed her cheek and held her for another few seconds. They both needed it. They stepped away at the same time.

"Come on, we're too close. We need to get to Melina's place on the other side of the city." He took Harper's hand, and they trotted down the alley.

They zigzagged down silent streets that would remain

asleep for several more hours before shop gates rattled open to the new day. Through hushed neighborhoods of twenty-story apartment complexes, she quietly followed, completely trusting in him. For over a mile they slinked through the city, traveling basically northeast toward the airport and the Cauca River. They didn't speak.

From half a block away, lights shone brightly ahead, partially illuminating the neighborhood street. The muffled sounds of cars and people filled the air. Keeping to the darkest shadows as they approached the corner, Rafe stopped short. Plastered against a tall stucco structure, they listened for footsteps on the adjacent sidewalk. When they heard nothing, they both peered around the edge of the building. The street was lit as bright as day and had just ruined her night vision.

"It's the InterContinental Hotel. I can get a cab there. We'll attract too much attention together. Go to the end of this block and turn right. I'll have the cabbie pick you up at the far corner. Be ready to jump in." He gave her a quick peck, and her heart jumped. His light touch was all it took to set her aflame. Yeah, it might have been the adrenalin that flowed like a flooded river through her veins, but Harper knew it was the man. He was protecting her.

"And this time, do as you're told." The seriousness in his voice matched the expression in his dark blue eyes. She didn't like taking orders, but she'd make an exception just this once.

"I'll be there," was all she told him as they turned their separate ways. Rafe strutted around the corner as though he owned the night.

Rafe knew the city better than she did, and riding in a cab sure beat running fifteen miles. After killing two men, and hours of sex with Rafe, she'd been tired before they'd escaped. Plus, she wasn't embarrassed to admit she wasn't back to her full strength after the cocaine reaction. When she came off this adrenalin high, she was going to crash hard.

Harper jogged to end of the street, keeping to the shadows. She peeked around the corner and saw the sidewalk was populated by the night shift of hookers. The last thing she needed was to stand out.

She stripped out of Rafe's sweats and oversized T-shirt then rolled them with the guns and extra ammo inside. After she'd raked all ten fingers through her sweaty hair and fluffed it a little, she tucked the bundle under her arm and sauntered into the sales zone in short shorts and sports bra.

She'd never played a hooker before. There had never been an opportunity for it in the Middle Eastern countries where she'd gone under cover with the Army. Still, she'd watched enough television to believe she could pull off the role well enough to get to the end of the block. Hide in plain sight was her plan.

Every set of eyes assessed her value as she sashayed down the sidewalk.

"Flaca bitch, no one's going to want that culo," a bleached blonde with a huge ass held in by the stressed stitches of a dirty pair of capris told her pimp.

Harper knew at least one man who wanted her ass, and she hoped he was waiting for her one hundred yards ahead.

"I'll give you something to remember, baby," a stout man offered as he hitched his jeans up under a beer belly.

She ignored his offer and the stained knees.

"Hey, puta, want to do this together? I'm sure Jesus here could handle both of us." The twenty-something flipped waist-length raven hair to the side so the man in the car could see more than her cleavage. She'd probably been pretty once. His smile broadened, and Harper caught a flash of his gold front teeth.

I don't think I'll quit my day job for this, no matter how many people shoot at me.

A toss of her hair allowed a casual look at the cars lined up at the curb, and Harper added a kick to her hips as she slowly strode down the busy sidewalk. A yellow cab creeping down the street in her direction caught and held her attention. When a back window lowered, she saw it wasn't Rafe, but a sicario. If he was looking for her, or recognized her, she was screwed. A shot of fear rang through her body, but she kept on walking.

Another cab stopped at the corner. When Rafe stepped out, he was instantly surrounded by both men and women. He towered over most men, but in the seedier part of Cali in the middle of the night, he looked like a lighthouse to her. His smile beamed as he waded through the offers to her.

"You. I want you." That was all he needed to say as he grabbed her hand and plowed through the throng, suggestions and bargains thrown at him from every angle. He shoved her into the back seat and followed her, slamming the door.

As he enveloped her in his arms, he whispered in her ear. "Pretty smart of you, Tambini. I almost didn't recognize you. I was looking in the shadows, and there you were, bold as day, strutting your stuff with the prostitutes." He kissed her playfully. "So, exactly what did I buy?"

In the middle of all this, he was teasing her. How could she resist?

"You haven't bought anything, yet. I haven't heard an offer of money." She could be playful, too. Inside the cab, in his arms, she felt safe for the first time since Melina had called.

Crackling voices croaked over the cab's radio. Even though Harper spoke Spanish, she only caught a few words of the thick local dialect.

Suddenly, Rafe stiffened.

"Halcones." The single word whispered into her ear sent shivers down her spine. "They were describing us."

Rafe gave a new address to the cabbie. Whispering in her ear, he explained, "We're going to the Hotel Spiwak Chipichape. We'll catch another cab there, different company. Solis's gang may own this one."

Still in her role, she hung on Rafe, pawed him, kissed him, and made sexual suggestions filled with the local colloquialisms she'd heard during her one-block hooker lesson.

While he paid the cabbie, she caught the driver's envious stare and smirk. As if eager to get started, Rafe grabbed her barely covered butt and caressed it as they strode inside the ultra-modern hotel. They walked straight through the lobby, past the front desk, and turned down the hall toward the ballrooms. Rafe shoved the men's room door open, and the lights came on.

"Put your clothes back on," he ordered as he stripped off his camouflaged shirt.

"Um, Rafe, I'm going to take a minute while I'm here. Sorry, but a girl's gotta go when she's got the chance." She was sticky from sweat as well as their earlier sex and just wanted to wash off the dirty feelings from the shooting and her whore walk. She dampened paper towels on her way to a stall. Afterward, she washed her hands and scrubbed her face with water.

"Feel better?" His question was as tender as his touch as he brushed back a damp curl from her forehead.

"Yeah. Thanks." She'd heard the water running and knew

he'd availed himself of the facilities, too. "How close are we to Melina's?"

"She's almost straight east across the city. I didn't want the cabbie to report our location or destination. This hotel has over two hundred rooms and too many exits. They wouldn't spend time looking for us here."

They exited the restroom. "Pretend you're a guest out for an early morning run. Calle 35N is a one-block loop. I'll look for you after I snag another cab."

She reached down the neck of her dark T-shirt and fished around.

"What the hell are you doing?" He knit his brows together. She handed him the spare magazines and reached for the gun she'd lifted from the gate guard.

"Presents." She kissed him briefly.

His look said he didn't understand.

"You can give them back to me when you pick me up. If I'm jogging, these will just bang against my boobs."

Light dawned in his eyes seconds before he gently stroked her breasts. "I don't want anything to hurt these." He ran his thumbs over her nipples, covered only by the thin cotton T-shirt and tight sports bra. They pebbled at his touch. Her heart pounded from the heat he brought with light fingers, his husky voice, and possessive words.

She took his face in both hands. When their open mouths met, she devoured, she took, she claimed.

"Eh, hum." A cough followed the interruption from a man behind them when they didn't separate immediately.

Harper buried her face in Rafe's chest. His voice rumbled as he spoke, "Babe, you have a good run. I'll meet you at the room in an hour for our morning swim."

She stepped back, squared her shoulders, and winked at

the bellman as she passed him. "I love morning sex," she told the young man and put a little more swing in her step, knowing both men watched.

"Mine." Rafe's voice carried the length of the hall.

"Yes, sir," the young man acknowledged.

CHAPTER 20

MELINA DROVE THE SILVER BMW X5 WITH SKILL THROUGH a city that would sleep for another hour or two while Jacin reclined in the front passenger seat with an Uzi resting on his lap. She turned off her headlights before pulling into the parking lot of the F.B.O. side of the Cali airport, staying in the shadows as much as possible.

Harper handed Melina the three grease sticks she and Rafe had used to camouflage their faces. With unsaid agreement, Jacin's bloated and distorted face needed nothing more than the shades of purple, black, and blue it currently sported.

"Stay here," Rafe ordered as he checked his weapon again. "I'll check out the area first. Solis's men, or that idiot Pablo, may have Narváez's helicopter staked out." He slipped out of the SUV and disappeared into the night.

Jacin's muffled moans as he shifted in the seat were the only sounds in the vehicle. Harper knew he was in great pain and wished she could do something for him.

Rafe returned within two minutes.

"Those aren't my men guarding the chopper." His voice

was low as he slid back onto the seat and quickly mapped out the locations of all Solis's sicarios.

"I'll take out the sniper on the roof," Melina offered, "then cover you."

Rafe nodded and looked at Harper. "I'll clear the way on the ground. Stay close."

He turned to the man slumped down in the shotgun seat. "Jacin, you've got our six. Make sure no one gets past this vehicle."

The three stepped out of the car together and zigzagged through the shadows to the dark side of a small hangar. Rafe followed a step behind Melina.

Harper continually checked their rear. She was surprised when she came around the corner of the hangar and found Melina and Rafe face-to-face, eyes locked on each other.

"Rafe, you're such a good man. I…you were special to me." Melina went up on her toes and brushed a kiss on his cheek. "Good-bye, Rafe." She turned away, headed toward the sniper's perch.

Fast as a whip, Rafe grabbed Melina's wrist. She looked at it before meeting his gaze. He quickly released her. "You were special to me, too. Be careful."

Melina nodded and jogged away.

Harper didn't know what to make of the exchange and decided to worry about it later. Rafe was leaving with her, and it was likely he'd never see Melina again. But his words jabbed at her heart. She wondered if she was special to Rafe or just a convenient physical release.

Why the hell should she care? Rafe was temporary, like all men in her life.

"Ready?" Rafe's low voice brought her mind back to the situation.

"Ready," she confirmed and followed a few steps behind him.

Two men stood bored at the corner of the hangar, quietly chatting and smoking. Before he could react, Harper used the hand signals she'd learned in SpecOps training to tell him she'd take the one on the left, and he had the other guy. Rafe stared at her in amazement for a second before she moved toward her tango.

Harper silently glided behind the guard and took him out. She guided the body to the ground and dragged him into deeper shadows. She pointed to the next tango then indicated for Rafe to wait ten seconds before he ran to the chopper that now sat between the last hangar and the runway. He nodded then blended into the shadows.

Her second man was easier than the first. As she approached, his cell phone buzzed in his pocket. In a rookie move, he released his rifle to dangle by his side and dug out the phone. He was dead before he could hit the answer button.

She joined Rafe a few seconds later. With the thin beam of a red penlight, he went through the pre-flight checklist with ease and speed. Throttle: full open. Starter: engaged. Main rotor: on, turning. Engine and oil pressure… He flipped toggle switches and watched the gauges as the pumps forced fluids to the engines and gears.

The sound brought several sicarios running toward them. The distinct crack of .50 caliber bullets and the report of machine gun fire echoed through the darkness as Rafe pressed onward through the takeoff process.

Using night vision goggles, Harper kept track as one cartel soldier after another dropped. She silently thanked Melina, who made sure no one got close to them.

With the blades finally up to full speed, Rafe warned,

"Hang on." His voice was smooth and calm through the helicopter's communication system in their helmets.

Lift-off was bumpy, but they were above the ground. The blades weren't clear of the rooftops before shots were fired from the ground and immediately answered by Melina.

As the bird rose, Harper saw a sicario climb onto the far end of the hangar roof where Melina had established her sniper's perch.

Harper didn't think about it. She simply reacted.

The rat-a-tat staccato of her machine gun on squirt mode would have deafened both she and Rafe if not for the sound suppressors within their helmets.

"Got him," she announced.

As fast as possible, Rafe forced the chopper higher into the air and out of range. He headed down the deep Cauca Valley, keeping the Cordillera Occidental on his right and the higher peaks of the Cordillera Central on the left.

Once they were out of range, Harper asked, "You all right?"

Rafe didn't answer.

She whipped her head toward him, but the glow of dials didn't offer enough light for her to see him clearly. Her heart clenched. The thought of losing Rafe hit her harder than it should.

She watched him fight the stick.

"Rafe, are you hit?"

"No. I'm good. You?"

Harper grabbed a sharp breath as the mountains huffed a gust of cool night air into the valley and bounced the helicopter.

"Fine." Now that she knew Rafe wasn't bleeding.

"Damn, this thing is flying rough," Rafe complained, the stick in both hands.

Harper watched the high-resolution radar as it outlined each elevation with a colorful grid as they headed away from the lights of Cali and the men who chased them.

"Damn it!" Rafe hissed.

That didn't bode well.

"What?" she asked.

"Fuel's dropping fast. Tank must've gotten hit. Start looking for an LZ to plant this bird. It'll be a metal rock within minutes."

Thankfully, Harper recognized some of the mountains as the ones they'd flown over on their trip to Cali, and found the pass they'd used. She recalled there was farmland beneath them.

"Find me a field, fast." Rafe's total concentration was on handling the helo.

In the moonlight, Harper could see the wide river valley spotted with small farm plots. "Which side of that river do we need to be on?"

"This side. Popayán is on the Southwest side of the Cauca." His voice was cool and collected.

"You sure? Don't they have piranha and crocodiles here?" Harper didn't care much for the wildlife in Colombia. Too many things could kill, and humans weren't necessarily at the top of the food chain. "I don't need an up-close-and-personal encounter while trying to cross the river."

"I'm sure, babe." There was a chuckle in Rafe's voice. It was as if he'd read her mind. They worked well together.

The chopper lost altitude. Harper knew he had to power in, and engines sucked down fuel fast. Unlike airplanes, choppers didn't drift—they dropped.

"One o'clock. There's a small field. It looks silver in the moonlight." It was rimmed on two sides by trees, the third by the river. Three small buildings were tucked into the corner of the fourth side.

"That'll work just fine. Thanks, babe." Rafe pushed the machine, which grew heavier every second. He came in low over the river and lost the tail rotor. The rear started to swing around.

"Don't you dare, you big old bitch!" He cut the overhead rotors so they would auto-rotate the last few feet to the ground. As the chopper tail tried to make a complete circle, the skids thunked on the ground. The right skid caught, and the chopper tried to flip. It bounced hard, but remained upright.

"Follow me and stay close," he ordered and jumped out his door. He pulled the KRISS K-10 to his shoulder and swept the area over its sights.

Harper came up beside him, rifle to her shoulder, and used the infrared scope to search for approaching people.

"Clear. Run!" She ordered.

They zigzagged across the field of knee-high plants, keeping at least twenty feet apart. When they reached the tree line, they continued for ten yards before crouching at the base of a huge tree.

They once again scoped the area. "Clear and safe," he declared.

Harper took a deep breath and leaned against the tree then jerked to standing.

"Up." She couldn't hide the hint of fright in her voice.

"Are you all right?" Rafe's apprehension radiated from him.

Prickles—or were they tickles?—ran down her spine from his nearness. His sincere concern for her demolished some of the walls she'd built around her heart.

"Hell no." She shuddered. "There are anacondas in this

goddamned jungle. The small ones are twenty feet long and weigh over three hundred pounds. I hate snakes."

"There are also jaguars." He swept the rifle upward. "While I was with the SEALs, we dropped in the other side of the Occidental Centrals and had to hike through a really dense jungle before we hid out for a week just watching this guerilla camp. My buddy, Doc, decided to sleep under a tree, and when he woke up, there was a two hundred and fifty pound jaguar napping just above his head. It's always a good idea to look up. Sorry I didn't think of it first."

Rafe scanned the branches above them for wildlife. "We're good," he finally announced.

Harper plotted on her GPS with a frown. A straight line through the jungle meant hours of hacking and whacking at the fast-growing vegetation for each mile gained. The river wound its way leisurely down toward the ocean, but they needed to travel upstream against several sets of class three and four rapids. She smiled at the thought of running it in a kayak.

"Good news?" Rafe asked, encouraged.

"No, it seems I'm always headed the wrong way." She pointed to her GPS screen. "These would be a blast to run in a kayak, but we need to move upstream, against nature. It's never easy."

"We could boat our way up to this point then cut across the jungle here." He ran a finger across her screen. He was standing so close, her whole right side felt the heat from his nearness.

His hand lightly brushed over hers. The jolt was electric, and she startled. He must have felt it too because his gaze met hers and held. In that moment, she remembered his tender touch in the soft sheets at La Comunidad only a few hours ago. How he'd brought her to completion so easily. He seemed to know her body and exactly what it needed. She wished they could have stayed there instead of running for their lives, chased through the Colombian night.

Rafe's eyes softened in the light of the tiny illuminated GPS. He reached up and cupped her cheek, his fingers sliding through her hair, and pulled her to him. The kiss was soft, gentle. Adrenalin pushed through her veins, but she needed this tenderness, and he seemed to know it.

He pulled back and stroked his callused thumb over her cheek. "I'm sorry we were interrupted and torn from the bed. I wasn't finished exploring your gorgeous body. Hell, I'd barely gotten started. I promise, when this is over and we're safe, we'll finish what we started. It may take days before I've made love to you all the ways I want you."

Just the thought of days in bed with him and the ways she wanted Rafe made her ache between her legs. If he touched her right at that moment, she'd explode within seconds.

Harper guided his face to her and kissed him hard, forcing his mouth to open to her. She shoved her tongue inside and tasted his need. He tangled his tongue with hers and thrust into her mouth, the way she wanted him inside her, much lower. He rocked his hips, and she felt him harden against her.

Snap.

Every muscle in her body froze. Bushes rustled about twenty feet away. With an efficiency of movement, Rafe stepped back and yanked the rifle to his shoulder, head tilted into the stock for optimum vision through the scope. Harper fumbled slightly and had her rifle up as well.

He snickered.

"We have an audience. Monkeys." He pointed.

Harper looked through the IFR mode of her scope. Six or seven small bodies with red and yellow heat signatures sat in a perfect row staring back at her. She couldn't hold in her giggle.

"We were about to show them how humans have hot monkey sex," Rafe teased. "I wonder if they'd learn anything."

"You're bad, you know that?" She swatted at his arm.

"No, I'm actually very good, but you know that." He brushed a kiss over her cheek as he ran his free hand over her bottom then smacked it lightly. "Let's move. It'll be light soon."

Harper took a deep breath and clicked the GPS back on. "You're right."

Rafe pointed toward the far end of the field. "We've got company interested in the chopper."

Two men approached the field where the downed helicopter sat glinting in the moonlight. Their stance was curious, not military trained, as they pointed at the helo. Their white shirts shone brightly in the night, opposed to her and Rafe's own black camouflage.

"How many?" Harper asked.

"Only two," Rafe replied.

Harper made a command decision.

"I've got this. Cover me." She stood and boldly walked out of the woods toward the two men. She removed the black watch cap that secured her hair. Her gold highlights glittered in the pale light of the moon. She wiped the black and gray paint from her camouflaged face with the black handkerchief she kept in her back pocket.

She took off her black shirt and tied it around her waist as she crossed the field. She wanted them to see her tank top and bare arms, to be sure they saw her as a woman.

"Hello, gentlemen," Harper called in her best Spanish to the two men who stood beside the field she was quickly crossing with determined strides. She knew she was safe because Rafe remained hiding in the woods and would continue to scan the surrounding area for any threats.

The two shacks from which they had emerged were typical of indigent residents, slapped together to protect them from the heat of the day and creatures of the night.

She smiled and spoke loud enough for them to hear since she was still fifty feet away, "I'm sorry our helicopter crashed and ruined your field. In payment, we give it to you." She and Rafe didn't need that chopper anymore, and Narváez wouldn't ever use it again.

These were simple farmers, eking out a bare existence. Their fields were planted for food for their families to consume, not cocaine. They looked like father and son.

She moved closer to them as they silently stared at her. "Well, hell," Harper said, wondering if they hadn't understood her Spanish. In this part of Colombia, many spoke dialects far older than the country itself.

The boyish one smiled, eyes growing wide. "You're American? Tourista?"

"Yes," Harper lied easily, seeing his exuberance for international travelers literally dropping in on them. "We need a boat. Do you have one?"

"Yes, ma'am." The young man gave her a hopeful smile as he looked at the helicopter. "The boat, it's not big, but it doesn't leak."

The older man smacked him on the back of head and mumbled.

"It leaks a little," he admitted. His large brown eyes were apologetic but turned hungry as his gaze stole back to the chopper.

They needed the boat so Harper offered, "You can have it. There are many good parts on the helicopter. It has a strong engine, compressors, many items you can salvage. That should cover the cost of your boat. I'll leave it several miles upriver. I don't want to keep it."

"Thank you, ma'am." The older man tentatively held out his hand. Maybe he was afraid to touch her. Harper smiled warmly and took his hand in both of hers. These men were short compared to the men she knew and very thin with lean working man's muscles, not like the gym-pumped men at the ATF.

She turned toward the trees and signaled for Rafe to join her.

Looking back at the older man, she asked, "What danger will we find up river?"

The older man smiled. "How far do you go?"

She ignored his question and asked, "Do guerillas control the river? Who is their leader?"

"Yes, often I see them when we fish, but they know me and don't bother with my family. We are too poor for them. We trade fresh vegetables, and they bring my wife cloth sometimes."

"Thank you. You are very kind." She watched their eyes climb upward and fear cross their faces.

She could feel Rafe, his growing presence, as he walked up behind her. She didn't need to look to know he was there. He was so familiar now.

"Would you please show my friend to your boat?" she asked in a gentle voice, hoping to reassure the older man, who then ordered the boy to take them to the river.

Rafe told the older man, "We were never here. You never saw us. Sicarios from the other side of the mountain crashed that helicopter and said you could have it for parts before they headed on foot to the highway." He pointed toward the looming Cordillera Occidental range and in the general direction of the road.

With short nods of his head, the old man agreed.

Rafe added in a more gentle tone, "We have to keep my woman safe." He put his arm around Harper possessively and switched to English when he whispered in her ear, "It'll be dawn soon. We need to move."

All she could think about was his arm around her. It felt so right. His heat warmed her all the way to her heart.

No, she couldn't go there. She wouldn't let a man into her heart. She'd been a pillar of strength for so many years, fighting her way through life alone. The mere thought of sharing the burden with someone else was an enticing invitation, but she knew how that ended.

Rafe and Harper followed the farmers to the river where they all looked down the steep bank at the small flat-bottomed boat that currently held two inches of water. It was two feet across at its widest point and looked like a tiny barge had mated with a canoe. The front was pointed, but the back was squared. A single board crossed in the middle area, created a seat. The paddles were new and plastic though.

Harper wasn't sure if both she and Rafe would fit. It would be a miracle if the boat didn't sink under their combined weight. Neither was small by anyone's standard.

"It doesn't have much of a keel," Rafe noted.

Harper beseeched the older man, "I hate to ask this of you, but is there another boat?"

"We only have the one." The boy shrugged, then lit up. "The men down the river have a big motor boat. Very loud. Very fast. It can even go through the rapids."

Harper smiled at the small, disheveled man. "How far down?"

"Two bends." Maybe this little thing could get them that far.

"Thank you," she said sincerely to the weatherworn man. "You should strip the helicopter immediately and drag it into the woods before the guerillas see it and start asking questions." Harper glanced toward the chopper then at the plowed and planted fields. She caught sight of an antiquated tractor and hoped it was powerful enough to drag the crashed bird away before anyone saw it.

Rafe looked at her. "Let's go steal a motor boat."

CHAPTER 21

RAFE CONTEMPLATED THE SMALL LEAKY BOAT AND FROWNED. He motioned toward the wet wooden hull. "Sorry, babe, but it'd work best if you'd put that pretty little ass of yours on the floor in the middle. Your lower center of gravity will stabilize what little keel is there."

"Let's dump the water out first, please?" Harper begged.

Rafe didn't blame her. The bottom of the craft looked disgusting and smelled worse. He motioned for the younger man to help, and together, the three of them lifted the small boat. "Christ, this thing's heavy as hell," Rafe complained.

"But making me happy is worth it." Harper's smile lit up the night. And his world. Yes, making Harper happy was high on his list.

Once righted, Harper planted her butt on the bottom of the boat and faced forward, legs crossed. Rafe crouched as he stepped into the boat and went to his knees. If she leaned back, she'd be against his crotch. His cock twitched. *Don't go there. Keep your head in the game. We're a long way from safe.*

Rafe used the paddle and pushed off from the black

muddy bank. The powerboat was downriver so he maneuvered into the swift, tea-colored river. Dawn was only about an hour away. The swiftly moving water glinted now and again from reflected starlight, as if someone had thrown a handful of tiny diamonds onto undulating black satin.

Rivers were so different from the ocean waters he'd grown up on and trained in as a SEAL. Luckily, he'd done a little kayaking in college.

Harper was so close he could feel the heat from her back on his thighs. When he bent to dig into the water for a deep stroke, his chest came so very close to her head. He imagined taking her from behind, pumping into her from the back. His erection pushed against his zipper. He readjusted his position on the board but found little relief. Every time he leaned forward to dip the paddle into the water, he could smell her hair, her body, the unique scent that was Harper. He wanted her, again.

The sky slowly turned from black to deep purple-gray as they came around the second bend. The river widened to more than one hundred feet across.

Just as the native had said, ahead on the right sat a bright yellow fiberglass boat run up onto a sand bar. It was at least fifteen feet wide, very tall in the back, and about twenty-five feet long.

"How the hell are we supposed to drive that huge thing up the shallow river?" Rafe asked.

"At screaming speeds." Harper smiled. "It's a New Zealand-designed river runner with a draft of only five inches and powerful engines made for speed. The wide body stabilizes the boat in sharp curves. It was built to run twelve tourists at fifty miles per hour through the Shotover Canyon with a zero-turn radius." She grinned at him.

"You seem to know a lot about it. Have you ever driven

one of these?" Rafe's boating experience was limited to sailing yachts on the ocean, riding in rigid inflatables as a SEAL, and the little rodeo-kayaks on Virginia rivers. He'd never imagined a big boat like this one on a river that was no deeper than his waist in most places.

"No. My team was training in the Idaho mountains along the Snake River, and afterward, we played tourist. We rode one of those through Hell's Canyon. What a wild ride." Harper's eyes lit with excitement.

Damn, she was so beautiful.

"Got any idea how we're gonna steal it?"

"If I remember right, the controls are on the front left side. I should be able to hot-wire it, and we'll be on our way within minutes," she offered.

"We need to move fast." Rafe said looking at the sky. "The sun will be up within thirty minutes."

"I wish we knew how many were in camp," Harper said. "I could sneak through the jungle and get a head count."

"No, it doesn't matter how many. We'll handle whatever happens." He gave her shoulder a squeeze. "I'll paddle quietly to the far side of the big boat, and we'll climb in next to the controls. I'll establish lines of fire, and you get it started. We should be out of here before anyone knows we've been there."

Rafe quickly paddled the old leaking dinghy onto the sand bar beside the shiny new speedboat. He and Harper slipped soundlessly onto the deck.

As Rafe swept the area with the IFR setting on his scope, Harper crawled under the steering column. He counted seven asleep in tents and two walking the perimeter at the tree line. Good thing they weren't concerned with a water approach.

Harper popped her head out from under the dash. In a backstage voice, she said, "Rafe, press the start button."

Confident he knew where all the bad guys were, he looked down and found the red button. Thankfully, the powerful engines growled to life almost instantly.

Rafe barely heard the yelling from the far side of the guerilla camp, but when the gunfire started, he threw the boat into reverse.

Harper rolled into his shins as they jerked off the sand bar. Then, he over-steered and flung her to the right.

He heard a thud.

"Damn it, Rafe, give a girl a little warning."

"Sorry, this thing is really reactive. Stay down and hang on." He nudged the steering wheel slightly to test the response, and the boat moved several degrees. He corrected his course as he rounded the bend, leaving the boat's former owners shouting as they popped out of their tents like prairie dogs.

More color now pushed its way across the sky in streaks of pinks and reds.

"Is it safe to come out?" Harper's voice sounded muffled.

They were out of sight of the camp, so Rafe said, "Yeah, come on."

Harper crawled from under the console. The boat shifted, and she grabbed Rafe to steady herself.

He glanced down and found her hanging onto his hips, her face inches from his crotch. Thoughts of her lowering his zipper and freeing him tightened all the muscles in his legs. He wondered if she'd stroke his sensitive skin and taste his flesh before she took him into that sweet mouth of hers. Their brief time together in his bed hadn't given her the opportunity to explore his body the way he'd come to know hers.

He gave her a slow sexy smile, and her eyes went dark chocolate with desire. His cock swelled and pushed against the zipper's metal teeth, begging for freedom.

With mild regret, he grabbed her arm and effortlessly pulled her up.

"Later," he croaked out. One hand still on the steering wheel, he clutched the back of her head and pressed his lips to hers for a fast but deep kiss. He spun her toward the seat beside him and playfully smacked her butt. "Behave."

Rafe glanced up at the sky as it filled with deep reds that gave way to blush rose then tinged pink. "Red sky in the morning, sailors take warning."

"Yeah, there may be a storm headed our way later today," Harper added.

"I hope we can get to Popayán before it hits. Even though it rains every day, a storm could mean trouble. The trees don't have deep roots, and the wind blows them over easily. The jungle is not a good place to be," Rafe explained.

Harper pulled her GPS from a side pocket and checked their progress.

Within a minute, they flew past the farmer who'd lent them his old wooden boat. Harper waved as two heads darted out of the downed helicopter. She was glad they were working on it and hoped they could get several parts removed before the speedboat owners showed up.

"Can we take this all the way?" Rafe asked as he whipped around the next bend.

"No, there are a couple sets of tall waterfalls before we get to Popayán, but it is close enough to walk from there. It's extremely dense jungle, so it'll be slow going from that point until we reach the road."

Harper continued to scan the banks of the river looking for signs of human life and potential threats.

Rafe turned his attention back to the river, dodging boulders the size of small European cars. On a long, straight stretch, he backed off the power and speed and finally sat down in the driver's seat. He was sure they weren't being chased and took the time to check important things like the fuel levels and engine performance. Everything was fine—the tank was full, and the engines purred well below red line.

Harper monitored the GPS and their progress.

Rafe took in the white-capped mountains that towered on both sides, knowing it would be the last time he'd see them. The Andes were beautiful and dangerous mountains, part of the Pacific Ring of Fire. Eruptions were not uncommon, and Melina had warned them that Puracé was rumbling. Being on a river during an earthquake or, worse, an eruption, was beyond treacherous. He hoped they'd get to Popayán soon.

After nearly an hour, Rafe offered, "Want to drive?"

"I thought you'd never ask." Harper reached under his arms and grabbed the wheel. He slid up the back of the driver's chair as she stepped in front of his seat.

He didn't move. He couldn't.

She stood between his spread legs, her butt cheeks brushing against his erection with every rock of the boat and shift of her hips. He was slightly bent over her, his hands still on the wheel next to hers.

He kissed her in that special spot just under her ear, and she leaned back into him. He grew even harder. No real surprise there. He wanted her again, but as they flew up a narrow river filled with huge boulders at fifty miles an hour, he knew now was not the time.

"I've got this if you want to check our position," Harper said as she turned her head slightly, her mouth close to his, but her eyes still on the river.

"Sure." He let go of the wheel and quickly moved to the seat she'd vacated. He grabbed the GPS and held it at his waist to hide his bulging zipper. He studied the map displayed on the green screen and looked at the surrounding mountains, orienting himself.

The opaque white sky was splotchy with large dusky blue clouds banked against the mountains. He hoped the rain would hold off until they were in Popayán.

Harper whipped the rear of the boat dangerously close to a solid wall of rock on the far bank as she zigzagged around the local wildlife.

"You trying to knock me out of this fuckin' boat?" Rafe shouted above the engine noise. "Maybe I shouldn't have let you drive,"

"I love this boat! It handles like a fighter jet running down mountain ranges. This is living. Woo hoo." Harper's voice echoed off the thick jungle on both sides.

With each set of rapids, they climbed higher up the mountains, and the river grew shallower as they passed convergences of other streams.

"Whoa!" Harper backed off the power to an idle in a large pool at the base of a waterfall. "I think we're at the end of the line." Picture-perfect rushing water dropped from a height of thirty feet into a natural pool that was crystal clear to its deceiving depths.

"Confirmed." Rafe pointed to the GPS screen.

Harper expertly drove the boat over to a tree that had fallen into the pool, and Rafe tied it to a large branch. They could practically walk off the boat onto the branches then to the shore. Whoever found the boat could have it and fight with the cartel farther down river over its ownership.

"I need a shower." She looked at the gorgeous waterfall. "And so do you."

They'd been on the run for hours. Adrenalin had heated their bodies, and sweat soaked their clothes. The warm breeze from the boat dried their clothing, but the sour smell remained.

Plus, with very little sleep during the past two days, Rafe hoped the cold mountain water would wake and invigorate him. They still had a long way to go before they were safe and reached a place where they could be rescued.

"You okay?" Rafe was concerned as his eyes raked over her. Dark smudges had appeared under her beautiful brown eyes that now drooped. She looked exhausted.

Rafe wished they could rest for a few hours, or days. But not yet. He'd carry Harper if he had to. He had to keep her safe and get her out of Colombia as soon as possible.

"I'm tired, and it'll be hours before we get to Popayán. Maybe we can hitchhike. That's why I need this shower. The way I smell, they'd dump me off within a mile of where they picked me up." She sniffed. "And you're just as bad."

Rafe helped her to the branch and followed her to the shore where they hid while he scanned the area through the scope on his rifle. While Harper unloaded their backpacks and weapons from the boat, he scouted the circumference of the pool, looking for trails and signs of human life.

"Only game trails and animal scat," Rafe announced. "We're pretty far off the beaten path. I think we're safe enough for a swim and a shower."

Harper sat on the rocky edge of the pool, and Rafe joined her. They took off their boots then emptied the contents of their pockets into them. With a fleeting look at each other, they ran into the water, clothes and all.

Rafe dove under the surface and stretched out as he swam through the clean mountain water. It was warmer than he'd expected, but as refreshing as he'd hoped. He surfaced, face toward the sky that was milky blue with bruised gray clouds that threatened rain. He moved beside Harper and heard her take in a breath. He reached for her and pulled her to him. He kicked for both of them as she wrapped her long legs around his waist.

Her lips were cool, but the kiss was hot, demanding. She opened her mouth to him. He dove in, thrusting the way he wanted his cock to move within her, the way she liked it. When they finally broke apart, they were breathing rapidly, and this time it had nothing to do with adrenalin.

"Let's wash these clothes then take a shower while they dry in the sun."

He liked her suggestion—they'd soon be naked—so he started to kick his way to shore. She clung to him, just along for the ride. And ride him was exactly what he had in mind.

When he could stand, Rafe held her as she slowly slid down his body. The cool water hadn't affected his erection one bit, nor did it drop the temperature of his blood. He needed her.

He took her face in both hands and kissed her. He kept it easy, careful not to reveal the depth of his need—not just desire, true need.

Harper pulled back and reached into her pocket. She pulled out the small bar of soap. She started with Rafe's shoulders and ran her hands over and down his chest, leaving suds in their path. He loved the feel of her hands on his body, even through the clothing. She seemed to need this control, and he gave it to her. He'd give her anything she wanted.

She moved up and down his arms. No one had ever given him a bath with his clothes on, and it was the most erotic feeling. His muscles quivered under her touch.

Finally, she reached around him to soap his back. He automatically mirrored the motions, matching her stroke for stroke.

When she stopped, he looked down at her dark eyes. They

were filled with passion that matched his own. He lowered his head and kissed her tenderly. She was special, valuable to him, and he cared for her in a way he'd thought had died years ago.

"My turn," Rafe said and stepped back. He peeled off his long-sleeved black shirt. They exchanged soap for his shirt, and then Harper rinsed the suds and squeezed out as much water as possible before she threw it ashore. He'd never seen Harper as domestic before, but the movements seemed natural to her.

Rafe's hands swept over every inch covered by her cammie shirt, but it felt as though he touched her skin as the wet cloth clung to her body. He spun her around so her back was to his chest. He pulled her to him and reached around to caress her breasts as he washed the front of her cammies.

He skimmed over the front of her pants and unfastened them. The baggy utilities came off and tufts of suds drifted downstream.

Harper reached down and removed her socks while Rafe washed the back of her tight black tank top. She stood up, and he once again cuddled her breasts before he caressed her from neck to hips. His fingers curled around the bottom of the tank, and he pulled it over her head. She rinsed the garment then threw it on shore.

Laundry as foreplay. This was a first for Rafe.

CHAPTER 22

HARPER STOOD IN HER SOAKED LACY BLACK BRA AND matching panties. Her tanned skin glinted from the clear mountain water.

She was so beautiful.

Rafe noticed the scar under her collarbone, the same one he'd found that first night before supper at the Narváez compound. He traced it with a fingertip.

"I took a bullet," Harper claimed with pride. "When I was twelve, Mom and I interrupted a burglar. The bastard shot my mom, so I rushed him, knocked him down. He got me here then shot me in the back as he ran out the door." She turned so he could see the fine white lines on her golden-brown back. "I wish I'd known then what I know now. I'd have killed him."

Rafe said nothing. He knew she was a different person today than the ballsy pre-teen who'd attacked a gun-wielding criminal. He wished he could have taken the bullets for her.

"I'm proud of what I did that day, and with my life since." She looked defiant. She didn't allow anyone to see her vulnerable side, but he knew she had one. He'd seen it.

Rafe reached out to her. "Oh, baby, I'm so sorry. You told me your mother had died, but I had no idea she was murdered."

Harper stepped into Rafe's arms. His heart swelled with an emotion he'd never felt before. He knew this was a rare expression of trust for Harper. A moment of comfort. He'd gladly give her that, and anything else she needed.

"Like my body, I've healed and moved on with my life." She sounded proud.

Rafe kissed her temple and just held her. It seemed to be what she needed.

For long minutes, the relentless waterfall thundered and pushed water past their thighs, but with their arms wrapped around each other, neither wanted to let go.

Clouds collected above them and blocked direct sunrays, but the temperature and humidity increased by the minute. Rafe was hot from an internal heat, one that seemed constant for the woman in his arms. He couldn't get enough of her. Their short interlude in Cali had been just a taste of heaven for him. His tented silk boxers were evidence of that.

She rocked against his erection. Her innocent Bambi eyes had turned into those of a Cleopatra-like seductress. She wanted him. He couldn't hold back his grin.

But Harper stepped out of his arms. "Let's lay out our clothes to dry while we shower in the waterfall." She headed toward the shoreline where their twisted clothes had plopped.

Rafe followed her out of their private nature-made pool. Damn she had a great ass, tight and the perfect size for his large hands. He wanted to grab her hips and nestle her sweet bottom against him. His erection throbbed as he picked up his cargo pants and squeezed out more water before he shook them and laid them in the sun to dry.

Harper hadn't looked at him while she tended to her own

clothes. His were ready and drying on rocks within a minute, but she continued to readjust hers. Nervous? That was hard for him to believe.

Enough. Rafe stepped beside her and took the black high-tech tank top she played with and quickly laid it next to the rest of her clothes. Then he turned to Harper and took her in his arms.

He was gentle because she seemed edgy. As he drew her close to him, her wet bra-covered breasts pressed against his chest and rivulets of water dripped down his abdomen.

"Let's get rid of this." With the snap of his fingers, he released the two small hooks. He ran his hands up her bare back and shoved the straps over her shoulders. He flung the bra next to the other quickly drying clothes and returned his attentions to Harper.

This time, when he pulled her to him, her soft breasts caressed his chest. She felt so wonderful, so right in his arms.

She stroked up his chest, and then her arms came around his neck. With an open mouth, she took his with fervor. She was demanding, but he liked that. She knew what she wanted, and he was more than willing to give it to her.

"You won't be needing these." Harper panted out the words when they broke apart. She hooked her thumbs in his soft, wicking boxers and kneeled as she pulled them down over his erection.

She stopped.

She stared at his cock for a long time.

"Like what you see?" Rafe certainly did. The sight of Harper on her knees in front of him, her warm moist breath heating his cock even more—he had to fist his hands to control the urge to press her face to his erection.

"Oh, yeah." Harper looked up at him with a Cheshire-cat smile. Then she licked him…just the tip.

He almost came.

Get control.

He'd wanted her again from the moment he'd left the bed back at La Comunidad.

When she took him into her hot, soft mouth, he thought he'd lose it for sure. She knew what she was doing as she sucked, but when she cupped his balls in her warm hand, he'd had enough.

He grabbed her by the shoulders and forced her to her feet. He thrust his tongue inside her mouth as his hands went to her breasts. Her nipples were hard pebbles as he ran his thumbs over them. He needed a taste.

Rafe lowered his head to one nipple and sucked. Hard. Harper's gasp satisfied his primal need to know her pleasure. His other hand slid down her hardened abs and under her lacy panties. When he slid a finger between her soft folds, she was wet and her clit taut. She pressed into his hand and moaned.

Yes, she wanted him.

He rubbed her center hard and sucked her other nipple deep into his mouth. She grabbed his shaft and squeezed tight.

Oh God. She gives as good as she gets.

Harper's ragged whimper almost knocked him over the edge. "Not yet, honey," he managed to say.

He slid a finger into her hot, wet sex. She rocked her hips, forcing his finger deeper. He glided in another finger, and she hummed.

"Rafe, now." Both of them were breathing as if they'd just sprinted up a mountain.

"Anything you want, baby." Rafe cupped her butt in both hands and picked her up. His boxers were still around his knees so he kicked them off. Her heat was pressed up against his pounding erection, separated by only the thin lace of her panties.

He set her down on the nearest boulder and grabbed for the scrap of lace. Harper beat him to it. She arched up and scooted them over her hips. He placed his hands over hers, and together, they slid them down her shapely legs. She shivered at his touch.

Damn, she was so responsive to him. No woman had ever been like this for him before.

He ran his fingers lightly up the inside of her thighs, separating them as he stepped to her.

When she put her hands around his neck, he needed no more invitation. He positioned the head of his cock at her opening. He took her slowly so she could adjust to his size.

Harper thrust forward, forcing him into her quickly.

"Christ," Rafe moaned. What a woman. He withdrew slowly then thrust again, all the way to the hilt. He continued to move in and out, taking his time. He wanted this feeling of pure physical pleasure to last.

Harper's hands were on his shoulders, her head thrown back, her eyes closed. The smile on her face told him everything he needed to know—she liked this.

He felt her tighten around him deep inside. She drew her powerful legs around his waist and pulled him deeper.

Oh God. Rafe didn't think it could get any better, but it had.

He strained to hold his release. She had to come first.

Rafe reached between them and found her center, full and hard. He rubbed his thumb over it with his every thrust and was rewarded with clenched muscles.

"Let go, baby. Take us both." On his next drive, she cried out her release. He fell with her. He kept moving within her, drawing out their pleasure for what seemed like the longest orgasm he'd ever had.

He could barely stand, so he braced his knees against the rock and let his hands fall beside her hips. When she fell backward to stretch out on the warm dark boulder, she pulled him over onto her. Thank God. He wasn't sure if he could remain upright another second. She'd milked every ounce of energy from him.

The mind-blowing sex had been the best in his life. No woman, not even Beth, had ever made him feel so hungry then so sated. Could it be like this every time with Harper? He'd make it his mission to find out.

"Christ, you're good." Harper finally spoke, her breathing still labored but recovering.

He wasn't sure if he'd ever get his breath back. She thinks I'm good? No way. It was her. She's fantastic. The best I've ever had.

Harper ran her palms down his back, neck to hips, and back again. She was comforting him. He felt her touch all the way to his soul.

No. He couldn't let her do that. She was the wrong woman for him.

Sex. Yes. Definitely.

Into his heart? No. He could never let himself forget she had a dangerous job, which meant she could be taken away from him so easily.

"Just good chemistry. We're explosive together." That was all Rafe could admit to. It was only lust and had to stay there, in the physical.

Harper was the wrong woman. But she was the right woman for now.

He brushed away a stray strand of hair from her forehead and kissed the place it had been. She was beautiful, strong in body and mind. He nuzzled her neck and smelled the essence of Harper. He wished they were someplace safe where he could keep her in bed for days. Maybe then he'd get over his need for her. He kissed the spot she liked under her ear. Then he licked where his lips had just touched.

Damn, if he wasn't getting hard again. He was still buried inside her. Her inner muscles pulsed around him.

Harper rolled her head and looked into his eyes. "Really?"

Rafe shrugged. "See what you do to me? It's all your fault. I can't help myself."

She shoved him off to the side and slid out from under him.

"You're going to have to take care of that yourself. I absolutely need a shower now, and then we need to get moving."

Rafe stood, glanced down, and then to Harper's eyes, about to make another suggestion.

She stared. Her jaw dropped a fraction of an inch. Her sleepy, satisfied eyes flashed in disbelief.

He looked back at his erection.

"Oh fuck." No condom.

As though she could read his mind, she said, "We're tested constantly, and I'm healthy. I'm always careful."

"I'm clean and healthy, too." He spoke quickly. "I've never…" Rafe realized it was the truth. He'd never had sex without a condom in his life. Even with Beth. She didn't do well on the pill, so he'd taken responsibility and consistently been prepared. "I've always used a condom. I guess you could say you were my first." Maybe that's why it felt so different, so much better. "But you could be pregnant." Rafe hadn't thought about children in years, but he was sure he didn't want them with Harper.

"No worries. I'm on the pill. Have been for years. Female agents have to control our periods. One less thing to think about during a mission."

Thank God. Dodged that mistake.

She moved to him and wound her arms around his neck. Her kiss was comforting. There she was again, reassuring him, taking care of him. He could get used to that. He could get used to her.

"Let's go shower." She led him by the hand to the waterfall.

They stepped behind the roaring water that smacked at their feet into a five-foot wide space where time and millions of gallons of water had eroded away the rock. Someday, the rocks that jutted overhead would weaken and fall, and the process would begin again. For now, nature provided them privacy and a shower.

Rafe had grabbed the soap on their way behind the thundering water and turned Harper so her back was to him. His erection throbbed as it poked her butt cheeks, but he concentrated on soaping his hands. Her body was warm against his chest as he reached around and began at her neck. He placed a kiss into her wet hair, and she leaned into him. He cuddled each breast in a hand and smoothed suds around and over her nipples before he slid his hands down her body and between her legs. She was ready for him again when he pulled his fingers up and down her center.

She arched her back, nuzzling her ass into him. Damn, he'd like to just bend her over and take her again. "Rafe...please?"

"Are you sure?" His voice was husky as she turned to face him and took him in both hands. Christ, what she could do to him with only a touch. Her kiss alone could make him hard, but when she touched him, he almost shattered.

"Oh, yeah. I'm sure." Rafe picked her up, and she guided him in as she wrapped her legs around him. He backed her against the wet stone wall and pounded into her, fast and hard. She came almost at once, and he wasn't far behind.

He rested his forehead on the cool rock surface beside her head. It felt so good on his overheated body. His muscles were no longer able to hold his bones together, to say nothing about standing and holding on to her, so he slid to the shelf smoothed by time and nature.

Harper rode him down with her legs loosely over his hips, straddled his lap, and dropped her head onto his shoulder. She let her arms fall to the sides. He held her, close, hands cupped on that perfect ass of hers, his head resting on her shoulder.

Sunlight shone through the sheet of water that unceasingly sprinkled droplets on them from the backside of the falls. Rafe wasn't sure if he'd slept, or if it had just taken a long time for his brain functions to return. He ran a hand up Harper's back, and she roused, as if she'd actually been asleep. He was sure she needed to sleep though. She'd physically and emotionally been through so much in the past few days.

"We need to finish our shower."

With eyes barely open, she kissed him. Her lips were cool and wet from the mountain river that poured over them.

He rubbed her back with long strokes from nape to hips, enjoying the feel of her. He listened as each breath she took became deeper than the last as she forced herself awake. He liked the feel of her soft breasts against his chest rubbing up and down with each expanding breath. It felt right to hold her as she pulled her brain and body together from the depths of sleep. This is what it'd be like to have her awaken in his arms every morning.

"You're right." She stood, a bit shaky at first, but soon

caught her balance and then moved toward the rush of water. Rubbing her hands together, she lathered the soap.

Mesmerized, he watched her run nimble fingers over her body, leaving a trail of bubbles that clung to her breasts as long as they could before they slipped down her flat stomach. Some caught in the fine hairs at the apex of her legs before she stepped under the waterfall. He was getting hard again. He stood and walked into the cool mountain water, drenching the fire that built within him, again.

CHAPTER 23

HARPER TOOK THE LEAD AS THEY FOLLOWED THE RIVER toward the road that led to Popayán. She knew Rafe had put her in the front so they would move at her pace, and he could keep an eye on her. It was the right tactical decision—she would have made the same choice if she were the leader—but it irked her on some basic level.

She and Rafe were a team, and a good one. They'd watched out for one another, covered each other, been there for the other person when needed. She let Rafe take the leadership role in this team, thus silently agreeing to follow. But why had she let him be in charge?

Was it because he was a man? No, she didn't think so.

Was he a better leader? Maybe. She was woman enough to admit that he probably had more experience in that role.

Did he have more skills than she did? He'd been a SEAL, but she'd had the same training…and more.

Or was it because he'd proven himself to her and she trusted him? Harper trusted Rafe with her safety, her body— and the pleasure he'd brought her in bed was beyond anything she'd ever experienced—and her life. Could she trust him with her heart?

She'd already broken her own rules with him and had sex during a mission, several times. But it was worth it. She'd needed that release and loved what they'd shared. More sex was in their future if she had anything to do with it, but it'd only be sex, no emotions involved. Once she got him out of her system, she'd boot him out of her bed, just like every other man.

But Rafe was different. The why of it made her brain ache almost as much as her muscles. Trudging up the steep mountains was hard work for her abused body. She winded easily. The drug reaction had severely damaged her stamina. Lack of sleep and lactic acid buildup made every muscle hurt as they stretched and pulled.

Rafe climbed right behind her and pushed her butt when she needed a boost. She liked the feeling of his big hands on her ass. Actually, she liked his hands on her anywhere, everywhere. He had talented fingers. Maybe it was the thought of what those hands did to her that caused her heavy breathing.

At the top of a ridge, Harper stopped and bent to catch her breath.

"We can rest if you need to. We could even take time out for a combat nap." He sounded so concerned for her she almost melted into him, and not just from the oppressive jungle heat which seemed to dissolve her strength.

No. She'd push herself until she dropped, literally.

"I'm fine," she snapped and stepped away. "It's very steep, but I'm making it."

With a brief nod, he said, "I'll scout ahead and see if there's another route." He pointed to an animal trail that led off to the side. "Even the animals don't go straight up."

Harper watched Rafe's tight butt and muscular back as he disappeared into the jungle. Damn, he had one of the best bodies she'd ever had the pleasure of touching. She plopped down on a boulder and dug in her backpack for a bottle and the miniature water purification pump.

He was an amazing lover. Rafe seemed to know just how she wanted it and could bring her to climax faster than any man ever had. For that alone she might keep him around a little longer. She leaned down and stuck the draw tube into a small eddy that formed before the clear water cascaded to create an even higher waterfall than where she and Rafe had showered.

They were good together, worked and played well. He was able to read her as easily as her team members. That was scary because she'd been on the ATF team for nearly two months and she'd barely known Rafe two days—or was it three now? Didn't matter. They'd grown close in a way she'd let very few people in her lifetime. The little pump purred as clean drinking water filled her canteen.

Barely a rustle of ground scatter announced Rafe's return. He emerged from the thick foliage, over six feet of muscle and sinew. His confident stride and square shoulders dared man or beast to challenge him. He was formidable...and hers.

Yeah. She'd keep him for a few days of needed play time. Then they'd go their separate ways.

Harper held out the filled container to him. He shook his head.

"Ladies first. My momma raised me right." His smile and kindness brushed over her heart. Grateful, she took a deep drink then handed it to him.

After a long pull of decontaminated water, Rafe scanned her face with unhidden concern.

"How are you really doing?" There was that compassion, that honest caring. He sat beside her and scrutinized her face.

"I'm better," she told him, but she knew he didn't believe her.

"You almost died two days ago. It'll take weeks for you to regain all your strength. Pushing yourself now isn't going to help." He took her wrist and felt her pulse then nodded, satisfied. No lover had ever been so thoughtful.

"I found a better path that will take us to the road," Rafe said. "It's only another two miles. There should be more traffic this time of day. Maybe we can hitch a ride into town."

"Sounds like a plan." Harper got to her feet, brushed off her butt, and stowed her water bottle in the side pocket of her backpack.

"I don't like the looks of those clouds. I'd like to get to Popayán before the rain lets loose." Rafe was right. It looked like one hell of a storm was about to break.

They made good time, even though the hot jungle seemed to drain more energy from her with every step. Rafe had kept a careful watch on her and helped whenever she'd let him. She'd bet he was prepared to carry her if needed. That wouldn't be necessary because she heard the sputtering of motor vehicles.

They stepped out of the dense underbrush that clung to the roadside and saw the gray sky had turned pewter as storm clouds collided into the Andes mountain peaks. Daylight barely penetrated the water-soaked air six thousand feet above.

"It's going to pour in a few minutes," Rafe noted.

"Let's hope someone takes pity on us and picks us up soon." Harper checked the GPS once again and started walking down the pothole-ridden highway.

Rafe placed himself between her and the regrettably

empty road, protecting her, again. She wasn't sure if she was insulted or aroused by his thoughtfulness.

Thunder boomed above, and she kicked up the pace. They could always return to the jungle beside the road and hide under huge-leaved plants until the storm passed. It was an option if they didn't get picked up soon.

Traffic seemed to come in waves. Several cars and delivery trucks whizzed by without stopping even though they both stuck out their thumbs in the universal hitchhiking plea. Often vehicles swerved into the other lane to avoid them.

Light sprinkles fell on her face as a dark SUV approached from the direction of Cali. Rafe's hand instantly went to the grip of his holstered pistol, his only visible weapon. They'd stashed most of their arsenal in the backpacks so as not to scare off the good people of western Colombia, the kind of people they hoped would offer them a ride to Popayán.

"Look desperate," he encouraged, "but be ready for anything."

Harper turned toward the oncoming vehicle, waved, and smiled. They were in luck. The driver slowed and rolled down his window.

"We're headed to Popayán." The driver's Spanish was atrocious, heavily English-accented, but his smile was wanton as his eyes raked the length of her body.

"You're American?" Harper responded in English. He looked astounded and pleased, as if he'd been given a gift.

"Yes...yes we are. Hop in." He nodded toward the back seat.

Rafe and Harper slid onto the bench seat behind the two men and shut the doors just as the clouds opened up and poured.

Before they were settled, the front seat passenger turned

to look at them, his soft round face smiling, his New England accent undeniable. "We almost didn't stop. You looked like all those militants that are running all over Popayán." He blushed. "But then we saw you were a woman, and I just couldn't leave you in the rain."

Harper considered how many weapons she and Rafe carried on their bodies as well as in the bags. Militant was an appropriate description. Unfortunately, the two of them might need every weapon they had before they were safe.

"Thank you, sir. We really appreciate the ride. Ours broke down several miles back," Harper explained. It was the truth, especially if she counted the chopper as their transportation.

Rafe looked at her with a good-job smirk.

Stretching as he twisted, the passenger extended his hand over the back of the seat. "I'm Dr. James Coleman, and this is soon-to-be Dr. Kent Nyland. He has yet to finish his dissertation and present it to me." The two men exchanged a reproachful look.

Harper took his hand in a brief shake. "Good to meet you. I'm Harper, and this is my friend Rafe." She hoped they'd miss the fact she left off last names and titles.

"Call me Kent," the driver said as he waved and looked at them in the rearview mirror.

"Are you here for Puracé?" Rafe asked as he shook Dr. Coleman's hand. "We heard she's about to blow."

"Yes, and just call me Jim." His delight lit up his whole face. "We're predicting an eruption will happen within the next forty-eight hours."

"I take it you're volcanologists?" Harper asked.

"Yes, from the University of Washington." Kent spoke loudly over the pounding rain and flapping windshield wipers.

"I've brought several of my grad students down here to

help with the experiments," Jim explained. "It's Kent's first big blow." In the rearview mirror, Harper saw the driver's hazel eyes slide to the professor in disbelief. She bit her lips to stifle her smile. He was far too good-looking for her to believe that, but there wasn't even a little tingle for him.

Rafe's hand was warm as it captured hers. Jolts ran up her arm, her nipples pebbled, and her stomach jumped. She squeezed her legs together and knew she was already wet. Damn him that he could do that to her. Soon, she promised herself. She'd move him into her bed and wear him out. She'd get him completely out of her system, and then they'd go their separate ways. That was the plan. Maybe.

"Are you here for the volcano, too?" Jim looked at them with many more questions in his eyes.

"No, we're meeting up with friends. We've been spending some time in the jungle, and they're giving us a ride home." She pointed to their backpacks, filled with weapons and ammunition, but they could logically contain survival gear and camping equipment. The professor seemed to accept her answer and rattled on about his findings and projected timetable for the eruption.

The satellite phone buzzed in Rafe's side pocket. He looked at the display and depressed the Talk button. "Hey, buddy, I was wondering when you were going to call."

Harper looked at him, brows knit together.

He mouthed the word "Ops."

She nodded. What he'd said had to be code for he was not alone and not able to speak securely. Good. They were moving toward home. Relief tugged hope back into her.

"Yeah, we're almost to Popayán now." Rafe said in a too friendly voice for an operational check in, but perfect for their cover. "Where can we meet you?"

CHAPTER 24

Hidden in a narrow alley, across the Parque de Caldas from the mammoth cathedral, Rafe scanned the area.

Nearly fifty people wandered through the small city block filled with tall trees encircled by trimmed shrubs. Volcano-seekers, dressed for the equatorial heat in shorts and sleeveless shirts, strolled on the artful stone and brick pathways that rayed in every direction from the center statue in the city's most famous park. Locals, in lightweight pants and long sleeves, walked pointedly toward their destination.

"This place is crawling with paramilitary." Rafe's quiet voice was controlled, but concerned. "I've seen sicarios from at least five different cartels. Some are friendly with Solis, others, I'm not so sure. I've trained men from this region for Narváez's cartel buddies. They might recognize me, but I wouldn't remember them."

And fuck it all, that's all we need.

"There's the Catedral Basílica Nuestra Señora de la Asunción. Isn't that where we're supposed to meet your SEAL friend?" She sounded so tired.

They both needed to rest. He hoped they would get

somewhere safe, sooner rather than later. Answering her question, he explained, "Yes. It's the seat of the archdiocese with a direct line to the pope." The U.S.A. had used the religious connection on more than one occasion since he'd been in Colombia.

"Let's hope they like Lutherans." She was so cute.

Rafe smiled and brushed a kiss over her lips. The sensation was nice but way too brief. He wanted to grab her and kiss her mindless. Not there though.

Ever-present, the paramilitary were dressed like Rafe and Harper. They wore camouflage utilities, black boots, machine guns pointed downward but hands on the stock, ready for action. Only the tourists paid them any attention, giving the armed men nervous glances, never making eye contact.

"We need to get across the square. Any suggestions?" Rafe asked.

"Let's blend in. We'll swagger our way through the park and right into the front door." Harper rose from their hunkered position in the shadow of a white block building, which looked like every other structure in Popayán. "As my old teammate, Tori, would say…own it."

Damn, he liked this woman. She had more guts than most of the men he'd trained in Colombia. She was so confident in her skills…and where did she get those skills? She took out those tangoes back in Cali like a pro. He was sure she'd had hand-to-hand training in the Army, but she was too good at it. He'd ask her about it later.

Head high and proud, Harper stepped onto the sidewalk and sauntered out into the street. A taxi blared its horn as it screeched past, but she ignored the cab and everything around her. He could tell, though, she was hyperaware and missed nothing.

Rafe stalked beside her. Another car sped toward them.

They both glared at it, daggers flashed from their eyes at the driver, who immediately slowed and curved around them. They looked exactly like what they were: bad asses capable of killing anyone who dared to cross them.

An orange-vested policeman held out both arms, palms up when they approached the street in front of the cathedral and stopped traffic. Rafe and Harper continued their casual pace and looked at no one, especially the uniformed officer.

Rafe had always liked the clean lines of the cathedral's Roman architecture. Eight columns, their bases nearly six feet tall, stretched up more than forty feet in front of the centuries-old building. The blocky clock tower anchored the cathedral at the far end, like a square lighthouse directing the faithful. Everything in Popayán was bright white, as if clean and pure. Rafe knew differently.

This city was filled with the scum of the earth. Thousands of tons of cocaine that grew on the surrounding mountains and beside tributary streams converged in the ancient city. Eventually, the product was refined, packaged, and distributed to the young adults in the United States.

Rafe had tried, and failed, to stop that flow of poison. Those were regrets for another day. Right now, he had to protect Harper so they could both leave Colombia.

The lavish ivory, pale blue, and light gray of the interior sanctuary was adorned with opulent gold details, a sign of this area's beginnings. The gold mines still operated, but the artisans who used the precious metal to praise their Lord had died centuries ago and had been replaced by capitalists. The emerald-jeweled golden crown that sat upon the Virgin Mary was a replica. The real one, bartered years ago, lay in a museum in the States.

Harper gawked at the high relief fleur-de-lis that decorated the aisles and craned her neck to absorb the scope of the impressive dome. Aged locals pulled rosaries through arthritic fingers while sitting on unpadded ancient benches, no doubt praying they lived through the impending eruption.

Rafe furtively glanced back at the door when someone opened it.

Oh, fuck.

He dragged Harper through one of the side arches and forced her to kneel in front of tiers of burning candles. Reaching over for a long stick, he shoved it into a flame until it caught fire, then lit two candles huddled within short red glasses.

"What are you doing?" she whispered.

"We were followed. One of Solis's lugartenientes just walked in." With his head bowed, Rafe peeked back toward the main sanctuary and watched the uniform disappear behind a thick carved door.

"Are you sure he's one of Solis's?"

"Positive. I trained him." Rafe didn't add that he was one of the best in that group.

"Shit," Harper hissed.

"The toilets are this way, if you need to use them." The raspy American-accented English brought a grin to Rafe's tight-featured face. It had been far too long since he'd heard that coarse voice. As always, he was thankful for the sound of his old friend.

"Preacher." It was a statement, not a question.

"Who else would you expect to come to this God-forsaken country to save your sorry ass?" the man said just above a whisper.

Rafe started to move, but strong hands held him penitent as a friendly face appeared between Harper and him.

"Harper, this asshole is one of my best friends, Matias

Revas. Call him Mat or Preacher," Rafe instructed by way of introduction.

At the mention of Rafe's SEAL buddy, Harper had visibly relaxed. "You have no idea how glad I am to meet you." She started to extend her hand.

"We'll shake later." Preacher covertly looked around. "Hold. And the Lord said, 'Beware of false prophets, who come to you in sheep's clothing but inwardly are ravenous wolves. Matthew 7:15.'"

"Is that a warning about you or the priesthood here?" Rafe asked. Sometimes Preacher's Bible quotes were a little ominous.

"Both." Preacher covertly looked around. "The archbishop here enjoys his lavish lifestyle thanks to the many gifts from the local cartels, including one allied with Solis. You're not safe here. He'll turn you over to them as quickly as he finds you."

Three male voices and stomping boots echoed throughout the cathedral.

Preacher mumbled what sounded like a short prayer and lit a candle. "Wise that you've chosen Saint Anthony who looks after travelers. We'll need his blessing before this is over," Preacher explained.

"How do we get out of here?" Rafe asked.

Preacher readjusted his robes to completely cover their clothes and appeared to be a priest consoling parishioners.

"Patience." He squeezed Rafe's shoulder. "First rule in an op, or have you forgotten?"

"I haven't forgotten anything. Matter of fact, I've learned a few new tricks along the way." Rafe had missed this friendly banter, but he wouldn't miss this life on the edge.

The rapid thud of boots on tile and the low murmur of several men's voices created a Doppler effect as a dozen uniformed sicarios strode up the central isle and into the same side chamber as the first ones had entered.

"Word travels fast," Preacher warned. "They must know you're headed here."

Damn. It had taken them only a few minutes to cross the park.

"Follow me and stay close," Preacher ordered Harper.

The lower ceilings along the outside walls kept the three in relative shadows. Halfway to the lobby, Preacher shed the white robes and stuffed them into the corner of a pew. His American camouflage utilities were stripped of any identifying patches, and to Rafe, Preacher was the best thing he'd seen in five years.

A wave of comfort and familiarity washed over Rafe. For the first time in years, he was a member of a team and on the right side. Segundo was gone. Completely. He'd been a good leader, but Rafe's mind shifted into follower mode. Preacher was team leader now. His mental load eased knowing the SEAL team would share the responsibility of getting them out of Colombia safely.

Preacher opened a hidden side door and all but shoved them through it. Heat and bright sunshine poured over them, temporarily blinding them. Harper tripped on the uneven sidewalk.

"Be careful. The last earthquake buckled some of the pavers." When Preacher took Harper's hand, Rafe stiffened at the shot of jealousy that speared his heart.

She's mine.

But, no, she wasn't his. Not really. He wanted her, constantly, and enjoyed being with her. His? For now. He watched her tight bottom under dark camouflage pants and wanted to hold those bared cheeks in his hands again as he slid into her.

Damn it. Stop that. He was growing hard.

"Where are we going?" Rafe needed to get his mind off Harper's ass before he couldn't walk, say nothing if they had to run.

"Iglesia de San Francisco. It's not far. Only one block over and three blocks down." The directions were probably true, but they couldn't walk openly on the now cartel-guarded streets. So they slithered between buildings that had been patched with concrete blocks and mismatched bricks after previous volcanic eruptions every decade or so. They crossed small dirt courtyards where children kicked soccer balls, sprinted down cobblestone side streets, and backtracked several times.

When they popped out of another alley onto a three-lane street, they faced the solid yellow side of the five-story church. Halfway down was an entrance that seemed to magically open as the three approached.

"Hurry," an older priest commanded. He shut and bolted the ancient door behind them. "This way."

They passed several ornately decorated naves honoring saints then cut through one of the two-story arches. The old man moved fast, but Rafe took in the sanctuary where at least a hundred benches sat perfectly spaced down both sides of a wide aisle. A smattering of locals prayed or stared at the five-story tall altar and the life-sized statue of Christ on the Cross covered in gold.

Harper faced him for a brief moment and smiled. "Breathtaking, isn't it? I love these old cathedrals."

In the natural light from the clerestory windows three stories above, she reminded him of an angel. Sunshine kissed her cheeks and sparkled off lips she'd licked seconds before. Blonde highlights and uncontrolled curls encircled her face, backlit in a golden halo.

His knees almost failed him. He wanted to fall to them and beg her to be his forever.

There was no darkness within this woman. She fought the evil of the world and brought light and love to his battered heart. She was so beautiful, yet dressed in black camouflage with weapons strapped to her gorgeous body, she was also a warrior. His avenging angel. In that holy place, surrounded by danger, with light drenching them both, he knew.

He loved her.

He wanted to spend the rest of his life with her. When they got out of Colombia, he'd tell her. They'd go together to buy the perfect ring, and she'd be his forever, because he was already hers. She owned his heart.

His smile was ear-to-ear. Hers broadened, and she stepped closer to him while the older priest fumbled with keys to open a deeply carved door.

"Did I ever tell you how much I love your smile? I don't see it very often, but when I do, it takes my breath away." She'd used the word love.

If only Harper had said she loved him.

He bent and kissed her quickly. Was it okay to kiss a woman in a church, other than during a wedding? He didn't care. The light brush of her lips on his, the promise of more, was affirmation of his discovered love.

Well-oiled metal slid across metal as the bolt eased home. The dense cherry door opened silently on hand-hammered iron strappings that had been forged two hundred years ago.

Rafe glanced over his shoulder and took one last look at the gleaming man on the cross. Silently, he thanked him for bringing Harper into his life and prayed hers filled with the love he felt today.

Hand-in-hand, Rafe and Harper followed the priest while Preacher trailed them down a long whitewashed hall with rough wooden doors evenly spaced along the right side and the sanctuary along their left.

The hallway opened to a large formal garden encompassed by a square of two-story rooms with wide verandas. A tiered fountain at its center begged for silent contemplation.

"Inside, quickly." The nearly gray priest seemed incapable of longer sentences, but more words weren't necessary as his keys once again opened another door, this time to a hotel room.

CHAPTER 25

THERE WAS A COLLECTIVE SIGH ONCE THE DOOR WAS LOCKED.

"This used to be a monastery, but it's now Hotel Dann, one of the nicest places to stay in Popayán." More relaxed, the priest spoke directly to Rafe and Harper. "This room is exclusively used by the church."

"Show them," Preacher ordered.

With a nod, the priest moved to the paprika-painted accent wall and crossed himself before he gently slid the rough charcoal drawing of Christ aside. Beneath it laid a modern palm scanner and numeric keys. "Please join me."

In a room filled with heavy Spanish antiques, the modern electronics seemed out of place, but Rafe and Harper walked over to the panel.

"Senorita, place your hand on the screen then type in six numbers that you'll remember in an emergency." She complied then stepped aside.

"Rafe, you're next." Preacher commanded.

He did as ordered and then slipped the picture back in place.

"Now, let's try this again. Harper, if you would please."

Preacher seemed very familiar with this place, but Rafe wouldn't question anything as long as it got them all out of Colombia.

She swung the picture aside, placed her hand on the pad, and then typed in her six numbers.

The wall moved almost silently. There was enough room for a person to pass through the exposed space. They followed Preacher, who flicked on the lights.

"We're inside the church clock tower." Pointing, he continued, "That door leads to the sanctuary, that one to the street, Calle 4. It was the last street we crossed to reach the church. Those stairs lead to the top of the bell tower, which is also a good sniper position. That's where I'll be when you're ready to leave."

They stepped back into the luxury of the hotel room to find a tray of food on the sturdy old table but no sign of the priest.

"You've been here before," Rafe noted.

"You know I was in seminary before I joined the Navy." Preacher gave Harper a shy grin. "I was going to be a Jesuit priest. I started in Catholic pre-school, did the acolyte thing, went to a private Catholic high school, then Xavier University. I was destined to be a priest, like my uncle. Or so I thought." He paused and stared at the room around him.

"What happened?" Harper broke the silence.

"I did a summer in-service here after college graduation and met Mariah. We were in the same program helping the nuns at the orphanage and in remote medical facilities way up in the mountains. My room was on the top level across the way. Hers was a few doors down." He looked at his feet and smiled. "My uncle gave me some great advice when I left home that summer, 'This is your last chance to live it up before you give it up.' I took his words to heart. After sleeping with Mariah all summer, it was almost impossible to leave her, but I returned to seminary. Within three months, I knew the whole celibacy thing wasn't for me."

"So why the Navy?" Harper asked the question before Rafe could.

"I was raised Jesuit, the warrior priests. They're known as God's Marines for a good reason. I guess service to God and country was engrained in me all my life. I'd sailed since I was a kid, so the Navy seemed like the right choice. Obviously, it was. I'm still in and plan to make it a career."

"I'm glad you knew about this place," Harper told Preacher. "So how long do we have before we can get out of here and on our way home?"

"We'd like to take you out after dark, but with Puracé about to blow, we don't want to waste any time. We're set for thirty minutes after dark." Rafe watched his friend's eyes travel the length of Harper, assessing her with the discernment of a true leader.

"You look tired, Harper, worse for wear. You're safe here, for now. You should try to nap or relax in the tub a while, relieve those weary muscles." Preacher's smile was that of concern, not the least bit lascivious like Rafe's. The thought of all that warm water bubbling around them, soaping her breasts as she leaned against him, running his hands up and down her body until she arched into him…

"The tub is big enough for two." Preacher looked at Rafe and smirked as if he knew what he was thinking.

"Voice of experience?" Rafe chuckled.

"We lived here for three months." What do you think? was left unsaid.

"Well, gentlemen, if you'll excuse me, that tub sounds like the best suggestion I've heard in days." Harper started to unstrap the weapons from her body and lay them on the thick dark table. "Nobody has to tell me twice." She gave Rafe a knowing look.

God, he loved this woman. She was sexy as hell as she rested her foot on a chair rung and ripped the Velcro securing her knife and pistol to her thigh.

Rafe slid his arms around her. "I know you're sore and tired, baby. I'll join you in a few minutes." He kissed her temple.

He'd work up to the big three words. He wasn't sure she was ready to hear them, yet. Besides, telling her for the first time in front of his old friend—who had known Beth and helped him get revenge for her death—wasn't the right place.

Everything felt perfect with Harper in his arms, hers securely around his neck. Harper worked in the part of the world that would forever be in twilight, not totally black, but definitely not in the full light and warmth of day. A place where you had to be as frigid as the situation just to survive. He'd been there, worked there. He knew the toll it had taken on his soul, and he wanted to protect Harper from that deep, dark place. He wanted to bring bright sunshine and heat to her. He wanted to warm her in the fire she stoked within him.

He pulled her tighter against him. They fit effortlessly. She shifted, pressing her warm breasts into his chest. He wanted her. Now. Again. Always. He was hard as steel.

Rafe was aware that they were not alone. He grasped Harper's hips and stepped back. If he kissed her now, he'd lock them both in the bathroom and wouldn't care what Preacher heard through the door.

But his friend had more to tell him or he would have left by now.

"Why don't you go soak while I catch up with Preacher?" He couldn't help himself. He brushed a light kiss over her soft lips. It was a promise. "Give us a few minutes."

Harper grabbed his face and brought his lips back to hers. She opened immediately and took control, delving deep into his mouth with long thrusts of her tongue.

As quickly as it started, she ended it. "Don't be too long." The spark in her whisky-brown eyes held more than possibilities.

When she turned away, he playfully smacked her ass. Over her shoulder, she just grinned before stepping into the bathroom.

Once they heard water running, Preacher said, "I like her."

"Me, too. Fact is, I think I love her." He let the words roll around in his head before he said, "Yes, I love her."

"I can't blame you. She's pretty as can be and smart as hell." At Rafe's questioning look, Preacher continued, "I read her file. SOP, remember? That's one brilliant woman in there. And brave. You should read the shit she and her team of women got into in Iraq and Afghanistan. Fucking Army wanted to test them, to see if they could be as effective as Special Forces, which they were. Their HUMINT was invaluable several times, but I was more impressed with the ingenuity they demonstrated while accomplishing the mission."

That was news to Rafe. He had no idea about her past service and training. But the way she'd handled those tangoes now made sense.

"Rafe, you deserve a good woman," Preacher continued. "Beth's been gone for years. It's time to move on with your life."

All Rafe could do was nod. Needing to quickly change the subject, he asked, "When did you get here?"

"We dropped in last night. We were set for extraction from the compound on the Pacific Coast and in the air before we got the no-go. We were formulating plans for Cali when we were told you were heading west. I made the executive decision to come here since I know Popayán."

"Who's with you, and where are they holed up?" Rafe wanted to have all the details.

Preacher rattled off a list of Spanish names Rafe had never heard before.

"Did you pick every Spanish-speaking guy in Team 4?" Rafe chided.

"No, not everyone." Preacher grinned. "They had to look the part as well as be fluent. I also brought Doc with me, so shut the fuck up."

"Just jerking your chain. I'd do the same thing if I were in your position," Rafe admitted.

"My men have infiltrated the community, and their HUMINT is the reason you're here rather than in enemy hands. Besides, we're going to get you and Harper out of this country"—Preacher looked at his big black military watch—"in the next four hours."

Four hours seemed like an eternity to Rafe but not nearly enough time with Harper.

"I have men in place. You're safe here." Preacher looked around the hotel room before his eyes fell on Rafe. "You look like shit."

Rafe was sure he did because he felt as though he'd just completed a marathon. His friend rose and strode to the window where he peeked through the sliver of light between the thick drapes.

"Problem?" Rafe asked.

"No. I was just checking the street." Preacher slid a well-worn key from his hip pocket on the way to the door and held it out.

Rafe took the room key with a nod.

"I think your little warrior is waiting for you. Why don't you join her or scrub her back…or something? If anyone but me tries to come through that door, shoot to kill. Do you remember our code?" Preacher's hand rested on the door handle.

"Of course." Rafe shot back.

"Get some rest. I'll be back in three hours." His friend was gone, and Rafe was finally alone with Harper. He heard the water turn off.

Perfect timing.

~

Rafe's light blue eyes darkened to the color of a storm at sea when Harper peered around the bathroom door in a haze of mist.

"He's gone." Rafe's husky voice was confirmation. He wanted her.

Rafe rolled his shoulders, muscles rippling under the dark camouflage utilities. She imagined the feel of his hard abs under her hands and how his perfect ass clenched as he pushed into her. As he walked to her, he radiated sex.

She wanted him. Now. Hard. Fast.

Rafe's smile told her he wanted it the same way. The kiss proved it. He took her mouth with a vengeance, forcing hers open, and then thrusting his tongue into her mouth with long, hard, deliberate strokes. She laved her tongue over and around his before she sucked on it.

A low moan of pleasure vibrated in his chest. Yes. He wanted her as much as she wanted him. She thrust her hands into his long, soft curls and pulled his head to her, increasing the pressure of his mouth on hers.

He unfastened the large black buttons on her cammie

shirt and shoved it off her shoulders. He insistently stroked her bare shoulders then ran his hands down her sides. His thumbs smoothed over the curve of her breasts on his way to the bottom of her tank top. Her nipples ached for his mouth.

He left her lips for only a second to jerk her tight tank up and over her head. He placed his hands on her waist and began to unbutton her pants. Her brain caught up, and she fumbled with his buttons before he grunted and pulled away from her. In one smooth movement, both his shirt and black tee were gone, exposing a light dusting of dark chest hair and his mouthwatering torso.

Harper wanted more. She reached for the button on his pants, and he did the same. Their boots took a little longer, but they were both naked in less than a minute. His erection, long and solid, pointed right at her.

He stepped to her and wrapped one arm around her shoulders. But instead of pulling her in for a kiss, his other arm slipped under her legs and picked her up.

"Ack," Harper squeaked. "I'm too big. Put me down."

"With pleasure." Rafe placed her on the bed and slid one knee between her legs as he covered her with his body. He rocked his hips into her while he ravaged her mouth. He placed open-mouthed kisses down her throat on his way to her breasts. When he took her nipple into his mouth and sucked hard, she arched up to him, offering, needing.

"More," was her plea when he rubbed his thumb over the one he'd just left and pulled her other perked nipple into his mouth. He obliged and sucked. Streaks of pleasure ran from her breasts to where the tip of his erection rocked. Every muscle in her body tightened as she strained to reach her peak. She was so close.

"In me, now." Harper knew what she wanted and wasn't

afraid to ask. She was almost ready to beg. She needed him inside her.

He rolled enough to get his hand between their bodies and then slipped talented fingers between her folds, brushing across her swollen nerves. She gasped.

"Not yet," Rafe ordered as he slipped two fingers inside her tight channel. She was wet and ready for him. She rocked her hips against his hand, needing the pressure, teetering on the edge of orgasm.

"Now." She barely got out the word between pants.

"Open your eyes, Harper." He rubbed his wet tip against her, teasing her.

She struggled to obey and forced her eyes open. This wasn't like her. She was always in charge during sex. With Rafe, it was different, so much better. The things he said and did to her made her want him more and more.

"Look at me when I enter you." His words were a growl.

She smiled. His cock was right there, and she was more than ready. She thrust her hips upward and captured him.

His eyes went wide with surprise…and heat.

He grabbed her hips and held them still. "Do you have any idea how hot and tight you are?"

Held captive in his big hands, she acknowledged him by squeezing her inner muscles around him and smiled into his pained face.

He let out a ragged breath. "Christ, you're going to kill me." He closed his eyes and clenched his teeth.

"Uh-uh-uh. Open your eyes, big CIA man," she warned. "If I have to watch, so do you." Then she taunted, "I'm going to watch as you come. I want to see you surrender to me."

He opened his eyes and withdrew.

No, no, no, she almost begged aloud.

Then he readjusted her hips and thrust into her so deeply

she let out a sound, not sure if it was a moan or whimper. He quickly followed it with another thrust and another until she could barely catch a breath as he pounded into her. Her muscles tightened until she was afraid they'd Charlie horse. Then he found the magical spot, and she was back teetering on the edge again. Her eyes began to roll back, and her eyelids sank.

"Oh no you don't. Look at me, Harper."

Her eyes met his. His face was so tight with strain she knew he was on that edge with her.

"Take us both. Take us…now," she whispered and wrapped her legs around his waist.

His next thrust was to the hilt, and she'd given him all she had. He rocked slightly, and that was all it took. Her vision went white, but in those few milliseconds before she lost all sight, she saw the ecstasy on Rafe's face and his total surrender to what she'd given him.

She fell into the pleasure he'd given to her in return.

Damn, they were good together.

CHAPTER 26

Harper slapped at the nightstand in an attempt to hit the snooze button. She could really use another five minutes of sleep.

The ringing persisted. She couldn't find the damn clock.

The fact she had her eyes closed might be the crux of the problem. The ringing continued. Reluctantly, she opened her eyes.

Shit, it was the satellite phone, not the alarm.

Harper rolled away from the hard body next to her and immediately missed Rafe's arms around her.

Grabbing the phone, she pressed the Talk button and said, "Tambini here. Hold on. I'll get Rafe." She rolled back over. Rafe was fully awake and aware as she handed him the phone. He leaned in so she could hear.

"I woke you?" Preacher's voice was crystal clear. "Good. You've rested." Rafe smiled at her and ran a finger down her cheek.

Harper was rested and relaxed. She'd fallen asleep, or maybe she'd never come out of her last orgasmic stupor.

An hour ago, she'd woken alone in the bed, wrapped only

in the soft sheets. Water was running, and Harper figured Rafe was in the shower. She'd considered joining him then decided to roll over and sleep a few more minutes. He'd appeared beside her, picked her up with a strength and ease she'd come to admire, and carried her to the refilled spa. Still locked in his powerful arms, he'd stepped into the foaming tub and sat down with her in his lap. Warm water pulsed over them, massaging the lactic acid out of their tired muscles. She'd laid her head on his chest, and they'd fallen asleep in the tub, legs intertwined, heart-to-heart. When the water had chilled, they'd returned to the antique bed. That time, their lovemaking had been slow and seemed to last forever.

Pulling her brain back to the present, Harper sat up in the bed and surveyed the room for their clothes and equipment. She was fully awake.

"Be ready to move out in ten." Could Preacher really mean they only had ten minutes to get ready? So much for a shower—it would take her that long to dress in all her combat gear.

"We'll be ready." He disconnected the line, and Harper rolled into Rafe's warmth and strength. She wished she could stay there, snug and secure. It was easy to be with him. It was exactly where she belonged.

Fuck. No time to go there. They had to get dressed and get the hell out of Popayán before they were captured or killed by Solis's men or whichever of Narváez's men were stupid enough to follow Pablo. Or some other paramilitary group that was after them for the bounty.

As she stretched out naked next to Rafe in the quiet hotel room, safely wrapped in his arms, the world seemed so far removed.

"We only have ten minutes to get ready," she reminded him. He took her hand and placed it on his very hard erection.

"I'm ready now." Rafe smiled at her with a half-lidded, half-asleep look that sent electricity from her overactive brain to her toes. Every inch of her body tingled. She felt herself dampen with anticipation and wanted him inside her again. This insatiable need, one that only he could fill, was new to her. She'd always enjoyed sex, but with Rafe she also relished the times he merely held her, like in the spa. She felt safe with him, protected, which was weird. She didn't need a man to protect her. No, she didn't need a man period, but she wanted the one who lay gloriously bare beside her.

They had to get going. The SEAL team was probably moving into position while she was considering jumping on Rafe's offer.

"Sorry, Rafe. Not enough time." She wondered how much time she and Rafe had left together. She removed her hand from his cock, but she couldn't resist a tight squeeze first and a long stroke of his length. At his gasp, she ran her fingers over him again. She loved hearing proof of the control she had over this man.

She smacked his bare ass and jumped out of bed before he could pull her under him for another ride. His face promised retaliation. She looked forward to it.

They gathered clothes, dressed, and then checked their equipment with the speed of many years of practice.

Rafe peered at the street through the small slit between the drapes covering the window while she checked her guns.

Two rapid knocks followed by a slap on the door then the sound of a key in the lock sent both Rafe and Harper to their holstered weapons. Rafe quietly slid the deadbolt and positioned himself behind the door.

"It's Preacher," he called as the door cracked open. Neither relaxed their shooter's stance until the man was in the room and they were sure he was alone. At his side, he casually carried a solid-stock, custom-made sniper rifle with a Swarovski scope. Impressive. Definitely not Navy issue. In his other hand, he held two bulletproof vests.

"No change in plans, but there are some details you need to know." Preacher didn't look happy when he handed her the smaller of the two vests. "There's a million dollar bounty on your head. From there it gets confusing. We know Solis's men want you both dead or alive. There's another group running around out there who wants Rafe alive and Harper, you're not even mentioned."

Harper couldn't withhold the shudder that ran through her body. Rafe put a protecting arm around her and pulled her close. His solid body was comforting but damn…dead or alive. The words bounced around as her brain tried to grasp the concept.

"Bet that came from Pablo," Rafe offered.

At the mention of the name, Preacher piped in, "Yes, that's the guy who is after Rafe and doesn't give a shit about Harper."

Rafe shook his head. "That idiot doesn't realize how valuable Harper is. He just wants revenge because Carlos is dead."

"I'm the one who killed him," Harper announced. "Not you."

The well-armed SEAL continued. "Someone knew about Narváez's plans, and those assholes are offering a different million on delivery of Harper alive, plus a bounty on anyone who hurts or kills you. Those folks either don't know or don't care about Rafe."

Rafe stepped in front of her and lifted her chin. "We've got you, babe. I won't let anything happen to you. I promise." His arms encased her and held her tight as he rocked her gently.

Harper knew the hug was as much for him as it was for her. She'd faced danger before and led her team to safety every time. She could do this. She would do this.

As she'd been trained, she took a deep breath then another, finding her calm. She focused on the situation and what needed to be done. When she stepped back from Rafe's arms, she was in mission mode. She strapped the black vest over her shirt. It was a little large for her, so she tightened it as much as possible.

"There's more. Let's hear it." She held Preacher's gaze.

He nodded. His face relaxed, just a little. He seemed satisfied with her resolve. He reached into one of the many pockets of his utilities and extracted two comm units. As she and Rafe screwed them into their ears, Preacher said, "They're waiting for you, just outside that door."

He quickly added, "But my men are there, too."

Rafe stripped off his shirt and shrugged into the vest. The protective sections didn't reach around his sides as they should but fortunately the webbed straps were long enough.

"Sorry, man," Preacher apologized, "Most of my guys wear a medium. Be glad I was able to secure a large from the ship."

The thought of a ship somewhere close, waiting for them, made Harper's hope soar. She'd soon be headed home.

"No problem," Rafe said, sliding back into his night camouflage shirt. "This is better than those useless flack jackets they gave us on our first mission into Guatemala."

Preacher chuckled. "Those suckers were used in Vietnam before I was born." He turned his attention to Harper. "You ready?"

"As ready as I'll ever be." She gave him a confident smile. She was ready.

"I'll take my position in the top of the tower." Preacher pointed upward. "You and Harper need to stay together."

"May God be with you." He crossed himself and walked to the hidden door.

"And also with you," Rafe said in rote response.

Mid-step he stopped and slowly looked over his shoulder. "Bless you, my child."

Rafe smiled at him. "I've missed my brother-in-arms."

Preacher swung the picture aside, palmed the plate, and punched in numbers, and then he disappeared through the opened wall. They'd do the same when ordered.

Over their headsets, they heard someone say, "This fucking place is crawling with goddamn tangos."

"Ain't that the truth," another agreed.

"Quit bitching like a bunch of little girls and put one in your crosshairs," Preacher said. "Call it."

As each man designated his target, Rafe laughed out loud. "Damn, I've missed this."

"Yeah, we love you, too." Preacher's sarcastic voice was low, but the line was as clear as glass. "Don't get mushy on me. We're far from out of here."

Harper knew all too well what they faced.

"They want this woman pretty bad," one SEAL commented.

Preacher spoke with unwavering assurance. "They can't have her. She's coming home with us."

That touched Harper's heart, which today seemed open to so much. She liked Preacher's possessiveness, his protective demeanor.

Possessive. Protective. She could use those same words to describe what she liked about Rafe. Only, there was a huge difference. To Preacher, she was a job. She wasn't sure what she was to Rafe. Initially she'd been his job, but she was sure her feelings had gone far beyond that. She felt Rafe all the way to her heart. It felt right to her. What she wasn't sure of was what Rafe felt for her, beyond sex of course.

"Tangos covered?" Preacher asked.

A male chorus of "Aye, sir," sang in her ear. She took a deep breath. This was it.

"What's the plan?" Harper asked, pulling her mind away from self-evaluation and to the palm scanner.

Preacher instructed, "When you come out the tower door, head east. Cross the street and there's an alley about thirty feet down. There's a black Rover waiting there. The driver is expecting you. We've got you covered. Wait for my count. There are civilians in the square in front of the church."

Harper placed her palm on the scanner and punched in her numbers. The door slid open quietly, and she and Rafe slipped into the shadow beneath the stairs at the bottom of the colonial bell tower.

It seemed like hours had passed before Preacher broke the silence.

In truth, it had only been two minutes. Harper hated this part, waiting, anticipating. That summed up her whole job in the Army, hours of waiting interrupted by moments of sheer adrenaline and terror. She thought she'd never be placed in this kind of situation again when she'd joined the ATF team. But here we go, again.

"On my count." Preacher began to count down. "Three, two, one. Go."

Rafe pushed open the door to the outside and in two long strides plastered himself against the far wall, hidden in the shadows of the centuries-old covered walkway. Harper was right behind him.

Suddenly, the report from several high-powered rifles echoed in the empty small square in front of them. Out of instinct and training, Harper crouched to give them a smaller target. Pistol in hand, she tapped Rafe twice on the back, the signal to move.

Sun shone through the Spanish arches, leaving Rafe and Harper exposed in the bright semi-circles for two steps before they fell back into the shadows. Rafe made it through. Her turn. As Harper's boot landed on the sunny concrete, it exploded mere inches behind her heel. Small shards of old cement flew in every direction, nicking her calf as she leaped into shadow.

Rafe waited in the darkness between the arches. He grabbed her shoulders when she crouched and rubbed her leg.

"Were you hit? Are you all right?" He looked more than merely concerned, on the verge of anger.

"I'm fine. Just a sting from flying debris."

He hastily pulled her to him and kissed her temple. Just as fast, he let go of her. She scanned the area. From the depths of the darkened walkway, she couldn't tell the origin of the shots. She would depend on the SEAL team to take out the shooter.

"We'll cross the next one separately," Rafe told her.

"No. Together." Preacher's voice came over the comm unit. "We got him. Move now."

They ran through the next two lighted patches and hunkered down at the corner of the building.

Rafe quickly peeked around the edge. "There's a tango partially protected in a doorway about fifteen feet down from us with a machine gun pointed our way," he reported.

"He's mine," Preacher said.

Rafe peeked again. He leaned in, close to Harper's mouth, eyes intent on hers. He was going to kiss her. Her stomach jumped in anticipation.

What the hell was that? The closeness of a man had never done that before.

Rafe lightly brushed his lips across hers. She felt his touch drop from her lips to her heart.

The fact he could do that to her in the middle of a gunfight pissed her off. She'd allowed him too much control.

Get your head in the game, Harper.

Rafe took another quick peek, turned back to her, and nodded. They exploded like sprinters out of the blocks, running for their lives as bullets flew all around them. They zigzagged, separated by several feet, and varied their gait as they'd been trained to avoid getting shot.

A shot flew past her from behind, and she heard boots slap too close.

"I don't have a clear shot," Preacher said, his voice calm through her comm unit.

"I can't chance it," was heard from another.

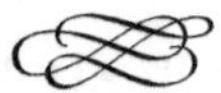

CHAPTER 27

Harper knew what she had to do.

She planted her next step, spun around, and dropped to one knee for a more stable shooting stance. She brought the pistol up. The shooting mantra began as time slowed for her.

Identify. The tango's left arm pumped in time with his long strides. He struggled to hold the pistol in his right hand steady, his arm out straight, the gun pointed at her.

Target.

Like a movie in slow motion, the ingrained training and muscle memory took over. Breathe. Relax. Aim. Sight. Squeeze.

She felt the recoil of the first shot as the barrel of the gun lifted. She leveled the gun and began the embedded BRASS again. She knew she'd shot him in the chest. It was a clean shot to the heart, but he'd only staggered. He was a big son of a bitch. Then she noticed the body armor. No problem. Her next two shots were to the head.

Harper didn't bother to watch him fall. She was up and running.

Rafe was already to the alley. When her boot hit the

pavement, she lost her balance, and her foot rolled to the side. Before she could catch her equilibrium, she was falling. On her way to the street, everything moved.

The earth roared. It sounded like a freight train was inches away. The ground shook as she attempted a skydiver's landing roll in the middle of the street. Her calf, thigh, hip, and shoulder hit unforgiving asphalt. She used the momentum and rolled across her back and onto hands and knees. The earth continued to agitate.

She looked up at Rafe and screamed from the bottom of her lungs.

Bricks pelted him as he stood frozen, watching her from between buildings so close together they'd scrape car mirrors if the driver wasn't extremely careful. The world moved in dizzying waves.

Harper wasn't sure if it was from her fall or the earthquake.

All shooting had stopped.

Civilians screamed and spoke rapid Spanish as they ran into the street, emptying homes that fell into rubble even as she tried to stand.

Harper couldn't keep up with their words. Translating took a few seconds. Time she didn't have. Then she caught the same word in several different voices. Puracé.

Was the volcano erupting?

Buildings undulated as though they were alive and desperately trying to catch their balance. Whole walls of white brick and block rolled while the earth itself roared deafeningly, drowning her screams.

"Move," she begged Rafe.

He looked up as falling white bricks hailed down. He disappeared into the alley.

Harper's world crashed. The entire wall on Rafe's left

crumbled like a surfer's dream wave, curling over the top of him, enveloping him inside nature's powerful fist.

"No!" Her scream was just another in the chorus of panic.

No. I can't lose him. Not now. They'd just found each other. She'd just found…whatever it was didn't matter. Only Rafe was important.

On her feet and ignoring everything around her, she raced toward where she'd last seen him. Dodging children who stood in the middle of the street, jaws open in awe, she ignored the pain in her ankle. She almost plowed down an elderly woman with a cane who'd emerged from a weather-roughened doorway.

Impatient, Harper scooped up the aged lady and placed her in the street.

At the entrance to the alley, patches of concrete clung to the sides of broken bricks, too weak to hold onto each other when its foundation rocked. The pile came to her waist. Harper planted her feet, bent her knees to absorb any more ground movement, and reached for the first brick. She tossed it aside and grabbed for more. Her hands moved with blurring speed. Getting to Rafe was her only thought.

She had to find him. If she hurried, he'd have a better chance of survival. SEALs always had a medic on the team with magic fingers for extracting bullets or neatly sewing up cuts and gashes. She'd seen their work before in the desert.

Rafe would head home with them. With her. She picked up another brick in each hand and tossed them aside.

They'd go to her condo in D.C., and she'd take care of him for as long as it took. She had vacation time coming. She'd take it. If anyone at USSOCOM gave her any grief, they could go to hell. The pile of bricks to the other side of her grew, as did her determination to find him alive.

"I saw what happened." Harper glanced up into the now-familiar face of Preacher. Her heart leapt with thanks at the sight of his dust-covered cammies and the rifle slung across his back. She nodded at him, but her hands continued their tossing motion. A fist had grabbed her throat from the inside, so speech wasn't possible. Rafe. She had to get to him. She had to save him.

Oh God, please let him be alive.

The silent prayer seemed appropriate as she glimpsed the bowed head of Rafe's friend, code name Preacher, who concentrated on grabbing and throwing bricks as fast as she. As if he'd heard her prayer, he looked at her with an encouraging smile.

Olive-colored hands appeared beside her, and bricks disappeared.

"What a clusterfuck," the SEAL declared. "You must be Harper. Call me Doc. I'd shake, but my hands are busy trying to get to my patient." After a few seconds, he added, "Rafe was my first CO when I joined the Teams. He's one of the good guys."

Damn. These were good men. After all these years, their bond with Rafe was still there. They were his friends, his teammates, his family. Family. That was the way she felt about Rafe. She was now part of his family. He was part of her family. No, not exactly. He was part of her.

Brick in hand, she stopped. She looked at it, not seeing its white painted side or the crumbling concrete. She loved Rafe as much as she loved her own teammates, as much as she'd loved her mother, just different. She smiled at those differences.

Large hands grabbed her face and forced it up.

"Let me look at you." Doc was in medic mode. He

covered Harper's eyes with his hand then quickly pulled it away.

"Eyes equal and reactive. No concussion." His hands groped through her hair, gently testing her scalp.

Harper had been through this routine many times and realized what Doc was doing. It wasn't her head that had been impacted. It was her heart. She batted away his hands.

"I'm fine." Harper smiled. "I'm better than fine." She was in love, and the love of her life was buried under the debris in front of her. She returned to the pile with a vengeance.

"Sure you're okay?" Preacher asked as he tossed two bricks to the side.

"Yeah," Harper choked out. Dust filled the air, burned her eyes, and clogged her nose. "I'll be a whole lot better once we reach Rafe."

Preacher spoke quietly into his comm. "Perimeter check."

A Spanish-accented man replied, "Secure."

"Status," Preacher demanded.

"Chaos in the street behind you. The tangos weren't focused on their mission. Typical. Most have disappeared. If they're local, I'd bet they went to check on their families. How much longer?"

"Unknown." Preacher's answer disturbed Harper. They had no idea what shape Rafe would be in when they got to him. Broken bones? Concussion?

Harper couldn't think about that right now. They had to get to him first.

Although it seemed as if she'd been digging for hours, it had been only a few minutes. Her biceps were burning from the repetitive motions. The pile was disappearing quickly with all the help. They'd moved a few feet into the alley.

Doc had picked up a large chunk and turned to throw it onto the pile at the end of the alley. Harper reached for the next piece and saw the black outline of a battered boot. She kneeled and threw off bricks. A calf. His leg was bent as if he'd curled up into a ball.

Preacher was right beside her. When Harper turned and tossed the next brick, she saw Doc pulling his stethoscope out of his backpack.

He had to be alive. He had to be. She couldn't lose him now.

On their knees, she and Preacher handed pieces to Doc, who handed them off to someone else. Others had joined in their rescue.

Harper lifted another large piece and found battered metal. Fast as their hands could move, she and Preacher passed debris to others. Rafe had tried to cover himself with a trash can lid, but hadn't completely succeeded.

Gashed and dented stainless steel covered his head and shoulders. When Harper lifted the circular metal, Rafe's hand was still clenched around the handle. His arm moved up with the lid.

He's alive.

Just as relief began to wash over her, his hand slid out of the hole and fell lifelessly next to his hip. He'd curled as tightly as his large frame would allow against the wall of one of the few buildings left standing whole.

Rivers of blood formed paths on either side of his off-center nose and drew red lines across his angular face. His wavy dark hair was matted with drying blood. Eyes closed, he lay so still, limp. Nothing moved, not even his chest. He wasn't breathing.

He was dead.

She knew it in her mind, but her heart wouldn't let her believe it.

Tears ran down Harper's dirty face. She couldn't catch

her breath. She sat frozen on her knees, hands listlessly at her sides. She had no strength left to lift them. She wanted to touch him, but she was afraid to know the truth. Afraid to know her greatest fear was real.

"Let me in there, goddamn it." Doc bulldozed his way past Harper. "Do something with her," Doc said over his shoulder to Preacher.

Doc kneeled next to Rafe's body, blocking Harper's view.

Preacher gripped her shaking shoulders and stood her up, out of the way. She could now see Rafe. He lay motionless amidst the broken debris.

Rafe was dead.

She couldn't breathe.

She was racked with pain from her head to her aching feet, but nothing matched the hole where her heart had just been ripped out.

Her entire body shook with uncontrolled adrenalin, exhaustion, and fear.

Preacher pulled her into a hug before her legs gave out. The words he said were incoherent mumblings, unable to surpass the screams in her mind.

Harper never took her focus off Rafe.

"Thready, but I've got a pulse." Doc's words were like water thrown on the raging fire that had been destroying Harper's heart. She didn't know love could hurt this much or that losing the man she loved could destroy her in the process.

That wasn't going to happen.

He was alive.

She let out a breath she didn't know she'd been holding. Probably why she couldn't catch her breath a minute ago.

You have to let it out in order to breathe in.

She forced in the next breath and huffed it out.

Breathe. Just keep breathing. Doc will take care of him.

"Heartbeat is very weak," Doc told anyone who was listening, stethoscope still in his ears. "Help me lay him flat."

Harper withdrew from Preacher's embrace and both assisted in carefully moving Rafe. She didn't want him to feel any pain. He could have broken bones or internal injuries.

Stretched out at the end of the alley, Rafe finally moaned and moved his head.

"He's coming around." Doc pulled a small tablet from his backpack then placed a cuff on Rafe's bicep that would transmit all his vitals to the miniature computer. He clipped a small device on his index finger and red numbers flashed onto the LED screen.

When Doc began unbuttoning Rafe's shirt from the top, Harper quickly started at the opposite end. Together, they removed his Kevlar vest then tore his T-shirt down the middle.

Doc placed five quarter-sized patches around his torso then touched a button to watch Rafe's heart in 3-D. With the swipe of his fingers, he rotated the picture to inspect it on all sides.

"Looks good," Doc announced.

Thank God. Rafe was going to be all right. She could see on the monitor that his heart was beating steadily. A heart she now considered hers.

"Harper, talk to him. Bring him out slow."

Harper knew this routine. When a warrior was knocked out during battle, he'd often come back to reality fighting, literally, as if no time had passed and he was still in the dangerous situation that had knocked him out. Getting punched was not high on her list of things to do right now, so she laid her hand on his chest, careful of the transmission pads, and leaned close to his ear.

"Rafe, come back to me." Out of the corner of her eye, she watched Preacher and Doc exchange a raised brow. Fuck them. She didn't care if they knew she'd fallen in love with Rafe. Hell, if he woke up, she'd scream her love for him from the bell tower—after she told him of course.

His hand moved and covered hers. He grunted at the exertion.

Harper placed a kiss next to his ear. "Rafe, you're safe now. You're with me, but you're hurt."

He tightened his hand on hers.

"He understands," she told the men.

"Pull him out further," Doc ordered. "I need to know if he's in pain anywhere other than the motherfucking headache he's got to have. We need him to wake up and stay lucid."

His hand had gone slack but rested over hers.

"Rafe, I need you to wake up. You're safe. I'm right here. You have a head injury, probably a concussion. Wake up, Rafe."

He took a ragged breath. He was forcing himself back to her.

Just as hope began to build, he slipped back into unconsciousness. His hand slid to his side.

"Well, fuck me to tears." Doc caught himself and looked contrite when his eyes met Harper's. "Pardon me, ma'am." He quickly looked back down and tended to Rafe's many wounds, cleaning and inspecting at the same time.

"We need to move him," Preacher announced. "I'd rather he was awake, but we're not safe here."

Someone handed Preacher a solar blanket. Rather than cover him with it, he laid it out next to Rafe. "Two more sets of hands, lefties if we have them," he ordered into his headset.

Without words, they carefully lifted Rafe onto the blanket and centered him.

"Try again while we wait for the others," Doc suggested.

Harper did as ordered. What could she say to wake him? Wake up now, or I'll never have sex with you again. No. He'd know that was a lie. She'd have sex with him as soon as he was well enough.

She looked the length of his still body, and her heart ached. His face was covered in dust-caked blood, his utilities torn, revealing scraped skin, especially at the knees, which were raw. She'd thought she lost him, and now she still had a chance at something new with him. When she kneeled this time, she knew what she had to say.

Her lips only a fraction of an inch from his ear, she whispered, "Rafe, wake up so I can see your eyes. I need to see them when I tell you that…I love you."

Rafe took a deeper breath then another, even deeper. His shoulders moved, and his lips twitched. His hand came to his face and followed its sharp angles to Harper's cheek. She watched his herculean effort as he opened his eyes.

"Again," he croaked out as sea blue eyes stared into hers.

She couldn't hold back her smile.

Male hands grabbed her shoulders from behind and quickly pulled her away to a standing position.

"Harper, front left corner." Preacher's command wasn't to be ignored.

But Harper wanted to finish what she'd started. Rafe was awake. She'd said the words, and she'd meant them for the first time in her life. She'd never said those words to a man before. She'd never felt this way before.

Resigned, she took her place, twisted the corner of the blanket, wrapped it around her hand, and fisted. Her gun slipped into place, and she was mission-oriented once again, on alert.

"Rafe. Look at me," Doc ordered. "Stay with me, man. We're going to move you now. I need you to be aware of every pain so I can treat them when we get you into the vehicle. Do you understand?"

Whether it was a grunt or a croak Harper couldn't say, but it was acknowledgement.

"On my count." In unison, everyone lifted the blanket with Rafe nestled atop. An SUV pulled up to the street in front of them.

Harper noted they were surrounded by armed guards, one of whom opened the back of the vehicle before he took up a defensive position. They slid Rafe into the back, and she climbed in next to him. Doc kneeled across from her doing his medic thing, speaking to Rafe who answered in a gravelly voice.

Gunfire broke out in the street.

Harper and Doc threw themselves over Rafe's body. The back door slammed shut to the renewed screams of the civilians diving for cover.

Bullets hit the windows, creating chrysanthemum patterns, but it didn't shatter. She heard return fire from all around her.

Harper wondered where they'd found a bullet-resistant truck. Deep down, it didn't matter. She and Rafe were together, headed to safety. His very capable friend and former teammate was caring for Rafe's wounds.

The side doors opened, and several SEALs jumped in, dragging in the smell of gunpowder. Small white clouds wisped from the end of their submachine gun barrels.

The Rover moved forward, climbing over thick debris. Harper was thankful for the high suspension so they could make their escape. She ignored their direction and the damaged scenery and concentrated on helping Doc as he worked on Rafe.

CHAPTER 28

Fuckin' A, his head hurt. Rafe's right leg felt as if a million little pins poked him with every bounce of the Rover. He wished he had moved faster in that alley. He hadn't been able to pull his whole leg under the trash can lid before the world crashed in on him.

He recognized their location as soon as he'd sat up. Doc told him he had a concussion, a broken rib, a few bone bruises on his leg, and lots of soft tissue injuries, the worst in his right shoulder.

No shit. He felt every one of them.

Still, none of his external injuries could match the pain he felt inside. He'd heard Harper's words. He was sure it wasn't a dream. She'd said she loved him. That should be good news, but the past thirty minutes had proven to him what he'd known all along. This life, in the shadow world filled with life-and-death danger, was hers. She'd admitted she loved the adrenaline rush. It was her job, and she loved it.

He wanted out. Out of the darkness of the underworld. Away from flying bullets. Away from fearing for his life. He wanted to be normal again.

Rafe wanted a life like the one his parents had found when they escaped to the United States. They'd known this world. They had lived in fear for many years before leaving Colombia and making a wonderful life for him and his sisters in their new country.

He was now headed home to the good ole U.S.A. He would quit the CIA and find a job. He knew getting over his love for Harper—and damn it, he loved her—wouldn't be easy, but he'd do it.

He'd have to.

She wasn't the right woman for him. He refused to have darkness in his home. He wanted a family, a wife, children, even a damn dog. He wanted a job that didn't follow him home. He'd lived his job, day and night, for five years now. He was tired of being on alert every minute. He was just plain tired.

Harper held his hand and looked at him with those big almond-shaped eyes. She was so damn beautiful. He wanted to touch her, hold her, protect her from all the bad shit in the world.

But they didn't want the same things for their lives. She wanted this world.

He gazed at the webbed glass where the bullets had been stopped.

No. His participation in this world stopped here. He was going home where he'd build a new life in the light of freedom and forget all about Colombia, Iraq, Afghanistan, and any other Third World shithole he'd seen in the past ten years.

It would be best if he ignored the words she'd said. He'd pretend he never heard them. They'd get on the rescue plane and fly out of here, and it would all end. Here and now.

Yeah, they'd had some pretty great sex—okay, the best

sex of his life—and he'd give Harper her due. She was an amazing woman. Just not the right woman for the rest of his life.

Rafe figured the plane would take them to a ship and he and Harper would go their separate ways. Ships were big, and he could avoid her. They'd be back home soon, and he'd never see her again.

He slid his hand from her grasp and steadied himself on the bumpy road. He closed his eyes to avoid seeing the hurt on her face, the disappointment in those big brown eyes of hers.

No one spoke as the last traces of daylight turned the world from soft gray to black.

The headlights speared into the night as they stopped in front of an airport Rafe knew well. He'd flown Carlos out of there several times before, less so in the past two years. Maybe it was the shadows cast by the sliver of moon, but the concrete block terminal didn't look right. He squinted in an attempt to merge the two buildings into one.

Fuck. He had double vision. He held up two fingers in front of his face. Yep. Four digits. No wonder his stomach had rolled with every bump.

"Osprey is five minutes out," Preacher announced. "Kill the lights."

The SEAL team leader turned and asked, "Everyone all right back there?"

Harper's voice was barely audible and clipped. "Fine."

"Yeah, fucking wonderful." Rafe's voice was as raw as his nerves.

"Doc?" Preacher asked. The medic gave a run-down of Rafe's condition.

"Add double vision to that list," Rafe said.

"Shit," was Doc's response.

"Osprey in two minutes," another SEAL announced.

"Move out," Preacher ordered then turned to Rafe. "Can you walk?"

Rafe had decided he was going to walk away from this vehicle on his own. He'd been a Navy SEAL, one of them. Then he'd been Segundo to one of the most powerful capos in Colombia. He was tougher than any lugartenientes in this God-forsaken country. He would show no pain.

Rafe took a deep breath, and Christ if that didn't hurt. Broken rib, idiot. Shallow breaths. He gingerly slid out the back of the Rover without making eye contact with Harper.

"Take it easy," Doc warned him.

He shook off Harper's hand on his elbow. "I'm fine. A few bumps and bruises. I've had worse." He straightened and had to hold in the gasp from the broken rib. His vest hadn't protected the right side of his torso enough when a brick found its way between the Velcro straps. That one was going to hurt for weeks.

Thank God the headache would go away within a day or so, but it was the damn double vision that threw him off. He lifted his hand to rake fingers through his hair but touched the bandage that wrapped his head and blood-matted hair. Head wounds bled like a son of a bitch. He felt the dry blood crackle on his face as he plastered on a fierce attitude. He'd feel much better after a shower on the ship.

"What can I do to help you?" Harper's voice was pensive and right beside him as he made his way to the uneven runway.

"Stay the fuck away from me." Rafe knew his words were harsh, but it was what he had to do. It had to end, and now was as good a time as any. "It's over, Harper. Get it through that pretty little head of yours. It was fun, and you were one of the finest fucks I've ever had...but we're done." He slid a glance her way as he diligently stepped over rough ground, making his way toward the point where a SEAL had popped a white phosphorous grenade to designate the landing zone.

The bright light reflected in the tears that gathered in her eyes. Damn, he was a douche bag. But he had to do it. Like a Band-Aid, he'd ripped it off fast.

Her head turned as she looked around at the SEALs, but she remained at his side ready to catch him if he fell. Yeah, he knew he'd said it loud enough so they all heard.

"Harper, with me," Preacher called from twenty yards in front of them.

"Gladly." She looked at Rafe with indescribable pain then jogged toward Preacher, who was busy with his team.

As she trotted past the corner of the terminal, a shadow emerged.

"Com—"

It wasn't a complete syllable, but Rafe knew it was Harper. His head popped up from his concentration on the ground. His brain bounced within his head, and nausea crashed over him. He closed his eyes until the world stopped rocking.

When he opened them, every muscle in his body froze.

He couldn't see even one Harper, let alone two.

With one sweep he took in the scene, attempting to filter out the dual images. All the SEALs had weapons at their shoulders or in their hands, pointed at the terminal.

He reached for his weapon, but his shoulder protested loudly. There was no way he could hold a gun up and peer down the sights. He managed to shift the gun to his left hand, but he wasn't a very good shot that way. Hell, he couldn't even align the sights with the fucking double vision.

"Anyone got a shot?" Preacher's voice came over his headset. Until that moment, Rafe had forgotten it was still in his ear. *Shit. Every man here heard my tirade berating Harper, loudly.*

"Negative," sang in a multitude of tense male voices.

As Rafe and Doc approached the corner, Doc held him back and shook his head. He signaled that he would take a look. Rafe's Alpha leader inner-self roared, but then he realized that he was looking at two Docs and acquiesced.

After a quick peek, Doc whispered, "They have Harper."

No, no, no. The alive or dead bounty bounced from his brain to his heart.

Doc signaled for them to move through the shadows to the right to give the SEALs a safe shot.

From behind a crate, Rafe saw a man holding Harper. Her arms were pinned to her sides, his pistol to her temple. The position looked very familiar. That was the way his men had captured her, the way Harper had looked the first time he'd seen her. Except it had been his men before, and he'd known they wouldn't kill her. These men might not hesitate.

Harper wore the same defiant expression now as she had then. And, damn, there it was. That brave face he'd come to love.

Yes, love.

"Try to stop us, and I'll kill her," the captor yelled.

Rafe understood those words all too well. The man started to walk back toward a van, where two machine gun barrels jutted from open doors.

He watched Harper's eyes as she courageously let the man pull her along.

"No," Rafe yelled, unable to stop himself.

Her head snapped to him, and their eyes held. She gave him a small grimace, as if she, too, was remembering a gun to the head at an airport. She closed her eyes and took a deep breath.

After Harper's eyes met his again, she glanced to the ground then back to him. She repeated the movement.

"You do that…and you'll be dead before she hits the ground," Rafe taunted the man…and answered Harper's question.

"Be ready to shoot," Rafe told the SEALs though his comm unit. "She's going to give you an opportunity to take him out."

Preacher quickly gave instructions to take out the guerillas in the van. "Rafe, my two best snipers have him in the cross hairs." Except her head is in the way, was left out.

Rafe had to trust Harper's life to the SEALs. They knew what to do and were the best trained in the world.

"I won't let you take her," Rafe warned loudly enough for everyone in the area to hear.

Harper went limp in the man's arms. Her sudden floppy weight forced him off balance. She slumped forward, away from his head.

In the next instant, the man flew backward several feet. Shots seemed to come from every direction.

Two men fell out of the van and hit the asphalt.

Rafe immediately scanned the surrounding area, watching for movement of any kind.

Then there was silence.

No one spoke. No one moved.

Harper lay in a heap, face down, hands over her head, next to the feet of the man who'd held her captive mere seconds ago.

A SEAL approached the van, knees bent, gun out in front, leading his quick, methodical search of the vehicle. "Clear," he announced as he bent to check for pulses on the men who had fallen from the van. The hole in the middle of each forehead told the story.

"Clear," another said and stepped into the light at the opposite end of the runway. "I got the two over here before I took out my guy in the van."

Rafe stared at the pile of woman that was Harper Tambini. He couldn't take his eyes off her, but his feet were frozen to the ground.

Move, damn it, he ordered them, but like his heart, they were afraid of what he'd find.

No, she couldn't be hurt…or worse. He couldn't bring his mind to even consider…worse.

Harper stood up and shook like a wet dog. "Damn. Do I have brains or guts on me?" She twisted to inspect her arms as she ran her hands all over her shaking body.

Rafe didn't know when he'd started to run, but the next thing he knew, he was in front of her. He shoved his hands into her soft hair and pulled her face to his lips. He felt the tremors deep within her.

"Thank. God. You're. All. Right." He kissed her between each word, reassuring himself she was there and in his arms again. He tucked her head under his chin and squeezed her tightly. He never wanted to let her go.

Harper almost didn't hear Rafe's words in the overwhelming noise as the aircraft descended. The Osprey was in vertical mode so it could drop nearly straight down onto the buckled runway. It sounded like a helicopter rather than a plane and kicked up debris that sandblasted them.

She stood frozen, surrounded by Rafe as he kissed her face, her lips. But Harper couldn't kiss him back. His words repeatedly drove a knife into her heart. It's over. Over. Over. We're done. Done. Over. Each time she remembered his words, the way he'd spat them at her just minutes ago, she wanted to cry. She'd been a fool.

For a few minutes there, while the sicario held a gun to her head, she'd wished that he'd just shoot her and put her out of her misery, a long-term solution to a short-term problem. And, yes, Rafe Silva was a short-term problem.

Over. Done. Her heart ached. She was in love with this ass. But he'd said she'd been the finest fuck he'd ever had. Well, good. Maybe when he was cold and alone at night he'd remember that part of their relationship. But a man like Rafe would never be cold or alone. He was so good-looking in his rugged way. He could find a woman anywhere. Hell, he'd found her in this horrible country, and she'd fallen right into bed with him. What an idiot she'd been to believe he might actually fall in love with her.

Harper was now sure that the spark she'd felt had been nothing more than adrenalin or the post-adrenalin spike for reproduction.

"Oh, babe, I thought I'd lost you," Rafe told her as he kissed her cheeks.

Harper took a deep breath and steeled her resolve. She yelled over the dat dat dat of the Osprey's rotors, "You have."

She took a shaky step backward, out of Rafe's arms, just as Preacher materialized at her side. She was shuddering all over and couldn't make it stop. The worst part was Harper wasn't sure if it was from the kidnap scene that had played out differently minutes ago from what it had four days earlier, or if it was because of the man who'd rejected her love. At this moment, all she knew for sure was that she was broken: body, heart, and soul.

Preacher slid an arm around her and spoke close to her ear. "Come on. Our ride's here." He pulled back and gently grasped her chin, turning her face toward his. His eyes searched her face then held her gaze. "You're shaking. Can you walk?"

"I'm fine." Harper stood up straight and took a deep breath. She glared at Rafe. "I can't wait to leave everything here behind me," she yelled so he'd be sure to hear her every word.

"Take care of him," Preacher ordered Doc, who'd appeared through the dust and stood next to Rafe.

With his arm still around her shoulders, Preacher guided her to the Osprey. She heard him grumble, "Fuckhead."

Preacher pointed to one of the jump seats that lined the sides of the plane. She all but fell into the webbing and worked the familiar harness straps into place.

Light from the fading white phosphorous grenade silhouetted Rafe as he hobbled up the ramp, Doc at his side.

It had been a long time since Harper had been inside a military aircraft. She'd jumped out of enough airplanes and been picked up by several types of helicopters that she was content with her surroundings.

Lately, she'd been flying around in the deluxe comfort of the corporate-style Cessna jet with its butter-soft leather seats that reclined for in-flight naps. No chance of that in these utilitarian seats.

The gray interior of the Osprey lacked the covered cabling and hoses that screeched and hissed as it gained altitude and rotated from chopper-like mode into an airplane form.

Preacher checked each man on his team. He'd thankfully seated Rafe on the opposite wall. She wasn't sure what she would have done had Rafe sat beside her. She didn't want to see him or speak to him right now. Never would be too soon.

Over. Done. She shivered as his cold, hard words coursed through her body. Crossing her arms over her breasts, she huddled into herself. With her head lowered, her hair curtained her face. She refused to look across the hold area to where Doc tended to Rafe and a SEAL who'd been hurt.

Without the thick insulation of commercial aircraft, the space grew cold as their altitude increased, so Harper hunkered down even more.

Dusty boots appeared on the floor in front of her. She prayed it wasn't Rafe. She couldn't handle him right now. But when the man sat on his heels, she saw it was Preacher. Neither spoke. It would be fruitless with the Rolls Royce engines screaming just beyond the skin of the aircraft. He slowly lifted her chin and gazed at her. She managed a small smile.

"You okay?" he mouthed.

No, not really. But she was a big girl, and she'd get over Rafe. Or maybe he wanted to be sure she hadn't been hurt by the man who had held her captive just before liftoff. There was that little incident.

"I'm fine." At her silent words, he smiled and shook his head. His large thumb swiped her cheek, and he showed it to her. Blood.

Harper's hands instantly went to her face, fingers searching for any cuts. She found none. She shrugged and mouthed, "Not mine."

This time his smile was one of relief. Preacher rose and disappeared for a few minutes.

The SEALs on each side of her had closed their eyes and were breathing normally. Just another day at the office for them. Maybe they'd gone to sleep. Harper wasn't sure she'd ever sleep again without remembering Rafe's arms around her, his warm body spooning her, or the feel of him sliding inside her from that same position.

Stop that!

Preacher reappeared with a gallon of water and a roll of paper towels. He swatted the SEAL on her right and hand signaled to him. The man—and now that he was close she could see he was so very young, barely in his twenties—dug in his pack and handed his CO a small mirror. Preacher handed it to Harper then patted her on the shoulder.

Well, at least she could clean up some.

Just as she was pouring water onto a wad of paper towels, they hit a small pocket of turbulence. Preacher stood steady in front of her, but the jug bounced, sloshing water onto her lap. Well, doesn't that figure.

She capped the jug and looked at the woman in the mirror. She didn't recognize herself. The grit from the downwash had been absorbed in the blood spatter and created ugly brown bumps. She didn't want to think what else she could have on her. That was just too yucky. She began wiping away the results of the past few minutes and wished it was that easy to cleanse her heart of Rafe Silva.

A pile of paper towels in her now dry lap, she presented her face to Preacher with a did-I-do-okay grin. He smiled down at her and held out his big hands. When he took the water jug, he handed her a solar blanket. Glancing around, Harper saw that all the others were snuggly wrapped in the reflective cloth.

"How long?" she mouthed to Preacher.

He leaned in next to her ear. "About an hour and a half." He took the blanket from her hands and shook it out with a snap. He tenderly tucked it behind her shoulders as he told her, "He can be an asswipe, but he's one of the good guys. Really. He's asked me at least a dozen times if you're all right. He cares for you, Harper. He's just pretty fucked up at the moment. It scared the shit out of him to see you at gunpoint."

She chuckled. "It wasn't the first time he'd seen me with a gun to my head."

Preacher stepped back with the oddest expression on his face.

"Ask him," she suggested.

He shook his head. "Try to get some sleep," he said and then disappeared toward the cockpit.

Sleep, yeah, like that's going to happen.

She glanced across the deck where Rafe stared back at her. He started to mouth something to her, but she shook her head then lowered it. She couldn't go there, not right now. She closed her eyes and was out before she exhaled her breath.

CHAPTER 29

HYDRAULICS MOANED, AND METAL ON METAL SCREAMED IN protest as the Osprey slowed and rotated the powerful engines.

Rafe was instantly awake. For a moment, he thought he was back with his old SEAL team. His body ached everywhere. He'd felt this beat up after almost every mission, and the gray interior of an aircraft, the smell of familiar mechanical fluids, fooled him temporarily. He skimmed his gaze over the camouflaged men who stirred in the jump seats that lined the cargo bay. He stopped when he came to Harper.

The fist around his heart tightened.

Worn and torn, she was still the most beautiful woman in the world to him. He had to get her back. He'd been stupid to think he'd be able to live without her by his side, every day and every night. She was his, and he belonged with her.

No, he belonged to her.

After a bounce and slight roll forward, everyone began to unbuckle and gather gear. The tailgate protested piercingly as it lowered to the ship's deck.

Medical personnel wheeled a gurney up the ramp as Doc signaled them to the injured SEAL. He'd been grazed deeply by a bullet. The hot lead had practically cauterized the wound, but there was a serious chance of infection.

Three corpsmen began to paw at Rafe, and he batted their hands away. "I'm fine," he insisted.

"You're going to see a doctor," Doc informed him and the rest of the medical staff. "I want his head X-rayed. I want to be sure there's a brain in there. He wasn't using it when we left Colombia, that's for sure."

Rafe looked around for Harper as he was shoved into a wheelchair and pushed down the ramp. Damn it, he could walk to sick bay. He tried to lift himself out of the chair, and his rib grabbed all the nerves in his side and squeezed like a son of a bitch. He settled back into the chair. Okay, he'd ride.

"Make a hole," someone yelled. "Captain coming through." The words parted the sea of medical people, flight crews, and SEALs who staggered toward a shower and a bed. The man in the white uniform adorned with plenty of gold led a wake of other officers in a direct line to Harper.

"Ms. Tambini, welcome aboard the USS Ronald Reagan. Let me assure you, you're safe aboard my ship." He held out his hand, and Harper was soon encircled by Navy officers.

"Sorry, sir, that the captain didn't welcome you with a tidal wave of officers. She must be someone special," the corpsman apologized.

"Yes, she is special." And I'm a dumb fuck for shoving her away.

Although to him it seemed like days, an hour later Rafe walked on his own out of sick bay. They hadn't told him anything new, but they had given him some nice painkillers.

He had to find Harper. Now.

He'd spent enough time on board ships during his five years in the Navy that he regained his sea legs almost immediately, and the double vision was merely odd moving shadows now. He found his way to the executive officer's miniscule space under the guise of getting a place to sleep. His admin, a petty officer third class, was more than willing to tell Rafe where he'd find his fiancée. Yeah, she wasn't his fiancée, yet, but as soon as he got to talk to her and made her understand, he'd ask her to marry him.

"Sir…uh…you're not allowed to have…uh…relations while onboard ship." The young man all but tripped over himself to get it out. Damn, they're making PO3s so young these days. Either that or Rafe was getting older. At the moment, he felt every one of his thirty-two years.

Rafe found his way to the female quarters and was just checking the numbers when a door opened. A small-framed woman with blonde hair pulled back in a fierce bun stepped from the room. Her khaki flight suit insignias indicated she was a pilot.

"Lieutenant, I'm looking for ATF Special Agent Harper Tambini. I need to speak with her immediately." Rafe used his most authoritative voice, and from his height, he towered over her. He'd been the same rank when he'd left the Navy, but that had been years ago.

She crossed her arms and purposefully placed her feet shoulder width apart. She stared at the white-bandaged stitches at his hairline and assessed him all the way down to his dusty and well-worn combat boots. He felt the twinge of being out of uniform during an inspection. He hadn't had time to shower and change. This was more important.

She sneered and looked him in the eye. "Are you the dickhead who dumped her?"

Ah, shit, Harper had been talking about him. Now he felt even worse. But if this little flight sprite would tell him where he could find her, he'd make Harper very happy…for the rest of their lives.

He grimaced. "Yes, I would be that dickhead."

"She doesn't want to see you." She stared at him but didn't move a muscle. She stood steadfastly in front of the door.

Okay, maybe he needed to explain, but he wanted to be telling Harper this, not some female guard.

"You see," Rafe started, "I love her."

The door flew open, and there was Harper, more beautiful than ever. Fresh and scrubbed. Not a drop of makeup, not that she ever needed any in his opinion. She was wearing a borrowed Navy T-shirt and sweatpants, ones that fit her much better than his had yesterday, or was it the day before? He didn't care. Harper was there, in front of him.

She gaped at Rafe from behind the pilot's back.

"Did you hear that, Miss Tambini?" her bodyguard asked.

Harper opened her mouth then closed it. She opened it again. It was as if she couldn't speak but wanted to say something.

"Uh…I think so," Harper managed to say.

Rafe looked up and down the passageway. A crowd was gathering at each end. His supersized body and the petite pilot filled the small space, and no one wanted to interrupt since Rafe was obviously not a member of the aircraft carrier's crew. But since he was on one of the Navy's newest nuclear carriers that meant he was important.

Hell, he didn't care who heard him. "I said I love you, but things got all…confused as we left Colombia. I was a prick, and I know it."

"I called you a dick, not a prick," the little pilot corrected.

Rafe gave her a what-the-fuck raised eyebrow.

"Just saying," she retorted.

Once again, Rafe looked at both ends of the passageway. It was stuffed with men and women in the uniform of the day.

Some had started yelling advice.

"Grovel a little more."

"No woman's worth this shit."

"Hey, honey, if you don't want him, I'll be happy to show you why helicopter pilots get it up faster."

"Bet my cockpit is bigger than his."

"Can we please talk about this in private?" Rafe really didn't want to bare his soul in front of half the officers on board, whose numbers seemed to be gathering exponentially at each end.

Harper laid her hand on the pilot's shoulder. "Thank you, Nancy."

"I'm here for you," Nancy said and eased her stance. "Are you sure?"

"Yes, I'm sure." The two women hugged, but Nancy glowered as she stepped out of the way.

"Show's over, folks. Carry on," Rafe instructed before he stepped into a typical officer's stateroom. Bunk beds filled the far end and lockers lined the walls. The space was small to begin with, but with both Rafe and Harper standing inside, there was barely room to move.

Rafe wanted to take her in his arms and hold her forever. He stepped toward her. She backed up, cocking her head to the side with a warning glare. He stopped.

"Harper, I love you. And I'm sorry for all those things I said back in Popayán." Rafe considered that a good start. He'd practiced that part. For the rest, he was resigned to wing it, but he wouldn't leave until she said yes to his proposal.

Her big brown eyes had lost a little of their steely resolve, and her face had softened. She didn't smile, and the corners of her eyes were tight. She folded her arms across her chest, which of course made him look at her breasts. He wondered what color bra she wore. *No, I can't go there.* And if he didn't get this straightened out right now, he'd never be allowed to go there again.

He lifted his eyes to hers and went on.

"When that sicario had a gun pointed at your head, I thought I'd lost you forever." He closed his eyes. The whole kidnap scene had played out like a movie in 3-D—without the colored glasses—thanks to his double vision. He'd felt detached, as if he'd watched it all from a front row seat.

Someone had pointed a gun to Harper's head and would have killed her. He could have pulled that trigger, and she'd be the one lying dead on the asphalt.

Rafe opened his eyes and tried to read her eyes. "You didn't even look afraid."

"I was though. But I knew the SEALs were out there, and they'd kill him. I just needed to give them a clean shot." She sounded almost nonchalant about it, but then again, she'd had several hours to deal with the adrenalin.

"Besides, it wasn't my first time." The sardonic smile Harper gave him never reached her eyes.

"Oh, babe, I'm sorry for that too." Rafe stepped closer, and this time she didn't move. She stiffened her arm, placing her flattened palm on his chest, and gave him another one of those cautioning glares. He rocked back on his heels.

"I know." Her words were quiet. "Neither of those were your fault."

"I thought I would lose you, and we've just found each other." He couldn't lose her now. *Oh God, how he loved her.*

Her feral eyes glaring at him, she seethed. "You didn't lose me. You shoved me away."

"I didn't mean what I said. I love you, Harper."

"I completely understood the words, 'stay the fuck away from me' and 'it's over.' Those words were very clear. Now you don't mean them? You claim you love me, but how soon will it be before you no longer mean those words, too? Tomorrow? A week? A month?"

"They're more than just words, but they're the only words I have to tell you how I feel about you. I want you in my life forever, Harper, and I mean forever."

She dropped her hand from his chest, and it instantly felt cold over his heart. She didn't meet his eyes, instead choosing to stare at the floor. She shook her head, her breathing became erratic. It seemed as though she was having an internal debate.

When she finally looked at him, her eyes were filled with regret. "You were right. It was fun. And you were the best fuck I've ever had, too. You were right to end it. We'll be home in a few days and go our separate ways. You can't love me. We haven't known each other long enough to fall in love."

No. This wasn't what Rafe had planned. He needed Harper in his life. Forever. And damn it, he did love her.

"Yes, it's only been a few days, but I did fall in love with you. We've spent more time together than people who have dated for years. We've been through more in the past three days than any couple faces in a lifetime. I've been there for you…except for that brief time when I lost my mind."

"You didn't lose your mind," she accused. "You probably have a concussion, but that didn't cause you to push me away."

He loved the way she called him on his bullshit.

"You're right. I admit it. I got scared. Give me another chance, Harper. I promise I'll always be there for you."

She took on the world with fervor, the way she took on him. He didn't want a passive woman in his life. He needed a woman who was as balls to the wall as he was, someone who could keep up with him. What he really needed was someone to challenge him. Why hadn't he seen that before?

He couldn't stand it any longer.

Rafe pulled her to him and kissed the spot where the maniac had placed the barrel of his gun. He stroked her back slowly. "I can't let you go."

He took her mouth with a kiss so possessive that it took his breath away when she returned it just as forcefully. She was perfect for him. He loved everything about her. He loved that she was smart and strong-willed. He loved her fortitude. She'd need all that to put up with him. They were matched in every way possible, and he loved her to his soul.

He couldn't lose her now. He couldn't let her go.

Harper brought her hand to Rafe's face and ran her thumb across his lips. Her touch was warm. He hadn't realized how cold he'd gone. When she lightly brushed her lips over his, heat shot through him in that now familiar jolt. He wrapped his arms around her and pressed her against his entire body.

"I love you, Harper. And I know you love me."

She leaned back and gave him a quizzical look.

"I heard your words in that alley," He confessed.

He took her hand and placed it over his heart. "You're in me now. And I don't want to lose you. Ever." He kissed her, pouring all the emotions he didn't have words for into their connection.

"Harper, I love you. I want you in my life, every day. I know what you do for a living is dangerous, and I respect the hell out of what you do for our country. But when you're done, I want you to come home to me." Rafe looked into familiar eyes, but he couldn't read them. "Marry me."

Harper stared at him for the longest time. He could almost see the inner debate.

"Yes," was all she got out before he captured her mouth with promises for their life together.

"Ahem." A deep familiar voice sounded from behind Rafe. Rafe didn't want to stop kissing Harper. She'd said yes.

"Rafe, Harper, sorry to interrupt, but there's an important message." Preacher's voice sounded urgent.

Rafe kept one arm around Harper as he turned them toward the large man who filled the doorway.

"I see your brain reconnected. Are you through being an ass?" Preacher admonished.

With a silly smile he couldn't wipe away, Rafe announced, "She said yes. We're getting married. Want to be my best man?"

Smile on his face, Preacher held out his hand. "Congratulations." They did that manly one-armed hug, back-thump thing before they quickly separated. Preacher held out both arms to Harper, who practically threw herself into him.

"Hey, that's my woman." There was a shot of jealousy at the sight of his best friend holding his fiancée. Yes, the woman who would, very soon if he had his way, be his wife.

Harper stepped out of Preacher's arms and back into his. She gave him a little squeeze. Damn, if that wasn't the best thing he'd felt in years.

"Hey, man, I'm here because your boss is burning up the

airwaves. You need to do the E.T. thing and phone home. The captain told him you were in sick bay, so he bought you some time."

"Thanks, Preacher. I appreciate it." He really didn't care about his boss. Harper was going to marry him.

"After you shower, let's meet in the wardroom, say…in thirty minutes. You both need to eat, and I'm starving. I've got to check on my men. Later." With that, his friend left them alone.

Rafe turned to Harper and affectionately held her face in his hands. He searched for the answer to his unasked question as if it was somewhere between her lips and her eyes. He said nothing, just scanned her every feature. He needed to hear the words she hadn't spoken since Popayán.

That's when she got it.

"Yes, Rafe. I love you." She kissed him but didn't let him deepen it the way he wanted. "Go." She stepped back. "Go shower and make your call. I'll meet you in the wardroom."

He couldn't help himself. He stepped back in for a quick little kiss then ran for his assigned room and a shower.

Five minutes later, Rafe stepped out onto a catwalk and into the past. The familiar heat of the flight deck radiated through the soles of his boots. The smell of jet fuel and hydraulic fluids invaded his lungs. Wind created by the forward motion of the ship combined with the natural hot breezes south of the Tropic of Cancer forced Rafe to lean forward or he'd have been blown over.

There had been a time in his life he'd loved this. It'd meant a mission for his team.

Instead of one hundred pounds of gear strapped to his back, weapons secured to his legs, and a helmet heavy with night vision and infrared equipment on his head, tonight Rafe wore a borrowed lightweight flight suit. Its khaki color stood out from the deck crew's navy blue working uniform pants and jerseys, which were colored depending on their job. It always amazed him how many people scurried around the ship in the wee hours of the night.

It was the city at sea that never slept. The first time he'd been on an aircraft carrier, the salty chief on his team had told him a carrier was a man-made steel island with an airport on top, a nuclear power plant in the basement, and five thousand people crammed in between. Every single person onboard had a job to do, and as a SEAL with shiny new silver lieutenant junior grade bars, his was to be sure he was ready to do anything his country asked of him when the orders were given.

For just over ten years, first as a SEAL then as a CIA agent, he'd done everything they'd asked of him. That would end tonight.

Rafe watched the crews' red, blue, and green lights bounce around the flight deck as they secured equipment from the last launch/recovery cycle. The Osprey that had rescued them wasn't the only plane in the air from the Reagan. An E2C Hawkeye reconnaissance plane had tracked their every movement from twenty-three thousand feet above the earth. The Navy's newest fighter jets, F/A18F Super Hornets, met them the second they hit international airspace and escorted them back to the ship. Hundreds of sailors had been involved in their rescue. Rafe wished he could thank each and every one of them. He was so glad to be out of Colombia and headed home with Harper at his side, forever.

He lifted his head to the stars, as if he could see the numbers he'd punched into the satellite phone travel through space.

"School Boy reporting in." He couldn't wait to get rid of that handle, or any code name.

"About time. The old man's been stomping around waiting for your call. Putting you through." The man at Ops Com Center didn't wait for his reply.

"School Boy, you should have called from the rescue plane." Deputy Director Tom Gillpatrick was not happy with him.

"Yes, sir." Rafe knew his double vision, which thankfully had disappeared, and the noise of the Osprey were not excuses. He should have contacted CIA headquarters as soon as they were safe. Or at least as soon as they'd landed on the Reagan. He'd screwed the pooch on that one and was due the wrath.

"Miss Tambini is now safe, thanks to you and the SEALs. You're still responsible for her and must assure her safety to D.C. Report to Langley as soon as you hand her over to the USSOCOM guys at Dulles Airport." There was a backhanded thank you in there someplace.

"Yes, sir." Rafe had anticipated that last part.

"Plan on staying there for a few days, maybe even weeks. You have a lot to debrief."

Well, hell. In the five years he was with Carlos Narváez, he'd reported in regularly, and no one had seemed very interested. Now they wanted to pick his brains to pieces.

"Yes, sir." Those two words were all that Rafe seemed able to say.

"You have quite a bit of vacation time accumulated. Take thirty days to decide where you want to go next. With your language skills, we have several countries available." Gillpatrick already had him leaving the U.S.A., and he hadn't gotten there yet.

No. That wasn't going to happen.

"Sir, as soon as I reach Langley, you'll have my

resignation." Rafe was through with the CIA, but for several long minutes, the DD tried to convince him to stay.

Finally, Gillpatrick said, "Do you want to transfer to another branch of government service, or do you have a civilian job lined up?"

"No, sir. Neither. I've given our country ten years of my life. I'd like to give the civilian world a try. I'll find something."

There was a short pause before Gillpatrick offered, "Have you ever heard of a company called Guardian Security?"

"Yes, sir. Harper mentioned them. They offer bodyguards and security systems."

"That's not all they do, son. They…almost exclusively… employ men with your…training and are—" Gillpatrick's hesitancy suggested he had chosen his words carefully.

"Sir, I have no desire to become a mercenary, even one under U.S. government contract. I want to get away from this life." Rafe had rudely interrupted the man who was still his boss.

The chuckle was crystal clear, although it had traveled thousands of miles into space and back to the ship. "No, no. They specialize in high-risk corporate security, both personal and facility. Check them out. I know one of the owners very well and would be happy to recommend you."

Flabbergasted at the generous offer, all Rafe could do was say, "Thank you, sir. I'll do that." Rafe hesitated only a second, but he had to know. "Sir, may I inquire as to the status of Melina and Jacin? Did they make it out of Colombia?"

There was a long pause, so Rafe braced himself for the worst. When DD Gillpatrick finally spoke, it wasn't what Rafe expected to hear. "I know you and your handler became close. It's a situation we, as an organization, do not condone, but we understand the strain on agents who have been under a long time. Because I don't believe your resignation has anything to do with her, I'll tell you that Jacin is hospitalized and expected to make a full recovery. Thank you for assisting them. We'll talk when you get to Langley. Gillpatrick out." The line went dead.

Rafe stared at the phone in his hand. Parts of that conversation had gone better than he'd imagined. He was glad Jacin was home safe in the U.S.A. But his boss really hadn't said anything about Melina.

Rafe stuffed the cell into his side pocket and headed to the wardroom. He couldn't remember when he'd last eaten.

Food in the middle of the night was proof they were special. Even though it would be hours before breakfast was served, they had hot food available.

Rafe picked up the glass plate emblazoned with the USS Ronald Reagan crest and heavy silverware. The culinary specialist stifled a yawn as he waited for Rafe's order.

"I really appreciate you being here. It's been a long time since I've eaten American food," Rafe admitted.

The CS, who couldn't have been more than nineteen, smiled at Rafe. "Then, how about a burger and fries? Nothing is more American than that. It'll just take a minute. I'll bring it out to you, sir."

Rafe piled salad onto his plate then joined Preacher and his team. He pulled up a chair next to Harper, who'd made a thick sandwich from the cold cuts on the salad bar.

"So did Daddy yell at you for not calling as soon as you were safe?" his old friend egged Rafe from the other side of Harper.

"Yeah." Rafe bit into fresh lettuce and a cherry tomato drenched in creamy ranch dressing. It tasted wonderful. He was hungrier than he'd thought.

"I'm sure you have to report to Langley," Harper said.

Rafe nodded and swallowed. "He said my debriefing might take a couple of weeks. Have you talked to your people?"

"Yes." She glanced around the table at the men then shrugged. "A colonel from SOCOM will meet me at the airport. I'll be debriefed, a.k.a. grilled over open flames."

At the acronym, the men all stared at her.

Preacher threw his arm around her. "She's a sister in arms. And one kick-ass Army captain."

They seemed to accept his explanation and returned to their food.

A double cheeseburger with the works appeared on the table in front of Rafe. "This looks awesome. Thanks," Rafe said over his shoulder.

"If you want another, sir, I'm right over there," the CS said with a broad smile and pointed to the grill.

"Hey, can I get one of those?" a SEAL from across the large round table asked. Before the CS could answer, requests came from several other team members.

"Sure, the grill's hot." He left to fill the orders.

"Damn, this is sweeeet," one of the SEALs commented. "We usually eat a power bar and pray it holds us over until they serve breakfast. You two must be really important." Realizing that he may have said something out of line, he looked at Preacher for admonishment. When none came immediately, the enlisted SEAL lowered his head and continued eating with greater speed.

Rafe remembered those days and was thankful for the VIP treatment tonight.

He dragged a fry through a puddle of catsup. "I told him I quit. I'm free after the debrief."

"Whoa, man. So, what are you going to do? Look for a

civilian job?" Preacher stared and popped chips into his mouth.

"Have you ever heard of a company called Guardian Security?" Rafe asked. "The DD said I should check them out. He knows one of the owners and actually offered to make a call on my behalf."

"No shit," said one of the SEALs. "I've heard it's pretty tough to get a job with them." The twenty-something man looked at him with increased respect.

"My old CO runs the Guardian Miami office," Doc said. "He told me to call him when I decided to get out. They pay really well. But doctors make a lot of money too, so I'm thinking med school."

Harper interjected, "My friends know those guys. When they're home in D.C., we go out clubbing and they always have a Guardian bodyguard."

"Who are your friends that they need a bodyguard?" Although one of the older SEALs across the table had asked the question, Rafe wanted to know the answer too.

"They work for the government, like me. They're nobody famous or anything. Not sure why they need a bodyguard. Maybe it's because he gets to carry a gun inside the beltway." Harper shrugged and sipped her soda.

"Are these women hot?" Preacher asked.

"They're all beautiful." She smiled at Rafe's old friend. "Call me when you get to D.C., and if they're in town, I'll introduce you."

"Me, too," the chorus of single men sang around the table.

"Hey, I don't want all you guys calling my wife when you hit the States. Find your own women." Rafe didn't like the idea of any man calling Harper. Especially horny SEALs. He'd been one of those guys and knew exactly how far they'd go to get laid.

She leaned back and crossed her arms. "Rafe Silva, I'm not your wife…yet."

"You will be by the time these guys get leave." He had plans for the two of them. None of this long engagement shit. He wanted Harper in his life, in his bed, immediately. Permanently.

He turned his whole body toward Harper and dropped his voice. "I've got to finish some things with the CIA, but I plan on taking Deputy Director Gillpatrick up on his offer about Guardian. Wouldn't it be great if I could work for their D.C. office? If not, I'll find some other job. There are plenty of beltway bandits around there. Then I'll find us a great place we can call home." He squeezed her hand. A kiss would be too much PDA in the open wardroom with the SEAL team watching.

"I have a great place I call home in D.C. It's a big condo with a wonderful view, and, hey, Guardian Security must also do residential because they protect my place. I'll talk to Katlin, I think she knows the owner."

"That's divine intervention if I've ever seen it," Preacher announced. "Your boss and Harper both have connections to Guardian. Doc, too. I have a good feeling about this."

Harper concentrated on her sandwich for a long minute. When her eyes returned to his, she had a look of resolve and hope in her melted chocolate eyes. "Will you move in with me, Rafe?"

"Hey, look guys." One of the SEALs pointed to the large flat panel TV on the wall, where sparks flew from a volcano lighting the night sky with reds and golds.

"Looks like we left too soon," another said. "Puracé just blew."

"No," Harper declared. "We had plenty of fireworks of

our own in Colombia, especially in Popayán." She squeezed Rafe's hand, letting him know the double entendre.

He loved this woman and would for the rest of his life.

"I'll stick to the Fourth of July fireworks over the National Mall from now on, thank you very much." Harper leaned in close and whispered into his ear. "We can watch them from our bed."

EPILOGUE

FOUR DAYS AFTER RETURNING STATESIDE, RAFE PRESSED THE button to release the electronic fence to the secure parking area at Harper's condo. It had been one hell of a week. Debriefing at Langley was never a picnic, but at least they had given him the weekend off and allowed him to stay with Harper rather than locking him down at CIA headquarters. He wasn't one hundred percent sure why he was getting this preferential treatment, but he was not going to complain. He was pretty sure Deputy Director Gillpatrick was his guardian angel.

Rafe pulled his new truck into the second parking space allotted for Harper's condo and got out. As he headed toward the front door, he looked around the crowded lot. Three identical black Land Rovers sat side-by-side. He wondered if they were some kind of a fleet car or if the building's residents just had an affinity for the expensive vehicle. With nearly every space now filled, he considered that someone may be having a party, it was Friday after all. He hoped if that was the case, they wouldn't be too loud. He was looking forward to spending a quiet weekend alone with Harper. Getting out of bed would be optional.

When the elevator door opened on the top floor, Rafe was bombarded with thumping music and nearly a dozen voices. The party had spilled out of the first apartment into the hall where all three doors stood wide open.

He was instantly upset with his fiancée. There were so many pilferable items in their home, not to mention all their guns and computers filled with classified information.

"Excuse me," Rafe said to the man big enough to be a running back for any pro football team.

With a smile, the man turned and held out his hand. "You must be Rafe. I'm Griffin." The big guy stuck his head into the first apartment and yelled, "Hey, Harper, your man is here."

When he heard her familiar voice, his whole world righted itself. Peering in, he watched Harper roll off the couch while laughing and trying desperately not to spill the wine in her hand.

"Rafe, come on in." She wove her way through small groups of people munching on hors d'oeuvres. "I want you to meet my friends."

She stepped out into the hallway, went up on tiptoes and kissed him. She tasted of wine and shrimp and love. Forgetting that he'd ever been upset with her, he deepened the kiss letting her know with his mouth and tongue just how much he loved her. His hand moved up her spine as he dug his fingers into her soft hair and changed the angle of the kiss.

"Get a room," someone called from inside. "Or I'm going to sell tickets to the show. I'm not into voyeurism, but I do like good porn."

Harper's smile broke the kiss. "Oh, Nita, shut up," she threw over her shoulder.

He couldn't miss the heat in her eyes when they met his.

"Come on. There's a lot of people here I want you to meet." She took his hand and led him inside. "Hey, everyone," Harper called loudly, and the room hushed. With a huge smile on her face, she announced, "This is Rafe Silva, my fiancé."

With a depth of pride he had never seen in her, she held up her left hand and flashed the ring they had selected together their first day back on U.S. soil. Damn, he loved this woman.

Starting on the left side of the U-shaped couch, she dragged him over to meet her friends. "This is Katlin." When the blonde stood so did the Latino man next to her. He seemed to favor his left knee and had a large bandage over his right bicep.

"Nice to meet you." She surprised him by enveloping him in a hug. "Thank you for helping Harper escape. The two of you went through hell to get out of Colombia."

Rafe knew his jaw dropped slightly as his gaze shot to Harper. Had she told them everything?

Katlin smiled. "I read your after-action report."

How the hell could she have done that? Who the fuck was this woman?

"Rafe, I'd like you to meet my friend Alex." She'd purposefully pulled his attention away from that line of thought, and they both knew it.

As he shook hands, Rafe asked, "Do you work for the government, too?"

"Not if I can help it," Alex answered with a grin and a glance toward Katlin. There was more to that statement than he was willing to say, but Rafe would let it pass. "I run a security company. One of our offices is here in D.C."

"Good to know." Rafe filed that information away aware

he would soon be freed from the CIA and would need to look for a local job. He could take his time though, because he had received a very pleasant surprise upon returning to the states. He had five years of government paychecks sitting in a bank account.

While working for Carlos Narváez, Rafe had no need for money. Anything he wanted was his for the asking. He'd also had a sizable income from the cartel that still sat untouched in a bank on the Caribbean island of Grand Turk. That was just another secret he would never reveal to his current employer. He had earned every dime of that dirty money. Someday he would put it to a good use.

"There's hot hors d'oeuvres in the kitchen, food is spread all over the place, and we'll probably call for pizza in about an hour." Katlin's gaze swept the room. "I have one rule in my home."

A battered woman with curly dark hair handed Rafe a beer from a local craft brewery with her good arm. The other was secured within a blue sling. He noted that her wrists were bandaged in gauze. Under the puffy yellow and green bruises, he could see the girl-next-door face.

With a nod toward the bottle Katlin continued, "The first time you're here, you are my guest. We'll serve you. After that, you're family. Get your own damn beer. If we're out of beer, or you don't like what kind we have, see rule one, get your own damn beer."

Rafe liked this woman. "I can handle that." He smiled and took a swig.

Turning toward the newcomer in the conversation, Harper gestured, "Rafe, this is Nita." She carefully hugged the woman who stood beside her. "We've been through a lot together." Her gaze wandered around the room. "We all have."

Rafe wasn't sure what connection these women shared, but it was tight, as tight as his SEAL team had been. He knew his fiancée kept secrets, but all women did, at least in his experience.

"Nice to meet you, Rafe." Nita's handshake was firmer than he'd expected for a woman as obviously injured as she. The smile she gave him was filled with mirth and fun-loving. "We're all glad you put a smile on Harper's face. Keep it up."

By the twinkle in her eye, he could tell she meant the pun.

"That's not a problem." Rafe wrapped an arm around Harper's back and pulled her to him. "I try hard to keep her happy."

"I'll just bet you do." Nita raked her gaze down his body then back up to meet his eyes. "She's one lucky woman."

"Nita, quit eye-fucking my man," Harper chastised. She glanced around the room before suggesting, "Go find one of your own. It looks like there's plenty of candy to choose from."

Nita sighed. "Sounds like good advice." Her gaze wandered to the chaise portion of the couch where a man with dark curly hair and nearly black eyes lay stretched out. A neat row of small stitches held together a two-inch gash on his left cheek. Under his sun-weathered skin, Rafe could see healing bruises. He too had wrists wrapped in gauze. "I think I'll go keep Chase company since he took the majority of the beating meant for me."

When Nita walked away, Rafe couldn't help asking, "What happened to them?"

"Fucking fundamentalist zealots," Katlin spat out.

"They were kidnapped?" Rafe asked.

"No. Captured," Alex answered as his gaze slid to the couch where Chase gingerly moved his legs to make room for Nita.

Rafe glanced around the room at the men and women who seemed to be enjoying each other's company as they casually ate what looked like high-end restaurant catered snacks and drank craft beer as he tried to piece together what he knew. He took a long pull of the delicious brew.

"So, you guys all work black ops for the government?" Rafe looked at Harper for confirmation and suddenly wondered if he knew the woman at all. If he hadn't glanced at Katlin that second, he would've missed the imperceptible nod.

Harper took a deep breath before she explained, "All the women in this room are active duty commissioned military officers. The men all work at Guardian Security for Alex." She hesitated and he could practically see the debate on her face to say anything more.

"Since you are going to marry Harper and will be around us on a regular basis, I'll tell you the truth." When Katlin took over the conversation, Rafe sensed relief fill Harper's body. "I know you have been sequestered at Langley, so I don't know if you saw the news where UN forces destroyed an actively producing nuclear facility in Iraq earlier in the week." She held his gaze. "That was us. And, yes, Harper was supposed to be there with us."

Fuck. No. His gaze shot to the bruised and battered couple sitting on the couch. Then he looked into the eyes of the woman he loved and waited for the dread to overwhelm him. It didn't come.

"I know exactly how you feel, Rafe," Alex consoled. "I'm right there with you. But I've seen these women in action and they are as well-trained, if not better, than you and I were."

Rafe assessed the man.

Alex continued, "You were a SEAL. I was Marine Raider. Every man in this room served his country in special operations. Every woman still does. The woman in your arms is more special than you know." He hugged Katlin to him and closed his eyes as he kissed her temple. "And it sucks every time they get called out on another mission. But there is nothing in this world like the feeling you get when they arrive home safe."

Katlin picked up the conversation from there. "And that's why we're celebrating tonight, another successful mission for the Ladies of Black Swan and the two of you. Thank you, Harper, for wiping out another of America's top ten. Hopefully with the removal of Turi Solis, and Carlos Narváez, the flow of poison into the United States will slow at least for a little while."

"We can only hope," Harper agreed. She looked at Rafe. "Are you ready to meet some other people?"

He would follow this woman anywhere. "Sure."

Harper sat on the huge Ottoman in the center of the three-sectioned couch in front of a man and woman in a deep conversation about sniper scopes. Even though she was sitting, Rafe would put her height at nearly six feet. With her bronze-colored skin, her heritage could be anything from African, Middle Eastern, or even Native American. Most likely a mix of all three and more.

At a natural pause in the conversation, the two looked at them.

"Rafe I'd like you to meet one of my best friends, Tori. She lives next door to us," Harper explained. She then looked at the sandy haired man and shrugged. "I'm sorry, but I don't believe we've met."

"Reed Delaney." He held his hand out and Harper shook it before he leaned forward to meet Rafe's hand. "I run the Los Angeles office for Alex. Nice to meet you both. I overheard you were a SEAL. I was Army Special Forces, but we ran into SEALs all the time on Forward Operating Bases. Mostly West Coast guys."

"I spent my Navy career on the East Coast," Rafe admitted. "I've been in Colombia ever since."

"But now he's home in the U.S.A. and living down the hall with me." Harper wrapped her hands around his arm and nuzzled into his neck.

"And we are so glad to have her back safe and sound." The pretty redhead plopped down beside Tori. "Hi, I'm Grace." She thrust her hand toward Rafe and gave it one good hard shake. Then she quickly stood up and hugged Harper before sliding back into her seat. "When's the wedding?"

Wedding? That was a good question. Rafe wanted Harper in his life forever but suddenly realized that meant a wedding. They hadn't discussed one yet. He had no idea if he could convince Harper to elope to Las Vegas or if she had hoped for the big white wedding dress surrounded by all her friends. He stole a glance at each woman in the room and suddenly realized how much these women meant to each other. She would probably want them all to partake in the ceremony. If so, he'd be in deep shit trying to dig up enough groomsmen.

"We just got engaged the other day." Harper casually laid a hand on his thigh and gave it a gentle squeeze.

Heat ran the six inches up to his cock which jumped to life. He wondered how long they'd have to stay at this party and how soon he could get her out of her clothes and into bed.

"We haven't even had a chance to talk about it yet." Harper looked at him beseechingly. The smile she gave him warmed him all the way to his soul. He didn't care what kind of wedding she wanted. He'd give it to her, even if it meant he had to spend every dime he had to throw her the party she deserved.

"Please don't pick pink for the bridesmaids' dresses," Grace implored her.

"Good God no," Nita called from the other couch. "No woman over the age of eighteen looks good in pink. And for fuck sake, don't you dare pick anything with ruffles on the boobs or butt. Katlin's breasts draw enough attention, and I already have too much that jiggles on my ass."

With a broad smile, Harper noted, "Got it. No pink. No ruffles. Any other mandates?"

A petite Asian woman with hair that flowed to where her butt met the ottoman sat down beside Harper and hugged her for a long minute.

"Rafe, this is Lei Lu," Harper made the introductions.

"A pleasure to meet you." Long black lashes over dark brown eyes turned toward Harper. "A destination wedding would be nice."

"We can go to Katlin's house in Costa Rica, and you guys can get married on the beach." At Grace's suggestion, Rafe watched Harper's eyes light up.

She turned to him and tightened her grip on his thigh. "Your parents and family could stay at the resort next door. It's beautiful down there."

Although that was a hell of a lot closer to Colombia than he ever wanted to be again, he wasn't a dolt. If this is where she wanted to commit her life to him, then so be it. "If that's what you want, it's fine by me."

"Katlin?" Grace called to her friend now in the kitchen. "Can Harper get married at the Costa Rica compound?"

"Sure," Katlin said as she stuck her head around the corner. "Just give me a few days' notice so I can contact the staff so they can prepare the food. It would be easier if we could have the reception over at the resort. The compound's kitchen is only set up to support twenty to twenty-five people."

Rafe was overwhelmed at how quickly his wedding came together, and how little input he had into the event. It suddenly dawned on him, his family didn't even know he'd returned stateside or had gotten engaged. He couldn't wait for his mother and father to meet Harper. Mentally setting a schedule, he decided they should fly to Charleston just as soon as he could get away from Langley. He tilted his beer and drained the bottle.

"Congratulations," Griffin said as he sat down beside Grace who instantly began to fidget. "I heard you and Reed talking. Did he tell you I was a SEAL, too?" As the big man ran through names of commanding officers and others they'd served with, Grace looked more and more uncomfortable.

Finally, Harper asked, "Grace, are you okay?"

Grace abruptly stood up and snatched the empty bottle out of Rafe's hands "I am such a terrible hostess. Let me get you another beer." She dashed off to the kitchen.

Rafe caught the raised eyebrows and silent communication between Tori, Lei Lu, and Harper. He smiled inwardly as he remembered entire conversations his sisters would have without a single word. He couldn't wait to see them again. They too would love the woman who would soon be his wife.

Several hours later and filled with pizza, beer, and some of the best hors d'oeuvres he'd ever eaten, Rafe was ready to leave.

As though she could read his mind, Harper stood. "We've had a tough week, so I think we will call it a night."

They said their good-byes to everyone in the living room and made their way toward the kitchen where Katlin and Alex were putting away the remnants of the food. As the women hugged, Rafe held out his hand to Alex. "Since I live here now, I guess I'll be seeing more of you."

"Actually, I travel a lot, and so does Kat," Alex explained. "But you'll probably see me as we both pass through Washington, especially if we're here at the same time. I'm glad we met. Kat's uncle, Tom Gillpatrick, mentioned you this morning. He tells me you're getting out."

Snap. So many pieces of the puzzle just clicked into place. The beautiful blonde in front of him was the link between Guardian Security and the CIA.

"Yes." Rafe was adamant about getting out, but unsure what he wanted to do afterward.

"Excuse me, Alex," the man with reddish-blond hair, who Rafe hadn't met yet, interrupted. "Sorry to interrupt, but if you still want me in Dallas by Monday, I really should catch the redeye out tonight for Miami."

"Good plan, Jonathan." Alex extended his hand. "Thanks for helping me out. You know you're stepping into a hornets' nest down there, but I'm sure you'll help Quin straighten things out."

"Yes, sir. I'll do a good job. You can depend on me." Jonathan's enthusiasm was barely contained.

"I know I can." Alex's smile showed his confidence in the younger man. "Call the D.C. office, and they'll give you a ride to the airport."

"Will do." Before he stepped away, he held out his hand to Rafe. "Hi, I'm Jonathan O'Neil." Rafe and Harper quickly introduce themselves realizing the man had much to do before morning.

"As you can see, I'm shuffling my management people around," Alex told Rafe. "I have a vacancy in New York City, but I'm pretty sure I know who I'm going to put there."

Katlin smiled. "I think Ryleigh will like it there."

At the name, Harper perked up. "Are you putting Ryleigh Davenport in New York City?"

Katlin nodded and Alex confirmed.

"She's awesome," Harper declared. "She trained with us you know, Alex."

"Why do you think I'm hiring her as the first female field agent?"

Harper threw her arms around Alex. "Thank you. One more glass ceiling busted."

"So, who is going to replace Jonathan in the Miami office?" Katlin asked.

"Griffin has asked for Dane Anderson," Alex replied.

"So that leaves you short in the D.C. office, right?" At Katlin's question, all eyes turned toward Rafe.

"I'll be hiring from the outside for that one." Alex looked pointedly at Rafe. "You interested?"

"Who would I have to interview with, and when?" He volleyed back.

Alex chuckled. "Me. And you just did."

Rafe felt Harper tense beside him. If he had a job waiting for him right there in D.C. as soon as he finished with the CIA, they would both breathe easy.

"Thank you. That would be wonderful. How about I call you in a few days when Langley is finished probing my memory?" He looked at his now very sleepy fiancée. "I need to get this one home and into bed."

Alex glanced to Katlin. "I think we both have the same idea."

As Rafe and Harper walked down the now quiet hall to the last door, she asked, "Any news on Jacin and Melina?"

"Yeah, matter of fact Mr. Gillpatrick told me he's still in Fort Hood, Texas recovering. Melina is supposed to be here sometime next week to begin her debrief."

"Should we offer her a place to stay with us?" Harper's sweet heart was one of the things he loved most about her, but having his former lover under the same roof with his fiancée wasn't going to work for him, even if she had helped both of them escape from Colombia.

"They'll probably put her on lockdown at Langley for at least the first couple weeks." Rafe was no longer surprised at how much leniency he'd been shown by Deputy Director Gillpatrick.

Rafe locked the door behind him and set the alarm, noticing for the first time the light gray Guardian Security logo on the keypad.

He turned to follow Harper into the bedroom to find a path of her clothes leading him to her naked body as she leaned against the door jamb.

"You're overdressed for this party." Her husky voice made his cock stand at attention.

His new life was going to be good. For all the horrible things that his college friend Carlos had done, he had brought this beautiful woman into Rafe's life for which he would be forever grateful. Freeing her from Narváez's velvet cage, set Rafe free as well.

The End

Continue reading for a
Sneak Peek at
Rescuing Melina
Jacin & Melina's story
A crossover novella between
KaLyn Cooper's **Guardian Elite series** and
Susan Stoker's Delta Force Heroes series

Excerpt from
Rescuing Melina
KaLyn Cooper

"He's coming around."

Jacin Torres had known pain, but he'd obviously moved beyond the point where it registered in his brain. He felt nothing.

Absolutely nothing.

Am I dead?

His mind was so screwed up. The voice sounded like a woman, yet, there had been two men who had taken turns beating the shit out of him. Men he'd known for more than a year. He'd worked beside them as a lieutenant in Turi Solis's cartel…until he'd made the biggest mistake of his life.

Jealousy, as much as fear for her life, had driven him to her that night.

His whole body bounced inches into the air before landing hard on the thin mattress.

Pain shot through his back. Yes. He was definitely still alive.

Had they finally finished the grueling torture session and shot him?

Jacin gasped, but he couldn't force air into his lungs. He felt like he was back in BUD/S, trying to qualify as a SEAL and nearly drowning in the pool.

Don't panic, he instructed himself. You can handle this. You know what to do.

SEAL training had taught him well. He reached to clear the mouthpiece of his scuba gear, but it didn't feel right. His hand slid over the device as though it were smooth and not attached to a tank. Was he wearing a rebreather?

Everything was so confusing.

And what was that beeping? Were they testing a new warning system?

A black curtain was covering the edges of his brain, forcing him into unconsciousness. He needed oxygen. Now.

He tried desperately to suck in air, and a knife stabbed into his back once again, just above the kidney.

"We're losing him."

"Hang in there, Jacin. Don't you dare leave me now." The warm hand of his angel slipped into his and squeezed.

Palm-to-palm, heat traveled through his body as the darkness closed on hot memories of the two of them, together, in her bed.

The next time Jacin surfaced, he cracked his eyes so as not to alert his captors he was conscious once again. He immediately slammed them shut. The room was too bright. They must've moved him from the cellar where they kept him a prisoner for nearly a week.

Slowly, he tried to fill his lungs to help shake off the drowsiness. No pain this time.

His eyelids felt like they were weighed down. When he tried to rub them, he discovered he was still tied to some immovable object. He yanked as hard as he could to no avail. At least the new bindings didn't cut into his oversensitive wrists.

For a fleeting moment, Jacin wondered if Solis had a new torment in mind for him.

"Jacin? Are you awake?" his angel asked in her sweet, melodic voice.

Thank God she was with him.

No! Solis's lieutenants would be back soon and find her there. They would torture her, too. They knew she was not who she claimed to be. That's how they'd discovered he was a spy. He needed to protect her.

"Run." He tried to scream the word, but his voice came out as a croaked whisper. He swallowed what little moisture he could gather in his mouth. Stronger, he managed to open his eyes a fraction.

Several seconds passed before he could focus on the most beautiful woman in his world. Flowing black hair matched dark eyes that seemed intensified by her light caramel face. She'd come for him, to save him, but she was the one he had to protect.

Gathering every ounce of energy he could muster, he warned, "Get out of here. Now."

"I'm sorry, I don't understand what you trying to tell me." She patted his hand. "I'm going to go get the nurse."

She was going to get…what? Help? In spite of everything, he chuckled. She would find no help for him in the home of Turi Solis.

She walked away. The natural swing of her hips and movement of her fine ass was the last thing he saw as he went under once again.

At the sound of voices, Jacin's mind stirred. He was feeling oddly refreshed, as though he'd had a good hard eight hours sleep.

"You've already started to bring him out of the coma?" A deep male voice posed the question.

Coma? Had he hit his head? Then Jacin remembered the beatings he'd taken for days. Men he'd once called friends had used his head as a punching bag. He figured he had a concussion, but had they pounded him so badly he'd fallen into a coma? That would explain a lot. Given the antiseptic smell and the incessant beeping and buzzing, Jacin concluded he was in a hospital.

But where? He could only hope it was in the United States and he was finally free of the drug cartels and Colombia. He raked through every memory he could stir trying to remember how he got out of that disgusting basement in hell to here—wherever here was—but he continued to come up blank.

"Yes. We're going to bring him out of this slowly," a second male voice announced.

"Is his wife here yet?" the first man asked.

Wife? He didn't have a wife. Maybe there was someone else in the room and they were working on him.

"No, but she should be shortly." The baritone voice continued, "Are the interns on their way?"

"They're waiting for you to give us the go-ahead. By the way, I've brought your neurological residents as well," the second man noted.

"That's fine. Get them in here. He's responding well to the medication."

Jacin seemed to be more and more aware of his surroundings every second. He'd always been hypervigilant; he had to be as a spy undercover in one of the most dangerous cartels in the world.

Louder, and perhaps even jovial, the deep voiced called, "Come on in. All the way around the bed. Keep moving."

"Dr. Tobias, on behalf of all the new interns, we just want to thank you for allowing us to experience this. It's a great honor to watch the Chief of Neurology for the entire Army in action." Kiss ass. There's one in every crowd.

"It's my pleasure to be here. Darnall Army Medical Center sees almost as many wounded and sick soldiers evacuated from the wars as we do at Walter Reed. This is only the second time I've had the opportunity to work in the new hospital. If everyone is in, let's get started." In a professorial tone, he continued, "Mr. Torres came to us ten days ago with a traumatic brain injury and a collapsed lung due to one of his four broken ribs. He had multiple bruises and abrasions, most significantly the ones around his wrists, ankles, and neck. Although I cannot tell you how Mr. Torres got in this condition, as much of it is classified or unknown until he recovers and gives his official statement—which will still, no doubt, be classified above my pay grade—I can tell you he'd been captured and tortured. As future physicians for the U.S. military, unfortunately you may see these conditions again."

Jacin was probably more thankful for the update than the soon-to-be doctors in the room. Since they were speaking English, he assumed he was somewhere in the good old U.S.A. He wanted to kiss the ground and throw away his passport. There had been too many times he'd almost given up hope of ever returning home.

His doctor continued, "We placed Mr. Torres in a chemically induced coma so his body, and especially the brain, could heal. He had significant brain swelling which we were able to reduce pharmacologically rather than surgically, our preference whenever possible. Mr. Torres's body has been put under enough stress without the invasion of surgery."

Mumbles around the room confirmed agreement.

"Well, then, let's give Mr. Torres a little more neostigmine and see how he does."

Jacin wasn't sure how he could be refreshed and still be sleepy. His body seemed to be having that mental debate he often had five minutes before he knew his alarm would go off. Should he give in and allow himself to return to sleep for a few precious minutes, or wake up and face the day which would be five minutes longer than usual. He succumbed to sleep.

"Excuse me."

At the sound of her voice, he awakened a little more and sighed with relief. She was there.

"I'm sorry, I need to get through."

Shuffling of feet was the only indication Jacin had of her progress.

"Dr. Tobias, I apologize, I was on a conference call with Washington."

Jacin silently chuckled. Knowing Melina, she could have been talking to the director of the CIA as easily as she could have been speaking with one of her agents still on the ground in Colombia or her brother stationed somewhere in Texas. She lied so easily and convincingly.

Not for the first time, he wondered if her words spoken softly in bed were also lies. When they were together, completely alone and sure no one was watching, his words had come from the heart.

"Just in time, Mrs. Torres," Dr. Tobias greeted. "In the next few minutes, you are going to play an important role for us." He raised his voice and spoke to everyone in the room— well, everyone except Jacin. "During your careers as military physicians, you're probably going to have to bring a soldier awake. I can tell you from experience the procedure is often dangerous, especially with a TBI. Unconscious, the brain does not calculate passing time so when awakened, the soldier may believe he is still in the situation which put him in hospital. It is not unusual for them to come awake fighting. Let me assure you, we have trained these men and women well. They can kill using only their hands and before their brains have time to realize their current situation, you could already be dead."

Jacin felt his hand lift and the restraint around his wrist tighten. His muscles contracted in a twitch at the brief pain. A memory of rough nylon rope attached to chains affixed to a block wall jolted to the front of his mind. A mental photograph of his personal torture chamber came into clear view. Why couldn't it have been a picture of Melina laying naked on the pastel yellow sheets in her bedroom, her nearly black hair fanned out on the pillow next to his?

As though struck by a Mack truck, Jacin realized Dr. Tobias had called Melina, Mrs. Torres.

Another lie.

But perhaps for good reason. If he'd been brought into the hospital unconscious, he'd probably spent time in the intensive care unit. Perhaps he was still there. Jacin had been in and around hospitals enough to know that only family was allowed to visit someone in the ICU. He remembered pacing the waiting room, barred by wide double doors and stern-faced nurses, when a SEAL teammate had taken three bullets. Only their commanding officer had been allowed in to see their friend—limited to ten minutes every two hours—until his family arrived from Oklahoma. Jacin warmed at the thought she'd wanted to be close to him, come see him even though he was unable to communicate with her.

"What do I need to do, Doctor?" Melina's voice was sultry and musical.

Jacin was sure that was by design. Their CIA training included classes in seduction. That's how they'd met. He was her final exam. Voice modulation, tone, and even pacing of words could be used to ignite a fire or douse struggling embers in a man.

"Hold his hand, and most importantly, reassure him he is home and safe now." Dr. Tobias' suggestions sounded just fine to Jacin.

This time, Jacin felt the drugs enter his body through the IV and race throughout his system with every heartbeat. He didn't know what they'd given him, or even care, as it brought him more and more aware. He dragged in air and caught the delicate scent of gardenias and spice that was Melina. No other woman in the world smelled quite like her.

"That's it, Jacin. Come back to me." She squeezed his hand and a different kind of warmth chased the medicine through his body then shot to his soul. She wanted him in her life.

"We're in the United States." She didn't bother to hide the tinge of excitement, or maybe he just knew her that well. "You're in a hospital on Fort Hood Army Base." Okay, they were in Texas. He wondered if it was the same base where her brother was stationed.

"Keep talking to him," Dr. Tobias suggested. "He's coming around nicely. Mr. Torres, can you squeeze your wife's hand?"

Well, no. I don't have a wife.

"Jacin, please, squeeze my hand." She'd asked sweetly, so with herculean effort he did as she requested.

"He did it. I felt his hand move." Melina sounded more excited than he thought she should.

"Excellent. Let's bring him up some more." The doctor moved beside him. Little by little Jacin became more awake and responded to his orders. "Mr. Torres, your eyes are still slightly swollen, but I need you to open them on your own power. Can you do that for me?"

He peeked them open the tiniest bit and slammed them shut. Damn, it was bright.

"Close those drapes and someone catch the lights. It's been days, perhaps weeks, since he's opened his eyes." Dr. Tobias patted Jacin's shoulder. "I'm sorry. I should have been more considerate."

Jacin dragged in a deep breath and tried to reassure

everyone in the room. "It's okay." His throat was so dry the words rasped out. "Water…please."

"Certainly." The doctor had an underlying eagerness as he continued, "Quickly, get the man some water and a cup of ice slivers."

A flurry of motion filled the room.

In a quiet voice Melina reassured him, "I'm right here, Jacin." When she wrapped her fingers tightly around his, he clutched hers in return.

The hum of the motor preceded the movement of his bed as it lifted his back up. He heard water pouring over ice.

"Now, Mr. Torres, if you'll open your eyes, you can have this water. But I need you to open those eyes, both of them."

Damn it, he wanted that water. This time when his lids lifted, the room was gratefully dim. His gaze found her quickly and when their eyes met, she gifted him with a real smile.

He sighed her name, "Melina."

A plastic cup with a bent straw appeared in front of his face, and he jolted back.

"Very good, son. Just a few sips. We have to get your body working again. Your system may reject food at first, so we'll start with water."

Well, isn't that fucking great? He couldn't remember his last meal. Matter of fact, he couldn't remember much. As instructed, he sipped the water and relished the cold on his tongue cleansing the roof of his mouth and soothing his throat. He'd swear he could feel the cool liquid move all the way down to his stomach.

The second man from earlier cleared his throat. "Mr. Torres, I'm Dr. Cassidy. I work very closely with Dr. Tobias on cases like yours." The short man who couldn't weigh a hundred and fifty pounds, moved through the crowded room to stand between Melina and Dr. Tobias. "Now, can you please tell me, who is the president?"

Without thinking, Jacin answered, "Juan Manuel Santos."

Snickers filled the room.

"Isn't he the president of Colombia?" asked the kiss ass.

"Jacin, he meant the president of the United States of America." She held his hand tight until he finally answered the question correctly.

"Good," Dr. Cassidy complimented and looked over his shoulder at the young faces. "You start with easy questions and work up to harder ones." Returning his gaze to Jacin, he advised, "I'm going to give you three words and I want you to remember them."

For the next ten minutes, Jacin was quizzed on everything from math to spelling. All too often, he answered in Spanish or gave the Spanish spelling of a word rather than English.

After the second time, his angel saved him. Lying, once again, she told the psychiatrist, "Spanish is Jacin's first language, and he has recently been immersed in a Spanish speaking country." She looked around the room with a big smile. "He was never very good at spelling to begin with. Thank goodness for spellcheck and auto correct, or I'd never be to be able to read anything he wrote." That won her chuckles and giggles from the future doctors.

All lies. Jacin had been born in the United States to a Puerto Rican mother and Venezuelan father who had seen the world together while working on cruise ships before settling in southern Florida and finally raising a family. Un-accented American English was most often spoken in his childhood home, but his multilingual parents also taught him and his sister Portuguese, Spanish, French, German, and even a little Italian.

Finally, the Inquisition came to an end when Dr. Tobias

took pity on Jacin. "I think our patient is tiring. We don't want to push him too hard; especially since this is the first time he's been awake in nearly two weeks."

Although chastised by his colleague, Dr. Cassidy rallied, "You're absolutely right. Mr. Torres, thank you so much for allowing me to show these young interns some of the challenges of psychiatry. I'll be back to see you several times before you can be discharged."

And won't that be fucking great?

No agent ever enjoyed the mind probe necessary to work for the CIA, but this grandstander seemed to be even worse. Given the vast amount of classified information in Jacin's brain, he hoped Langley would spring him from this hospital soon and get him to Washington D.C.

Several of the younger people in white coats filed past him quietly thanking him. A tall lanky young man waited to be last.

"I'll bet you were in Colombia, weren't you? Were you undercover or something? DEA? CIA?" His questions flew at Jacin too fast to answer any given one. They almost hurt his brain.

Marlena stared daggers at the eager intern who couldn't be twenty-five-years old. "Young man." The tone of her voice commanded attention and everyone in the room stopped and looked at her. "You are in a military medical facility. You have already been told that information is classified. What you need to learn is that knowing that kind of information can get you killed."

At the shocked look on the young face, Jacin's avenging angel reiterated, "Hear me and understand…Information. Can. Get. You. Killed. I want you to forget you ever met Jacin Torres. I want you to forget what he looks like. You're a security breach waiting to happen. Your questions just got your personnel file tagged with a big red flag. I can assure you, you will be watched very carefully, which is a shame for such a bright young man with such a promising future."

Bright eyes looked to Dr. Tobias for help but found none.

"I told you when your class first came into this room that as a military physician you will be exposed to highly classified situations," Dr. Tobias said. "You just failed this first test. You are dismissed. Please join your class for rounds."

Anger flashed in those young eyes before he acquiesced. "Yes, sir." His gaze went to Melina. "I'm a fast learner, and I completely understand."

She didn't back down. "You'd better."

"Yes, ma'am. Message received." He spun on his heel and left.

"He'll make it," Dr. Tobias glanced from Jacin to Melina. "I don't believe either of you have anything to worry about, but I too received your message loud and clear. His file will be flagged, and he will be watched, especially for the next year. I don't know who you really are or if those are your real names." He shrugged. "In truth, I don't really care. You're my patient, and I'm here to help you get better. We each serve this wonderful country of ours, but in very different ways." He stared into Jacin's eyes and held his gaze for a long minute. "I want to thank you for everything you've done. You took one hell of a beating for our country. I'm just glad I was here to help put you back together."

He reached down and wrapped a big hand around Jacin's forearm well above his sore wrist. "I'm sure you want to spend some time with your beautiful wife. I'll be back at least once a day until you're released."

Finally, Jacin and Melina were alone.

"Come here," Jacin commanded.

He tried to reach up only to realize he was still restrained. "Can you unfasten me?"

She smiled and went to work on the padded cuffs. As soon as his hand was free, he pulled her head toward his. When their lips met, for a brief moment she hesitated before they both gave in and were consumed with each other. His world—which had been tilted for far too long—was once again righted.

This was the way his life was supposed to be. Melina was his, and they were together, hopefully forever.

This concludes your Sneak Peek at
Rescuing Melina
Available only on Amazon
https://kalyncooper.com/rescuing-melina

For more of the **Black Swan series**, continue reading for a
Sneak Peek at
Unexpected Love:
Griffin & Grace
Black Swan Novel #3

Excerpt from
Unexpected Love
Kalyn Cooper

"Lady Eagle, ready," Grace Hall spoke softly into her miniaturized communications unit without lifting her cheek off the stock of her custom-made sniper rifle. She lay on her belly, flattened against the yellow earth on a ridge five hundred yards from the Islamic radicals' encampment. Through her scope, in infrared mode, she watched two red blobs casually pace the perimeter on the west and north sides. She'd been watching them for over two hours as the insertion teams sneaked close and prepared to breach.

She listened while several more teams checked in with the United States Special Operations Command Control Center half a world away.

Her tangoes had met once again at the corner. When they seemed to be exchanging something, she knew they would stand next to each other for at least two minutes as they smoked cigarettes. Good. She wouldn't have to move the gun much at all to quickly take out both vile excuses for humanity.

Lady Eagle thought about the fourteen little girls who had been kidnapped from their schools, some as young as nine years old. Not for the first time, she sent a quick prayer that they would be able to find the girls swiftly and extract them without injury to the U.S. team.

"Gray Two, ready." The sound of Parker "Griffin" Mitchell's smooth Southern drawl through her com sent a shiver down her whole body. She'd reacted as though he'd whispered sweet sonnets in her ear while lying naked in bed. Not that they had ever done anything more than kiss good night—and she could count those on one hand—but a girl could dream. That darn man had the most beguiling effect on her…mostly confusion.

"Operation Save the Children is in position and ready. Do we have a go?" Lady Hawk's voice broke through Lady Eagle's reverie.

She refocused her attention on the crimson forms leaning against the wall at the northwest corner.

"You have a go." General Lyon's baritone came through loud and clear.

"On three," Lady Hawk instructed.

Lady Eagle inhaled deeply.

"One." Lady Hawk counted down.

Lady Eagle released her breath as she aimed and wrapped her index finger over the trigger.

"Two."

She tucked in tight and chose her first target.

As her team leader said the word "three," she pulled the trigger. She was too busy lining up the second shot to watch the first man drop to the ground. Immediately after acquiring the second tango, he lay sprawled on his back from the force of the .50 caliber bullet to the head.

Part of her mind registered two other shots on the far side. Only two shots. Good. Lady Falcon had also been successful. Her friend would remain in place and cover the extraction team.

For a long five seconds, Lady Eagle stared through the small circle checking for any movement. She was sure of her shots, but the slightest gust of wind that she hadn't calculated for could move a supersonic bullet a fraction of an inch along its flight and graze rather than kill. She had to be ready to correct that mistake.

No movement. Not even a muscle twitch. With one last

scan of the area out to half a mile, Lady Eagle ignored the yellowish green indicating residual heat rising from the high desert. Seeing no red, she came to her feet and flipped down her night vision goggles.

"Lady Eagle on the move. North and west sides secure." She was down the ridge and sprinting toward the compound.

"Lady Hawk is in." Leave it to her team leader to be the first one into the valley of the shadow of death.

"Gray One is in." It was no surprise that Alex Wolf would be right behind her. To keep things simple for USSOCOM, the men from the Guardian Security team had agreed to use codenames for this mission, rather than their former military handles.

"Lady Harrier is in," their team doc announced.

Lady Eagle mentally checked off each person as they entered the makeshift compound.

Please God, protect our team as they do your will and release those little girls from the evil men who kidnapped them. In the name of Jesus Christ, amen.

When she was halfway to her entry point, she slung the sniper rifle onto her back and pulled her M4 across her chest. Her hand automatically dropped to check the position of the pistol she wore strapped to her right thigh. With every step, she felt the other gun at the small of her back. Her first mission, several years ago in South America, had taught her that her backup needed a backup.

Out of the corner of her eye, she saw movement. With her next footfall, she went to her knee and brought her rifle to her shoulder. No one from the rescue mission was supposed to be in that position. She watched the crouching figure stand then hobble toward the ridge she had just left.

It was a child. Had one of the girls managed to escape out the backside?

She moved to intercept.

At twenty feet away, the child began screaming in an Arabic dialect that was unfamiliar. She couldn't allow anything to attract attention to her. She tackled the small frame and slapped her hand over the screaming mouth.

In the Arabic she'd been taught at language school, she tried to reassure the child.

The body under her stilled.

As best she could, Lady Eagle explained that she was there to rescue her and the other girls. She asked the child to promise to be quiet.

When the little head under her nodded, she raised her hand a fraction of an inch.

Sitt, Arabic for woman, was the only word she caught.

She had to smile. Most people were surprised at the fact her team, the Ladies of Black Swan, were all female. She replied with a nod and the Arabic word for yes.

Large brown eyes stared at her. The child spoke again, too quickly for her to completely understand.

Bacha bazi and iinqadh were the only two words she recognized.

Lady Eagle's heart broke in two.

Never, in all the hours of planning this mission, had anyone considered the possibility there might be kidnapped boys. Bacha bazi, translated into dancing boys or boy play. Sexually abusing young boys was an acceptable practice in some Middle Eastern cultures and had been quite prevalent in Afghanistan. As the Taliban and their followers had been pushed out of that country, many had migrated into the area where the borders of Iraq, Turkey, and Syria were little more than constantly disputed lines on a paper map.

Lady Eagle wasn't positive which of those countries she

was in at the moment. It made no difference. Only the lives of those innocent children mattered.

She rolled off the boy, who looked to be around ten, and told him he had to be very, very quiet.

"Ladies…I repeat…Ladies." All chatter in her ear went silent.

"Lady Eagle," the new commander of USSOCOM sounded concerned. "Are you injured?"

"No, sir. But we have an additional situation." She stared into a dirty round face. "I have rescued a bacha bazi." The boy's whole body flinched at the term.

Male voices whispered curses. "Christ."

"Jesus."

"Yes, gentlemen. He has brought these innocent young boys to our attention." With command in her voice, she added. "We need to find them and take them with us, too."

"Make it so," General Lyon ordered.

A chorus of "Yes, sir," followed.

Thinking quick, Lady Eagle asked the boy if there were others like him in the compound. When he nodded affirmatively, she hesitated before she asked in Arabic, "Can you show me where they are kept?"

Frightened eyes darted between her and the horrific place he had just escaped.

"We need to rescue them as well." Either way, she had to go through those hovels to get to the extraction point.

In the light of a crescent moon, she watched the boy inhale deeply and square his shoulders. He quickly stood and reached for her hand. He slowly and carefully said his next words asking her to follow him.

The plan was for her to enter through the north side, but he was pulling her in the opposite direction. "Lady Eagle on the move toward the southwest corner. Someone else needs to clear from the rear."

"Operations, Gray Three. I've got it."

Lady Eagle wasn't sure exactly who he was, but all the men on the Guardian team had once been Navy SEALs, Army Special Forces, or Marine Raiders. Whoever he was, he could take her original job and handle cleanup. She had young boys to find and save.

"Operations, Lady Harrier. I found the girls." There was audible sigh from several people. Then the other shoe dropped. "Only eleven of them. Obviously, some of the men are using the others."

"We're on it," Gray One announced.

Bat, tat, tat. The three-round burst of rifle fire signaled that they were no longer covert, and everyone needed to expedite the mission.

The boy stopped and turned huge round eyes toward her.

"We have to hurry," Lady Eagle explained. When they neared the corner, she announced. "We're heading down the south side. Lady Falcon, please don't shoot us."

"I've got you covered," her friend assured. "You're clear."

They had only taken two steps and the boy disappeared. He had been right there in front of her and now he was gone.

Her gaze swept the length of the building then the barren landscape. Nothing moved.

She felt a light tap on her boot and looked down at a small hand jutting out from the foundation. She kneeled and the boy's slight face appeared. He frantically waved his hand as though signaling her to follow him.

At five feet, seven inches, and 132 pounds, there was no way she could fit into the small hole that didn't look big enough for a woodchuck back home in Iowa. Disappointed she couldn't go after the boys herself, she tried to explain to him, "I need you to be a hero. You were strong enough to escape, so I know you are strong enough to help the others. Bring them here and give them a boost. I'll pull them through and together we'll get all of you to freedom."

When the child hesitated, she gave him a big smile she hoped was reassuring. "You can do this. I have faith in you."

With a jerky nod, he disappeared for what felt like an hour. Because she checked her watch several times, she knew it had been less than five minutes. She hated being this exposed. She'd slipped around the corner twice to check her six and Lady Falcon had her covered.

A long string of automatic rifle fire nearly drowned out Gray Two's voice. "Die, you child fucking pigs." Through his miniature microphone, everyone heard two young female voices screaming. In Arabic, he kept repeating the words rescue and safe. Lady Eagle was relieved when she heard Griffin finally announce, "I've got two of the girls. Heading your way, Lady Harrier."

Less than a minute later, Lady Hawk confirmed she'd found the last of the girls.

Thank you, God. Please protect all of us as we get these innocent girls… she looked down at the hole then added… and boys, to safety. In Jesus's name, amen.

"Sssst."

Her attention flew to the small opening. Obviously, the child didn't realize how whispers, especially S sounds, cut through the night. All covert operators knew to speak very quietly, barely moving their lips in low tones that blended with the night. But he was just a child, bravely helping others, placing his life in danger if caught.

"How many?" Her question must have confused the child. His face disappeared and two very small hands emerged from the hole. Lady Eagle grabbed the tiny wrists and pulled a slight body from the dirt. A child, missing his eye teeth, smiled up at her and immediately began jabbering. Then he threw himself at her legs. Her left arm wrapped around him, and she pulled her rifle to her shoulder and scanned the area to see if they had drawn unwanted attention. Seeing no movement, she instructed him to lay down flat off to the side.

The next boy seemed a little older and a little larger than the first, but his gratitude was not an ounce less. Prepared this time, she gave him directions as she pulled him to her. The process repeated twice more before she pulled out the boy she'd caught running away. He stood in front of her, almost at attention, as the others rushed to him for a group hug.

"Are there more?" she asked.

As he spoke, she understood his hand gestures better than the words. He indicated he had found all of them.

"Operations, Lady Eagle. Five boys rescued. Moving to the extraction point now." She looked at the first boy and instructed, "Line them up. You, at the end." It took longer than it should before she had the boys holding hands and ready to move out.

They'd nearly reached the end of the south side when she heard the distinct shot of a high-powered sniper rifle. Lady Eagle whipped around, automatically bringing her M4 to her shoulder and sweeping the area behind her through the sights. A man at the far end fell to one side.

"You're welcome," Lady Falcon bragged. "But you'd better get moving faster."

Thank you, God, for my wonderful teammates and their skills.

"Roger that." Lady Eagle looked at the open expanse they had to cross to get to the next ridge. Not far for a trained special operator, but a long way for five little boys. The original evacuation plan had been for the entire mission team to surround the girls and shuffle their way across. She could wait there with the boys and extract all the children at once.

More gunfire erupted inside, this time it seemed far too close.

"Escape route blocked. We're taking the girls out on the northeast end," Lady Hawk informed everyone.

Okay. So much for that idea.

"Operations, Gray Four. Charges set. I'm on the south end behind the resistance forces. Do you want me to take them out or exit?"

"Gray Four, operations. Exit as planned. We'll get those fuckers with the bombs."

"Operations, Gray Four, ready to exit."

"Gray Four, Lady Falcon. You're cleared to exit." The statement reassured Lady Eagle that she and the boys were still safe.

"Gray Four, operations. Move east to assist Lady Eagle."

"Roger that, operations. Gray Four on the move."

Thank you, God. Not that she was calling General Lyon God, but she wanted the Lord to know how much she appreciated his answer to her unasked prayer for help.

Without being told, Gray Four moved to the back of her line of boys and hand signaled her that he was ready. Lady Eagle grabbed the smallest boy's wrist and instructed the children to run as fast as they could. Her order was rapidly repeated by the older boy using different inflections and word accents.

As soon as they started a cross the open field, word came over the com that the others had cleared the compound. There was a brief exchange of fire before Lady Hawk declared everyone clear.

Gray Four slowed his steps and looked over his shoulder.

Holding a device high above his head, still keeping pace with the boys and scanning the area all at the same time, he announced, "Fire in the hole."

Lady Eagle stopped, gathered the boys, and forced them to the ground, covering as much of them as she could. Gray Four's body joined hers a second before the earth shook and a gust of power blew over her back, pressing them into the soft earth.

Chapter 2

Parker "Griffin" Mitchell dropped his huge duffel on the concrete and leaned his ass against the military jeep that brought him to the base's hangar on the far side of Batman Airport in western Turkey. The other Guardian team members of Operation Save the Children milled about, chatting in small groups. Griffin didn't feel like talking to anyone. He was still pissed that Grace had been left outside the compound, by herself, then taken on the responsibility of five little boys. Sure, his buddy Quin had finally joined them, but she had been out there alone for hours.

At least she'd made it back to the base safely. He hoped to see her before they bunked in for several hours sleep before flying out at night, but that hadn't happened. She'd taken charge of the children while their team leader had found the kids a safe place to live.

He crossed powerful arms over his broad chest and made himself as comfortable as possible while they waited for the Ladies of Black Swan. The armed guards surrounding their ride home wouldn't even let them in the building. At least they were following orders.

He had shed his operational handle as Gray Two as quickly as he'd stripped out of the desert camouflage uniform and boots. He only wished the shower on the surprisingly modern military base had washed away the horrors he'd witnessed on the rescue mission. Looking at the body language of his teammates, he wasn't the only one.

Quin Barrister, the newly promoted manager at the Dallas Guardian Security Center, parked his butt a few feet away and stretched out his long runner's legs. "Sometimes I wonder why the fuck I do this, then I think about those kids." He lowered his head and rubbed a hand across the back of his neck. "Christ, what those monsters did to them. Those little boys were…" He sighed heavily. "So grateful. When Grace and I finally got them to the extraction point, they just held each other and bawled their little eyes out."

"Yup," was all Griffin could say around the fist in his chest.

Jonathan O'Neil, assistant manager at the Dallas Center, walked up and fist bumped his new boss, Quin, before shaking hands with Griffin. "It was really great to get to work with you again."

Even though he and Jonathan had been on several covert missions together in the past few months, the man had worked for him for several years in what they all considered to be their day job—protecting residences and businesses, as well as personal protection. "We miss you at the Miami Center." Griffin looked over at his counterpart. "You realize you got one of my best men."

Quin's smile said he knew the truth in that statement. "He's mine, and I'm pretty sure his new girlfriend isn't about to move to Miami."

"Fiancée," Jonathan corrected. "And no, Dallas is home for me and Gwen."

Congratulations and handshakes were exchanged as Alex Wolf—their boss in the field and as the managing partner of Guardian Security—walked up and stood in front of them.

"Great job out there, men." He looked at the dust cloud pluming on the horizon. "In case you hadn't heard, the girls will be returned to their parents, provided they'll take them back. If not, they'll join the boys at a Catholic orphanage in Italy."

"Good." Griffin knew the social norms in that area of the world often shunned children who had been subjected to sexual abuse. "Did Katlin make those arrangements?" He asked of the Black Swan team leader.

Alex didn't bother to hide his smile at the mention of his lover, who also happened to be his business partner. "Yeah, with the help of her uncle, Monsignor Francis Callahan."

"That's some serious pull she has," Quin noted.

Looking down the road to where several vehicles were approaching, Alex commented, "You have no idea."

Griffin chuckled. "Yeah, she has pulled us into USSOCOM and pulled us into taking on missions that don't even involve Americans."

Jerking his head around, Alex informed them, "Our target was to take out the leader and his lieutenants of this rebel band of zealots. Those assholes weren't even Iraqi. The Taliban wasn't fundamentalist enough for them back in Afghanistan, so al Abib-I-don't-give-a-fuck brought his faithful followers here to build a new caliphate." He slowly swiped his hand over his face. "Only Kat and I knew about that part of the mission. When General Lyon took over USSOCOM, he found lots of holes."

Griffin stood. "You think we have a mole?"

"No." Alex shot back. "But it looks like they might. We all agreed that only the three of us would know the true purpose of that mission." He grinned. "Why do you think I had Quin blow the place to hell? And Katlin kept Tori sniping until after Lei Lu and the Turks landed the helicopters to extract us?"

The fact that no one got out of there alive made Griffin feel vindicated. He hadn't thought beyond the satisfaction of sending all those men to meet their maker. Now it all made sense.

Just then, three ancient Jeeps pulled up and stopped next to the ones that had brought the men. A curtain of dust passed over, coating everyone in fine yellow sand. Griffin ignored the grit and watched the Ladies of Black Swan emerge from the newly arrived vehicles. All five were dressed in black flight suits; the only identity patch was the U.S. flag on their left shoulders. A definite contrast to the polo shirts and khaki slacks the men from Guardian Security wore.

Katlin Callahan approached them. Undeniably, the blonde was gorgeous—and sleeping with his boss as often as possible. As an active duty Navy lieutenant, and mission commander, she had to maintain her distance throughout the planning phase at USSOCOM in Florida and during the op. Looking at their relaxed demeanor, it seemed as though they'd been able to find each other in the post-adrenaline sexual spike. Lucky bastard. Griffin had taken care of himself in the shower while dreaming of sliding into Grace...someday.

"You guys ready to head home?" Katlin looked to the west where the sun was slowly turning the clear sky shades of peach. "I'd rather leave under the cover of darkness, but I want to get the hell out of here. Dusk will do."

Grunts of affirmation came from men.

"Na, na, na, na, na, na, na, na, na, na, na, na, na Batman!" Nita's smile, amidst the girl-next-door face, was contagious. She trotted toward them, arms outstretched, singing the theme song to the old television show. Stopping in front of them, she dropped her hands to her hips and looked around the very small airport. "If this is Batman's airport, where the hell's his cave? What the fuck is he doing hiding here in Nowheresville, Turkey?" She looked at each man. "Well? Ideas?"

Quin smiled and threw his palms up. "I got nothin'."

"I'll bet when I landed that big black jet here a few nights ago, it scared the crap out of anyone who dared to be around." Grace's light laugh drove into Griffin's chest and grabbed his heart. When she flipped her dazzling auburn hair over her shoulder, the remaining sunlight caught the red strands infusing them with rose gold. The tightness in his core migrated south and took a firm grip on his cock.

"They probably thought the man himself had arrived." Neither Tori's quip, nor the nearly six-foot tall former model's poise as she joined the group, could tear Griffin's gaze away from Grace. Her green eyes filled with laughter and sparkled like a deeply faceted emerald.

Damn, he wanted her in every way a man could.

Griffin had been attracted to Grace Hall, a.k.a. Lady Eagle, from the first time he'd seen her striding out of the Miami condo in her sexy green, formfitting club dress and sinfully tall high heels. She'd been dressed to kill that night and the arrow had shot straight through his libido. She and her friends had contracted Guardian Security for bodyguards. Griffin, like so many other men who worked with him, had taken them for exactly what they looked like…socialites out for a good time in the big city.

But Grace had seemed different from the others. She never swore, and although she danced provocatively, she never went home with a man. She and Katlin seemed to be older than the others, or at least more mature. One evening, as he was handing over their personal protection duty to Miguel,

Grace had asked if Griffin would take her home, claiming that she wasn't feeling well. He'd been more than happy to oblige.

Before he could assist her into the back of the company Land Rover, she'd deposited herself in the shotgun seat. Griffin grinned as he remembered her saying that the loud music and too many writhing bodies were remaking her nervous. She'd touched his arm as she'd turned toward him and asked if they could stop for ice cream. It had been the first of many evenings that he and Grace had left her friends at a pheromone-filled club, opting for the virtue of coffee and strawberry ice cream.

Griffin's brain still had a hard time equating that seemingly innocent socialite with the war-hardened Navy lieutenant five feet away. He glanced at the big duffel bags at her feet containing her sniper rifle—the stock custom-cut shorter to fit her smaller frame—her M4, several pistols and probably a grenade or two.

Last night, he'd seen a glimpse of that big heart of hers as she rescued those five boys. Once back on the Turkish base, she stayed with them for hours making sure they were fed and properly clothed. He had wanted so much to be the man to back her up, cover her and be sure she was safe, but his assignment had been to stick close to Lady Harrier and help her get the girls out without harm. Every time Grace had spoken, he had been distracted, downright concerned about her, too often taking his attention away from his own job.

He was in deep.

And it was high time he did something about it.

The squeal and creak of hangar doors brought Griffin back to the present. He'd obviously missed a great deal of conversation. When he scanned his surroundings, he noticed the sun had completely disappeared behind the horizon painting the high desert in deep purples fading to grays.

He grabbed his bag and jogged past his teammates who were amiably talking as they walked toward the hangar. "Grace, hold up."

She stopped and spun to look at him, giving him a questioning smile.

He dropped his bag and pulled her into his arms. He didn't care everyone was watching them. "You are so fucking amazing." When he saw her shocked eyes soften, he didn't need any more permission. He crashed his mouth on hers, taking her with a ferocity that he was no longer going to hold back. No more gentle, chaste good night kisses at the front door of the Miami Beach condo. No. The woman warrior in his arms could handle anything he gave her.

This concludes your Sneak Peek at
Unexpected Love
Available in all formats
<u>Unexpected Love</u>: Griffin & Grace
Black Swan Novel #3
He never believed in love, but he never expected to find her.
https://kalyncooper.com/unexpected-love

If you've enjoyed *Uncaged Love*, please tell others what you liked about this book by leaving a review on your retailer's site.

Please consider these other books by KaLyn Cooper:

Black Swan Series
Military active duty women secretly trained in Special Operations and the men who dare to capture the heart of a Woman Warrior.

Unconventional Beginnings Prequel (Black Swan novella #0.5) ~ He's dead. But they can't allow it to affect her. She's too important.
Download FREE https://dl.bookfunnel.com/uec4utb66d

Unrelenting Love: Lady Hawk (Katlin) & Alex (Black Swan novel #1) ~ Women in special operations? Never… Until he sleeps with the most lethal woman in the world.

Noel's Puppy Power: Bailey & Tanner (A Sweet Christmas Black Swan novella #1.5) ~ He's better at communicating with animals than women, but as an amputee she knows firsthand it's the internal scars that can be most difficult to heal.

Uncaged Love: Harper & Rafe (Black Swan novel #2) ~ The jungle isn't the only thing that's hot while escaping from a Colombian cartel.

Unexpected Love: Lady Eagle (Grace) & Griffin (Black Swan novel #3) ~ He never believed in love, but he never expected to find her.

Challenging Love: Katlin & Alex (A Black Swan novella #3.5) ~ A new relationship can be fragile when outsiders are determined to challenge that love.

Unguarded Love: Lady Harrier (Nita) & Daniel (Black Swan novel #4) ~ She couldn't lose another sick baby…then he brought her his dying daughter.

Choosing Love: Grace & Griffin (A Black Swan novella #4.5) ~ Hard choices have to be made when parents interfere in a growing relationship.

Unbeatable Love: Lady Falcon (Tori) & Marcus (Black Swan novel #5) ~ Scarred outside and in, why would his beautiful friend ever want more with him?

Unmatched Love: Lady Kite (Lei Lu) & Henry (Black Swan novel #6) ~ Scarred outside and in, why would his beautiful friend ever want more with him?

Unending Love: Lady Falcon (Tori) & Marcus (Black Swan novel #7) ~ Their life together is not over. He has to believe it…or it will be.

Guardian Elite Series

Former special operators, these men work for Guardian Security (from the Black Swan Series) protecting families in their homes and executives on the road, but they can't always protect their hearts.

Double Jeopardy (Novella #1 Guardian Elite series crossover with Hildie McQueen's Indulgences series) ~ Guarding a billionaire and his wife isn't easy when you can't keep your eyes off your bikini wearing, gun carrying partner who is lethal in stilettos.

Justice for Gwen (Novella #2 Guardian Elite series crossover with Susan Stoker's Special Forces World) ~ She's not what she seems. Neither is he. But the terrorist threat is real. So is the desire that smolders between them.

Rescuing Melina (Novella #3 Guardian Elite series crossover with Susan Stoker's Special Forces World) ~ When Jacin awoke stateside, he remembered nothing about his escape from the Colombian cartel or his torture. He was sure of only one thing, his love of Melina, his handler. When she disappears, neither bruises nor the CIA will keep him from rescuing her.

Snow SEAL (Novella #4 Guardian Elite series crossover with Elle James Brotherhood Protectors World) ~ Terrorists want her…but so does he. The chase isn't the only thing that heats up when the flint of the former SEAL strikes against the steel of the woman warrior.

Securing Willow (Novella #5 Guardian Elite series crossover with Susan Stoker's Special Forces World) ~ Guarding her wasn't his job, but he couldn't let her die…even before she stole his heart. When he discovers the temptingly beautiful foreign service officer is being threatened, his protective instincts take over.

SEAL in a Storm (Novel #5 is part of the Suspense Sisters new wave of connected books, Silver SEALs featuring a seasoned hero and heroine, second chances, and edge of your seat suspense.) ~ With a hurricane bearing down on the tiny island, they only have days to find and rescue ten kidnapped young girls and their chaperones…and keep their hands off each other.

Cancun Series

Follow the Girard family —along with their friends, former SEALs and active duty female Navy pilots—as they hunt Mayan antiquities, terrorists and Mexican cartels in what most would call paradise. Tropical nights aren't the only thing HOT in Cancun.

Christmas in Cancun (Cancun Series Book #1) ~ Can the former SEAL keep his libido in check and his family safe when the quest for ancient Mayan idols turns murderous?

Conquered in Cancun (Cancun Series Novella #1.5) ~ A helicopter pilot's second chance at love walks into a Cancun nightclub, but she's a jet fighter pilot with reinforced walls around her heart.

Captivated in Cancun (Cancun Series Book #2) ~ His job is tracking down terrorists so he's not interested in a family. She wants him short-term, then needs him when their worlds collide.

Claimed by a SEAL (Cancun Series crossover Novella #2.5 with Cat Johnson's Hot SEALs) ~ How far will the Homeland Security agent go to assure mission success when forced undercover for a second time with an irresistible SEAL?

Never Series

The mission brought the five of them together, disaster nearly tore them apart, a mystery and killer reunited them forever.

A Love Never Forgotten (Never Series novel #1) ~ Dreams or nightmares. Truth or lies. He can't tell them apart. Then he discovers the woman who has haunted his dreams is real. Is she his future? Or his past?

A Promise Never Forgotten (Never Series novel #2) ~ As a Marine Lieutenant Colonel, he could take on any mission and succeed. Raising his two godchildren…with her…just might kill him.

A Moment Never Forgotten (Never Series novel #3) ~ The moment he realized she was in serious danger…he couldn't protect her.

ABOUT THE AUTHOR

KaLyn Cooper is a USA Today Bestselling author whose romances blend fact and fiction with blazing heat and heart-pounding suspense. Life as a military wife has shown KaLyn the world, and thirty years in PR taught her that fact can be stranger than fiction. She leaves it up to the reader to separate truth from imagination. She, her husband, and Little Bear (Alaskan Malamute) live in Tennessee on a micro-plantation filled with gardens, cattle, and quail. When she's not writing, she's at the shooting range or paddling on the river.

For the latest on works in progress and future releases, check out KaLyn Cooper's website

http://www.kalyncooper.com/

Follow KaLyn Cooper on Facebook for promotions and giveaways

https://www.facebook.com/KaLynCooper1Author/

Sign up for exclusive promotions and special offers only available in KaLyn's newsletter

https://kalyncooper.com/kalyn-cooper-newsletter